Fortune

PAUL-LOUP SULITZER

Fortune

A NOVEL

Translated from the French by Susan Wald

LYLE STUART INC.   SECAUCUS, N.J.

Published by Lyle Stuart Inc.
Published simultaneously in Canada by
Musson Book Company.
A division of General Publishing Co. Limited
Don Mills, Ontario
Queries regarding rights and permissions should be
addressed to: Carole Stuart, 120 Enterprise Avenue,
Secaucus, N.J. 07094
Manufactured in the United States of America

Library of Congress Cataloging-in-Publication Data

Sulitzer, Paul-Loup, 1946-
    [Fortune. English]
    Fortune : a novel / Paul-Loup Sulitzer ; translated from the
French by Susan Wald.
        p.   cm.
    Translation of : Fortune.
    ISBN 0-8184-0446-9 : $15.95
    I. Title.
PQ2679.U457F613   1987   87-20912
843'.914—dc 19   CIP

Any resemblance to real persons or events is,
of course, mere coincidence.

To my father, my mother, and my daughter Olivia, who has
her specialty . . .
To my friends: Claude, J.-R. Hirsch, Albert and Catherine
Blanchard, Marc Sulitzer, J.-P. Rein, Pierre
Douglas, J.-F. Prevost . . .
to Lyne Chardonnet and Anouchka Auspitz

As it was not possible to take into account the recent fluctuations in the exchange rates, it is understood that in all of the financial operations mentioned in this book, the dollar is set at 5.00 FF.

Prologue

In mid-September 1976—September 18, to be precise—it was just over three months since I had become involved in buying and building a giant casino-hotel in the United States. A real casino! Once completed, it would be able to accommodate twenty-five or thirty thousand gamblers at one time. That's not peanuts; it's enough, anyway, to rival Caesars Palace or the MGM in Las Vegas. The proportions are the same or just about. As for the scope of the deal I was involved in, three figures will give a sufficient indication—the total investment was $500 million, that investment normally should be recovered in three and a half years, the expected annual revenues were 100 million.

Minus taxes and fees.

On September 18, 1976, a taxi dropped me off before the entrance of a building on East Sixty-fifth Street, Manhattan, New York. It was eight o'clock in the evening, give or take a few minutes.

"My name is Franz Cimballi. Mr. Olliphan's expecting me."

The armed guard consulted a list on his desk, stared at me, and nodded. I walked toward the elevators. The man called me back.

"There's a private elevator to Mr. Olliphan's apartment."

He led me to a door of polished oak, strangely lacking a handle or any means of opening it.

"Please look at the camera."

I had to raise my head, and the single eye of the lens dropped toward me. I gave it one of the charming smiles I'm known for. Ten seconds. The lockless door swung open silently to a kind of boudoir lined in watered silk, furnished with two straight-back Adam armchairs; between them, a Louis XVI chest. I entered, and the door closed behind me. I didn't feel the cage move, nor did I notice the very slight shake marking the end of the ascent. A door opened, sixty-four stories up. A blank-faced Puerto Rican butler helped me out of my raincoat.

"This way, please, Mr. Cimballi."

The apartment was a duplex, judging by the very narrow ebony staircase off to one side, and was of unparalleled luxury. The man who had invited me to dinner was waiting at the end of a wood-paneled hallway, in a huge library. As I entered, he laid in its case a violin that I would bet was worth as much as the duplex and its contents. He smiled. He was a man of about fifty, tall, slender, very handsome, superbly distinguished, silvery temples, tanned complexion, green eyes shining with intelligence. His name was James Montague Olliphan. It was he who sold me the Crystal Palace, acting as an intermediary.

"Would you like something to drink, Mr. Cimballi?"

"No, thanks."

His green eyes examined me.

"I knew Scarlett," he said softly.

Philip Norman, called Scarlett. Corporate lawyer. Now dead—he had died in a fire of his own making to put an end to a horrible disease. But just before his death, he had helped me, allowing me, in a single stroke, to put the finishing touch on my revenge and my fortune. I stared at Olliphan and a strange sensation came over me, arousing my distrust.

"You seem to know a lot about me."

"Your name is Franz Cimballi. To look at you, one would think you were no more than twenty-two or twenty-four years old. In fact, you're slightly older. But not much. But you have pulled off several remarkable coups in the financial arena. And in terms of your total wealth . . . shall we go into dinner? Are you hungry?"

"Always. Especially between meals."

The strange impression I got from watching Olliphan was that of a man besieged by an incredible case of nerves, even to the point of despair, yet perfectly controlled.

He finished his sentence. "In terms of your wealth, I would say it probably exceeds $80 million."

I followed him as he walked and talked. We entered the dining room. The sight before me literally stunned and froze me in place for several seconds. She was a woman, or rather, had been a woman, years before. Now she was a monster, a huge mass of fatty, gleaming, billowing flesh. She sat, or, rather, was propped up, at the end of the long table, inert but living. Two black eyes, of an oppressive icy fierceness, targeted me as soon as I entered. And they never left me.

"Dearest," said Olliphan, with extreme gentleness, "may I present my friend, Mr. Franz Cimballi? My wife, Mr. Cimballi. My wife Angelina."

I held out my hand, but the monster did not make the slightest gesture to take it. She was already eating, or rather, gorging, grabbing handfuls from dishes placed all around her. Nauseating. And the worst, perhaps, was Olliphan's attitude. He treated this wife of his as though she were the most beautiful woman under the sun. Repeatedly, during dinner, he spoke to her, seeking her corroboration of what he said to me or what I replied to him, seeming never to notice that the octopus did not open her tiny voracious mouth except to stuff in squid dripping with tomato sauce or handfuls of spaghetti. And each time he spoke to her, with complete naturalness, his voice was filled with tenderness.

"Coffee, Mr. Cimballi?"

We had finished dinner. No, no coffee. And no after-dinner drink, either. To tell the truth, I had only one desire, which was to get the hell out of there, out of that room and that house.

Yet Olliphan announced, "I'd like to show you something."

He led me up the narrow staircase—why narrow? To prevent the ghastly Mrs. Olliphan from using it? We reached a landing.

"Was I wrong a little while ago when I estimated your fortune?"

No. Except that he had forgotten to subtract the $25 million I'd had to spend to buy the Crystal Palace. Olliphan pushed open a door. Suddenly the temperature rose several degrees. We entered what was actually a greenhouse. The air was damp and warm, perfumed by the scents of tropical plants, which encircled an oval basin about twenty-five or thirty feet long—a real swimming pool.

"Do you like it, Mr. Cimballi?"

"Yes, Bwana."*

*Swahili for "mister."

I raised my head. It was all glass, through which you could see the half-starry, half-cloudy sky of Manhattan.

I asked Olliphan, "Do you know Martin Yahl?"

"I've never met him."

My abrupt question certainly did not surprise him. It was as if he were expecting it. He laughed softly, his eyes seeming paler in the shadow, as we walked along the paths of that amazing exotic garden perched sixty-five stories above the darkness of Central Park.

"I know Martin Yahl is a Swiss banker," he said. "I know he hates you, and that you hate him as well. I know that the two of you have clashed, and that you bested him twice.

"Follow me, there's something else I'd like to show you."

He opened a sliding glass door. Behind it was a terrace that occupied the entire area of the roof not covered by the greenhouse. The temperature difference between its stuffiness and the New York air was at least twenty degrees. Olliphan walked straight ahead in the darkness. He was already three or four yards away, and I could barely see him.

"You don't have to follow me," he said.

But I caught up with him anyway, sinking into shadow myself. Gradually it brightened as my eyes adapted. The ground on which I walked was black, a kind of tar with a dull surface. I crouched down and brushed it with my fingers. It was indeed asphalt. Olliphan continued walking forward. Around us, the sky was growing ever brighter. I began to make out chimneys to the south, etched in profile by the lights of the Empire State Building.

"Do you work for Yahl, Olliphan?"

A slight laugh in the darkness. "No."

"Have you worked for him or with him?"

"No."

"Is there any connection between the Crystal Palace and Martin Yahl?"

"Not that I know of."

I heard him laugh again. I took a few more steps to reach him, and that's when it happened. The ground under my feet, perfectly flat up to then, suddenly began to slope. I immediately froze, gripped by fear. What the hell kind of game was this? I looked straight ahead—emptiness.

EMPTINESS.

For several seconds, I thought it was a hallucination. But no, there could be no doubt. In front of us, no question about it, the railing that circled the terrace stopped for at least ten yards. My heartbeat quickened suddenly.

"Look at your feet," Olliphan said.

I lowered my eyes and read the figure "5," written in white on the black tar.

Olliphan continued, his voice amused, "I couldn't decide. Gradations in yards or in meters? I finally opted for the metric system, which will be universal one day. The scale goes from one to twenty. Up to five, the slope is almost imperceptible. Then it increases. It goes from a 5 percent slope at five to ten, from 10 percent at ten to fifteen, to 20 percent from fifteen to twenty. Of course, after twenty, there's nothing, except sixty-five stories of empty space. Isn't it a clever idea?"

I gulped. "Hilarious. Is it yours?"

He nodded, smiling. In the darkness, his Irish eyes grew paler.

"Personally, I've gone as far as seventeen."

"The world's record, I assume?"

"So far, yes, It's because you have to account for the wind. And when it rains, it's slippery, of course. But records are made to be broken."

I chuckled. This guy was nuts.

"At least go as far as ten, Mr. Cimballi. The risk is almost nil."

That "almost" worried me. But I took two or three steps, then another three or four. I was at "9." And I thought, "Cimballi, you're even crazier than he is. What are you doing here, you idiot?" I slid the sole of my shoe warily forward and touched the white circle of "10." Beyond, I could feel that the slope increased. Olliphan, for his part, was at "14," hands in his jacket pockets, hair tossed by the wind.

"You really won't come as far as me?"

"Not without a parachute."

"But I thought you knew how to take risks."

An alarm signal began buzzing in my head.

"Not this type of risk," I answered.

I could see pretty well by now. I made out the figure "20," just a few inches away from empty space. Olliphan turned his back to me, hands still in his pockets. He stepped forward one more meter.

"Buying a casino is a risk, Mr. Cimballi . . ."

There we were. Olliphan went down another meter.

"I would say it's equivalent to going up to the eighteenth mark on a windy day, in the pouring rain."

Silence. Finally, I said, "What's that? A warning?"

He had stopped for a moment, but now he resumed walking straight ahead and down, hands still in his pockets.

"Olliphan, I asked you a question."

He shook his head and kept walking. I could already see myself explaining how, after a stupid game, my host of the evening had taken a swooping plunge of sixty-five stories to be squashed on the sidewalk.

"Something else, Olliphan?"

"I like you a lot."

Okay, that was enough. I turned around and very cautiously made my retreat, until I once again felt solid and perfectly level ground beneath my feet. I looked behind me. Olliphan continued to go forward, putting the weight on his heels. Finally he halted.

"Eighteen-and-a-half. A new record."

"Is there a trap in this casino deal?"

"Not that I know of."

I couldn't see his face, but I heard his laugh.

"I was the intermediary between my clients and you, in your purchase. Do you really expect me to tell you the deal isn't sound?"

I was crouching down, suffering from slight dizziness. I stood up.

"I'm leaving Olliphan. Thanks for dinner. Good night."

"Good night."

On the lower floor, the butler came forward as soon as I appeared on the narrow wooden staircase. He handed me my raincoat. I followed him through a series of rooms. The dining room was now empty. But not the living room.

There she was, Mrs. Olliphan in person, sunk in an armchair, crushing it with her weight. How much could she weigh? Three hundred pounds? And she looked at me as she dipped into a box of chocolates.

"Good evening, Ma'am."

No answer.

Then I ran. Literally.

Easy does it, Cimballi. Don't get carried away, like you usually do. Begin at the beginning.

18

1. Ice Cream from the Imam

1

I did a lot of thinking afterwards. It was really all Sarah's fault. (She doesn't agree.) After all, the idea of buying a hotel—no, correct that, a chain of hotels—that idea was hers.

In the spring of 1976, the ludicrous ups and downs of my speculation in coffee were nearly six months old. I took vacations and kept myself more or less quiet. Of course, I speculated a little, here and there, changing a few million dollars into gold, German marks, Swiss francs, Japanese yen, even Brazilian cruzeiros. I bought a few Canadian and Australian bonds, but nothing out of the ordinary. It was merely a question of keeping my hand in, and the rest of the time I behaved myself.

I traveled. I went back to Maria Cay, to that desert island which belonged to me, at the very end of the Bahamas archipelago. And there we played Mr., Mrs., and Junior Robinson Crusoe—me, Sarah Kyle, and my son, Marc-Andrea. We went from Tahiti to New Zealand by way of Peru. Sarah even had me visit her native Ireland, which I had seen only between flights. We did a lot of skiing with a friend who was an instructor in Aspen, Colorado. We flew over Canada with him in a helicopter to find new, virgin trails. The rest of the time I relaxed, watching my son grow up and watching Sarah manage her hotels. She wasn't the owner, just the general manager, even though I had frequently offered to buy the lot.

In the spring of that year, 1976—months before I heard of the Crystal Palace, Olliphan (the man with the terrace), Henry Chance, or Caliban—Sarah told me one day, "You're vegetating, Franz."

I looked at her, surprised. At that very instant, I was lying in a hammock on the edge of a beach in Montego Bay, Jamaica, and my naked son, with his feet together, was jumping on my stomach.

"I'm *what*?"

"You're vegetating."

"So?"

"And what's more, you're getting fat."

She thought it was time I arose from my torpor. She could see I was starting to get bored, she said, and she could understand that. After all, I was only twenty-six years old, and it was my nature to gallop around the world.

"So, you've had enough of me, is that it?"

That wasn't it at all, but in her opinion, I should extricate myself from that hammock and do something. And she had just the idea of what that should be—buy a hotel chain.

"I suppose you'd be the manager."

"Absolutely not! If there's one man in the world I wouldn't want for a boss, it's you, my pet. I'd rather clean houses."

For the simple reason that she liked her independence more than anything else. Twice already, I'd asked her to marry me. NYET. "Why not?" "We'll talk about it when you're grown up." It was at times like that she annoyed me the most. She was definitely the only person in the world who didn't take me, Cimballi, seriously. The only one, that is, besides me, Cimballi.

One thing was certain. I didn't feel any kind of enthusiasm for building or buying a hotel chain. Because for $80 million, you can't get much, anyway. And besides, playing dice with thousands of hotel rooms didn't excite me. I could see myself running from one hotel to another to make sure that my various managers weren't stealing my silver spoons.

Nevertheless, for the sake of pretending, and to satisfy my favorite lady, I contacted Marc Lavater in Paris and asked him to send me a study on the hotel industry around the world.

I received his material a month later, in the form of a five-hundred-page report that I didn't in the least feel like reading, in which was laid out the organizational structure and finances of the Hilton, Sheraton, Holiday Inn, Hyatt, and other chains. About as fascinating as the phone book.

But one of Marc's assistants had seen fit to underline in red a single sentence, which stated: "Sixty percent of the profits created by all the branches of the Hilton chain around the world come from the Las Vegas International Hilton alone." And in the margin, Lavater's aide had given an explanation for this phenomenon: "Because of the casino located at the Vegas Hilton."

That's where it all began. And I went on the warpath.

"A casino?"

It must have been about the middle of June, the fourteenth, probably. The weather in New York was splendid. Philip Vandenbergh sat across from me. He looked at me as if I had just suggested drug trafficking or turning over an entire girls' school to prostitution. Quite obviously, there was a good share of playfulness—almost complicity—in the dislike we felt for each other. In five years, he had never smiled at me. We had never lunched or dined together. He had always refused to call me by my first name, and when we happened to be in the same room, he made sure he was as far from me as possible. If we met at Yankee Stadium, we'd probably need loudspeakers to communicate. But it was this same Philip Vandenbergh who had once jumped in up to his eyebrows, even involving his own relatives, to find me the thirty-odd million dollars that had ultimately saved me. For my part, while never failing to display my animosity toward him, I had sought his advice for five years and paid for it at the price of gold.

"A casino," I said. "I'd like to buy one or have it built."

He leaned back in his chair, pressed his neck against the back, and placed his fingertips together in a deliberate way.

"Do you have any idea of the capital you'd need to invest?"

"I want a big one."

"Then you'll have to think in terms of hundreds of millions."

"I'll break my piggy bank."

"What do you know about the gambling industry?"

"Absolutely zero."

Which was the wretched truth. Sarah regularly fleeced me at gin rummy, and even in War, I was beaten by my four-year-old son. And I had lost $2.50 on my last trip to Vegas.

"Have you ever heard of something called the Mafia?"

"I saw *The Godfather* twice."

"Very funny," said Vandenbergh.

He had a cold smile on his face. Clearly, he felt sorry for me. And did I know that the Mafia had always been involved and was still extremely interested in gambling, whether in Vegas, Atlantic City, San Juan, Puerto Rico, the Bahamas, or various Latin American countries? Did I realize that I could barely get my feet wet in that milieu without running up against the Mob?

Vandenbergh went on.

"In Vegas, in the fifties, everything or almost everything was in the hands of the Mob. Things have changed a bit as a result of various scandals. One involved the Silver Slipper, where they discovered wide-scale cheating that made it possible to launder huge sums of money from the drug trade. The state of Nevada, with its gambling commission, cleaned things up. It could do that because of licensing and its power to grant or withdraw them. As a result, other investors arrived, and they elbowed out most of the Mob families—oil companies, movie companies, hotel chains, or billionnaires like Howard Hughes in search of new investments. In short, financial giants."

His implication was perfectly clear. What was I doing, with my paltry $80 million, between those giants on the one hand and organized crime on the other? I'd be pulverized in an instant.

"And other places besides Vegas?"

Philip Vandenbergh gave me a compassionate look.

"Forget it. It's true they've just authorized gambling in Atlantic City. But everything indicates that the situation will be the same as in Vegas in the fifties. Maybe worse. The New York underworld is a thousand times better organized than in Nevada, and it's geographically closer. Forget about it. You won't come out alive. And I'm not just talking about money."

Everything clicked that instant, with that last sentence. I took it as a challenge to me, especially coming from Vandenbergh. Sarah was right. These last few months I'd kept a low profile, meek and passive. Now something was beginning to stir inside me again. For heaven's sake, I was only twenty-six years old! And already retiring?

I didn't underestimate Vandenbergh's warning. If I came to see him first, rather than Joe Lupino, Jimmy Rosen, or even Lavater, it certainly wasn't because of any fond feelings for him, which I didn't feel. But I'd learned to appreciate the workings of that computer he had for a brain. I knew he was right. Well, almost completely right. But I also knew I had made my money by trusting my own instincts more than all the advice I'd been given. I smiled at Vandenbergh.

24

"Let's say I ignore your warnings."

He shrugged.

"You want to execute this project in the United States?"

A dumb question. I didn't see myself trying to buy the Enghien casino or the one in Monte Carlo! For heaps of reasons—reasons of scale, to begin with.

Vandenbergh, the human computer, started up again.

"In that case, you'll need to meet three basic conditions."

He raised his thumb.

"One—as soon as you begin to plan a large operation, you'll need several million dollars. Say five hundred. That means 20 percent from your own pocket, your personal share. A hundred million. You don't have it. You'll need partners to put up all the guarantees. In all areas. You don't have that yet. An oil company or any other giant of that magnitude would reject your offer because it doesn't need you. As for the usual financiers, they'll refuse to invest in a gambling project. Any other candidate would be suspect."

He raised his index finger.

"Two—the license. You're not an American citizen, and no gambling commission will issue one to you. Those licenses are name-bearing, personal. They're granted to individuals, never to a company. So you'll have to recruit someone with U.S. citizenship, who's never had any trouble with the law, who knows gambling and casino management inside out, who has no suspect contacts near or far, who is scrupulously honest, whom you can trust—to the extent that you trust anyone—and, finally, who is free and willing to help you."

He was teaching me the ABCs, as far as I could see. He annoyed me.

"Child's play," I said.

Vandenbergh raised his middle finger.

"Three—the site, developed or not. I mean the site on which you'll build your casino. Buying a place all set up and ready to operate would be unbelievably costly. Five hundred million wouldn't be enough, you'd need twice as much. In your place, assuming I were crazy enough to get involved in something like this, I'd choose to build or renovate. The site you're looking for is in either Vegas or Atlantic City. It will have to be located within a certain district. In Vegas, that means on the Strip or close to it, and in Atlantic City, on the Boardwalk or close to it.

Such locations are rare. There's competition for them. Their prices are going up every day, they stagger the imagination."

Vandenbergh's cold smile became openly sadistic.

"Three conditions, Mr. Cimballi. Do you think you can meet them?"

And of course, I answered, "What do you want to bet?"

I paid similar visits to Rosen and Lupino as I did to Vandenbergh. I informed them of my project, also. They both had an identical reaction. With slight differences—I was crazy.

Jimmy Rosen reached for a memo pad and began making calculations.

"Franz, this represents at the low end an investment of $4 to $6 million."

"I might get away with less."

"I'd be very surprised."

He was a little offended. He couldn't stand for anyone to question his figures.

"Jimmy, we can always try, can't we?"

"You've always had outlandish ideas, but this one is by far the worst."

But since it mattered so much to me, okay, he would try.

Ditto for Lupino. Except that he choked with laughter at my first words.

"Here we go again! I was surprised, too, to see you snoozing in the sunshine all these months. How big do you want your casino, and where do you want it?"

The strangest part was that I hadn't the slightest idea. Eight or ten days went by. My three lawyer-counselors put their teams to work, looking for something to buy or rebuild that would satisfy the conditions laid down by Vandenbergh. Those three conditions did seem to me indispensable, necessary, and sufficient. And each of them was unbelievably difficult to satisfy. I clearly remember my state of mind in that June, 1976, while the United States was celebrating its two-hundredth birthday—a huge uncertainty, and from one day to the next, either a desire to call everything off, or, contrarywise, a fury to begin.

To the point that when Marc Lavater phoned me, around June 25, I didn't tell him anything. He asked if the portfolio he had sent me on the hotel industry was useful. I overdid it and told him that my request for a study was mere curiosity, that I hadn't made up my mind about anything. Which was true on the twenty-fifth or twenty-sixth, and was still true two days later, when Lupino reached me by telephone. He called me at the Pierre, just as I was getting back from a quick trip to Quebec, where I had gone to cast an eye at the gigantic James Bay construction project, for which the government of Quebec was issuing bonds that interested me as investments.

"Franz, I think I've found something for you."

"Vegas?"

"Atlantic City."

For a second, I felt kind of disappointed. I didn't know Atlantic City. For all I knew, it was some sort of ghost town.

"And it's worth it?"

The gleeful voice of that blasted Lupino.

"It's worth about $30 million, at any rate, my friend."

At first, I thought he was kidding. Unlike Rosen and Vandenbergh, who were as funny as a mausoleum, Joe Lupino had a sense of humor.

But he added, with all seriousness, "Franz, it's worth it. You should go and have a look."

No enthusiasm on my part. My dream of a casino, rather vague to begin with, went along with sunshine, the desert, and the special atmosphere of Las Vegas. And here I was, being offered the fog of a tiny seacoast town that seemed to me to have no future.

"Franz, time is short. We're not the only ones interested."

"Tomorrow."

We agreed to leave the next day at one o'clock in the afternoon, by car. Joe Lupino sketched a fast picture of the "big deal." A hotel with about four hundred rooms, dating from the turn of the century, pretty run down but with huge drawing rooms, located on the beach, in the very heart of Atlantic City, with access to the Boardwalk, and its own private dock. Plus five acres of land. In terms of facilities, it needed everything. With an additional drawback: the building was classified an historical landmark.

"And I'm supposed to pay $30 million for this pile of garbage?"

"We can always bargain. But according to my guys, it's worth it."

I doubted it. I felt as much like going there as I felt like hanging myself. But in the end I said, "Okay, Joe. One o'clock tomorrow."

It's always been true: Things always come in pairs. There must be some kind of law that makes "everything happen at the same time." Proof? That same evening, I had dinner with the Rosens. Jimmy's older son was getting ready to leave for Europe, Paris, in fact, where he would spend a year before going to college. Jimmy was a little worried about his son being lonely overseas, especially in France, the land of perdition if there ever was one. I offered to have the Lavaters, Marc and Françoise, look after him.

"I'll call them tomorrow morning to let them know."

Which I did. The exclamation of Marc's Parisian secretary told me that something important had happened. She let out a cry.

"What a coincidence, Mr. Cimballi! I was just going to dial your number in New York when the phone rang. Mr. Lavater has some important news for you."

And, indeed, I immediately heard Marc's voice, subdued for once.

"Franz? It's about Hassan Fezzali. He's just surfaced again."

2

He was my father's friend before he was mine. Hassan Fezzali, under the carefully maintained guise of being a carpet dealer, managed the fabulous wealth of a Saudi prince, a petrodollar billionaire, prior to his disappearance. He had never given me anything for free, naturally, but whenever I needed an ally, I had found him amiable, ready to listen to my arguments, though not always ready to agree with them. A year and a half earlier, he had disappeared. Abruptly. He was supposed to have left his office in Cairo on his way to the airport to catch a plane. He had never arrived at the airport. No one had ever seen him again. I believed he was dead.

"He's alive, no doubt about that," Marc Lavater told me from Paris. "I have proof of it."

Aside from my friendship and my curiosity to know what had happened to him, I had yet another reason for being very pleased by the news of his return. Shortly before his disappearance, Hassan and I had contracted a speculative venture in oil. The details are unimportant. What counts is that we had transferred funds (19 million for Fezzali, 10 for me, one for Lavater) to a Liechtenstein account. A special clause provided that not one dollar of that money could be used without the unanimous consent of the partners or their authorized representatives. As Hassan could not be officially considered dead, those funds were frozen. Finding my favorite Bedouin meant, therefore, that I would again be able to make use of my $10 million, which had been unusable for eighteen months.

For this one would at least make the trip from New York to Paris. I did so. I phoned Lupino to put off our visit to Atlantic City, despite his protests, and jumped on the first plane.

"The letter arrived in Vaduz, two days ago. Here's a copy of it."

I took the paper Marc Lavater handed me. The document beneath my eyes was short, a few handwritten lines. It was in English: PLEASE TRANSFER SPOT VALUE ON NEXT 29TH JUNE 61,551.86 U.S.$ TO ACCOUNT 1543 ZSM WEINER BANK ZURICH ATTENTION MR. GUNTHARDT. Nothing else except the access code (secret—only Hassan, Marc, and I knew it, besides the banker) and the signature. All in all, it was only an ordinary transfer order given to the Liechtenstein bankers.

"In fact, Franz," Lavater said, "you know as well as I do that the bank in Vaduz cannot execute this order as it stands, owing to the clause requiring the unanimous consent of the three company shareholders—Hassan, you, and me. Hassan knows it too."

So Fezzali had sent this letter for the sole purpose of alerting us.

"That's the only explanation. He was sure that the banker in Vaduz would let us know immediately. Which he did, for that matter."

I studied the photocopy. The writing was a little shaky, naturally, but it was unquestionably familiar to me.

"You had it analyzed. Is it Hassan's?"

"There's practically no doubt. Besides, don't forget the secret access code."

"And why this bizarre amount, $61,551.86?"

"Beats me."

Why hadn't Hassan rounded off the sum to sixty-two thousand dollars for instance? I knew he was stingy, but still.

"Marc, Hassan was trying to tell us something. I'd stake my life on it."

But what? The frustration was infuriating. Nevertheless, this transfer was undoubtedly a call for help. And there was no question of leaving that call unanswered. Anyhow, before coming to Paris, I had set another process in motion. Since I couldn't yet involve the regular police, I had alerted a private-detective agency whose services I had already employed on several occasions. Its head was the man I call the Englishman. He was as blond, as stolid, and as well-groomed as ever.

"Everything's in place," he told me. "I did what had to be done as soon as you called me from Kennedy Airport. I have a team in Vaduz and another in Zurich in the vicinity of the Weiner bank and a third ready for any eventuality. As soon as the transfer goes through between Liechtenstein and Switzerland, we'll hit the trail. Provided, of course, that our Swiss friends agree. They have some very backward notions about banking secrets."

And he gazed at me stolidly as though he had just revealed some crucial information.

Once again, the agreement of the two other partners—in this case, Marc and me—was absolutely imperative so that the transfer Fezzali was asking for could be made. Therefore, we countersigned the photocopy, and, to be even safer, I left immediately for Vaduz. Hassan's letter arrived on the twenty-fifth. I landed in Paris on the twenty-seventh, in the early afternoon. I was in Liechtenstein on the evening of the same day. I made sure that the transfer would be made on the twenty-ninth.

And, in the meantime, I pondered my riddle. 61,551.86. I tried all the possible combinations. It might be a telephone number; though the hint might be a little obvious, you never know. After all, by shifting the comma and period, you get 615.51.86. In Paris, for a princely sum, Lavater put his own staff on the trail along with another investigative agency. The results soon poured in. Does anyone want to know how many seven-digit telephone numbers there are in the world? I happened to find out: 1,628,000 and a bit. But my sleuths discovered a grand total of only forty-nine subscribers answering to 615.51.86. The first was an invalid old lady in California, the second was a laundry in Rio, the third lived in Australia. . . .

And the whole thing was a flop.

I dropped the telephone numbers. I tried zip codes. Forget the details, they're stupefying. If we tried to perform a check, it would take months. I gave up on that, too.

"Maybe it's some kind of settlement," Marc suggested on the telephone. "Hassan is obviously someone's prisoner, and that person has forced him to pay . . . I don't know . . ."

"His gas bill."

I chuckled, but with clenched teeth. I was exasperated by this puzzle that I couldn't' solve. Yet I was convinced of two things—the transfer order contained a message and that message was meant for me personally. And I didn't understand it!

Time was short. If I didn't do something before the transfer reached Zurich, the sixty-one-thousand-odd dollars would get lost in the banking maze, along with our trail. On the morning of the twenty-eighth, I was in Zurich, after nearly beating down the door of that Gunthardt whose name appeared on the transfer order. He was a very ordinary banker who played dumb with the greatest courtesy.

"What name did you say?"

"Fezzali. Hassan Fezzali."

I went through my explanation again. Hassan's sudden disappearance, our setting up a company in Liechtenstein together, the matter of the frozen funds, the message, and so forth.

Gunthardt stared at me, indecipherable. "Mr. Cimballi, surely you must be familiar with the laws that govern banking secrets in our country."

"But a man's life is at stake!"

A brick wall. I couldn't get anything out of him—that beast would sooner have been killed on the spot. I rejoined the Englishman who had accompanied me to Switzerland and was waiting for me on the Paradeplatz.

"Only the Swiss police could do something," he said.

I'd thought of that. But I knew in advance what response the Swiss authorities would give me. Did I have evidence?

No, there was only one solution. The next three hours were insane. I used them to find an airplane that could take off immediately and travel twenty-five hundred miles, since using a regular airline would waste too much time.

I finally took off just after three p.m., Zurich time. And it was still light when I touched down in Riyadh, Saudi Arabia. Alerted by Lavater, who had phoned them from Paris to announce my arrival, two young men dressed in European style but with red-and-white-striped shmaaghs were waiting at the end of the passage that had been set up especially for me, in order to spare me the formalities of customs. I didn't even have time to feel the heat. They put me into an air-conditioned Rolls.

"Is this your first visit to our country?"

I said yes. I was a bit taken aback. The Rolls cut a swath through the traffic with loud horn blasts.

"Prince Aziz is waiting for you, Mr. Cimballi. He has a lot of affection for Hassan Fezzali."

"So did I."

Prince Aziz was my age. I had met him only once, years ago, at the Hotel de Paris in Monte Carlo, over a lobster souffle and braised bass with lettuce. We had nearly become friends then. He listened to me tell the whole story.

I wound up, "I am now convinced that Hassan is alive. Or was, three or four days ago."

Silence. Suddenly I had the unpleasant feeling that my listener not only knew what I had just finished telling him, but knew more about it than I did.

Anyhow, he said, "I thought you knew. Hassan disappeared in January of last year. Since February, I've been paying two hundred thousand dollars every month to keep him alive."

The prince beckoned. Photographs were brought in, dated on the back from month to month, from February, 1975, to June, 1976, nearly all identical except for a few details. All of them showed Fezzali sitting or standing, holding a newspaper whose masthead made it possible to tell the date on which the pictures were taken.

I asked, "Where is he being held?"

"We don't know, of course."

The background of Hassan's pictures gave no indication. It was a plain, white sheet, apparently stretched over a wall. As for the newspapers, they were from all over the world.

"Who's holding him?"

"We don't know that, either."

I gazed deep into the Saudan's dark eyes. I didn't understand.

With the enormous resources at his disposal, why hadn't he tried to find out? I didn't even have to ask the question. He guessed it, and explained: "The ransom money is paid on the first day of each month to a numbered account in Switzerland. The first time, we tried to trace that money . . ."

He interrupted himself, pointing to the stack of photographs.

"Look closely at the picture marked 'April.' "

I did so. Without noticing anything, at first.

"The left hand," said Aziz.

I jumped. Hassan now had only four fingers on his left hand!

Aziz continued, "We made a second attempt, two months later, taking every imaginable precaution. Look at photograph number six, marked 'July.' "

This time, I shuddered in horror. After the pinky, they had cut off the first two knuckles of the ring and middle fingers.

"And they warned us that the next time, he no longer would have a hand at all."

He smiled, without the slightest pleasure.

"Mr. Cimballi, I feel a very special friendship, even affection, for Hassan. I'm not eager to have him cut up, piece by piece. I offered a huge sum for his release. They didn't even bother to reply. I don't know who's holding him, I don't know why, I don't know for how long. But I want to keep him alive. And I'm warning you—do something, anything, that jeopardizes his life, and there no longer will be a reason for me to like you."

He stared at me, and I remembered I was in a city at the end of the desert, where justice was eagerly dispensed with an ax.

Nevertheless, I made a final attempt. My conviction was firm. I was sure that in one way or another, Hassan had used that letter to Vaduz to alert us, to give us a new trail to follow, a different one. It seemed clear to me that sixty-one thousand dollars had nothing to do with the two hundred thousand paid each month as ransom. They were two separate operations.

"Hassan succeeded in setting a trap for his kidnappers. We both know how shrewd he is. By not answering his appeal, we're condemning him for good."

And by myself, I couldn't blast open the Swiss safe. But if he, a Saudi prince, who could involve the government in Riyadh, agreed to intercede with the Swiss authorities through diplomatic channels, then the Swiss . . .

I spoke in vain. Aziz rose.

33

"You're wasting your time, Mr. Cimballi."

I played my final card.

"And if I decode Hassan's message? If I'm able to understand what he tried to tell us?"

"I read that letter you showed me. I don't believe it contains anything other than a transfer order."

I could have left Riyadh forthwith. But I hung on, refusing to be defeated. The prince's aides had obtained a suite for me at the Riyadh Intercontinental, where foreign missions in search of a few petrodollars gathered. I phoned Marc in Paris. There was no news. At least, as far as Hassan was concerned.

"On the other hand, Joe Lupino called twice. It's about a hotel in Atlantic City. Joe's demanding a quick decision. Franz, I don't know what this is about. You want to buy a hotel?"

To hell with Lupino and Atlantic City! I really wasn't in the mood to concern myself with . . .

"Franz, Joe's being awfully insistent."

In Marc Lavater's tone, I clearly discerned a bit of spite. He was certainly the man I trusted most in the world, and I had not yet told him about my casino project. But things had gone so fast.

"I'll tell you about it, Marc. Later."

He hung up first, and I could tell he was put out. Too bad. He'd get over it! I plunged again into contemplation of the photocopy made in Vaduz. It was turning into an obsession. "Please transfer spot value . . ." My fury mounted, and it got to the point where I called Rosen in New York more to get my mind off things than because I really wanted to.

"Jimmy, it's about this casino business. Joe Lupino says he's found something interesting in Atlantic City. Find out but don't let him know. I want you to make a study independently of Lupino and anyone else."

He agreed, without comment; he would get to work immediately. Everything should be ready in two weeks. Not before; otherwise, it wouldn't be a thorough job.

We had barely hung up when I placed another call. This time to Vandenbergh, to ask for a report on Atlantic City.

"You have two weeks," I told him.

I went on to a third phone call. Lupino's voice betrayed his impatience, not to say his nervousness.

"For God's sake, Franz, where are you?"

Night had fallen in Riyadh. The Saudis didn't worry about time zones. Each day, they based the time on the sun's rise and setting.

"Where are you, Franz?"

"On camelback. Joe, shut up for a minute, please. All right, you swear to me that the Atlantic City deal is fabulous, and so okay, I'm going to give it a try. But please keep your cool. Go see your sellers and ask them in my name for a one-month option."

"They won't go along. You're not the only potential buyer . . ."

"Do the best you can. A one-month option." I quickly calculated. The sellers Joe had found were asking $30 million for their old hotel. "Offer them two hundred thousand for the option."

"It's going to be tough."

"I'm not paying you to see the Cosmos play in New York. And if this deal turns out to be a lemon, you're going to pay me back the two hundred thousand."

At that very second, I nearly yelled out loud.

During the whole time I had been on the phone, between my call to Marc and this one, I had been looking at the photocopy of the transfer order. And suddenly one word, a single one, literally jumped out at me, a shining light. For God's sake!

"Joe, get a move on. I'll call you back tomorrow."

I hung up without giving him time for another objection. In the next few minutes, the desk at the Intercontinental sent up to me the various lists and information I requested. A few simple operations on my pocket calculator, and the game was on. I rushed back to my telephone. The truth was I really had no time to lose. If I hadn't gotten it mixed up, as I usually did, it ought to be about eight p.m. in Paris and Zurich. That left me, roughly, twelve to sixteen hours before the sixty-one thousand dollars left Vaduz. But I was practically hopping with excitement. A good fifteen minutes of discussion, pleading, threats—no, His Highness was not at home, His Highness was attending a reception at the Al-Ma'ather palace, and His Highness . . .

At last, the voice of Aziz.

"Mr. Cimballi, I hope you're not disturbing me for . . ."

I cut him off with absolute irreverence.

"I've got it. I know where Hassan is."

35

SPOT!

It simply means "cash." But it's not so simple. Because a regular banker or financier, like you or me, would almost never use it in a transfer order. He would write or Telex "Please transfer (or forward) immediately . . ." Or in extreme cases, if he's fanatically precise, he would use the word "cash."

"Spot" is a term used by exchange brokers, those specialists who, all year long, send and receive transfer orders from one currency to another, from the dollar to the Swiss franc, from the Dutch florin to the Mongolian tugrik (although there was rarely a call for that). I had engaged in this type of operation, but without comparison to Hassan Fezzali, who had always been a very major exchange broker. Aziz stared at me.

"You took me away from the reception to tell me that?"

I handed him one of the lists that the Intercontinental desk had given me. It showed all the currencies traded in the world, ranked in alphabetical order by the countries that issued them, from Abu Dhabi (where a Rolls is purchased with Bahrein dinars) to Zambia (where a secondhand bicycle is paid for with two or three tons of kwashas, which in turn are divided into ngwees).

I explained, "Hassan used the word 'spot' in his message, whereas he might have left it out or used a different word. It's clear. He wanted us to think about currency trading. Now, consider this figure: 61,551.86. It's not a round figure, to say the least. So I took this list and searched it. What is the only currency in the world, the only one, in which on June 29 at the start of trading, $61,551.86 changes into a round figure? I did my calculations. There's only one currency."

I allowed myself a small pause, just to show how devilishly clever I was.

"There's only one, Your Highness: the riyal, or Yri, of the Republic of Yemen. Hassan is a prisoner somewhere in North Yemen."

3

It's extremely easy to convince the Swiss police and bankers to violate banking secrets and get them to tell you how much Mr. Schmmuuggluff has in his account, where he gets the money, and what he plans to do with it.

All you have to do is satisfy three conditions.

1. Have an income of around $1 billion a year, after taxes.

2. Have the unconditional support of a legitimate, sovereign government whose foreign debt is close to zero.

3. Give the Swiss a really good reason.

I know it's fast and easy because Aziz did it. In record time. No sooner had I finished speaking than he got in touch with his cousin, the prime minister, who spoke to his cousin, the foreign-affairs minister, who phoned a second cousin to both of them, who was ambassador to Switzerland. And the latter, on the dawn of June 29, represented to the Swiss government that a crime indeed had been committed, namely a kidnapping, against the person of the closest adviser to a member of the royal family, as evidenced by the ransom demands and payments and the diligent investigations by the Saudi and Egyptian police, and others, in January, 1975, and during the following months. By means of which, from one government to another and one police force to another, an understanding emerged that the banking secret, indeed, should be broken. But caution: Just as much as was necessary, and no more.

Thus, on June 29, around two o'clock in the afternoon (or about noon in Switzerland), the Englishman was able to call me from Zurich and stolidly announce, "We've found the trail. At least the beginning. The man who opened the numbered account in Zurich is named Belkacem. He gave a London address. We checked. The address is false."

"Do you know what will happen to the sixty-one thousand dollars?"

"It should be transferred today to Luxembourg. The Swiss police have a rogatory commission; we can trace the money wherever it's transferred."

The Englishman was optimistic. So was I, but never for long. I had not left Riyadh, mainly because Aziz had asked me to stay, for personal reasons this time. An invitation that had a disturbing aspect. Clearly, I was responsible in advance for what would happen to Hassan Fezzali. Thus, I weighed the fragility of my conclusions. What if I were wrong? What if I had simply overestimated my old friend's craftiness and capacity for resistance? The photos I'd seen of him showed that his captivity had taken a great toll on him. The main argument I employed to convince Aziz to act and to make his government act in Switzerland was this—I was convinced that Hassan had managed to bribe one of his guards by offering him more than sixty thousand dollars (a fortune in Yemen) behind the backs of his other kidnappers.

But if I were wrong, and my actions led to endangering Fezzali, surely the world would not be wide enough to shelter me from the thunder.

Lupino again. While all this was going on, he'd obtained the option I asked for on the hotel in Atlantic City.

"But for two hundred fifty thousand dollars and only two weeks, Franz, that's all I could wring out of them. You now have until July 21 to make up your mind."

In other words, if by that date I had not picked up my option and confirmed my purchase of the hotel—a hotel I had not seen, good heavens!—I would lose a quarter of a million dollars.

"As for the purchase itself," Joe continued, "the sellers are still asking for 30 million, but I think we can make them come down a little. Say 27 or 28."

"We'll see."

The same day—that is, the twenty-ninth—Lavater also phoned. I told him I'd finally managed to wring a decision out of Aziz. He instantly spotted the weak part of my situation.

"If your intervention results in more troubles for Hassan, Aziz is going to be really upset with you."

"Thanks for reassuring me."

"You should have left it to the police. Turning the whole business over to the Englishman only increases the risks you're taking."

"I have more confidence in the Englishman than in all the cops in the world. And if I succeed, it will only add to my credit."

Those weren't the only reasons. In truth, Aziz didn't know I was using the Englishman. He must have suspected I'd resorted to private detectives, but knew nothing about them. I'd refrained from any revelations on that point, out of caution. I hadn't forgotten that the Saudis' second attempt to follow the trail leading to the kidnappers had ended in failure, despite "every imaginable precaution." The result—two fewer fingers for Hassan. I had no wish to add to the carnage.

And it was on that same June 29 that the Englishman, in very guarded words, let me know the point he had reached.

"The money didn't stay in Luxembourg even for one hour. An order has just transferred it to Rome."

To a bank that the Englishman put under surveillance immediately, with the cooperation of the Italian finance unit. Without results. Two days passed without anyone seeming to take an interest in the sixty thousand dollars. As for me, I was still in Riyadh, where I had truly seen everything there was to see, from a former U.S. Vice-President literally going door to door on behalf of a company that made bulletproof vests, to a bank managed solely by women, open only to women (the Koran, it seemed, was in agreement), and where I was escorted from the door by armed female guards as soon as I tried to set a curious foot in there.

Finally, on July 2, things moved in Rome.

The Englishman: "A new transfer order has just arrived. Its next destination—Beirut."

"An order from where?"

"A London bank, but it acted only as a relay. The real origin is Cairo. One of my teams has just left."

He, the Englishman, followed the sixty thousand dollars to Lebanon. He had the same feeling I did. Such an almost ridiculous wealth of precautions in transferring a relatively modest sum might mean that someone was having a joke at our expense. But we rather believed we were dealing with an amateur trying to erase his tracks, one who was certainly aware of a few banking procedures, but was not a true specialist, nonetheless. In other words, my initial hypothesis was taking on greater cohesiveness—one of Fezzali's kidnappers was acting on his own behalf. The true authors of the kidnapping, those who had been receiving the ransom for eighteen months, had demonstrated much greater skill.

"And I think Cairo is the final destination," the Englishman concluded.

He proved right. On July 3, the Beirut bank did credit an account to the Maha & Moore Bank in Cairo. Contrary to what he had done so far, in Vaduz, Zurich, Luxembourg, Rome, and Beirut, the Englishman did not make contact with the bank's management, nor even with the Cairo police. He relied on his instinct, he said, and now wanted to work only with his own men, without any official assistance. He went to Cairo, where he called me on the morning of the fourth.

"The man we're looking for is here."

Three hours later, after a rather grim discussion with Aziz, who reproached me for using too much of my own discretion, but still consented to let me leave Saudi Arabia without first slicing me into pieces, I boarded a plane for the Egyptian capital.

"That's him."

Through the car's rear window, I could see a young man of about twenty-five, dressed European-style. We were in the Choubra district. The car in which the Englishman had come to pick me up at the airport was just at the entrance to Guezireh el-Badrane, which was the busiest route in the area where Cairo's Christians—Syrians, Lebanese, and others—were gathered. The man was coming in our direction and had to pass us sooner or later. He was short, rather swarthy, with a small mustache. He certainly didn't look as if he had invented warm water.

"Why him? Why him in particular?"

"First of all, because he works at Maha & Moore, as a clerk. Second, because we're operating on your initial hypothesis, your secret message concealed in a trading operation. And it seems you've hit the nail on the head. I don't even know why I say 'it seems.' You *have* hit the nail on the head. Our man is Yemenite. He was born in a dusty hamlet in what is now North Yemen. Five weeks ago, he took his annual vacation and went home to pay a visit to his family. The usual thing. What is unusual is that he came back to Cairo after spending only six days in his village. We made the rounds of the airlines. Upon his return to Cairo, he took a plane to Beirut, Rome, Zurich. Probably traveled by train—he doesn't have much money—between Zurich, Vaduz, and Luxembourg. In Luxembourg, took another plane to London, and came back from there. To here. Naturally, we photographed him with a telescopic lens and sent his picture to the bankers in Vaduz and Zurich. They recognized him. He's Belkacem—the one who transferred the sixty thousand dollars."

"And his name?"

The Englishman deigned to remove the Craven-A from his lips for a second.

"Yussuf Somebody-or-other."

The man passed alongside our car. If I had stretched my arm out the open window, I could have grabbed him.

"And does he have something to do with Fezzali's kidnapping?"

No. The Englishman had a theory that dovetailed pretty well with mine. Yussuf, back in his native village, had learned in some way of Fezzali's captivity and had swindled him out of sixty thousand dollars. Perhaps by promising to call for help.

"But Hassan was even cleverer than he. So that means he has to be in the vicinity of that village."

"Exactly," said the Englishman.

The man disappeared from our sight, in the midst of the world's most tumultuous throng, walking toward the central station and the statue of Ramses II. I was surprised that he wasn't being followed.

"He is. Five of my men are keeping him covered."

"I never see your men."

"That's why they work for me. Otherwise, I'd fire them. Mr. Cimballi, there are three possibilities. First, we can turn him over to the Egyptian police, or even the Saudis, for being an accomplice to a kidnapping and extortion case. Or we can take care of it ourselves and make him talk. And believe me, we'll make him talk."

I met his glance. What next? I couldn't see myself becoming involved in torture, directly or indirectly. Even if they only planned to tickle him.

I said, "The third solution."

"It's your money."

"So I've noticed."

The third solution, of course, was not to try anything with Yussuf, not to appear to know that he even existed, and, meanwhile, to go and take a panoramic and searching glance at North Yemen.

"Which Yemen is a people's republic slightly to the left of Stalin?"

"The South. Ours is the North."

"So we can go and look around and try to find Hassan. That's easier said than done. What I know about Yemen would fit on a postage stamp, but I have a feeling you can't go there like you go to Switzerland. It's probably an untamed wilderness."

"It's worse," said the Englishman. "The place is called Rub al-Khali. The government in San'a—that's the capital—has only nominal authority there. The natives are still armed to the teeth, and we'd be as conspicuous as a London banker wearing tweed in a nudist colony."

He smiled at me, very pleased with his joke.

As for organizing a commando made up of sharpshooters recruited as mercenaries, Hollywood-style, whether financed by me or by Prince Aziz—we both agreed it was better to forget about that. Even though I toyed with the idea for a few hours. But aside from the fact that I was slightly lacking in experience in such matters, I was afraid that a forced evacuation would put Fezzali's life in danger, and that was a risk I didn't want to take. And anyway, how could such a commando be recruited without word getting around? On that July 4, I had not yet informed Aziz about our discoveries. The fact was that I had a few suspicions. The more I thought about it, it seemed to me entirely possible that one or more persons in the prince's immediate entourage might benefit well by Fezzali's absence, and might benefit even better by his final disappearance, which would create an opening. Who could tell? No, all things considered, I would operate alone.

Especially since I believed I had two assets that would enable me to act in my own way, nonviolently. First was the Englishman, who had found someone who knew someone who knew someone who was completely familiar with the desert around Rub al-Khali and the two Yemens, North and South.

Second, I had an idea. A preposterous, farfetched, even crazy idea—call it what you will—but one that pleased me immensely.

4

In Cairo, I took a suite at the Nile Hilton, which, as its name indicates, was built directly over the river. On the evening of July 4, I had just put through my telephone call to Adriano Letta in Rome when the Englishman popped up again. He told me he had found the person who knew someone who, etc.

"He's here. You ought to see him."

"One moment."

To Adriano Letta (he was one of my safest occasional-collaborators in Europe) I explained what I wanted him to do and how he should go about it. He expressed not the slightest surprise and merely wanted to know how much time he had. "The sooner the better." He said okay, he'd take care of it. That was one of Adriano's qualities I prized the most. Had I phoned him to say I'd just bought the Eiffel Tower and the Brooklyn Bridge and was planning to make them into pipe cleaners, all he would ask is, "How much should I sell these pipe cleaners for?" The Englishman, however, who had followed the conversation, lost his composure for once and stared at me in dismay.

"You're really going to do that?"

"I've got to let Hassan know that I got his message and understood it and that I'm going to take care of him."

"No comment," said the Englishman, stolidly as ever.

He then ushered in the specialist from Yemen, who in and of himself made the trip worthwhile. I'm not extremely tall myself, and many times I have to lean my head back in order to look people in the eye. Well, for once, it was the reverse. The person the Englishman had brought me was at most five feet tall. He was as wide as he was high and wore a colonial helmet like Kitchener's—you might have thought he was Henry Morton Stanley, in a distorting mirror. And he regarded me with hatred (I quickly learned that he regarded the entire world with the same hate-filled eyes, since he detested the entire world without exception). What I knew of him amounted to very little—a former corporal in the British army, he had been stationed in Aden and environs under the British Empire, had fallen madly in love with Yemen, remained there after the departure of His Majesty's army, and tried to unify the two Yemens. Without the least success. In the end, they'd thrown him out. In short, he was a failed Lawrence of Arabia, a two-bit one, you might say.

He said to me, spitefully, "And you think it's easy to retake one of al-Chaafi's prisoners? Is that what you think?"

I was baffled. Who was this al-Whatsisname of whom I'd never heard? The specialist snorted contemptuously. Al-Chaafi was undoubtedly the man holding Hassan Fezzali in his fortress.

"It can't be anyone but him, the swine. Your Yussuf's native village is the one ruled by al-Chaafi."

He spit on the Hilton's carpet, consenting all the same to explain to me that the aforementioned al-Chaafi was a kind of local warlord, reigning supreme over a fortress village in the heart of the Yemenite mountains, on the edge of the Rub al-Khali, which was an absolutely terrifying desert. And that he would do anything for money.

"Even going so far as to kidnap a financier like Hassan Fezzali in the streets of Cairo?"

I shouldn't have said that. Lawrence of Arabia II looked at me as if I were an absolute half-wit.

"That son of a bitch al-Chaafi doesn't even know where Cairo is. No, if he's got your Fezzali holed up in his hide-out, it must be because another piece of garbage put him there for safekeeping."

The Englishman and I exchanged a glance. Now my suspicions were confirmed. They hadn't kidnapped Fezzali solely for the ransom. Someone in Aziz's entourage obviously had a hand in it. Perhaps out of jealousy, perhaps at the instigation of Martin Yahl. All told, I'd done well not to let Aziz know of my present and future actions.

"And can we try a raid on this village?"

Lawrence of Arabia II went into a fit again. A parachute division would not be enough. And al-Chaafi's first reaction upon their arrival would be to get rid of his prisoner, even if he had to make him into shish kebab.

"Can we buy him off, then?"

A kind of frenzied whinnying was his reply to my question.

"And how do you expect to get in touch with him? By telephone? They're in the Middle Ages down there. Don't even have a highway to get there. And," he added, "even assuming I hop on a camel to go down there and try to negotiate, the best thing that could happen to me would be that I would be captured too."

At that point in our conversation, Lawrence of Arabia II began to exasperate me. He must have some kind of solution, for Pete's sake!

The Englishman said to me, laughing;

"You should tell our friend about that idea you had."

And, why not? Given where I was at! So there I was, explaining what Adriano Letta in Rome was preparing with his usual efficiency. I expected another volcanic eruption. None came. On the contrary. Silence. For the first time in our conversation, Lawrence of Arabia II looked at me with respect.

"At last, an intelligent idea," he said. "About time. Now, that might work. It's dumb as hell, but it just might work."

We took off from Djibouti on the stroke of eight a.m., July 7. We, being Adriano Letta (he spoke Arabic fluently, among other languages), plus the Englishman, plus Lawrence of Arabia II, plus a parachuting expert, plus me. At the controls was my favorite pilot, Flint, who had come specially from Florida. The plane was a DC-3 chartered in Addis Ababa, not without difficulty. Ethiopia was in the midst of revolution, and the plane's owner wanted to sell it to me.

The six containers equipped with parachutes were lined up beside the door from which we would drop them. I wondered how. A moment ago, I'd tried to lift one and had been unable to move it. Each of them, content and container, must have weighed 300 to 400 pounds. For a nutty idea, this was a nutty idea. What was I doing here, in this musical-comedy adventure, when I should have been in Paris, New York, St. Tropez, or Atlantic City, inspecting an old hotel that was already costing me $250,000, or, better yet, in Jamaica with my son and Sarah?

Below us, the Bab el Mandeb strait came to an end. Happy Arabia, otherwise known as Yemen, appeared to the left as well as the right in fabulously clear air. But there must be no miscalculation. While I had succeeded without too much trouble in obtaining permission to fly over North Yemen, which was pro-Western, I'd been flatly turned down in Aden, capital of the other Yemen, where they had taken the trouble to tell me that Soviet-made MIGs would be happy to shoot me down on sight.

The DC-3 puttered along at 150 miles per hour. The Red Sea disappeared completely. In its place, an ever more mountainous terrain rose toward us. Flint grumbled, as usual. For him, there was no doubt—this rented plane wasn't worth spit, we would shortly crash, and, in any case, we could never clear the over-nine-thousand-foot peaks that stood in our way. He conde-scended to show me on the map where we were—in the south-east and less then seventy-five miles from San'a, thus no longer very far from our destination. It was a matter of twenty-five min-utes or so. Lawrence of Arabia II had just settled into the co-pilot's seat. He recognized caravan routes, a water source fed by a wadi, a stream that appeared dry.

"We're getting close."

We passed Ta'izz and its high plateaus with their checker-board of cultivated fields. Here was what had been the true Happy Arabia of the ancients, but the dominant color now was ocher on a land that was becoming drier with each passing cen-tury. Flint slanted the DC-3's wings to the left, and there we were again, flying over a region of real mountains, atrociously barren and alarmingly arid. Yet here and there, capping some steep wall, rose a fortified village, its access slopes encircled by tiny rectangular fields. Sparse goat herds, no highway. The Mid-dle Ages, as Lawrence of Arabia II had said.

We were now flying north-northeast. The scenery became more and more arid, unbelievably parched, inhuman. The South Yemen border was no longer far off, while on our right and in front of us stretched the terrifying Rub al-Khali, one of the most desertlike deserts in the world.

"There it is!"

Lawrence of Arabia II leaned forward, trembling with excite-ment and also, perhaps, a feeling of nostalgia. According to his biography, he had spent thirty years of his life in this wild land. In any case, he pointed out a precariously perched fortress vil-lage.

Flint lost altitude. He made a first pass at less than ninety feet above the tiny stronghold which dominated the village, a square structure of ocher clay, pitted with moucharabiehs and tran-soms, its widows highlighted with whitewash. Men appeared, faces turned skyward.

"They're capable of firing on us, those bastards. Watch out."

Flint swerved and returned. The second pass. Lawrence of Arabia's prediction came true. They did indeed fire on us. With-out harm.

"But they're loading machine guns and heavy artillery."

Time to quit acting like clay pigeons. The parachuting expert opened the door.

"Here we go," he yelled.

Flint regained altitude. Two minutes later, the parachute of the first container unfolded in the sky over Yemen. It was quickly followed by five more. We hadn't lifted the containers—all we had to do was push them out the opening.

"Let's get out of here."

Mission accomplished. Or so I believed. But apparently, that was not Flint's opinion. He positioned the plane for a fourth descent, shaving the reddish-brown turrets. I screamed bloody murder—it was no use. That idiot Flint replied to all my cries of rage with a mad grin, showing me with a jerk of his thumb what was happening at the back of the plane. Clinging with one hand to the rim of the door that was still open onto thin air, Lawrence of Arabia II was pissing on the fortress village, while shouting some kind of challenge to al-Chaafi. The Englishman and the parachute expert were doubled over laughing. Even Adriano Letta smiled. I was the only one who didn't find it funny.

Below, the six containers had reached the ground. I could see men approaching them cautiously. Soon they opened them. And then they found, not only my offer to negotiate, but six-hundred quarts of ice cream as well. Not just any ice cream—it was stromboli, a vanilla-pistachio-chocolate mixture with nuts, candied fruits, and small morsels of chocolate. Hassan Fezzali's favorite. I'd paid so much attention to detail that I ordered the ice cream specially from the Milan factory which Hassan had once told me he thought was the best in the world.

There was nothing more to do but wait.

I waited, biting my fingernails. In arriving at the idea of parachuting the ice cream, I had piled theory on theory. If a single one of them proved false, I would probably spend my life regretting it. Aziz's Saudis would fix my wagon, even if it were only in the financial arena.

I left Adriano in San'a to wait for any response from al-Chaafi to my offer of negotiation. I went directly back to Paris without passing square one, i.e., Cairo. I arrived at Roissy airport on the morning of July 9. When he learned of my escapade, Marc Lavater threw up his arms—first a casino and now ice cream in Yemen!

"Franz, you really should see a psychiatrist!"

"It may work. According to Lawrence of Arabia II, it's a brilliant idea. Anyway, I'm brilliant."

I was beginning to find the whole thing hilariously funny. I sniggered and Marc sulked.

"If that's how it is, I'd rather not know about it," he said.

"And let me lose sleep all by myself? Selfish!"

We went to Lipp's for lunch. Pointing at Marc, I told Roger Cazes, the owner, "This guy thinks I'm completely crazy."

"Only madmen are truly interesting. By the way, good to see you again," Roger replied with his usual humor.

It was during that lunch, while I stuffed myself with red meat (my stay in Arabia had put me in a state of need), that Marc spoke to me of Jersey and the Channel Islands in general. He had spent a weekend there and fallen in love with the place. At first, this interested me as much as a boil epidemic in Senegambia, but then, as I listened to Lavater to make him happy, I began, almost in spite of myself . . .

"After all, why not?"

Marc raised his eyebrows.

"Why not what?"

"If I buy a casino, lots of casinos, a hotel, lots of hotels, which will combine to make even more casino-hotels, I'll need a company to manage it all. Why not in the Channel Islands?"

Strategically, it was the perfect place. And unless Marc was wrong—but he was never wrong about such things—there were considerable advantages in establishing a company there. Tax-wise, for instance. In Jersey, income taxes were 20 percent in pounds sterling, at maximum. That, in itself, was food for thought. And even better, one island in particular enjoyed a truly outstanding situation: Sark. If you live on Sark, you have a choice between two kinds of taxation. One consists of paying 10 percent of your crops if you're a farmer. The other (if you're not an agricultural landowner), of spending two days each year on pleasant chores, such as repairing roads. And if you prefer jogging, you can even get rid of that burden by paying ten pounds or about sixteen dollars.

I suddenly felt a tremendous urge to be a roadman.

Besides, I could easily see myself on my island, standing on a rock like Victor Hugo, in immediate proximity to the French and British coasts, addressing fond greetings to the finance ministers of France or the United Kingdom, in the event—absurd hypothesis—that a left-wing government one day took power in either of those countries.

48

"And how do you get to Jersey?"

Like everyone else—by plane. And Marc Lavater was right about one thing—it was magnificent, with incredibly varied scenery, quiet, and full of adorable little hotels and wonderful English pubs. We stayed at the Longueville Manor in St. Saviour, also known as St. Hélier, just long enough to indulge in a seafood orgy, and then, in fifteen minutes, a hovercraft took us to Sark Island.

It was love at first sight. What else was there to feel about this virtual garden poised on the sea, where there were no cars (except a few tractors), where crime did not exist because each one of the five hundred or so inhabitants took turns being policeman, where the only thing prohibited was dogs because some two hundred fifty years ago, a dog had bitten the hand of the lord's little girl?

I met the present lord. And he was patient, as far as listening to me. In truth, during the trip from Paris to Jersey, other ideas had occurred to me. Why not take full advantage of all the legal opportunities Sark offered?

Its special status—like that of all the other Channel Islands, by the way—stemmed from an accident. Jersey and Guernsey were mistakenly omitted from the treaty of 1258 in which the English kings renounced their rights to William the Conqueror of Normandy. Therefore the islands were not part of the United Kingdom, they were not represented in the London Parliament, they were self-governed, by a bailiff, and on Sark, by a lord. Their civil law was descended from old Norman custom, vaguely amended by English law—no inheritance rights, no value-added tax, no customs. That created a lot of possibilities, *non*?

"You could set up a bank here, or a free zone, or both."

The lord was still listening to me with complete courtesy. We were touring the island on foot, from the small port of La Maseline to the village.

"What would be necessary for a free zone?" I continued. "A mere office would suffice, where records would be kept. We could register ships, as in Panama."

"A flag of convenience."

"Exactly. And there's nothing to stop each one of you citizens from heading a hundred or two hundred companies. It would take them at most fifteen minutes a week."

49

"And is all of this honest?"

"But of course," I said. "And there should be no lack of customers, enough to quickly solve all the financial problems the island may have. If there are any."

"Who doesn't have them? And you would take charge of finding those thousands of customers?"

Certainly. By opening offices in Geneva, Hong Kong, Outer Mongolia, or anywhere. On payment of an honest commission, naturally. We could also authorize the establishment of corporations of the Panama, Curaçao, or Liechtenstein type. It was legally possible. The lord had the right. And furthermore, we could set up a free zone, even better organized than on Jersey.

I talked on and on. At least I succeeded in forgetting my worries for a few hours, though failing to convince an unshakeably courteous lord. Our walking eventually brought us back to our point of departure, the manor itself, an old sixth-century monastery, remarkably kept up. Marc came out as we arrived. He had given instructions to his Paris office, mentioning our itinerary. A worthwhile precaution.

"Franz, they called you from Yemen. Adriano needs you urgently."

End of intermission. I left immediately.

5

Adriano Letta was waiting for me at the San'a airport.

His first words, as soon as we were out of range of indiscreet ears, "They made contact, Mr. Cimballi. Less than forty hours ago."

In the letter addressed to al-Chaafi that had accompanied the ice cream, I had mentioned Adriano's name and his address in San'a, a tiny "fondouk" (hotel) near the Bab el-Yemen port. We thought, I especially, that things would move slowly, and as the parachuting over the fortified village took place on July 7, we estimated it would take eight to ten days for any reaction. But only five days had passed when . . .

"I was in the street, I had just left my hotel. There were three of them, all carrying weapons, but that's nothing, everyone is armed here. They surrounded me without a word, and gradually pushed me inside a house. They said, 'Cimballi is the one we want to talk to.' I said you weren't there and that I was representing you. Nothing doing. They kept repeating 'Cimballi.' "

So, Adriano made an appointment for me. But distrustfully, he said. He hired bodyguards.

"Adriano, what are you, crazy?"

He shook his head.

"It's dangerous, Mr. Cimballi. Really dangerous. They didn't want a meeting in town. And once you're outside San'a, anything can happen."

"Does that mean the meeting is outside?"

More outside would be hard to find. I was supposed to meet the other parties in Marib-Fata.

"Never heard of it."

"It's the land of the Queen of Sheba," Adriano explained.

Come on, now. The Queen of Sheba herself was all that was missing!

"Call me Solomon."

A lunar landscape—an ocher plain with ravines and crevasses, pock-marked with tiny mesas, strewn with an infinite number of stones. The stones, also ocher or black, seemed to have been flung by an explosion. The sinking sun showed them in startling relief and all but brought them to life. Now that the engines had been stifled, the silence was crushing, oppressive. It made a ringing in my ears.

A ghost town if ever there was one, Marib-Fata, home of the Queen of Sheba, lay seven or eight hundred yards ahead of me, its rectangular structures perched on a row of black hills. Some buildings seemed 150 feet high. I could see the maze of clay bricks, the loophole windows, their embrasures sometimes rimmed in white, in the local fashion.

"Does anyone live there?"

"Three or four merchants who supply travelers with provisions."

I shifted the twin circles of my binoculars onto the dead city—not the slightest sign of life. If there were merchants behind those ramparts, you really couldn't accuse them of being aggressive with customers!

"Five minutes till meeting time," Adriano announced, in hushed tones (he was really doing all he could to reassure me!).

Then he continued in Arabic, apparently giving orders—the men in my escort spread themselves out, jumping from the Toyota trucks that had brought them from San'a. There were thirty of them, armed to the eyes with Kalachnikovs (Chinese-made, I heard) and with "jambias," huge daggers with carved handles, without which a true Yemenite would no longer be a true Yemenite. Bearded and mustached, their eyes hidden by sunglasses, they were a terrifying sight. I wondered who I was more afraid of—al-Chaafi, who was coming, or my bodyguards who were already there.

"Two minutes," said Adriano, more solemn than ever.

I stared hard at the small clay-brick structure halfway between the ghost town and me. Twenty minutes earlier, Adriano had gone to inspect it to make sure that it contained no trap.

"One minute."

Cimballi, you dunce, why aren't you in Montego Bay, on the beach or indolently wedged in your personal hammock? IMBECILE!

"Now," said Adriano. "And good luck."

Did he really need to whisper, on top of everything? He made my blood freeze. I walked the few hundred yards separating me from the shack, and with each step my conviction grew that I was behaving like a jackass. Especially since, in the deserted town ahead of me, nothing was stirring, nothing was happening, no noise could be heard. At best, I'd been stood up in Yemenite fashion. There I was at the shack. I walked around it and with some reluctance (I expected at any moment to hear the whistle of the saber that would slice off my head) glanced inside. It stank, but aside from that, it was as empty as the head of an investor in a Communist country.

As soon as I came back out into the open air, I heard the noise. No doubt about it—THEY were coming. From the home of the Queen of Sheba.

I was prepared for anything—a fierce, tumultuous charge of turbaned horsemen, as in a Moroccan fantasy, or the thundering of proud camel riders swaying on their desert ships, or even an Apache-style approach where you lift a rock as big as a fist and there are three or four of them hiding underneath, looking at you with a silent sneer.

Anything but this.

Three motorcycles. The first was a kind of Florida chopper with ultra-custom controls. Riding this first motorcycle was a young man about my age, bushy-headed, his face swallowed up by huge glasses with pink frames. He wore yellow silk pants, a black leather jacket with an eagle on the back, decorated with fake-fur stripes of a handsome mallard green. On his feet were beige sandals. Straddling the back seat was what I assumed to be his girlfriend, though you couldn't see much of her—aside from a black velvet cape that covered her from head to foot, she sported a pink veil through which you could glimpse only her heavily kohled eyes.

The machine halted six feet from me.

The youth smiled. "We're on time, aren't we?"

"You're not al-Chaafi."

"I'm his son."

I glanced at the other two motorcyclists. They were no older than my interlocutor. They were both armed with Sino-Soviet automatic rifles and wore them casually slung over their shoulders. Yet something told me that it wouldn't take much to turn them into sharpshooters.

"Where is Hassan Fezzali?"

A vague gesture.

"Allah knows."

This young man was making a fool of me.

I said, "Above all else, I want proof that he's still alive."

The leather-gloved hand plunged inside the jacket and came out with Polaroid prints. I turned them over and could barely repress a smile. They showed Hassan wolfing down my ice cream.

"How much are you getting to guard him?"

A short hesitation.

"Five thousand rials."

"Per month?"

"Yes."

That was eleven thousand dollars. Prince Aziz was paying two hundred thousand a month.

53

"Those you are guarding Fezzali for are cheating you. They're making three times as much as you."

I deliberately pared down the figures. First, in order to determine the exact degree of relationship between those who had kidnapped Hassan and those who were guarding him. Next, so as not to raise the stakes unnecessarily. My reasoning was simple. If the youth didn't know the exact figure of the ransom, it meant my initial hypothesis was correct—al-Chaafi and his village were mere stooges, with whom I could easily negotiate.

The boy knitted his brows and said simply, "Three times more?"

"Three times. They're robbing you. And yet, you're taking all the risks. Especially now that we know where Fezzali's being held and by whom."

"How did you find out?"

"I went to a clairvoyant."

I began to get over my surprise at seeing a biker who would have gone unnoticed in Florida appear in the midst of medieval Yemen. Besides, I had been expecting some kind of old-style negotiation. You know—sitting around for hours, smoking a peace pipe with an old chief after offering him glass beads and my scouting knife. No such thing. My interlocutor that day spoke perfectly decent English, which he certainly hadn't learned in his remote mountains—nor had he bought his Yamaha there. He had probably traveled. Perhaps he was one of the hundreds of thousands of Yemenites who had been forced to emigrate to look for work in, say, the Persian Gulf emirates. Or perhaps he had been a student, his studies financed by Papa al-Chaafi, who must have accumulated a bit of money by kidnapping people or holding them hostage. I would never know, and I didn't care.

"Five million dollars," said the man on the motorcycle.

I snorted. There followed an hour-and-a-half of discussion in which I learned that Papa al-Chaafi had died three years ago. It seemed Lawrence of Arabia's information was a little out of date.

"I'll pay you a year's board, that's all."

"Five million."

"Hassan Fezzali is no longer young. His extended captivity . . ."

"He's in perfect health."

"Except for those fingers you cut off."

"That wasn't me, that was my uncle," the young man said. The uncle had died, also, seven or eight months ago.

"Three million."

"Fezzali is old and sick. If he dies, you won't get a penny. But the Saudi army will come and slice you in pieces one day. Four hundred thousand."

We finally came to an agreement on four hundred fifty thousand dollars. In cash. I thought the bargaining was over.

"That's not all, Mr. Cimballi."

And he laid down his final condition. I looked at him, flabbergasted. Was he serious?

"Take it or leave it. The money is for me. The rest is for the village. Otherwise, they'll never be wiling to release your friend."

I said okay. We shook hands. He and his friends got back in the saddle. They disappeared into the ancient dwelling place of the Queen of Sheba. I rejoined Adriano Letta, and his worried face really didn't help matters. I went into convulsions of laughter.

A WHAT? "Marc Lavater asked me.

"An ice-cream factory. That was their nonnegotiable demand. And they want it set up in their little town for their exclusive use. They liked my ice cream a lot. Except for the nuts. They don't like pine nuts much. They would have preferred almonds."

We hadn't lost a second. From San'a, Adriano hurried directly to Milan and began hunting. He phoned me in the late morning of July 16. He'd found the necessary equipment, plus the no-less-essential kerosene generator. A cargo plane would load up the lot that very evening, bound for Yemen.

"And the candied fruits? The almonds?"

Adriano had thought of that—a ton of each. We made inquiries. The manufacture of stromboli requires ice cream (milk, eggs, sugar) and whipped cream. No problem there. Adriano provided two and a half tons of frozen whipped cream, for starters. Ditto for the milk, which would be powdered. Sugar was not a problem either.

"The eggs, on the other hand," Adriano explained, with a gravity that almost made me choke, "are a trickier proposition. There are two possibilities. Either we supply the Yemenites with powdered eggs, but then the ice cream wouldn't taste the same, or we sign a contract with an Egyptian company to deliver seventy dozen nearly fresh eggs to San'a each week. According to the stromboli expert in Milan, seventy dozen eggs is what they'll need in Yemen to make enough stromboli for 309 people, at the rate of two servings per person per day."

I laughed so hard I nearly cried. Not Marc. He felt even less like laughing when I asked him to do his share of the work.

"After all, Hassan's release will help get back your money too. Do you or don't you have a million dollars tied up in Liechtenstein? So shake your butt a little."

His mission consisted of legally paving the way for the export operation. He was in San'a on the eighteenth when Adriano arrived in his cargo plane, and when I arrived after transferring the four hundred fifty thousand dollars from one of my accounts in the Bahamas to a Yemenite bank.

Thus, there should have been three of us. But there were four, and Marc Lavater regarded in amazement the small, bearded chap, all in black, who had accompanied Adriano throughout.

He breathed in my ear, "Who's that guy?"

"Can't you tell? He's an imam. A Moslem priest, you might say."

"And what in God's name is he doing in this crazy business?"

"In God's name—you said it. Yes, I know, I should have told you about it sooner, but everything went so fast. It was our pals in the mountains. They didn't want any old ice cream. They needed religious sanctions. In other words, each of Adriano's purchases in Milan and elsewhere—from the tiniest part of the whole operation to the largest, the purchase, the shipment, and soon the installation of the factory—were and will be scrupulously followed by the good imam. I recruited him myself, in a section of Paris where he was vacationing, castigating his countryman, the Shah of Iran."

Accordingly, we had just invented the first Islamic ice cream ever to be placed on the world market.

This revelation destroyed Marc. You could understand why.

It also put an end to Hassan Fezzali's captivity. There are limits to the absurd. I wouldn't go so far as to say that the Yemenite authorities were indifferent to Adriano and his paraphernalia, or

56

the technician who had come from Florence, or the imam—delighted with the trip, but still mumbling his antimonarchical curses—but in the end, thanks to "qat" (they begin chewing the leaves every day around noon in Yemen, after which the whole country falls into near-lethargy), things went off pretty well.

All day long on the nineteenth, the helicopter I'd been forced to charter made continuous round trips. By the middle of that afternoon, the "factory"—the establishment actually consisted of a single room—was in place. The first ice cream rolled out two hours later. Adriano and the Italian technician immediately withdrew and radioed the news to me. I was some thirty miles from there, to the northeast of San'a, accompanied by my bodyguards, their cheeks stuffed with qat. They had arrived in trucks. I had used a second helicopter, on which I left the four hundred fifty thousand dollars in care of Marc and the Englishman.

Twenty minutes later, the three motorcycles loomed on the horizon. And this time, it was not a Yemenite princess straddling the back seat of the big front bike but Hassan Fezzali.

The game was over.

And the first words from my Bedouin—exhausted as he was—were, "I'm not at all surprised—you picked the wrong street in Milan. The right factory is the one in the Crescenzago district."

In Cairo on the twentieth, we practically hopped from one plane to another. We rushed to London in order to take the shuttle to Jersey. I'd reserved two suites at the Longueville Manor.

"Why Jersey?" asked Hassan, who had let himself be pushed about without even having the strength to protest.

With that question, he fell asleep. He was at the end of his strength. I had found him terribly thin, emaciated, not very far from the breaking point. He mainly needed rest, I was assured by the doctors who, at my request, examined him right at Heathrow Airport in London. Why not Jersey, under those circumstances? And then, I still hadn't told Aziz. Hassan would do it. I could well believe there would be a few accounts to settle, in Riyadh or elsewhere, and I wanted nothing to do with it. Once again, it would be up to Fezzali to decide on what attitude to take, as soon as he had recuperated.

As for me, I didn't linger. I hardly had time for it. The option on the hotel in Atlantic City was expiring on July 21. And it was July 21 exactly, at 9:15 in the morning, when I landed in New York. Rather tired, but rather pleased with myself on the whole. Sarah wanted to see me shake off my Jamaican lethargy?

She and I closeted ourselves in a hotel suite for some twenty-six hours. I knew why we were so well-adjusted to one another. Aside from the fact that I was always at the ready with her, I discovered a new facet of Sarah's sexual needs. She loved to be spanked. I don't mean that she wanted to be beaten. But when I turned her over my knee and slapped those firm globes until they turned pomegranate red, the moisture in her began to almost bubble. When my rhythmic spanking began to elicit moans, I turned her over and literally slipped into that richly oiled canal.

Our joy was intense—and mutual.

When we had resumed normal breathing, I told Sarah about Hassan Fezzali. I wasn't concerned about the very large expenses I'd had those last few weeks. Hassan would pay me back. He could certainly afford to, and, if necessary, Aziz would help out.

One deal was ending, another beginning. And if, at that point in my story, I'd been asked what relationship there might be between one and the other, I surely would have replied, "None."

2. The Crystal Palace

6

But let's come back to the main story.

Exactly twenty-seven days earlier, Joe Lupino called to tell me, as he put it, that he'd "found me something," i.e., a place for building or renovating a casino. I asked him, "In Vegas?" He answered, "No, Atlantic City." I felt disappointed. I was like a person expecting Dom Pérignon who gets offered Coca-Cola. In other words, I wasn't wildly enthusiastic about the old seaside hotel.

"And now what do you think about it?"

I snorted.

Lupino began laughing.

"In any case, you'd do well to make up your mind as soon as possible. The sellers are expecting us today at five o'clock. Tell them yes, tell them no, but you have to tell them something."

He came to pick me up at Kennedy Airport, where Philip Vandenbergh and Jimmy Rosen were also waiting. A tourist plane flew us over Jamaica Bay and Sandy Hook and along the New Jersey coast. It was not yet ten-thirty when we began driving from Pomona Airport, which, in addition to Bader Field, serves Atlantic City. Now we were entering the city.

A Frenchman or a Briton would be reminded of Deauville, because of the big seaside hotels and the Boardwalk, its fifty-foot width stretching nearly ten miles. But the comparison hardly goes farther. Atlantic City had its glory days at the turn of the century, and in the twenties and thirties. After that, time passed, and fashion changed. The little town of fifty thousand inhabitants fell back into slumber and virtual abandonment. I remembered having talked about Atlantic City with Jimmy Rosen about three years before. At the time, I wasn't yet involved in the huge coffee operation that almost cost me so dearly. I was in search of investments. Somebody in an airplane had, as he put it, "tipped me off." "They're about to license gambling in Atlantic City, and when that happens, the lousiest rattletrap will be worth a thousand times its price overnight."

I had repeated the remark to Rosen. He shrugged his shoulders with his usual sad expression. "Franz, gambling in Atlantic City is a pipe dream." He went on to explain that for almost half a century, the state of Nevada had made its money from two basic industries—divorce (it was in Nevada where they cleverly invented "mental cruelty" as legal grounds for breaking up a marriage), and, above all, gambling. Gambling was legalized in Nevada in 1931. Since that date, no other state in America had followed Nevada's example. This meant that the state gambling commission there had an exclusive and inordinate privilege, in a country of some 215 million people. And do you think they'd agree to share it? The Nevada gambling lobby was powerful. It had plenty of money and would stop at nothing to preserve its monopoly. People had been talking for a long time about legalizing casinos in Atlantic City. They were already talking about it before I was born, just as they talked about it in Miami and in the Poconos, a hundred miles east of New York. They talked about it, but nothing was ever done. It was a pipe dream. And the talking could go on for a hundred years.

Rosen was not a man who made mistakes very often. To my knowledge, it's the only mistake he ever made. He had, in fact, underestimated a crucial factor—the New York City budget crisis, and the subsequent crisis of the state of New Jersey—hence the pressing need for extrabudgetary resources.

The event took place at a time when I was up to my neck in the coffee deal and hadn't paid too much attention to it. They had held another referendum in New Jersey on the issue of legalizing gambling. Supporters of a "no" vote had won, of course, but by only one or two votes. The Nevada lobby became alarmed. It even changed its tactics overnight. And, resigning themselves to the inevitable, the men from Vegas and Reno took the next plane to the East Coast.

This had as its logical consequence a fantastic real-estate boom that meant I was being asked 30 million for a hotel that, three years earlier, I could have bought for perhaps one hundred times less.

I had only myself to blame. After all, four or five years earlier, when I was carrying out what at the time I called the "Sunbelt operation,"* I had done nothing different from what my sellers were now doing—buying up whole blocks of buildings which were then cheap, in order to resell them a very short time afterwards at a high price, the American real-estate market having fully recovered in the meantime. Hence, I was hardly in a position to criticize anyone and had no intention of doing so, anyway.

"Tell me about these sellers, Joe."

"I just told you. The meeting is at five o'clock this afternoon. You'll probably meet a man named Schimmel, assisted by one or two counselors."

Over the telephone from Riyadh, I had asked not only Joe Lupino but Rosen and Vandenbergh as well, for the records on the hotel that was being offered to me for sale. I received the three folders two weeks later. Naturally, I glanced through them, but without really concentrating. I was preoccupied with my ice cream. In the plane between the Channel Isles, London, and New York, I read everything again. My three counselors, though working separately, had come to the same two conclusions—it was a good deal, even at 30 million; and the aforesaid Schimmel was merely a front man for a New York family whom I will here call the Caltanis.

"The Caltanis won't be at the meeting this afternoon?"

"Not a chance."

Lupino, who was driving, turned off the air-conditioning and rolled down the windows. The warm air that entered the vehicle had a salty sea flavor.

"This guy Schimmel, and the Caltanis who are behind him, does he know what I want to do with the hotel they're trying to sell me?"

"These days, anyone who buys in Atlantic City is planning to set up a casino, large or small. Yes, of course, they know what you intend to do."

*See Money.

"Then if it's such a good deal, why don't they keep it for themselves? Why don't they set up their own casino?"

It was Rosen who chose to answer from the back seat.

"Because they need money. They're already in the process—I'm speaking of the Caltanis, not their front man—of setting up a casino. They've already invested, or are getting ready to invest, almost $100 million in it, plus a bank loan. They don't have the means to carry on both businesses at the same time, especially on such a scale. Even if both buildings, the one they're trying to sell you and the one they're renovating for themselves, are side by side, as is the case. In the beginning, they probably planned to run both places at the same time, to set up one big casino. But they bit off more than they could chew, and they have to spit out part of it."

I sought Vandenbergh's eyes in the rear-view mirror. He nodded.

"Same answer," he said.

He practically hadn't stopped clenching his teeth since Kennedy Airport. Probably because it hurt his pride to discover that I had asked my other two lawyers for the same study I'd asked from him, without letting him know.

"Joe?"

Lupino laughed.

"I couldn't have said it better."

He slowed down. For several minutes, we had been following a long boulevard, bordered on the left by hotels that fronted the sea, and on the right by the city itself, or what passed for it, a hodgepodge of empty lots and every style of building. The atmosphere was of a construction site with work going on in every direction and no overall plan. Here, a hotel or restaurant undergoing full renovation, swarming like an anthill with workers; there, an old roadside stand serving hot dogs and sandwiches. Explosions regularly rocked the air, sounding the demise of a condemned building torn down to clear the site. Lupino drove our car into a parking lot surrounded by a rusty wire fence, its entrance casually guarded by an old black man picking a guitar.

"Here we are, Franz. What you see behind you is the Crystal Palace."

In the United States, white elephants are what they call those large hotels built between the end of the last century and the

Great Depression. They are always gigantic structures, usually with hundreds of rooms, and with halls and lobbies so vast they could easily accommodate a Grand Prix auto race. Owing to the change in tourist habits, most of them had become huge mausoleums, with little if any commercial value. You don't find them only in the United States. I had seen them in Europe and elsewhere. Over the last fifteen years, some had been simply razed to make way for more modern, better designed hotels. But that was not always possible. It was sometimes felt in high places that these huge hodgepodges with their rococo façades and vaguely Victorian, wedding-cake shapes belonged to the American architectural heritage. They were classified as landmarks. Which is to say that if you wanted to renovate them, you were compelled to preserve the original style and especially not change the façades in any way.

"And that's the case with this thing; this Crystal Palace is one of those white elephants."

"How convenient."

We were now on the famous Boardwalk, much bigger than in Deauville, of course. The long gray waves of the Atlantic stretched behind us. The sky over our heads was about the same color. It pulled a long face, clouds covering its forehead. On top of everything, a chilly light wind was blowing, which did not, however, discourage the swimmers on the endless beach studded with a few operating piers. We were really a long way from Las Vegas, with its hot, dry air, its awe-inspiring desert ringing the city and exerting a strange fascination. The atmosphere here more closely resembled the cheerful gaiety of a French prison yard on the morning of a guillotining. I knew I was exaggerating, but I was tired from my plane trip which had brought me here from Yemen almost without a break.

I considered "my" hotel. It wasn't love at first sight. A white elephant, indeed.

"How many rooms?"

"About four hundred fifty."

"And the total area?"

"About five acres."

It was large. The structure itself did not occupy the entire ground surface. It was U-shaped, opening on the sea. The rear building—the base of the U—was rectangular, with about twelve stories and not too many embellishments. For the two

65

wings, however, the original architects had let their imaginations run wild. It resembled—from faraway and in a thick fog—the wings of the Louvre in Paris, seen from the Carrousel arch. Except that they had been extended even farther with low structures of barely two stories, with a flat roof and large bay windows embellished with scalloped garlands that must have been bright blue at one time but were now faded by the sea air. In the middle of the kind of rectangular inner courtyard formed by the U was a swimming pool.

"There's another one on the roof, under the skylight," Joe Lupino noted.

"I didn't bring my bathing suit."

"You'd break your neck. No water."

Lupino continued to display exasperating good humor. He annoyed me. I stepped back a little further to climb onto the landing stage that was also part of the hotel. In this way, I had a better view. Should I buy this piece of garbage for 30 million?

"Where's the other hotel, the one Schimmel and the Caltanis are keeping for themselves?"

"The one on the right."

I examined it. It looked like the twin of the first one. A bit smaller, of course, but in just as sorry a state. To transform these near-wrecks into Vegas-type casinos would surely require hundreds of millions of dollars. Where would I get it? No question that I was getting myself involved—if I was getting involved—in a monumental undertaking.

"And who owns the hotel on the left?"

Jimmy Rosen mentioned the name of a large movie company, which had already invested, years earlier, in one of the biggest casino-hotels in Vegas. With the profits from that it was able to recoup even the losses from its films. While he was at it, Rosen went on reciting to me the list of those who were positioning themselves in Atlantic City—Caesars, Hilton, MGM, Playboy, Sands, and others. As if to say that all of Vegas, without giving up Nevada, was implanting itself on the Boardwalk. And if all those biggies had decided on this investment, they must have had their reasons. I wouldn't' be in such bad company, when you came right down to it. Despite the gray sky and the gray sea, despite the cold breeze, despite the landscape—so different from what I'd been dreaming of—for the first time I felt the fever, the true one, that has always taken hold of me on great occasions. I smiled at Lupino.

"If that's all true, you've really found me some sweet deal, you lousy macaroni."

My eyes skipped over those miles of boardwalk, followed a few of the strange wicker armchairs, mechanized and on wheels, that moved up and down the planks. With just a little sunshine, this wouldn't be so bad.

It was probably at that moment, perhaps without yet knowing it myself, that I decided to buy the Crystal Palace.

7

The hotel I was buying had an ordinary history, as told to me by Rosen. From 1929 to 1964 (not to go back too far), it had belonged to one MacAteer, who, having lost enough money, sold it—in '64—to someone named Baumer, a New York hot-dog merchant. Baumer knew about as much about hotel-keeping as I knew about Japanese theater, but he was a sweet knucklehead who wasn't trying to make a profit. He was only too happy to hold a kind of Oktoberfest at his place from time to time, inviting his old buddies from Manhattan to come and drink beer. In this way he held out for several years, balancing his accounts as best he could, losing in Atlantic City what he earned in his New York delis. At which point, Cupid struck. Baumer met an apparently very affectionate golddigger, with whom he eventually flew off to the Caribbean beaches, neglecting to make his payments to the bank from which he had borrowed to finance his purchase of the hotel. This resulted in several court orders, which in January, 1975, were finally declared ineffective for reasons of death. And the Schimmel-Caltani group had taken over everything, mortgage included, in the spring of 1975. Or about one year before gambling was legalized in New Jersey.

"Franz, from all the evidence, it seems the Caltanis made their bid because they knew gambling would be allowed sooner or later. You can't blame them for it. You would have done the same thing in their position. Of course, it's rather irritating to think that these people are going to sell back to you for thirty million what they themselves bought for six or eight hundred thousand fourteen months ago, but that's how it goes."

It was 5:30 in the afternoon on that July 21. Schimmel was sitting across from me. Of course, I'd already made my decision. I was ready to pick up my option and confirm my purchase. But I wanted another postponement, of one month this time, even if it meant paying another two hundred fifty to three hundred thousand dollars. The reason I intended to give—the fact that my sellers would be my neighbors, hence my competitors.

And now, after the first few minutes had passed, the other party was giving me reasons to delay the sale by placing two conditions on it.

"We'd like you to give us a ninety-nine-year lease on a small strip of land."

We looked at the plans. The parcel in question was located on the very boundary between the two future casinos. Having the use of it would enable Schimmel and thus the Caltanis (but their name was never mentioned in the meeting) to satisfy the safety standards laid down by the Atlantic City government, particularly in regard to firefighter access.

"That's negotiable," I said.

In principle, I was supposed to deal mainly with Schimmel. Yet as the minutes passed, he barely opened his mouth, and the negotiation was actually conducted by a green-eyed lawyer. With my infernal habit, so un-American, I hadn't caught his name while we were introducing ourselves. The lawyer smiled at me.

"We'll negotiate. But we're only talking about a strip six yards wide and twenty yards long."

"That's negotiable."

The second condition the other side was placing on the deal— part of the payment would have to be made, officially, in the United States, the other, more discreetly, to a company account in Curaçao.

"You are taking no risk, Mr. Cimballi. Not being an American citizen, nothing prevents you from transferring money to such an account."

"I'll think about all this."

The figures were named. Ten million dollars to be transferred

68

to the account of a company headquartered in Trenton, New Jersey, and another 15 million to Curaçao (for, of course, I jumped at the cancel to knock 5 million off the sale price). Thus, the Crystal Palace would wind up costing me 25 million. In reality, I was buying a company, whose principal asset was, of course, the Atlantic City hotel, but which also included a kind of hot-dog stand in Greenwich Village, a small furnished studio nearby on West Eighth Street, and—even more picturesque—two or three broken-down automobiles, the newest of which had a hundred thousand miles on its meter, plus a small timber plantation in Austria with an adjacent farm. The lawyer smiled, as if to apologize.

"A legacy of the company owned by the late Herman Baumer, who owned the hotel before my clients bought it."

So much for this heterogeneous assortment. When the time came, I would ask Marc or Rosen to sell the lot. I'd make enough money to pay my bar tabs. We had begun the negotiation at five o'clock sharp, in a conference room at one of the nearby hotels. It was nine-thirty when we concluded it. Making use of the conditions imposed by the sellers themselves, I had obtained another one-month option for three hundred thousand dollars. I had every reason to be satisfied.

The green-eyed lawyer visibly maneuvered to be at my side as we all left the room together.

"I hear from Joe Lupino that you've just arrived from Yemen?"

"I went there to deliver some ice cream. Sorry, but I didn't catch your name."

"Olliphan. James Montague Olliphan."

He smiled at me, rather winningly.

"May I hope to have you over for dinner one of these days as soon as this matter is settled?"

"Why not?"

Significantly, it was that very day that I first met Olliphan, who would play an essential role in the whole Crystal Palace episode. It was in July. The dinner I related in the beginning did not actually occur until two months later, on September 18.

The month which followed—from July 21, the day on which I saw the hotel for the first time, to August 21, the date that had been set for signing the deed of sale—was marked by fierce activity. We were not idle—we consisting of my three American teams, plus Marc Lavater, whom, of course, I had asked to join me. Everything that could possibly be done to prepare for buying a large hotel and its immediate conversion into a casino-hotel, and to provide for its future profitability, we did.

In terms of financial analyses, part of the work was already done, since Rosen, Lupino, and Vandenbergh, working separately, had pretty well done the spadework in order to present me with the folders I'd received while I was running around the Arabian peninsula parachuting in ice cream. We went back to square one with the assistance of Marc, who is all the more useful in these matters for being a born pessimist. To him, any new enterprise is automatically doomed to disaster.

That financial analysis was combined with others. Buying the hotel was one thing, turning it into a casino was another. How much would it cost? Beginning on the morning of July 22, the day after the meeting at the Hotel Dennis in Atlantic City, I had put four teams of architects to work, two of which had already proved themselves by renovating or building casinos in Vegas. I gave them until August 15 to present me with viable plans. They made their deadlines to within twenty-four hours.

At the same time, I got several investigations going. On Schimmel, of course, but also on the Caltanis—on their financial position, particularly with regard to the casino they were planning to set up next door to mine; on any hidden reasons for that ninety-nine-year lease they were asking for; on their request for payment in two separate phases and any risks I might incur as a result.

I also did an investigation of Olliphan, for the simple reason that the man intrigued me, both for his distinction (which did not fit too well with his role as official counselor to a Mafia family) and for his obvious interest in me, to the point of inviting me to dinner.

As was my habit, I carefully compartmentalized this whole process. I applied the watertight principle known to sailors and spies. Rosen didn't know what Vandenbergh was doing, and he didn't know what I had asked Lupino to do. None of the three knew the nature of operations for which he was not directly responsible. And even for the least important investigation, the one concerning Olliphan, I had doubled the precautions by hiring two separate teams of private detectives, each working without the other's knowledge. One person besides me had an overall view of these entire preparations, and that, of course, was Marc Lavater. If I couldn't trust him, after six years of working together, then trust didn't exist. But let me make one point clear—I would never regret having relied on him.

July 21-August 21. The results I was waiting for were beginning to flow in. And this hard labor was beginning to bear fruit. A few days before my second meeting with Schimmel and Olliphan, I was able to draw some conclusions:

1. The four plans the architects had submitted to me required an investment (including the land purchase) which varied, depending on the options, from $300-$400 million. My personal preference was for the plan submitted by a California firm, which ranged around $375 million. (My spine tingled, and Marc nearly fainted.)

2. BUT—the most exacting financial analyses all predicted, for an establishment of the size I was contemplating, an ANNUAL profit of $3-6 million! After repaying the loan, of course. For a loan would be necessary.

3. As far as Schimmel was concerned, he was nothing more than a front man, of no interest at all. My sellers were, indeed, the Caltanis. And those gentlemen were two brothers, Joseph and Larry. They represented the third generation of the Family. The first one, grandpa's generation, had made its debut in New York in the '30s, alongside such estimable characters as Longy Zwillman, Dutch Schultz, Albert Anastasia and Charley Luciano. Real high society. Joseph and Larry, officially, were as respectable as one could wish. Very seldom had they had any dealings with the state or federal police, and each time had come out of it unscathed. Financially, they were entirely comfortable and ran a small empire consisting of a restaurant and deli chain, plus—it was said— shares in a Vegas casino in partnership with a Chicago Family. They also had shares in a few import-export businesses, particularly olive oil. In Atlantic City, they were about to invest $85 million in their casino, for which, in addition, they were about to contract a bank loan in the amount of $320 million more, all quite legally.

Nothing suspect in that request for a ninety-nine-year lease. The Caltanis really did have access problems as a result of the city's strict safety code.

I incurred no risk by agreeing to a two-step payment.

The closeness of the two future casinos, the Caltanis' and mine, was in no way unusual. All the casinos, under construc-

71

tion or planned in Atlantic City, were in the same situation. This wasn't Vegas, where gambling establishments were sometimes distant from one another.

Finally, Olliphan. His professional qualifications were beyond question. He'd done brilliantly at Harvard. He could have chosen a musical career, being a violinist of great talent. He was considered extremely cultivated and refined. Nevertheless, there was no doubt that he was the Caltanis' official legal adviser, their number one in that area. The Caltanis did nothing without consulting him; he represented them in everything. Not without reason—twenty-two years earlier, he had married Angelina Caltani, the only sister of Joseph and Larry, who thus were his brothers-in-law.

August 21, ten a.m. In Jimmy Rosen's office, Olliphan smiled sympathetically at me:

"Ready to sign this time?"

"Completely ready."

As were the documents, every comma of which had been gone over with a huge magnifying glass those last few days by my counselors and me. By noon, everything was settled. Olliphan returned to the attack in regard to my dinner invitation.

"Any day you like, Mr. Cimballi."

"Give me a week or two, and I'll get back to you."

He replied, with that odd mixture of melancholy and mocking irony that characterized him, "Okay, I'll grant you a third option. For dinner."

I left New York that same evening. Apart from two miserable weekends that I'd managed to steal from my overloaded schedule those last few weeks, I practically hadn't seen my son and Sarah since the start of the Fezzali operation. For Marc-Andrea (he bore my father's first name, and that of Marc Lavater, his godfather), I felt more than love: adoration. I had to sit on myself not to bring him to New York, where I would have kept him with me twenty-four hours a day. I hadn't done it for the simple reason that it would have forced him to spend his life in a hotel room and to hop from one airplane to another. And as a matter of fact, I firmly intended to put an end to this crazy life I was leading, I mean, to change it completely.

"Sarah, I'm serious. I'll get this casino off the ground and call it quits. All we'll have to do from now on is go to Atlantic City once a month with a big suitcase to collect the profits. I'll give you five dollars a month to burn on MY baccarat tables, and whether or not you break the bank while I'm talking with my accountants, we leave Atlantic City that same day. I swear it."

Anyone else, in Sarah Kyle's place, would have shown some skepticism, made an ironic comment, or done something outlandish, like bursting into tears or breaking out the champagne to celebrate the news. Not Sarah Kyle. My favorite Irishwoman merely stared at me, with her idiosyncratic way of looking at me through narrowed green eyes, her face slightly tilted back. With no comment. She had an incomparable, and yet inexplicable, talent for always keeping things in the right proportion. She calmed me. I would be quite incapable of defining the feeling that existed between us since our first meeting six years earlier in Kenya, then later on, when we met again in Hong Kong and Jamaica. It was a feeling that had survived my own marriage and divorce. At the very least, it was a silent complicity based on a look. Sometimes I had the feeling she could see right through me, and she was unquestionably the only person in the world to whom I felt, God knows why, I owed an explanation.

I asked her, "You're not telling me you're against my casino idea?"

"You know very well what I think of it, my pet."

"At least come and see it."

She would come, she promised. As soon as she could get away from the three or four hotels she supervised. And when she came, she would bring Marc-Andrea.

I spent twelve days in Montego Bay, more than I'd expected, but each time it was getting harder and harder to leave my son. Yet I left again, on September 3, and headed for Jersey, where Hassan Fezzali was still staying. The Son of the Desert was his old self again. He was almost completely well, except for a slightly irregular heartbeat that occurred from time to time.

He chuckled in his lounge chair, "So, you're in the casino business now."

Thus, he'd been informed, without leaving Longueville Manor, of my Atlantic City project. And since I was certain it wasn't Marc who had told him, the information must have come from Aziz. I deduced that the prince had come to St. Hélier—and that a few heads must have wobbled, back in Riyadh or Cairo, when it came time to find out who was responsible for Hassan's kidnapping.

"And what did you talk about, you and His Highness?"

"A fellow named Cimballi. A rather shady kind of international financier who sometimes has outlandish ideas. His Highness thinks well of him, Allah knows why."

And while we were at it, Hassan asked me for an exhaustive account of my expenses for all of Operation Ice Cream.

"Down to the last penny, young Franz. You shouldn't have to pay out of your own pocket. Send me the bill, if you please."

"I will."

"I'll get mad if you don't."

The weather in Jersey was magnificent. Candy-pink English people showed off their sunburns. A Sealink ferry van entered St. Aubin Bay and hid Elizabeth Castle from our sight. During World War II, twenty thousand German troops occupied the Channel Islands, and there was only one death during that occupation, a Frenchman escaping from France who had thought he was landing on free British soil. A silence came between Hassan and me. I would have liked to ask him a few questions—how was he kidnapped, by whom, why, had the real perpetrators been identified, was my hypothesis correct that there were instigators in Aziz's very entourage, what was Martin Yahl's exact role, and what had now happened to the guilty ones?

Far too many questions. And I knew my old Bedouin too well. If he had wanted me to know the answers, he would have provided them.

He reached out and touched my forearm.

"Thanks, Franz. Thanks for everything. I don't expect to die in the next few days. And if, one day . . ."

I stood up. I had to get back to New York, where a pile of work was waiting for me.

"Insh'Allah, Hassan. Or Mektoub, if you prefer."

His big bony paw half crushed my dainty wrist, and I was off. I was in New York on September 6, one of those hot sticky days that New York is famous for, extremely trying even for me, and I have a taste for ninety-five degrees in the shade. The following days were feverish. For, having settled the purchase, other problems immediately cropped up.

Such as financing.

An easy problem—to raise. Solving it is another matter. Of the four plans, I had chosen finally the one by the California architects, thus opting for a total investment of $500 million. As a result of Vandenbergh's efforts, a Philadelphia bank declared its willingness on September 14 to grant me a $400-million loan. On two conditions. That I bring them irrefutable proof that I actually had what is called up front money, that is, my personal contribution, or $100 million. And second, that it be clearly established that my partner or partners, if I acquired any, would have no contact, direct or indirect, with what my bankers coyly termed "illicit persons."

I had already paid $25 million. I expected to pay out as much again. But not more. A payment of $50 million on the $90 million I possessed already seemed exorbitant to me—never in my life had I played for such big stakes; there was no question of my getting in deeper.

It remained, therefore, to find one or more partners. Those good fellows, whose names I did not yet know, had to possess several characteristics. They would have to believe in the profitability of a casino, not feel an incorrigible hatred toward gambling in general, not be afraid of, let's say, the Godfather's heirs, and above all, not be themselves Godfathers, sons of Godfathers, nephews or cousins of Godfathers, even very, very remotely. In addition to that, they had to have $50 million to lay out immediately.

This may be hard to believe, but people having all those qualities don't grow on trees.

I was at this rather gloomy stage of my thoughts when Olliphan called on September 15. I had tried to reach him on my return from Jersey, but his office informed me that he was on vacation and out of town.

"My invitation still stands," he said.

We agreed on the evening of September 18. . . .

And so things have come full circle.

For indeed, on the evening of the eighteenth, I went to have dinner at his house and after a ride in a private elevator found him putting away his violin. I dined with him under the dull and terrifying eyes of Mrs. Olliphan, née Caltani, who was a monster such as I had never seen before and who made me sick to my stomach. I followed him onto his madman's terrace, where I cringed in terror, and I left him without having managed to dispel the least little bit the mystery of this man, for whom, in spite of it all, I could easily feel sympathy, indeed, friendship.

The next day was, of course, September 19. At nine o'clock, my suite at the Pierre was invaded by a horde of architects, decorators, and various would-be suppliers whom I had invited over. Also arriving were three of my lawyer-advisers, Marc Lavater, Jimmy Rosen, and Philip Vandenbergh. I described the scene of the previous evening to Marc. He shrugged his shoulders.

"You're the one who wanted to buy a casino."

"Let's not start that again."

We'd already discussed it, endlessly. For Lavater, it was all very simple. When you have $90 million, you sit back and relax, you don't court adventure. But the truth was that each time I had confided in him about one of my projects, his first reaction was to throw up his arms and tell me I was crazy.

He added, "Okay, we got the information on Olliphan that you wanted. He a character, no doubt of that—his terrace is famous. But professionally speaking, his record is clean. He's not like his clients."

We'd talked quite a bit about that, too. Not only Marc and me, Vandenbergh and Rosen had also gotten into the act in the weeks leading up to my purchase of the Crystal Palace. All three of them had put their two cents in. And they all said the same thing. These people I was buying from were not regular sellers. In fact, I was dealing with a New York Mafia Family, hidden behind a few front companies of the usual type. Of course, everyone knew there was no such thing as the Mafia. I answered, So what? Do you need a seller in order to buy? Do you know another one? And anyway, it's an honest transaction, isn't it?

"Marc, let's not start that again."

He raised his arms again, but this time as a sign of resignation. "Okay." A closed book. I concentrated on my architects and decorators, with whom I had planned to spend that entire day. They brought all kinds of plans, working drawings, maps, even scale models. Enough to keep us merrily occupied for hours. And hours actually passed, filled with discussions and some snacks that I had room service bring up.

It was late in the afternoon when the second event occurred. For me, it marked the true beginning of the Crystal Palace affair. There must have been a knock on the door that led to the hallway, but I heard nothing, wrapped up as I was in explaining an idea I'd had, that with my usual modesty I considered simply brilliant. Marc went to the door. He came back with an odd gleam in his eyes.

"It's for you, Franz."

"Not now. Whoever it is, write a check."

As a matter of fact, I was in a great mood. The Olliphan episode was long past, and my discussions with the architects were ever so much fun. Marc shook his head.

"You really ought to go."

There was nothing ominous in his tone. He rather seemed to think that what was happening was funny. I abruptly left my architects, decorators, and businesspeople, who had completely covered my bed and my entire room with their papers. I crossed the large living room, where Jimmy Rosen was working. Beyond it was an entrance foyer.

There stood a little girl. About eight or ten. Blond, with long golden locks, huge blue eyes, dressed in what I thought was a Tyrolean outfit. Cuter than words could express. On her chest she wore one of those white plastic badges that are pinned on children traveling alone by plane. I had never seen her before.

"Yes?"

No answer. She was content to stare at me, strictly imperturbable.

"Are you alone?"

She didn't blink then either.

"Is it me you wish to see?"

She crooked an imperious finger at her badge. It read, in English: IN CARE OF MR. FRANZ CIMBALLI—PIERRE HOTEL, NEW YORK CITY, NEW YORK, UNITED STATES OF AMERICA. Not one word more. I felt a presence behind me, and discovered several presences. There were at least a dozen people watching this spectacle. Including Marc, who laughed outright.

"There you are," he said. "That's what happens to Casanovas who go around making babies everywhere. One fine day—poof! They pop into your life."

"That's clever."

I shrugged my shoulders. If there was one thing in the world I was sure of, it was that this little blonde number wasn't mine. No way. I turned back to the girl.

"And what's your name?"

Silence, her big blue eyes staring right into mine.

After English, I tried German, taking into consideration her Tyrolean costume.

It worked. She spoke and answered, "Heidi."

"Heidi what?"

She frowned, leaned her head on one side, pretty as a picture, and answered with a question.

"Are you really Mr. Franz Cimballi?"

"*Jawohl*," I said. "In person."

Pow! I didn't have time to put up the slightest defense. She wore adorable wooden clogs—no doubt about it—wooden clogs all adorned with tiny pink and blue flowers engraved in the wood, but hard and sharp as hell. And the tip of her right clog had just struck my left shin with unexpected force. I began to dance on one foot. With a kangaroo leap, I dodged the left clog aiming for my right shin. That lout, Marc, laughed till he cried.

Having put myself out of reach, I asked Heidi, "But why on earth are you kicking me?"

"Because it's my specialty," she answered, with the satisfaction of one who has fulfilled her mission. "And because all four of us are penniless because of you, you thief."

3. In Which the Bombshell Doesn't Know She's a Bombshell

8

"I'm starving," she said. "Anything to eat in this joint?"

I stopped dancing in place and put myself entirely out of reach of her right and left clogs. Hiking up my pants leg, I glanced at my shin.

"You don't even have a dent," she said.

"That's not your fault. You did your best."

Marc Lavater continued laughing stupidly behind me. Heidi turned her big, cornflower-blue eyes to him.

"Who's that guy over there?"

I jumped at the chance (Marc didn't understand a blessed word of German).

"He's the one who told me to take all your money. It's all his fault. He made me do it. I didn't want to."

She nodded gravely, still staring at Lavater with a marvelously innocent expression. Then she was moving toward him, her hand outstretched, a big smile on her face like a senator on a campaign tour.

"You see," Marc crowed, "all you need is an honest face! Children can always tell."

POW! The next second, he, too, was howling and hopping on one foot.

"It's my specialty," Heidi said with delight.

Well, well. Supposing we tried to make sense out of this?

"So. I took all your money?"

"Yeah."

"And who else's?"

"My sisters'."

"How many do you have?"

"Three. I'm starving. I could eat a horse."

I lifted the receiver of the wall phone in the foyer.

"Chicken and ham, is that okay?"

"Do they have any apple strudel?"

I translated the question for room service. They had it, or the next best thing.

I said to the little girl, "They've got it."

"I don't want any," she said. "I just wanted to know."

"Ham and chicken and pastries," I said to room service. I hung up. "And what are your sisters' names?"

"Anna, Christel, and Erika. I'll take the chicken, but I want some milk, too, and some ice cream. And an American hot dog. And American corn flakes. And some American ice cream pops. Lots of everything."

I placed the order.

"Anna, Christel, and Erika What?"

"You're trying to get me to talk, huh?"

"Yeah."

"Fat chance."

She gave me a faint sarcastic smile, walked past me (I again got out of her way with a leap that should have qualified me for the Olympics), and began inspecting the apartment, handing out an equal number of polite guten morgens and kicks to the spectators, half of whom were soon dancing.

"For heaven's sake, Franz, where did she come from?"

"Damned if I know. Her name is Heidi and she has three sisters. And I'm supposed to have left them all penniless. That's all I know." I raised my hand to ward off his comment. "Yes, Marc, I know, maybe it's only a joke someone's playing on me, but there could be something behind it."

I picked up the phone again and questioned the front desk.

Yes, they had seen a little girl go by, dressed in strange clothes. She had even kicked the porter and one of the bellhops. As for the flight attendant . . .

"What flight attendant?"

The one who was with the little girl when she came into the hotel, who inquired about my suite number, who came up with the little girl, saying she wanted to surprise me, who had just left.

"Go get her. Fast!"

Too late. The flight attendant had left the hotel, climbed back into the cab that was waiting for her, and disappeared.

"However, she left a letter addressed to you, Mr. Cimballi."

Thirty seconds later, a messenger brought me a manila envelope without a stamp, which, therefore, had not gone through the mail. It was labeled: "Mr. Cimballi, Pierre Hotel, New York," with a further inscription in the upper righthand corner: "Strictly personal." Inside were two other, smaller envelopes, also sealed and bearing my name. I opened the first one. The letter was hand-written in German: "Mr. Franz Cimballi, you have left us penniless and homeless. We don't know where to go. However, we were told you are a nice man. So, please, take care of Heidi. Heidi is very bright and very nice as well, except that she likes to kick people in the shins. But she doesn't mean any harm, it's all in fun, she's really very intelligent, you'll see. P.S. Don't dress her in wool next to the skin, it makes her break out." Signed: Anna Moser.

If my eyes were popping like Marc's, to whom I translated the letter as I went along, we must have really been a pair.

"And the other envelope?"

It contained three sheets. I quickly realized that they were all the same text, written in three languages: German, French and English. It said: "I, the undersigned, Anna Moser, in my capacity as guardian of my sister Hildegarde-Heidi Moser, authorize Mr. Franz Cimballi, residing at the Pierre Hotel, New York, New York, United States of America, to keep my abovementioned sister with him. Salzburg, Austria, September 9, 1976." The signature was the same as on the other letter, but this time it was accompanied by two official seals, illegible as usual, and by two other signatures of illustrious strangers.

You can't say we didn't try. For two hours, there was a general mobilization, rather comical and certainly disproportionate, I admit, which she surveyed with a highly sarcastic detachment. We all turned ourselves inside out—three of the best business lawyers in the country, a former high-ranking inspector of the French Treasury, a highly talented international financier (I'm speaking of myself), and several widely known architects and decorators—with the sole aim of discovering what in the world I could do about this little blond monster who had fallen into my lap.

The Austrian consulate general in New York? On that Friday evening the place was all but deserted, except for a staunch resident staffer who thought this could all well wait till Monday morning.

The mysterious flight attendant? It was fairly easy to identify her, thanks to her Austrian Airlines uniform, with a few telephone calls to the arrivals department at Kennedy Airport. It was official. Little Heidi Moser had entered American soil quite legally, traveling from Vienna in the company of one Elizabeth Dressler. Who was where? On vacation or on leave for nine days. In what part of the United States? They didn't know. Yes, with a boyfriend, perhaps, but the staff's personal life . . .

The police, then?

A woman police officer finally agreed to come over. And Heidi cleverly chose the precise moment of her arrival to throw herself into my arms and cling to me as if I were all she had in the world.

"And you say you don't know this child, Mr. Cimballi?"

"I've never even seen her before."

"Is she a threat to your safety?"

"Are you kidding?"

"Are you a threat to her safety?"

"Do I look like a child molester?"

"Child molesters look like anyone else, Mr. Cimballi. However, you yourself admit that your mother was Austrian. Perhaps this child is one of your relatives without your knowing it. Of course, if you don't want her, I can always turn her over to a welfare agency."

"An orphanage, you mean?"

The police officer gave a shrug. If I didn't want her, there was no other solution. I remember that at that moment I was kneeling. Heidi was clinging to me more tightly than ever, and, playacting or not, her soft blue eyes revealed panic and a sorrow that wrung my heart.

She whispered in my ear, "That lady, is she a cop?"

I nodded. Around us, huge by comparison, stood Marc Lavater, Rosen, Vandenbergh, the policewoman, and other spectators. We were the same height, Heidi and I, practically nose to nose, our eyes meeting.

She whispered again, her lips pressed against my ear, "I want to stay with you, Mr. Cimballi."

84

And then I began whispering too, while secretly blasting myself for being such an idiot.

"How do you think I can keep you?"

"Anna said I could stay with you. She said you're very nice."

"But she doesn't even know me!"

"Anna doesn't. But Goni does."

"And who is Goni?"

"Anna's husband."

"So Anna's married?"

"No."

"But she has a husband, you just said so."

"He's not really her husband."

"Her fiancé, then?"

Heidi chuckled.

"They sleep in the same bed, anyway. Stark naked. And Anna goes, ooh, ooh, ooh..."

"How old is she, Anna?"

"Old. At least twenty."

"And you love her?"

"That depends which day."

All of this in a whisper, and all in German. From time to time, I raised an embarrassed face to the others, who were watching us, speechless. I must have really looked smart, on all fours! I returned to Heidi.

"Do you live in Austria?"

"No."

"In Germany?"

"No."

"In Switzerland, then?"

"No."

"In Liechtenstein?"

The little Tyrolean made a very expressive face—never heard of what's-its-name. But undoubtedly she was leading me by the nose.

"Heidi, you're lying. Your nose is growing."

She felt her nose.

"No, it isn't. That's not true."

"You come from Austria. Anna's in Austria?"

"Yeah, I guess so."

"Where in Austria?"

"I dunno."

"You know very well. In Salzburg?"

"Not in Salzburg."

"Then where?"

"Anna told me not to tell you."

"But why did she say that?"

Heidi chuckled merrily.

"So that you wouldn't know, dummy!"

"Mr. Cimballi?"

The policewoman was getting impatient. So much so that she eventually left, after consulting with Vandenbergh and Rosen, whom she knew by name.

"The best thing," Jimmy told me, "would be for you to get a nanny."

"Who'd act as a chaperone?"

He smiled.

"That would be best."

He made a few telephone calls.

"She'll be here in an hour and a half."

He, in turn, left, and so did everyone else except Marc.

"Are you still hungry, Heidi?"

She shook her head, with that slightly glazed look that meant she was sleepy. Of course, for her, given the time changes, it was two or three in the morning.

"You want to sleep?"

And it happened very naturally, as though an old bond already existed between us. She crawled quietly into my lap and nestled there with her head on my chest. I lifted her and carried her into the bedroom where Marc-Andrea usually slept when, by chance, he was with me in New York. She had closed her eyes. I hardly dared to touch her and merely removed her wooden clogs and white anklets. Without opening her eyes, she said to me, "What about my braids? You have to undo them."

Marc Lavater had followed us as far as the doorway, but hadn't entered the room. He spread his hands, as if to say, "Oh, no, not me!" Undoing those damn braids took a long time. Eventually, her blond hair hung loose. She lay there patiently, her eyes still closed, barely turning and lifting her head only when necessary.

"You're nice, Mr. Cimballi. Anna was right."

Anna! I could have told her a thing or two, that one! Whoever she was. But at the same time, I was torn and uncertain. I covered Heidi with a sheet.

"Will you be warm enough?"

She nodded, looking as if she were already asleep, a tiny contented smile on her lips.

"*Gute Nacht*, Heidi."

"*Gute Nacht*, Mr. Cimballi."

I couldn't tear myself away. She fascinated me. When finally I decided to come out of the bedroom, Marc stared at me, shaking his head.

I asked him, "And what do you have to say?"

"Nothing, Daddy."

I felt like a complete fool. But it wasn't a bad feeling.

The next day I was on the phone with Li and Liu—they in San Francisco, I in my bed. As usual, I couldn't tell whether I was speaking to Li or to Liu (or vice versa). It was all very well their being merely cousins. It was all very well that I'd known them for years. I still couldn't tell them apart. Especially thousands of miles away.

Li or Liu said, "Would you like to repeat that?"

"Fifty million dollars?"

Li (or Liu) howled with laughter.

"Gleat Cimballi, he clazy!"

I had been trying to get them for several days, but they were traveling in China, which, for Chinese, is logical. I had just explained to them that I would very much like to have them as partners with me in the casino. Obviously, they were going to refuse. They refused. It was a huge disappointment for me, I felt almost sure of persuading them. Especially since they had the funds, they could probably line up several times that sum. And then I was hoping they would be interested in the couple of original ideas I'd had for making it a casino unlike any other. They refused.

"Franz, the answer is no. We don't even need to think about it. Gambling—that's not our job! We'd like to stay happy. Because, Franz, a joyful heart kills more germs than all the antiseptics in the world."

I didn't insist. I knew them too well to have any illusions about my chances of persuading them once they had said no. We spoke a few moments longer, and I hung up, not even able to resent them. But I had taken a severe blow to my spirits. Oh, shit on everything!

"Mr. Cimballi?"

I jumped so high I almost hit the ceiling. I hadn't heard her coming. And for good reason—she was barefoot—in fact, she was bare all over. But it wasn't Heidi, or else she'd doubled in size overnight. I recognized the Amazon-type Jimmy Rosen had found me as a nanny. She had arrived at 10 o'clock sharp the night before, just before Marc's departure, and had moved right into Heidi's room. The first time I saw her, in the doorway, I thought there were two of her, one on top of the other. The Amazon was over six-feet tall. She was a near-Olympic champion of hammer throwing who had sprung from the East German ranks. She had been in the United States for four months, and her stay in America agreed with her. Her official weight must have been some 175 pounds, but she probably weighed forty or fifty more—it was like looking at the back of a bus.

Standing there naked, she wept, "Heidi gone."

Ten minutes later—not even that—I was scouring Central Park in a bathrobe. I led a posse that included at least a dozen Pierre employees, plus the Amazon in an overcoat, plus about sixty unidentified joggers—all of this on the strength of the testimony of someone who thought he had, indeed, seen a three-foot-tall Tyrolean scampering toward the Wollman Memorial skating rink. As the minutes passed, other weekend marathoners joined us, rounding out the cyclists, roller-skaters and horseback riders. It's wild, the number of nut cases you can find in Central Park on Saturday morning, throwing themselves enthusiastically into a Tyrolean goose chase. Some of them, thinking it was some kind of television contest, even asked me, "And what do we win if we find her?" I was angry, amused and worried, all at the same time. What if this whole business was a set-up, to make me look like a sadistic child molester or something? It didn't make sense, of course, and I knew it, but I'm never very bright when I'm galloping like a horse.

I crossed the entire width of Central Park. I'd had enough. My tongue was dragging on the ground with all the running and talking. I hailed a taxi at the corner of Seventy-second Street, piled the Amazon into it, and we returned to the Pierre. Joe Lupino and Rosen had arrived while this was going on.

"We don't like this disappearance, Franz. We mean, this disappearance of a little Tyrolean after her appearance. It's suspicious."

Did they think I was delighted by it?

"Where's Marc?" Rosen asked.

"Someplace over the Atlantic."

"He's going to Austria?"

"Naturally."

I was in an increasingly murderous mood. I resolved to notify the police, and as the sergeant recorded my call, it was all I could do not to shout. No, the child was not my daughter, my niece, my cousin, or the child of friends. No, I didn't exactly know who she was. Her name might be Heidi, perhaps even Heidi Moser, but for all I knew, her real name might be Roswitha Tarteufel or Gudule Rabinowich. And I didn't have the slightest idea what she might be doing in New York, and at my house on top of it. No, I didn't know, either, if she had family or relatives here. I knew absolutely nothing about her except that I had put her to bed the night before, that she had corn-flower-blue eyes and braids—no, I had undone the braids—blond hair, anyway, and that she was dressed in Tyrolean costume and had disappeared. I hung up.

"There's what you might call a clear explanation," said Rosen, as he ordered breakfast for Lupino and himself (they like to have their breakfast at my expense).

I was furious over this disappearance, after the negative reply Li and Liu had given me, and because of the realization we'd had, Marc and I, the night before. Namely, that there must have been a connection between Heidi Moser (if that was her name), from Austria (now that had to be true), and the Austrian timber plantation that was part of the Baumer inheritance, which I had bought along with the hotel. It all matched. First, because Baumer himself was an Austrian immigrant. Next, because Anna Moser's letter was dated September 9 and September 9 was the day after Cannat, Lavater's assistant in Paris, acting on our orders, had sold everything in Austria, plantation and farm, that had belonged to the late Baumer.

"Am I clear this time?"

Jimmy approved.

"Not very, but I understand anyway."

"In other words," Lupino commented, "there's some connection between this kid and the White Elephant."

The telephone rang. It was the female police inspector of the night before.

"We have to know what you want," she told me. "Yesterday, you had one Tyrolean too many. Today, you're complaining that there's one missing."

Nevertheless, she had already completed a preliminary investigation. The kidnapping theory didn't hold, according to her. More likely, we were dealing with a runaway.

"Hotel staff members saw her walking around. First in the kitchens, then in the television room, where she asked for chocolate and apple cake, and they turned on the VCR so she could watch a movie."

"And she asked for all that in German? She speaks only German."

The inspector gave a hearty chuckle. Then the Tyrolean must have learned English overnight. Because it was in good English that she had asked to see a movie. She had also wanted to know how many miles it was to Disney World. And when she was told it was in Florida, she had asked for information on how to get there.

"And they let her go out?"

"No one saw her go out. But she went out anyway. A carriage driver in front of the Plaza Hotel got a kick in the shins because he refused to take her to Florida. He saw her enter the Plaza."

But it was futile to rush over there. She had nearly crippled, with her deadly clogs, one of the hotel's concessionaires, after which she had fled through the door that leads to Fifty-eighth Street.

"I think I'm going to have to ask my supervisors to sound a red alert before your kid disables half of New York."

At that point, another line buzzed. I went from one receiver to the other. Rosen, who had picked up, had a strange gleam in his eyes.

"Cimballi."

"Mr. Cimballi? This is just so you won't worry. I'm at the Empire State Building. Way at the top. It's fantastic!"

9

I'll always remember it. For, of course, I rushed to the Empire Sate Building, with the Amazon and Joe Lupino galloping at my side.

The elevator attendant clearly remembered having seen Heidi—oh, how well he remembered. He raised his pants leg and showed me his shin as proof. But, he said, he had nothing against the poor kid. Naturally she'd be upset after what I'd made her do. Yes, sir, absolutely, aren't you ashamed to make such a cute little girl climb up to the top of New York for something as worthless as a cigarette lighter! A cigarette lighter! He was choking with indignation. And did I think I was going to find it, my cigarette lighter, with those tens of thousands of visitors each year?

I shouted, "I DON'T SMOKE! I DON'T HAVE A CIGARETTE LIGHTER, AND I'VE NEVER HAD ONE! WHERE IS SHE?"

And anyway, if I wanted it so much, my cigarette lighter, I could just as well have gone up myself, instead of sending my daughter. And he'd heard I beat her, on top of it.

"Where is she?"

Gone down again.

"But she left you a message, poor kid. She was crying."

I opened the calling-card-size envelope. It was written in German, and it read: "I really got you, didn't I? Now I'm going to visit Grand Central Station."

So what the hell else could I do? It was turning into a game of hide-and-seek, but I had no other choice. After all, she was only nine or ten years old, and we were in New York, which isn't the safest city in the world, even on a summer Saturday. The Amazon, Joe, and I had made it to Grand Central Station, and as soon as we entered the cavernous lobby, I heard my name proclaimed by all the loudspeakers. I was being paged at the reservation counter for the Metroliner, which connects Boston, New York, and Washington. There I found no Heidi, but a clerk, explaining to me that my "niece," who was sorry she had lost me in the crowd and made me miss my train, had finally gone back to our hotel. And she had left me another message: "It's not as great as the Salzburg station. Isn't this fun?"

I vented my rage on the clerk, "And you let her go off by herself?"

"But she pointed to a lady and said she was her Russian governess. I believed her!"

Return to the Pierre. Naturally, that diabolical Tyrolean wasn't there. At the desk, they were beginning to look at me strangely. The Amazon burst into tears. Joe Lupino kept his composure.

"Franz, this kid is more resourceful than a squadron of Marines. There's no reason to be too worried."

"And the Russian governess?"

He agreed that the Russian governess might exist and thus was a source of worry. I had just emerged from the elevator and was putting my key in the lock of my door when the telephone rang. I rushed in. It was Sarah, and she guessed immediately from the sound of my voice.

"You're having problems, Franz."

"Yes and no."

"Can I do something?"

"You can leave your Jamaica and come to New York. For good."

Silence.

"I need to think," she said.

It was better than nothing. Usually, when I made that kind of offer, she simply shrugged her shoulders.

"Sarah—the sooner the better."

I hung up. It was around eleven-thirty in the morning. I hadn't even shaved, and I had spent the better part of the morning running around NewYork in pursuit of a little girl aged nine or ten. And I wasn't forgetting the bad news from San Francisco.

"Joe, I was able to reach Li and Liu. They refused to take part in the deal."

"Tough luck. Where are you at, exactly, with your bankers in Philadelphia?"

"I promised to bring them one or more partners with fifty million dollars by next Thursday. I was really counting on those damned Chinese. They told me they'd be in on my next deal."

"And if not, no loan?"

I was in the middle of shaving.

"No loan."

"You'll find other bankers."

"And I'll lose another month or two. And the other casinos in Atlantic City will all be open for business while I'm still running from one bank to the next."

"You can always pay a visit to your Arab pals."

I'd thought of that, of course. But with Hassan Fezzali still convalescing in Jersey, and Aziz probably in the midst of a huge spring cleaning among his entourage, it seemed to me a bad time to talk business. Especially since by asking the Arabs for $50 million right after I'd done them a favor, I would seem to be presenting a bill, like a plumber. And that would do considerable damage to any partnership relations we might have.

"The situation is basically simple," Joe concluded. He, therefore, ordered another breakfast at my expense. "You have five days at the most, including one Sunday, to find someone willing to invest $50 million who has absolutely no ties to the Maf—"

There it was again—the phone. I had just stepped out of the shower. As I lifted the receiver to my ear, a bloodcurdling shriek came out of it. It lasted at least twenty seconds. Then silence. Then Heidi's totally calm voice, "I scared you, huh, Mr. Cimballi? I gave you the creeps, didn't I?"

Up to the last second, I thought the little demon was playing me for a fool again. But no, there she was, seated primly at one of the outdoor tables at the sunken plaza in Rockefeller Center. In front of her was an entire collection of ice cream and cake, as if she had ordered the restaurant's whole menu.

"But she ordered the whole menu," the maître d' explained. "All of it. She was very insistent. Mr. Cimballi, your daughter . . ."

I didn't even protest at this attribution of paternity. Nor was I listening to the maître d'. My one intention, ambition, and ultimate aim in going to fetch her was to give the Tyrolean the spanking of her life. Ten seconds earlier, I was still dreaming of it—but not now. Her face, with its braids and blue eyes, peered out at me from between two piles of cakes. Is it possible to fall in love with a nine-year-old girl—not physically in love, of course, but in love to the point of feeling merely relief and tenderness at finding her again, as well as the beginnings of shared laughter? I sat down at the table across from her.

"You played a real good game on me, huh?"

"Yeah."

"Who was that Russian governess at Grand Central?"

With a shrug, "Just somebody. Some lady. I needed one. 'Cept she wouldn't let me go afterwards. She wanted to take me to my parents. She was a leech, that old lady."

While answering me, she surveyed with an expert eye the improbable heap of ice cream and pastries. There was enough there to supply a Tyrolean village for three days.

"They didn't want to let me order the menu, those creeps. I told them my daddy was a billionaire who lives at the Pierre, and if they bugged me, I'd have you buy the place. They believed me. People believe anything."

She picked right and left among the piles.

"This pastry isn't so great. You know Tomaselli?"

No, I didn't know Tomaselli. I gazed at her, stunned and, in fact, impressed by her monstrous nerve, her confidence . . .

"Tomaselli's in Salzburg, Market Square. They make whipped cream better than anyone . . ."

. . . her incredible prettiness.

"You didn't tell me you spoke English, Heidi."

"You didn't ask."

The waiter brought the coffee I'd ordered.

"And where did you learn English?"

"Dunno."

"Liar."

"Yeah," she said calmly. She went on picking, dipping her finger into everything, and making faces. "This stuff is disgusting. And expensive! Did you see those prices? These Americans are crazy."

"Don't change the subject. How do you happen to know New York so well?"

Her mouth full as she went on with her sampling, from her tiny purse she took and handed to me a guidebook in German. Inside, someone had drawn arrows on the map, tracing an itinerary that started at the Pierre, went through Central Park (there was an "X"), Avenue of the Americas down to Thirty-third Street, the Empire State building (an "X"), back to Park Avenue as far as Grand Central (an "X"), continued on to the Waldorf (an "X"), then St. Patrick's Cathedral (an "X"), and on to Rockefeller Center (an "X"). In short, the very path she must have followed.

"Who drew this tour?"

"Goni."

"Who's Goni? What's his real name?"

"Goni is Goni."

And vice versa, I guessed. Okay, I switched tactics.

"Do you know anyone in New York?"

94

A big smile decorated with whipped cream.

"You, Mr. Cimballi."

"And besides me?"

"No one." She raised her right hand, brandishing a half-eaten chocolate éclair. Scout's honor.

I went back to the map: the itinerary didn't end with Rockefeller Center, it went down to Washington Square, ran toward the Brooklyn Bridge, jumped over the bay to the Statue of Liberty, came back to Manhattan by way of the Battery and the twin towers of the World Trade Center, with a side trip to Wall Street . . .

"And you expect to see all of that?"

"If this place wasn't so expensive, yeah. But at first I only ordered hot chocolate, and I didn't have enough money to pay for it. So then, naturally, I ordered other stuff and called you."

To back up her words, she showed me the few coins she had left—thirty to forty cents.

"We don't have any more money since you took it all away," she went on. "Do you have any money?"

I did my best to chuckle.

"Obviously. Since I took it from you."

"You're a billionaire, huh?"

"You said it."

"You don't look like a billionaire."

"Heidi, you still don't want to tell me who Goni is, and where Anna and your other sisters live?"

"No."

"Or where you come from?"

"No."

"Or why you say I stole your money, you and your sisters?"

"No."

"Who is Elizabeth Dressler?"

She looked at me with wide eyes dripping with innocence.

"Who's she?"

"The Austrian stewardess with whom you went through customs when you arrived in New York."

"Never heard of her."

"You're lying again."

"Yeah."

Exasperating. I settled the bill. Good Lord, $117 worth of pastries and ice cream!

"Heidi, I have an offer to make you. I'll take you around to everything you want to see in New York, and you'll answer my questions. Is it a deal?"

She thought it over, head bent, frowning.

"Everything I want to see?"

"Everything I can possibly show you."

A contemptuous snort.

"You're hedging, huh?"

"I'm not hedging."

She thought some more, bending her head a little more, her golden hair sparkling in the September sun. I could have chewed her up, that little Tyrolean demon. I was melting like ice cream.

"Heidi, why did you run away this morning?"

"Anna."

"Anna what?"

"Anna told me to give you a hard time. Did I?"

Okay, I gave up. I took her hand in mine, and we went off to see New York. I may be a good talker, but she had shut me up, and no mistake.

It was one or the other—either she had been through an intensive training course in the Tyrolean mountains, or I had been suddenly struck with senility. Because we saw everything, or nearly everything, that she wanted to see, and at a rapid clip. She dragged me to the Bronx Zoo, got bored immediately, headed for the Statue of Liberty. A boat brought us back to Manhattan. Macy's, which we swept through like lightning. At an outdoor cafe in Greenwich Village, she wolfed down her seventh hamburger and eleventh milkshake. Next, the Brooklyn Bridge . . .

And the other bridge, the Verrazano? Why don't we go there? And Coney Island? And the Brooklyn Botanical Garden? And I want to see a game at Yankee Stadium and go to the top of the World Trade Center and . . .

The helicopter idea was mine. It was either that or end the day crawling on my hands and knees. It was six-thirty when, seated at last, we flew over New York, directly over the Hudson and East Rivers.

"Is this as good as Salzburg, Heidi?"

"Yeah. Not bad."

But her cornflower-blue eyes sparkled in the summer dusk. All the city lights were kindled one by one. The panorama beneath us was as fascinating as ever, but it was her I watched, amazed by the remarkable swiftness with which this urchin had got her hooks into me.

She'd been able to drag me into this New York merry-go-round, at a time when I had so much to do. In the first place, there was that partner I had to find, preferably within five days. The only excuse I could find to justify this waste of time with my Tyrolean was that I couldn't come up with any kind of solution. I had to do something—but what?

At each stage in our zigzag race through New York, I had telephoned the Pierre in case Marc had tried to reach me. He had to have reached Austria. Why didn't he give any sign of life, as we had agreed he would? It was already dark when a taxi brought us back from the heliport on East Thirtieth Street. We went through Central Park, where a band was playing. Heidi had grabbed my hand as soon as the helicopter blades began to turn and hadn't let go of it since. From time to time, she turned away from the spectacle of New York by night, and fastened her astonishingly serious eyes on me. Several times, I tried to get her to tell me about herself, without any success. She dodged all my questions with disconcerting ease. "She's really very bright," the person signing herself Anna Moser had written. There was no doubt about that.

Jimmy Rosen was waiting for me at the Pierre. He had learned from Lupino of Li and Liu's refusal.

"Franz, you won't find a partner by next Thursday."

"Call the bank in Philadelphia on Monday. If necessary, go there with Vandenbergh and ask them to give me a few more days."

"They won't go along, and you know it. They weren't all that hot about a casino venture in the first place."

"Try anyway."

The truth was that I had decided to try my last resort. I was going to see Hassan Fezzali, in spite of all the good reasons I had for not doing so. It didn't make me very happy.

"What about her?"

Jimmy Rosen, with a jerk of his head, indicated the little Tyrolean, at present engaged in a lively conversation with one of the hotel messengers who spoke German. Any normal little girl would be fast asleep by now, after her daylong travels. Not she. To all appearances, she was in fine shape.

"Marc didn't call?" asked Jimmy.

"Not yet."

I wouldn't be able to take Heidi with me, especially if I had to go see Prince Aziz in Riyadh. As for leaving her alone, even with the Amazon, in the suite at the Pierre—well, her disappearing act this morning was enough to dissuade me from that.

"Franz, I'll be glad to look after her while you're gone, until you or Marc find out why she's here. She'll live with us."

Jimmy Rosen had five children and lived in New Rochelle, a large, affluent suburb of New York. I had gone there several times. I'd even spent a weekend there several months earlier with Sarah and Marc-Andrea. I was certain Heidi would be happy there. Two of Jimmy's three daughters were more or less her age. That's what I tried to explain to her. It didn't go over too well. She burst into tears suddenly in the lobby.

"I don't want to leave you, Mr. Cimballi."

And then I could gauge how attached to her I had become, knowing almost nothing about her, and with the possibility that she could easily cause me some serious problems. In the end, she left with Jimmy. I dined alone, moodily. The prospect of having to wheedle $50 million out of Fezzali was not an enchanting one. But, no, he had been out of touch with things for a year and a half. It was Aziz I would have to face. I decided to leave for London the next morning, Sunday. I went to bed and had just fallen asleep, about one a.m., when . . .

Marc on the phone, "Franz, you listen to me! It's seven in the morning here, and I spent the whole evening and the whole night running from one village to another and one chalet to another. So if somebody's entitled to be grouchy, it's me."

Yes, he had found Anna Moser. She was sitting across from him as he spoke to me. No, he couldn't put her on the phone. No, she wasn't mute. She simply didn't want to speak to me. I nearly choked—what did that mean?

"It means that if you want an explanation, you're going to have to make a trip to the Tyrol just like me. She only wants to speak to you, in person, and at her home."

"Marc, have you been drinking, or what? Where are you, anyway?"

"Gasthof Post, in Kössen, in the Austrian Tyrol. And according to the lovely Anna, you have no choice. You'll come here for an explanation, or we'll both die imbeciles. Take it or leave it, Franz."

"But in God's name, is she really the one who sent me her sister?"

"Yes."

"But why?"

"She categorically refuses to say. Unless . . ."

Unless I went to the Tyrol to listen. One thing, at least, now seemed completely clear—if I thought Heidi was an outstanding example of a pain in the neck (adorable, but, nonetheless, a pain in the neck), her older sister had every record beat.

"Is she really Heidi's legal guardian?"

"Yes."

Thank goodness for that, at least. I wouldn't go to jail for kidnapping or detention of a minor.

"And is that all you were able to find out?"

Marc began to describe his Tyrolean odyssey in bitter tones. I cut him short.

"Marc, even in the best case, I could never be in that godforsaken hole before next Tuesday."

And even then, only on the condition that a meeting with Hassan in Jersey would produce a partner for me, because if I had to run all the way to Saudi Arabia—I hung up.

And picked up the phone again right away. It was Li or Liu.

"Franz, our consciences bothered us. It's true that we promised to go in with you in the next deal you offered us. We're well aware that we've put you in a fix. So we thought it over, we made some phone calls, and we may have found an answer. The perfect partner, the kind you were dreaming of—ready to invest almost any sum, not a Mafioso, charming, honest, nice eyes, fresh breath . . ."

Coming from anyone else, I would have thought they were crazy. But that was my Chinese friends' regular way of speaking. They had often proved to me that when it came to finances, they were as sober as Swiss bankers underneath their nutty façades. This time, though, they didn't add much to that impression.

"Having said that, Franz—he won't be a comfortable partner. Assuming, of course, that you manage to convince him. Do you know what a coat hanger is?"

I knew. Used in that sense, a coat hanger was a long, sharp

knife that someone sticks in your back by surprise because you haven't kept your promises.

I asked, "And I'd be able to convince this guy in such a short time?"

"Since it comes from us, and after we've made the introductions, yes, you have a chance. But don't waste any time."

I didn't. I canceled my reservations for London and Jersey, and the very next day, Sunday, September 21, I flew to Macao.

10

A package. Now I know how a (de luxe) package feels. I didn't even have to say one word, except "yes," when they asked me if I was indeed Mr. Franz Cimballi of St. Tropez. From then on, they took complete care of me. A Rolls came to pick me up at the airport. We drove for about two miles, up to the door of a helicopter that, unless I'm mistaken, was a Kawasaki made in Japan. Inside, it was "Champagne, Mr. St. Tropez?" They stuck a crystal flute in my hand before I could reply. "A little caviar, Count?" I was surrounded. They made sure I was completely comfortable. They massaged me, sponged me, and pampered me in every possible way.

As for me, I was rather glad that they kept so close to me, because "they" were four absolutely stunning Chinese girls, of the kind I didn't even know existed.

We flew over the Pearl River.

I had been in Macao once before, five years earlier. I had spent no more than a day there, and it hadn't made a deathless impression on me. Sarah, who accompanied me, had hated the place at first glance, and by mutual agreement, we had never set foot there again during the whole of our stay in Hong Kong.

The helicopter dropped straight down over the peninsula. For several seconds, I was afraid that our pilot had lost his mind and was deliberately trying to land on a lightning conductor. But at the last minute, a flat space opened up near the Jai Alai casino. We touched down a few yards from the playing court. They helped me out, with infinite precautions for my aristocratic person. Another Rolls. We drove. I recognized a few buildings, including the stunning, colossal Lisboa Hotel and St. Paul's Cathedral (nothing remained of it but the impressive, ultra-Baroque façade, rising into the clear blue sky over a flight of granite steps). We drove on. I didn't have the slightest idea where they were taking me, and each time I opened my mouth to ask a question, they kissed me sloppily on the lips to make me shut up.

What followed was in keeping with what had gone before. It was mysterious, vaguely disturbing, but certainly not unpleasant. The Rolls came to a halt inside a private residence. In the wonderful garden were vestiges of the old city walls, or at least I thought so. They showed me in, all but carrying me to spare me the slightest effort. They led me into a bedroom with an adjoining bathroom that couldn't have been more luxurious. There, they took my clothes off, plunged me into a round bathtub nine feet in diameter, washed me, massaged me all over with, at most, a slight smile when—I tried to think of prices on the stock market, but it was no use—I furnished the all-female attendants with incontrovertible proof that I was a male in perfect working order. This lasted a good ten minutes, without one of the bath attendants/bodyguards/chambermaids doing anything to remedy the situation. After which, they pulled me out of the pink-and-black marble bathtub, dried me, perfumed and oiled me to perfection, not neglecting the smallest part of my body, and then withdrew, leaving me completely naked.

She entered.

She was between twenty-five and thirty-five years old, and if the young women who had picked me up at Kaitak Airport in Hong Kong were already worth the trip, what could you say about her?

"Did the bath relax you, Mr. Cimballi of St. Tropez?"

"My name is Cimballi. Just Cimballi, nothing else. And I'm not a count."

Surely I owed this ennoblement to some joke Li and Liu had played on me. But for the time being, what worried me the most was my total nudity. I said, with all the dignity I could muster (a certain detail of my anatomy particularly embarrassed me), "I'm here because I have a business meeting with Mr. Deng."

"That's me," she said.

"You cannot be Mr. Deng."

That was obvious. All you had to do was look at her skintight, black-silk tunic dress—it looked as if it had been painted on her.

"But I am Deng," she continued. "And I'm the one you'll have to persuade."

"I would prefer to be dressed. I always put my hands in my pockets when I talk, and this way, I'm handicapped."

She snapped her fingers. Two pretty girls appeared, bringing my newly washed and ironed garments. They dressed me in a twinkling of an eye.

"This way, please, Mr. Cimballi."

Miss Deng led me through a series of rooms until we reached her office. On the table were two stacks of banknotes.

"When do you need this $50 million, Mr. Cimballi?"

"Thursday the twenty-fifth, at 10:30 local time, in Philadelphia. Do you think you will be able to give me a quick answer?"

She smiled.

"Messrs. Li and Liu have told me the nicest things about you."

"I'm grateful to them."

"You will have your answer this evening."

She indicated the bills on the table.

"Therefore, we won't waste time. You will understand that if I am to make up my mind in such short time, I need to be sure of some things. To begin with, there's a million Hong Kong dollars there.* It's two o'clock in the afternoon. I'll give you until eight."

With a big smile, "To lose it in my casino."

Every day, ten or twelve thousand gamblers disembark from the Hong Kong hydroplanes. They are in addition to the natives of Central Macao, those from the Taipa and Coloane Islands. In other words, at the exact second I entered the great two-story hall of the casino, I wasn't exactly alone. In fact, I was immedi-

*1 Hong Kong dollar = about U.S. $0.23

102

ately snatched up, borne along, submerged by a milling throng in which all kinds and both sexes mingled, from the most wretched coolie to the most upstanding businessman. It all went very fast, with the cold but smiling efficiency that had surrounded me since my arrival in Hong Kong and Macao. The girls of my escort abandoned me suddenly at the door of the establishment, with a final gesture of invitation: Your turn to gamble.

In the literal sense.

And my mission was to lose at these gambling tables the equivalent of two hundred and thirty thousand dollars. Clearly, I was being tested. It didn't cost much, because the beautiful Miss Deng, by having me gamble in her casino, would take back with one hand what she had lost with the other.

That wasn't the problem, anyway. The real problem was trying to understand exactly what was expected of me—trying to reconstruct the logic of my potential Chinese partners. Not an easy task. Apart from doing an eleven-foot high jump, I know of nothing more difficult than trying to second-guess a Chinese who's resolved to be devious.

I quickly made a decision. I would be myself, Cimballi. And knowing Cimballi as well as I did, I knew that he abhorred losing. Thus, I would try to win.

I climbed to the second floor. The crowd there was hardly less thick than below. There were even gamblers leaning dangerously over the handrail and throwing their stakes onto the tables fifteen feet below them, without anyone being surprised by this. The din was deafening, a cacophonous symphony, in which even the croupiers took part, calling the gamblers by name, shouting jokes to one another from table to table, one chewing a sandwich, another, with an almost tyrannical blow of his rake, squashing a hand he didn't like. And no shyness about the customary tips "for the employees." Each winner was automatically ransacked, his pockets turned inside out before he could say a word. Between this Far Eastern bazaar, and the hushed atmosphere of Las Vegas Strip—not to mention the European casinos—there was the difference between a rock concert and a low mass in the Vezelay cathedral.

From above, I completed my survey of the games themselves. At least a dozen in all, not to mention the slot machines, which were called "famished tigers" here. The tigers didn't interest me—the stakes weren't high enough. I was Cimballi, I had come here for $50 million, I wasn't going to fight over the price of a doughnut.

Likewise, I decided to ignore the fan-tan. A bowl of pearl buttons is turned upside down on the carpet, and the buttons are divided into groups of four, with four possibilities or ending. There can be only one, two, three, or four buttons remaining. You bet on one of the four possibilities. You had to be Chinese to like that, and the bets began at barely one Hong Kong dollar.

I also passed up sik po (gambling on throws of a dice cup) and keno, which is played in Vegas and is a kind of lotto, drawn twice an hour, with numbers written on ping-pong balls.

I found pai ko more interesting. This is played with dominoes, or, rather, a kind of dominoes engraved with ideograms. But a few minutes of observation sufficed to convince me, despite the explanations of a hostess, I would never understand it, even if I gave ten years of my life to it. Furthermore, my being a Westerner brought me a few sour looks. Forget it.

On to more serious pastimes. A glance at my watch, I still had five hours and fifteen minutes. The choice was between baccarat (which wasn't played in a closed room here), craps, blackjack (also known as pontoon), roulette, boule, and railroad. Roulette and boule were distinctly too passive. I chose blackjack.

What I knew of it didn't weigh too heavily on my memory. You play against the house, and the cards they deal you have to total twenty-one. In twenty-five minutes, I lost (with a ceiling on bids of HK$500) a trifling fourteen thousand dollars. I changed tables. That didn't work. I was down twenty-seven thousand. But I began to understand a few simple rules that as a mere beginner I had known nothing about. Roughly, the art of "staying" with the hand dealt by the banker. Another change of table to test my new knowledge. I won back four thousand. That was better. I took in fifteen additional pieces of information, and went back to seventeen thousand down. A jerk of the croupier's chin alerted me. Apparently, I was becoming dangerous, in the sense that I was beginning to win too much. We were in Macao, and I knew what happened to those who insisted on taking money from the house. At a certain point, their cards were simply taken away from them, whether they liked it or not. And it was best not to protest.

Unless, in the upper reaches of management, someone decided otherwise.

And that was apparently what was happening to me. For a hostess had appeared, dressed all in pink. She whispered a few words into the croupier's ear. He suddenly grew calm, smiled at me, and motioned for me to continue. The result was that forty minutes later, not only had I recovered all my previous bets, but I had won about fifteen thousand dollars.

The note reached me by an anonymous hand. No sooner had I turned than the messenger had melted into the crowd surrounding the table where I was seated. I unfolded it: YOU MUST LOSE. My turn to write: I AM NOT A LOSER. Without even turning around, I held up the folded note. An unknown hand took it. One hour later, I was up to sixty-five thousand dollars in winnings (I never knew if I was very lucky, or if someone had assisted my luck).

Sixty-five thousand dollars, a good part of which I lost at baccarat (in Deauville, they call it banco).

Winning back most of it at craps.

Immediately (in a manner of speaking, it took more than an hour) lost again at railroad.

At no time did I feel the high that gambling is supposed to produce. Perhaps I'm psychologically incapable of it. Or perhaps it's because I was gambling with money that didn't belong to me. I consulted my watch at regular intervals, astonished, nevertheless, at seeing time pass so quickly. At fifty minutes to eight, I returned to my first love, blackjack, that is. And there, whether by brazen luck or through some skillful manipulation by the casino employees, I won everything I wanted. At three minutes to eight, I had the initial million, plus an additional $195,000. From the corner of my eye, I spotted my bodyguards coming to get me. I yelled a resounding "STAFF!" in French, and yielded all of my winnings to the astounded croupier.

Whereupon the young ladies made off with me, gently but firmly.

"I asked you to lose that money."

"I can't lose. It's not in my nature."

She surveyed me for a moment in silence, her face impassive. Two or three girls were busy setting up a table for dinner for two. They had arranged the table so that once Deng and I were seated, we would be facing a bay window. Behind the window was the China Sea, dotted with junks. There was also a freighter whose flag I didn't recognize, but which must have come from Canton. Night was falling, and to tell the truth, so was I. I hadn't slept for thirty hours, and my back was killing me after running around New York on the heels of my pocket-sized Tyrolean.

"Are you hungry, Mr. Cimballi?"

"Starving. What should I call you? Deng?"

"Miranda."

I was stunned.

"Miranda?"

"Please sit down."

It was the noise that alerted me. A sort of metallic curtain was sliding the length of the bay window. The China Sea vanished. The lights in the room went out one by one. Before my eyes, there was now a projection screen.

"Watch as you eat, Mr. Cimballi."

The first picture already carried the message. The film was in Super-8, black and white, slightly jerky at times, with the awful insistence, the mute implacability of archive footage, of life stolen and not restored. A man's face appeared in huge close-up. He was Chinese, and with mouth stretched wide, he was screaming his fear or his pain in the thickest silence. I was lifting a strip of pressed duck to my lips; I stopped.

"Watch, Mr. Cimballi. His name is unimportant. Let's say that it's someone who gambled frequently in Macao, in an unidentified casino. And who lost more than he could afford."

The image did not budge. The camera stared. The man, however, moved: he shook his head, wept, his eyes bulged.

"He lost too much, Mr. Cimballi. And the security forces of the casino in question paid him a visit, asking him to clear his debt. He explained that he couldn't. He even gave excellent reasons."

A violent convulsion shook the speechless man. He disappeared from the frame, but returned to it very quickly, pushed by a gloved hand that could not have been his own and that forced him back in front of the lens.

"This man is not a coolie, of course. To be able to gamble on credit in a casino requires certain guarantees. It is up to the casino manager, its head—I mean the one responsible to the shareholders—to decide who may gamble on credit and who should not. And it is best for that manager if he does not make too many mistakes of that nature."

We were now alone, the Chinese woman—Miranda, since that was her name—and I. And she was commenting on the film while eating, in an indifferent tone, not even looking at the screen, like someone who had already seen the show and was not interested in it.

"Now, every casino is naturally inclined to grant certain big players the option of gambling on credit. That's business."

The camera finally moved. It moved down slowly, very slowly. It showed the neck, the shoulders, the torso, all naked. I realized then that the man was literally crucified, wrists and forearms bound with iron wire to a rough-hewn beam.

"The problem of credit gamblers is common to all casinos in the world, Mr. Cimballi."

Another camera movement, this time a fast zoom which put the skin of the victim's chest in tight close-up. I saw an ideogram, accompanied by what must have been its English translation: CHEAT. The characters might have been drawn on the skin with a red felt-tip pen, but it was obvious they had used the tip of a knife. And that they hadn't been afraid to cut too deep. But the worst was still to come.

"Mr. Cimballi, it is a problem that has no legal solution. What kind of remedy can there be? The question is worth pondering."

The worst came when the camera resumed its downward movement, when it showed, in a medium shot, the ripped abdomen, and in the gaping hole, a gloved hand. . . .

I closed my eyes and turned my head, about to vomit, my temples pounding and covered with sweat.

"Would you like to see more, Mr. Cimballi?"

"No. I get the message."

I even managed to finish dinner, forcing myself to eat. To be sure, the screen had once again given way to the panorama of the China Sea. We talked business, calmly and politely. We talked figures. As to the question of why Macao Chinese, otherwise solidly tied to Peking, would be willing to come in on a venture in the United Sates, Li and Liu had enlightened me. The revenues stemming from the Macao casinos, the hotels, the transportation services between Macao and Hong Kong, even the garment and other factories of the officially Portuguese colony—the Lisbon authorities' role was confined to maintaining a rather listless police force and modestly financing missionary groups—those revenues reached and probably surpassed three billion French francs per year. Peking took a good share, as did the local government. But this left some rather juicy profits. Investing them in Macao made no sense. There was not enough room. Hong Kong was self-sufficient. Li and Liu had been blunt. "Franz, you'll arrive at the right moment. They're looking for other avenues. If you can convince them your deal is sound, and that they can more or less trust you, they'll make up their minds very quickly."

"I promised you an answer this evening," said Miranda.

The girls cleared the table.

"You'll have it in one hour, Mr. Cimballi. I do, after all, have partners to consult."

She went out. And her departure was like a signal. The squadron of young ladies took charge of me again. They led me into the bedroom—and the bathtub!—I had already seen. And it began again: naked and into the tub. I tried to defend myself, but apart from the fact that there were now six of them and that they had hands like Scandinavian masseuses, they also made themselves comfortable and splashed in the water with me, making sure they did not avoid contact between their naked bodies and mine. One could do worse than to give in. All the same, I was pretty exhilarated by the time they carried me to the bed. I barely had time to wink before I found myself alone.

But not for long.

"I have your answer," she said. "You see that it didn't even take an hour."

This time, at least, to defend my modesty, I had a sheet. I wrapped myself in it like Marlon Brando doing Shakespeare.

"There's no hurry," I said.

In fact, I was beginning to get ideas in the back of my head. And not only there.

"What do you call your casino?"

"The Crystal Palace."

"It's a pretty name."

She was six feet away from me, perfectly still, arms and hands at her sides. I sat on the bed. Since arriving in Macao, I was conscious of having passed two tests—the million dollars to be lost or won, and the film. I now understood I would have to face a third one. "Cimballi, you're going to have to give your body to Finance." Noble and majestic, like Julius Caesar entering the Senate, I got up from the bed.

"There's one thing that concerns us, despite your explanations," she said, very calmly.

"What's that?"

"The man who will become the casino manager of the Crystal Palace. You haven't found him yet, and . . ."

"I told you how I was going to recruit him."

It was exactly as I feared—her tunic dress was fastened by millions of tiny buttons. I began undoing a few of them. With a rather startling thought. If I were wrong about the lovely Miranda's intentions, I would wind up impaled or at the bottom of a sauce for crab soup.

"That's true," she said. "But that's not the point. We won't be on an equal footing, you and us. Not really. You'll have half the shares like us, of course, but it's you who will appoint the manager. It's an unequal bargain."

Those goddamned buttons resisted fiercely. I had already undone twenty of them, but this one . . .

"It's a fake," she said.

"The future manager?"

"The button. This kind of dress comes off like a very tight shirt. You roll it over your skin."

She was right. It rolled. And underneath she had only herself.

I asked, "And what do you suggest, to create a balance?"

"An assistant manager. Appointed by us."

She raised her arms, or, more precisely, kept her arms raised when I lifted them for her to finish removing her dress. Her nipples were hard.

"And who would that assistant manager be? You?"

I kissed one breast.

"Not I."

"Too bad."

I kissed the other breast.

She said, "How long do you expect to keep that sheet on, Marc Antony? No, the assistant manager chosen by us is named Caliban. You're going to have a surprise . . ."

As she was speaking, I picked her up by the knees and armpits

109

and carried her to the bed. She finished her sentence lying down, inert, right heel on the toes of her left foot, palms under her neck.

"You're really going to have a surprise, Mr. Cimballi."

Typhoon is a Chinese word that means "big wind." In the second after her last word, I was hit by a typhoon. It engulfed my whole body. She seemed unaffected by whatever I did or said, and then suddenly, with a regular explosion, she took the initiative.

Several minutes of somersaults followed. End of the first round.

I asked, "Was that the surprise?"

"No. The surprise will be Caliban."

I launched a counterattack for the second round. Silence again.

Finally she said, out of breath, "By the way, the answer is yes on the fifty million."

"What a surprise. But I need it Tuesday."

"Ten-thirty. I've made a note."

For the third round, I didn't even hear the bell.

11

Marc Lavater came to pick me up in Munich. I told him I had found my partners and that I would have an assistant manager named Caliban.

"Funny name. Isn't that in Shakespeare somewhere?"

"The Tempest."

"I didn't know you were so up on literature," he remarked.

"I bought an encyclopedia."

We were driving through the countryside, on the Munich-Salzburg-Vienna highway. The date was Tuesday, September 23, and in that part of the world it was five-thirty in the afternoon. I was drifting a little: helicopter from Macao to Hong Kong, plane from Hong Kong to Tokyo, then from Tokyo to Amsterdam (the only flight that matched my schedule), then from Amsterdam to Munich. And now an hour and a half in a car.

"Anna's not alone," Marc said. "You'll have to face the three sisters."

"That's Chekhov." (I was half asleep).

"What?"

"Three Sisters."

He gave me a worried look, but launched into fresh news, or at least freshly learned. There were indeed four Moser sisters, Anna was the oldest and the guardian, the parents were dead. And Herman Baumer was the brother of the sisters' mother. Hence, he was Heidi's uncle.

"And there is indeed a connection between Heidi and the Crystal Palace."

"Affirmative."

"How did I leave the little things penniless?"

"For years they received an income from the timber plantation, or at least that's what they thought. In fact, the operation hadn't brought in any money in years, and it was Herman who paid out of his pocket, the equivalent of ten thousand dollars per year."

"When did Baumer die?"

"January '75. But he probably made arrangements, for the annual income of ten thousand dollars was paid as usual in '75 and '76."

"Then what's the problem?"

"Walcher. Ernest Walcher."

"Never heard of him."

"He's head of the loan department in a bank in the Bronx. It seems he was a buddy of the late Baumer, and for good reason— both of them came from the Tyrol, though they arrived in the United States at different times. Walcher is the executor of Herman's estate."

"I still can't see what the hell I'm doing in this story."

"Wait. Three weeks ago, at the beginning of September, Ernest Walcher wrote to Anna and her sisters, whose existence, he said, he had just learned of. He told them of the death of Uncle Herman, and at the same time announced he had liquidated the dead man's property. He was sending them everything he was able to salvage from the disaster—twelve thousand dollars. Anna Moser has nerve. By return mail, she asked about the annual income, which Walcher hadn't mentioned. Walcher's reply, he wasn't aware of the existence of that income, and, in his opinion, since it came from a timber operation, it would certainly no longer be paid, since the operation, like all the former landed property of the deceased, had been bought by the international financier Franz Cimballi. We're getting there."

A sign read Kössen. It was a gorgeous place, very tiny and typically Tyrolean. Marc steered the car toward an isolated farm.

"And here is Anna Moser."

"Please meet my sister Christel," she said. "And that's Erika over there."

All three had Heidi's eyes and hair. But Marc was right. While these three Tyroleans might not be bad to look at, Heidi would definitely be the beauty of the family.

I said, "Heidi is very well, in case you're concerned about her."

"But we weren't at all concerned. Of course, you'll both stay for dinner."

A majestic calm. She had made me travel halfway around the globe in a few hours, but, apparently, she was in no hurry to get to the subject of my visit. Nor were her sisters. There was a slight curiosity, amusement perhaps, in the looks they stole at me from time to time, but that was all. It was as if I were a neighbor who had come to spend the evening. I mentioned Walcher's name. Anna slapped my hand with a kindly smile. I told them about Heidi's pranks, making me chase her all over New York. All three of them shook their heads. "Yes, she likes to make mischief. She gets that from Papa." And they recounted all the tricks that that scalawag, Papa Moser, had played all over the Tyrol. When my eyes met Marc's, he shrugged his shoulders and frowned, as if to say, "What do you want me to do about it?"

The meal was gargantuan—goulash soup, paprika schnitzel, boiled pork with horseradish, tons of potatoes accompanied by fritters in bacon fat, cheese blintzes. After which came the pastries—Ischl tarts, apple strudel, plum fritters, etc.

"You don't eat like this every day, do you?"

112

A very serene smile from Anna. She certainly didn't look like a featherbrain who'd send her eight-year-old sister to a stranger in New York.

She explained, "We knew you would arrive today. And Goni told me you ate a lot."

Goni! I seized the opening and threw myself into it.

"Who is Goni?"

"Gunther Kraus, my fiancé."

Why hadn't I thought of it! Of course I knew Gunther! He was the Aspen ski instructor with whom I'd made friends and who had gone skiing with me, Sarah, and Marc-Andrea in Chile and then in the Canadian mountains where there was no towlift and we had to use a helicopter.

"I thought Gunther was in Colorado."

He was. But not always. From time to time he returned to Austria, to his native town, to give his fiancée a hug. And he just happened to be there—ski instructors take their vacations in the summer—when Anna received the second letter from Walcher in which he mentioned a certain Cimballi. Everything became clear. Well, almost.

"Goni assured me that Heidi would be safe with you, that you really liked children."

Anna smiled quietly at me.

"We have almost no more money, Mr. Cimballi. This farm we're living on belonged to our uncle, and you've sold it. We'll have to leave at the end of this month, next week, that is. That's why I sent Heidi to you."

"And Goni, I mean Gunther, agreed?"

No, Goni didn't know.

"Sending Heidi to you was my idea, Mr. Cimballi. Goni surely would not have agreed."

Then for heaven's sake, why had she done it?

"So that you would take care of her, and of us. And especially so that you would find out what happened to Uncle Herman."

Had anything in particular happened to Uncle Herman? Besides his death, of course? She didn't know. But in her opinion, it didn't make sense that a man so rich . . .

"In America, Mr. Cimballi, he owned several restaurants and a very big hotel. He was rich. The only time he came to see us, two years ago, he showed us photos. He told us he'd bring us all to live in his hotel with him. He went back to America and three months later he died. And what do I learn? That he left us only twelve thousand dollars. And I find out he died a year and a half later. No one told us anything. That's not normal. I say that something happened to him. And what can I do? Go to America? But you, you can. You're very rich, a thousand times richer than Uncle Herman said he was. You can do something. And that's why I sent Heidi to you. She's very intelligent. I told her to act in such a way that you would like her and be interested in her. And she succeeded, because you came to Kössen."

I couldn't manage to say a word. The most alarming part was the utter serenity with which she recounted her story. As though it were all perfectly normal. I even had the sense that Anna was rather pleased with herself, on the whole.

She continued, "I know I'm asking a lot of you, Mr. Cimballi. But if you could keep Heidi a little while longer and, at the same time, find out what happened to our uncle, that would really be very kind of you. We're going to leave this farm, my sisters and I. I found a job in Innsbruck and so did Christel. Next spring, Goni will return, we'll be married, and with the money we have left and what Goni has saved, we'll buy a hotel in Sankt Johann. Can you keep Heidi until then? Please, Mr. Cimballi."

She had Heidi's eyes, the same way of bending her head when she gently begged for something.

"Please, Mr. Cimballi."

What an idiot, that Cimballi!

All in all, I spent some fifteen hours in Austria. I left on Wednesday the twenty-fourth, before noon. A direct flight, Munich–New York. Marc came with me. We had planned that he would do an investigation on Walcher and the deceased Herman Baumer. For my part, I had to think above all about the meeting I had the next day, Thursday the twenty-fifth, in Philadelphia with the bankers. Moreover, Philip Vandenbergh was waiting for me at Kennedy Airport. He confirmed that, as arranged with Miranda, the Macao Chinese representatives had already arrived, equipped with all the necessary credentials.

From the New York airport, I called Rosen. Heidi was as well as could be.

"But she's asking for you, Franz. Did you see her sisters?"

I summarized my discussion with Anna. He was surprised. Was that all? Anna Moser had made me come all the way to

Austria for that? And anyway, what did she mean, "something unusual might have happened to the late Baumer?" He offered to do some research into the matter, but I said no thanks, Marc was taking care of it.

"And give Heidi a kiss for me, Jimmy."

Vandenbergh and I were at the Barclay Hotel in Philadelphia on the stroke of eight p.m.—two o'clock in the morning for me, as I was coming from Europe. There were three representatives, including a Chinese-American lawyer from California who knew Li and Liu very well, having had an opportunity to work for them. The $50 million constituting Miranda's share had, they told us, brandishing proof, been transferred that day to Philadelphia by the Hong Kong and Shanghai Bank. For my part, I showed them my property deeds to the hotel in Atlantic City, plus the proof of transfer of an additional 25 million, which I had summoned from Nassau. Hence, everything was ready. But the discussion of the partnership contract dragged on, to the point where, leaving Vandenbergh to wind up the details, I went to bed, dead with exhaustion. When I looked back over my schedule of the previous few days, it made me dizzy. Last Friday, Heidi had sprung into my life. Saturday I had chased her all over New York. Sunday I left for Macao, where I played blackjack and sported with Miranda. Tuesday I was in the Tyrol. And I had just completed a twenty-four-thousand-mile trip around the world. No wonder I was winded.

And I remember that my last conscious thought, before dropping off to sleep that evening, was again amazement at the ease with which that diabolical Anna Moser, behind her placid airs, had gotten me to agree to take care of Heidi. Oh, I was no dupe! With a bit of imagination, you can always find excellent excuses for doing what you feel like doing. In the case at hand, the reason I had given myself for keeping Heidi with me was, first, the interests of the little Tyrolean, and second, those of Marc-Andrea. I firmly intended to bring my son to live with me as soon as things had calmed down a little. With Heidi beside him, he would no longer be alone in the midst of adults, as he had been each time he had spent in my company.

The next morning, in fact, I was on the line with Sarah. A miracle. She made almost no fuss about giving up her hotels for a while. She had promised to think it over, and she had. She would take six months' leave at once, and we would all settle down in a house I would rent. "On the condition I choose it myself," she said. I promised everything she wanted. The main thing was that for the first time in my life, I would be able to live normally. A wife and children at home, my only job being to casually supervise the operations of my casino. For, of course, I had told Sarah the news about Heidi.

She laughed. "It seems to me that this Anna really put one over on you."

She suggested that we all go to Colorado for Christmas, where we would see Gunther, that is, Goni, again. And we could invite Anna, in fact, all the Moser sisters, until the Tyrol was depopulated. Why not, after all?

Half an hour later, I was with the bankers. We signed one by one. Everything was in order—the $400-million loan would be issued quickly, and construction could begin on the Crystal Palace. With the near-certainty of being able to officially open the casino in the spring of 1977, probably in April.

I had one more operation to carry out.

When I had gone to consult him about my project in mid-June, Philip Vandenbergh had pointed out that it was essential to meet three conditions. I would have to find land or a building to renovate (that was done). I would have to find partners (that had just been done). Finally, I would have to recruit a manager, a casino manager with the indispensable license issued in his name by the gambling commission and having superlative qualities besides. The time had come to concern myself with the third condition.

That same Thursday the twenty-fifth, as soon as I had finished with the bankers, I took off for Las Vegas. The man I needed was there. He wasn't alone, however. Also waiting for me in Vegas—Miranda's businessmen reminded me of it, in case I had forgotten—was the man who was destined to become assistant manager of Crystal Palace, his main job being to look out for my partner's interests. My incandescent Macao Chinese woman, between two typhoon blasts, had warned me, "You're going to have a surprise when you see him."

12

I almost missed seeing him. In fact, I went right by him without noticing him, hidden as he was by his golf bag.

A pressure on my arm. "Mr. Cimballi? Welcome to Las Vegas. Did you have a good trip, my colleague?"

Surprised? That was putting it mildly. To begin with, there was the fact that he spoke to me in French, and what French!— for all his distinctly slanted eyes and something heavily Asian in his features, he spoke French with a superb southern accent. You would have thought you were hearing a St. Tropez fisherman.

And in addition, he was at most three-and-a-half feet tall.

"One meter, seven centimeters exactly, my colleague."

I scrutinized him from the dizzying height of my five-foot-six inches.

"Caliban?"

"Himself. You look even younger than your picture. Are you coming? A car's waiting for us. Air-conditioned, of course. It's broiling outside. I swear, it's like being in a pizza oven."

I managed to recover myself.

"I guess you're a native of Macao?"

"Correct."

"It's your accent. There's no mistaking it—Macao."

We walked toward the exit. People turned and stared at us, but my companion obviously did not care about the curiosity he evoked.

"Is Caliban really your name?"

He smiled.

"Of course not. It's a joke between my cousin and me. She acted in *The Tempest* in college, and she gave me that nickname."

His cousin?

"She's the one you dealt with in Macao. We're cousins twice removed. My father married her father's second cousin. My real name is Hervé Casalta. A Corsican from Toulon on my father's side, Chinese from Macao on my mother's side. My cousin calls me Caliban, and I gave her the name Miranda."

He smiled, revealing perfect teeth.

"I admit I overdid the Toulon accent a while ago. I wanted to surprise you."

"Very successful."

One of the prettiest blondes I had ever seen came toward us, smiling a smile that unquestionably was meant for us. The figure of a fashion model, my height, slim and very elegant. The dwarf switched from French to an equally remarkable English. He made the introductions.

"Mr. Franz Cimballi, my wife Patty. Patty is kind enough to act as my chauffeur. I have trouble handling a regular car. My legs are too short to reach the pedals. When I have time, I have the car adapted to my proportions. But since we're only in Vegas for a short time . . ."

One always feels embarrassment and sometimes uneasiness in the presence of someone with a glaring handicap. I felt that way with Caliban for the first few seconds. But the feeling was already dissipating. He spoke in such a natural way of his dwarfism that he soon made me forget about it. And then I discovered him as a person, which made it worthwhile. I wasn't at that point yet. For the moment, he intrigued me. We got into the car, the young woman at the wheel, her husband and me in the back. Caliban talked. Either he thought it wasn't the right time to bring up serious things, or he declined to discuss business in the presence of a third person, albeit his wife. He contented himself with idle chatter. I learned that the couple spent half their time in California, half in France, that their marriage was already five years old, that Caliban himself was over forty (Patty seemed hardly older than twenty-five).

"As for Vegas," he said, "I know it well, of course. I worked there on two occasions, four years in all."

What kind of work? He didn't say. We arrived at the Strip, passing the Dunes on our left, and stopped in front of Caesars Palace. Twenty minutes later, Caliban and I were sitting in the living room of the suite that had been reserved for me. The lovely, graceful Patty had discreetly slipped away, contenting herself with a parting pat on her husband's hand, a gesture that revealed the tenderness that existed between them. Either she was an accomplished actress, or she was very much in love with her Lilliputian husband. In the latter case, it was one more proof, if one was needed, that Macao had not delegated just anyone.

"What should I call you?"

"Caliban will do very well. I'm used to it. At any rate, for my

Chinese relatives and friends, it's easier to pronounce than Hervé."

The armchair in which he was sitting was, of course, too big for him, and he had folded his legs under him to keep them from dangling. The waiter who had brought us fruit cocktails withdrew. Caliban gazed at me with his remarkable, glinting dark eyes.

"I hear everything went off well with the bankers in Philadelphia. Do we already have a date for the opening of the casino?"

"April."

I explained that was when the gambling season really began to get under way in Atlantic City. After all, the state of New Jersey had only recently granted legalization, and while a few establishments were already in operation, many others had hardly gone into construction. Crystal Palace would be the happy medium.

"May I call you Franz? We could even use the familiar forms in French, okay? Franz, do you have any experience in gambling?"

"None."

"I do," he said. "I'm forty-two years old, and it's forty years since I spun my first roulette, in Macao."

(I was later to learn that his father had been a Corsican from Indochina who had succeeded—a rare achievement—in marrying a Chinese girl from a family with major interests in Cholon and Saigon, as well as in Singapore, Hong Kong, and Macao. Caliban himself was born in Toulon, rather by accident, but he had eventually, especially after his father's death, lived in the Far East). He leaned toward me.

"First of all, let's get a few things straight, Franz. By chance, both of us were born on the southern coast of France, within a few miles of each other. That could create a bond between us. It's even possible that we might be friends."

"But you're in this business to defend your Chinese relatives' interests."

"Precisely. And I will do it, friendship or no friendship. Whatever the consequences may be for you. Clear?"

Curiosity had led me to skim through Shakespeare's *Tempest*. I'd bought the book in Philadelphia. The name of Caliban intrigued me. If I'd understood the story correctly—and there was no guarantee of that—Caliban was a "born demon," a rather

119

dreadful gnome, a brute force in its natural state, whom only a certain Miranda could get to obey. In other words, the character was not too reassuring.

I asked, "And the other things?"

Caliban smiled, putting together his small but powerful fingertips.

"There's just one more. I'm the world's top expert when it comes to supervising gambling, in casinos or elsewhere. I'm not bragging, Franz. The croupier or gambler who could cheat under my eyes without my spotting him immediately hasn't been born. You can believe me or not. That has absolutely no importance."

"I believe you."

"What's the name of that man you came to find here in Vegas, to be the manager of the Crystal Palace?"

"Chance. Henry Chance."

His name had been given to me two months earlier, at the beginning of July. The source of the information was my friend Paul Hazzard, from San Antonio, Texas, with whom I'd done some oil prospecting ventures. Paul's first, immediate reaction, when I told him about my project was "Franz, forget it. The gambling world is a hundred times worse than the oil business, and that's saying a lot. You'll have two kinds of adversaries. Either superstars, who'll drop one or two billion bucks on the table without batting an eyelash, or the others, those whose names end in vowels. In both cases, the stakes are too high." I pressed him. In the end, he mentioned the name Chance. "But he won't go along. I know him, I tried to put a deal together with him. He won't go along. Not after what they did to him." And naturally, I wanted to know what "they" had done to Henry Chance.

The story goes back to the 1960s—much farther, in fact, when you know that Chance's forebears had worked the riverboats on the Mississippi in the last century. In fact, it was a family tradition with the Chances. They were not gamblers, but dealers. Henry Chance arrived in Vegas in 1945, right after his discharge from the army. Before the war he had already worked as a croupier in Reno. When the notorious gangster Bugsy Siegel set up the first of the great casino-hotels on the Strip—the Flamingo— Chance was one of the first to be hired. He rose rapidly through

120

the ranks, especially after the death of Siegel, whose skull caught a bullet that happened to be whizzing by. Other super-casinos were established. Chance was recruited by them, and his rise was steady. He became assistant manager for the first time in 1954 and earned his marshal's staff five years later—casino manager.

Casino manager in Vegas is the equivalent of the White House for a politician or a seat on top of a double-decker bus for a Londoner. All the previous generations of Chances must have sung hallelujahs from their graves. For ten years, Chance stayed at the helm with exceptional integrity. But circumstances would work against him. The establishment he managed came under attack one fine day from the large American financial groups, which began to think that gambling was far too prosperous an industry to be left to hoodlums. Big Business brought in heavy artillery, with the support of local politicians and the Nevada Gaming Commission. Two teams of lawyers, one representing Howard Hughes, the other a superpowerful oil company, arrived at the casino where Chance was the manager (only the manager, not the owner) and handed down an ultimatum—sell within twenty-four hours to one or another of the two delega-tions. The Family which owned the place gave in to that caval-cade of dollars. Chance was fired. Not that they had anything against him, but he had been in the confidence of the former owners, and that was enough to brand him. He found himself out of work.

(What I knew of Henry Chance came from two sources—Paul Hazzard to begin with, but above all, the Callaway private de-tective agency, which I had hired on July 5. Their mission was to answer three questions—who was Henry Chance, what was he worth professionally, and what exactly were his relations with the Mob? Callaway handed me an initial report at the end of July, a second one on August 20—the day before the signing of the deed of sale to the Atlantic City hotel—and a third one on September 15. The three reports complemented one another, and were clear—Chance was the man I needed.)

With no job in Vegas, he left for the Bahamas, where the gangsters kicked out of Cuba by Castro had set up shop. He stayed there two years, but resigned—"for incompatibility of temperament," Callaway explained. For a while, he was in San Juan working on a casino-hotel project. He resigned again of his own accord, again for incompatibility of temperament. He traveled. His trail was found in Europe, Latin America, the Far East, wherever there were gambling tables. In short, he was a victim of his vocation or of family tradition. Nowhere could he find a job commensurate with his abilities. He then committed the one and only mistake of his life. He took up work again in Vegas as casino manager, not in a "clean" place but in one of the others which had remained in the hands of the Mob. Five months later, the story broke, and Chance was the man who brought on the scandal. He alerted the Feds to the illegalities committed in his own casino—rigged tables and laundering of drug money. He testified in court. Punishment was swift. He was beaten up and his right hand sawed off. And since he persisted in his charges, an accident occurred. While he was on vacation with his family on the Baja California coast, his car exploded. He got away and so did one of his daughters, but his wife and his other daughter were burned alive.

Callaway's comments: "The risk that the subject has maintained friendly relations with the underworld is extremely slight." I shared that opinion. There would be hard feelings, to say the least.

After the tragedy, Henry Chance left the United States. He went to live in Europe, in Monte Carlo, with his surviving daughter. She married. Chance, now alone, came back to Vegas after years of absence and settled down there. "Subject does not travel. He lives alone except for a housekeeper. He does not gamble. Nonetheless, he spends fifteen or sixteen hours a day in the gambling rooms of various hotels, going from one casino to another."

In 1976, Chance was sixty-one years old. According to Callaway, although he was not rich, he had easily enough to live on. The little haciendalike place he lived in, at the very end of Charleston Avenue, on the road to Boulder City, belonged to him. I had seen only three or four photos of him, attached to his file.

On September 26, the day after my arrival in Vegas and my meeting with Caliban, it was a few minutes to nine in the morning, and Henry Chance was before me.

13

Before *us* would be more accurate. Caliban accompanied me. Chance stared at us, from one to the other. He was strictly deadpan.

He said, "I was getting ready to go out."

I drew from my pocket one of the cards Callaway had provided. I read aloud, "Subject received no visitors in the last sixty-three days. His six-room house is kept up by a housekeeper named Ruth Martinez, age fifty-nine. Subject gets up at 8:15 every morning. He goes out at nine o'clock. His itinerary did not vary in sixty-three days of observation. He begins by driving to the Sahara Hotel, where he leaves his car. He spends forty minutes there, eats breakfast for ten minutes, then enters the gambling room. Leaving the Sahara, he makes a series of visits, of about one hour each, to all the major casino-hotels on the Strip. In unvarying order: Thunderbird, Circus Circus, Riviera, Stardust, Royal Las Vegas, Silver Slipper, Frontier, Desert Inn. He eats lunch—broiled meat and salad—either at the Desert Inn or at the Frontier, less often at the Royal Las Vegas. A taxi— always the same one, driven by Harry Martinez, son of Ruth Martinez—takes him from the Desert Inn to the Castaways. The subject resumes his rounds, in this order: the Sands, the Holiday Inn, Caesars, the Flamingo, the Dunes, the Bonanza, and the Aladdin. Subject generally dines at Caesars. Less frequently, he ends his evening at the Hilton, always alone. In any event, he uses Martinez' taxi to get back to his own car, between one-thirty and two in the morning, and goes home."

I raised my head.

"Should I go on?"

Silence. Henry Chance was taller than I, thin and carefully dressed in a beige suit. He gave off a striking impression of calm and reserve. You would take him for an observer on the moon. His hair was more than white, it was snowy. Light-colored eyes, but without that dreamy vacuousness that blue or gray irises often express. His gaze was full and hard, marked by an uncommon, almost discomforting keenness—the eyes of a hunter on the lookout. Especially at that moment, as he gauged me.

"So I've been under surveillance for sixty-three days?"

"A little more. I ordered an investigation of you that began in early July. But it's only been two months since my investigators began what they call close surveillance."

Chance smiled (only with his lips, his eyes remained icy).

"In that case, I must be getting old. It's only sixty-one days since I spotted your men. Four men and two women, taking turns. They all stayed at the Showboat Hotel on Fremont Street. They work for the Callaway agency in Los Angeles. Extremely professional."

I burst out laughing.

"But not enough to fool you."

Another smile, as chilling as the first.

"I am a difficult man to fool, Mr. Cimballi. And while I'm on the subject, I rather like the hotel you picked for your future casino. I assume you're going to use a facsimile of the London namesake as a logo in your advertising campaign?"

Things were beginning to move a little fast for me. I shot a glance at Caliban. But his dark eyes were impenetrable and were fastened on Chance. The dwarf and I had spent the previous evening together—the three of us, in fact, because the gorgeous Patty was with us. He turned out to be a real live wire, stealing the show from the professional comic on the stage. His imitation of a pivot by the Harlem Globetrotters left the entire room in stitches. Now I was looking at a completely different Caliban. This one, tense and alert, could easily send chills down your spine. The idea occurred to me that a team made up of Chance and Caliban would be ideal. Especially if Chance was only half as smart, wily, observant, and suspicious as he looked.

I asked him, "Okay, you spotted Callaway's boys, but how did you know they were working for me?"

"I've spent two-thirds of my life here, Mr. Cimballi. I know nine out of ten of the croupiers and all the staff of the hotels, bars, restaurants, and gambling halls personally. I know every policeman, public or private. For years, as a casino manager, I set up and monitored a huge surveillance network. My job was to attract gamblers to my place."

And one had a better chance of finding large bettors in the suites of Caesars, MGM, or the Hilton than in the motels for unlucky fortune hunters on the outskirts of Vegas. And he used his friendships, his past connections, as leverage. And when one of Callaway's men visited me the previous evening at Caesars to deliver his report . . .

"Cimballi. Your name meant something to me. But you're not a gambler."

"Not at all."

"If you'd lost more than a thousand dollars in the last fifteen or twenty years in any official casino in Vegas, Nassau, San Juan, or Macao, your name would be in my files. And it's not there. Last night I made a few phone calls. Who was this Cimballi who was having me followed for two months?"

"Reply—Crystal Palace."

He nodded, and from a small table, picked up a very fine, gold cigar case imbedded with seven diamonds. He opened it and placed five Havanas inside—a sign of luxury in the United States, where the importation of Havana cigars is prohibited.

"My ration for the day," he said, smiling.

He had used only his left hand. The other one was hidden in a leather glove of the same color as his suit. But I hardly noticed, for a word had struck me in what he had just said—files. He had files on large bettors, had kept them up to date for at least "fifteen or twenty years" and probably more. There was no mistaking that sign. He hadn't mentioned his files by accident.

In other words, he knew why I had come to see him, what I was going to ask him, and what his reply would be.

For that matter, so did I.

There are the figures, said Henry Chance, an hour and a half later. In that year of '76, nearly ten million visitors had arrived or would arrive in Las Vegas, by plane, bus, train, or car. Each of them, according to statistics, would stay four full days and would spend an average of $77 for food, drinks, souvenirs, and lodging. In addition to gambling. On that, the estimates varied at around $200 *lost* per visitor. One need merely do the arithmetic—two hundred times ten million.

Chance had taken us to the top of Landmark Tower, some three hundred feet above the ground.

"Ten million visitors per year. To see what? A city that's not even worthy of the name, in the middle of the desert. No monuments, no archeological ruins to visit. Churches, yes. There are more churches here, proportionally, than in Rome. You know why? Because gambling is considered immoral by nearly all religions. So each casino had one, five, ten churches built, for as many different sects, including the most obscure. It was the best way to get the clergy to shut up, whoever they are. They deposit their share of the profits and keep their mouths shut."

At some point, Chance had discovered that Caliban also spoke French. And it was in French, barely tinged with an accent, that his remarks were made.

"I have never gambled, Mr. Cimballi. Never. Even though I've spent forty-five years in casinos. Does that surprise you?"

If it made him happy. I hadn't come to Vegas to hear a sermon, but to find a manager for the Crystal Palace. A casino manager, as they say here. And when you say those two words in Vegas, it's like speaking of the pope in Rome. The evening before, even Caliban had done his part. He had sketched a portrait for me of the ideal casino manager—an expert, suspicious to the point of paranoia, capable of seeing at a glance which of his thousand of employees is getting ready to do something stupid, knowing all the tricks, past, present, and future, possessed of a powerful memory when it comes to figures, names or faces, capable of setting up an organization to rival that of the KGB. And at the same time, scrupulously honest toward his employers. And furthermore, likable, affable, courteous, gifted with dexterity, tact, savoir-faire, speaking several languages, knowing who's who, in Tokyo, London, Riyadh, or Chicago.

In short, a superman.

No casino was profitable without a good casino manager. For he was the one who personally watched all the money come in and go out, down to the last penny. He was the one responsible for each employee, over whom he had regal authority—he could fire anyone without warning or explanation, and his decisions were final. He had to seek out and attract good customers, large bettors, decide if he would grant them credit and how much. And this Renaissance man, in addition, would have to concern himself with entertainment for his establishment, hire this or that star, know exactly what the effect of those stars would be on the casino's volume of business, its "drop."

Out of curiosity, I questioned Chance on that last point. He shrugged.

"Sinatra's Number One. There's no one better for attracting large and small gamblers. At the other extreme is Barbra Streisand. She's the last one you'd want. Not because of her talents, but her presence would have a disastrous effect on the size of the bets. Someone like Elvis Presley would fill your halls with a record crowd, but in that crowd there wouldn't be a single large bettor. They'd go someplace else and wait for the commotion to die down."

And so on and so forth. We were still at the top of Landmark Tower. Chance stretched out his gloved hand.

"Look."

I couldn't see anything but desert, whichever way I turned—hundreds and hundreds of square miles of desert.

"Exactly," said Chance, reading my thoughts. "That's one of the secrets of the success of Vegas. Vegas is a dream in the middle of nowhere. There's nothing else to do but gamble. And that's exactly the function of this desert surrounding us, Mr. Cimballi—it's a buffer zone. Which doesn't exist in Atlantic City. And never will."

"And is it all that important?"

It made things more difficult. In Atlantic City, a gambler didn't have far to go to get away from the gambling world. For right behind the casinos lined up on the Boardwalk, there would, indeed, be a regular city, a normal life, which would interrupt the fantasy and restore the gambler's contact with reality.

"That will be the biggest problem in Atlantic City, Mr. Cimballi." (He insisted on never using my first name. It was clear that he intended to keep his distance.) "The biggest one, but not the only one. Here in Vegas, a cheater is a condemned man. Where can he hide? And the regular police are on the lookout. What will happen in New Jersey, with New York so close? If they apply the rules followed here, everything will be all right. Only the major problem will remain."

Up to then he had spoken French. But now he used the American expression, "To keep the mobs out."

There it was again, as always.

I spent a total of five days in Las Vegas. It was a way of learning the ropes as a future casino owner. And I had at my side two of the best experts in the world. It was hard to imagine two men more different than Chance and Caliban. There was their size and their physical appearance. But that wasn't the main thing—one was as introverted as the other was extroverted and expansive. Yet there was one point on which they were alike—their exceptional knowledge of casinos. To see Vegas with them was to watch a show from backstage. The other side of the fabric.

The first day, the atmosphere between them was decidedly

cold. You might even say it was funny. They actually competed with one another to see which would be the first to spot the tiniest abnormality in the halls we endlessly frequented. But very soon, a mutual respect grew up between the Chinese-Corsican from Macao and the Anglo-Saxon from Mississippi. Friendship was not far off. Just as long as it didn't develop behind my back.

Speaking of Caliban, Chance told me, "That midget is the most remarkable room monitor I've ever seen. For instance, when somebody's dealing cards, it can happen, and it does happen, that he takes the card from the bottom instead of the top of the pack. If the cheater's skillful enough, you won't see anything. But perhaps you'll hear it, because it makes just the tiniest click. Men who are capable of hearing that click are one in a million. In the roar of a gambling hall, it's something of a miracle. But your Caliban can do it. And he doesn't even need to be close to the table. Don't ask me how he does it, I haven't the slightest idea. But he does it. You want another example? He's the most fantastic countdown expert I've ever known, and I've known a few, believe me."

Naturally, I knew nothing about a countdown. It's easy to explain. You sit down at a baccarat table at the beginning of the shoe, when they've just finished putting new cards in the pile. You memorize the cards dealt—all of them. So that as the pile diminishes, you can tell which cards haven't been dealt yet. Easy to explain . . .

And Caliban, for his part, speaking of Chance, "Franz, I knew this man only by name. Your information is correct, and I'm going to tell Miranda that you kept your part of the bargain. This guy was born to manage a casino the way Nureyev was born to dance."

And he listed all the reasons he had for thinking so. Well, so far so good. As for me, I had learned more in these five days than I would have done if I'd stayed there ten years.

I knew:
A table, each table, absolutely had to yield as a profit 20 percent of the sums invested by the players. That was the sacrosanct percentage rule. If the percentage went down on a given evening, it automatically set off the alarm signal. If it went down for an entire week or even longer, the tactic for dealing with this

was blindingly simple—you kicked out the entire team of croupiers and monitors assigned to the table. If cheating could be
proved, so much the better, but if not, too bad. OUT!

The game is LEGITIMATE.

A croupier who starts limping from one day to the next, even
slightly, has probably slipped chips into his socks. (He has no
pockets except for this shirt pocket on his chest, where gamblers
can put tips, which, however, are immediately deposited in the
common fund.)

The 20 percent per table on the *drop* is called the *hold*. About
one-fifth of the hold is used to cover the entertainment costs and
to pay for the supply of drinks and food served free to the
players. If those costs exceed one-fifth of the hold, someone gets
fired immediately.

The game is LEGITIMATE.

A special piece of equipment makes it possible to infuse pure
oxygen into the room after two or three in the morning (at the
discretion of the casino manager or one of his assistants), in order to revive the flagging energies of the weary players and keep
them at the tables.

A casino must have a hotel as its natural complement. The
ideal capacity of that hotel is around 600 rooms. The hotel must
be lavish, but NOT TOO COMFORTABLE, at least as far as the
rooms are concerned. Otherwise those lazy gamblers would
never come out of them. And they belong downstairs at the tables. OUT!

A casino hall should have no direct exits. The gambler should
not know if it is day or night, sunny or rainy. Such details don't
concern him and would only be a distraction.

The game is LEGITIMATE.

The ladies of the night (one to two hundred dollars in '76),
whose job, semiofficially but very genuinely, is to "distract" certain players, must be imbued with a sense of their sacred
mission—to bring those players back to the table as soon as possible.

One casino worker (employed by the casino to create entertainment around a table and attract players) is called a shill. A
shill can become dangerous. There's a famous example. She was
one of the prettiest girls ever seen in Vegas, where the competition is keen. Apart from her exceptional beauty, there was nothing she could do. A casino hired her as a shill. In that role, she

was given three hundred dollars a day to play against the bank. It didn't matter whether she won or lost. In either case, it would all go back to the main coffers. So far, there was nothing extraordinary in this. Except all of a sudden, this young beauty—let's call her Lisa—began to be blessed with absolutely incredible luck. Although she bet low stakes, she won enough each day to buy herself a Cadillac. This wasn't a problem, because her winnings, like that of any shill, were collected by the casino as they accumulated. But things became complicated when real players, noting her fantastic success, began to imitate everything she did. And to win also, of course. Following her when she changed tables and staking bigger and bigger sums. The alarm signal went off. Was the beautiful Lisa cheating? Video camera recordings of the gambling tables revealed nothing. In the end, they decided it was luck, pure and simple. They figured it wouldn't last. It lasted. Then they brought in a team of psychologists, psychiatrists, and other specialists, who put the too-lucky shill on a couch and interviewed her. The diagnosis was surprising, but unanimous. The experts saw only one explanation. Such persistent luck could have only one source, Lisa's virginity. A virgin in Vegas is obviously a rare phenomenon. Don't forget that all of this—it's completely authentic—was happening in a world on the edge of fantasy. In Vegas, they believe in luck as an inexplicable phenomenon. Supposing there was a connection between luck and virginity? To determine this, the best thing was to relieve the young lady of her special feature. The most seductive staff members were assigned to the siege. The fortress remained impregnable (and Lisa kept winning). Customers were recruited and paid to offer the young lady fabulous rewards in exchange for a short trip to the bedroom. Nothing doing. They even resorted to a world-famous singer who agreed to do the favor and crooned on behalf of the management. Lisa remained firm as marble, remained a virgin and continued to win. At that point, there was only one solution, hopeless from the scientific standpoint, but effective (they had already lost a million dollars on account of that virgin). They fired her.

The game is LEGITIMATE.

The slot machines, and to a lesser degree, roulette, are essentially designed to occupy the wives and girlfriends of real gamblers, who can thus devote themselves wholeheartedly to craps, blackjack, baccarat, etc.

A casino must earn its money in three successive stages. First, on the tables or through the other games. Then, in a relentless combat with its own employees. Finally, in the collection of chips, cash, checks, credit-card receipts, and other tokens of indebtedness.

"Vegas statistics show that for every million dollars gambled on credit, you actually collect only 80 percent, or eight hundred thousand dollars. The other two hundred thousand dollars go under profit and loss. Which doesn't prevent each casino manager from urging his collectors to behave 'unpleasantly' when collections are difficult."

"Which means what?"

I already saw myself—without the least enthusiasm!—at the head of a team of hired killers who would terrorize my future customers when they didn't pay. Those "ladies of the night" were still sticking in my craw.

But Chance shook his head:

"No blood, Mr. Cimballi. Not even the slightest bit of violence. The collectors of a casino worthy of the name . . ."

"Like the Crystal Palace."

"If the Crystal Palace exists one day. The collectors of a casino worthy of the name are under permanent orders to be as polite as possible. They're public-relations people, above all. A debtor who's unable to pay is still a potential customer. As such, he's entitled to every consideration."

"But if he's a swindler?"

Try as I might, that 20 percent I would systematically have to give up kept bothering me. I did a quick calculation. For the Crystal Palace, the loss would be a million and a half dollars per year!

"If our background check shows that the debtor is actually solvent, if his unwillingness to pay can be proved, we use every legal means at our disposal."

"But since gambling debts are not legally recognized?"

"We sue anyway. And of course, we lose. But many of these negligent debtors have otherwise honorable reputations—otherwise, we wouldn't have offered them credit—and they hardly appreciate the publicity they receive."

Henry Chance was the king of euphemism. I said "swindler," he said "negligent debtor." Never a word of slang on his lips, whether he was speaking French or English. From him and from Caliban, I had learned a huge amount in five days. Not enough to attempt to become a casino manager. I didn't have the taste or the time for it. Or the capabilities, either, probably. No, the main thing was that I had fulfilled the third condition.

For, quite obviously, Henry Chance had said yes to me. Truth to tell, I'd obtained his agreement with so little difficulty that it surprised me.

"I was told that you wouldn't accept."

"By whom?"

"Paul Hazzard of San Antonio. He offered you a partnership, and you turned him down."

"I'm not interested in a partnership. That would be gambling with my own money, and as you know, I never gamble."

"Is that the only reason?"

"Paul Hazzard wasn't able to put together $500 million."

But the impression remained with me that there was still something else. Chance was certainly sincere when he said that he had turned down a partnership because he didn't want to invest his own money. I even thought I had uncovered the real reasons for his refusal. He belonged to that very rare sort of men who are admirably aware of their own limitations. To gamble on his own account would force him to become personally involved. In so doing, he would probably lose the best of his abilities, perhaps owing to an emotionalism that he so carefully concealed. Working for someone else, however, enabled him to remain that almost utterly perfect machine.

I began to laugh.

"Okay, I'll offer you a job instead of a partnership. And I've put together $500 million. But there's still something else."

He smiled—really smiled, for the first time since I'd known him. I read the amusement in his pale, piercing eyes.

"Duke Thibodeaux," he said. "You must surely remember him."

"He's not the kind you forget."

Far from it. I could still remember the taste of Duke's vile moonshine—homemade, in Louisiana. Duke Thibodeaux was more than an old friend.* In a really dark moment, I had even gone so far as to cry on his aged shoulder. Besides lending his

*See *Cash.*

132

shoulder to self-pitying Frenchmen, he was an oilman and a boiler of official, patented illegal whisky.

"And you know old Duke?"

"We're second cousins," Chance grinned.

Oh, for heavens sake! I would have to remember to compliment that damned Callaway on the thoroughness of his information!

On October 1, I was in New York. In descending order of size, there were waiting for me at Kennedy Airport, with identical smiles—the Amazon, Marc Lavater, Sarah, Heidi, and Marc-Andrea. Plus what was apparently a dog nearly four feet long, all black, red-tongued, and licking everyone to the point of idiocy, named Satan.

My family in full regalia.

14

"How long is she going to stay, Franz?"

I had just finished explaining to Sarah (for the second time, the first time having cost me a fifty-five-minute phone call between Las Vegas and Montego Bay, Jamaica) Heidi's special situation.

"We'll see at the beginning of January."

"Why the beginning of January?"

"Or during the Christmas holidays. Anna and all the Mosers will come from Austria to Colorado. We'll be there, too. It was your idea that I should invite them. And Gunther, whom you know, will also be in Colorado."

"Whom I know. He's very handsome, and he doesn't sneer at me when I ski on my behind. Unlike some others I could mention. But you haven't answered my question."

We were walking in Central Park, along the elm-lined path of the Mall. I was deeply engrossed in contemplating the statue of Shakespeare by one J.A.Q. Ward. That guy had a regular alphabet for a first name. Thirty feet ahead of us, Heidi and my son were talking about farming and laughing, incredibly spontaneous and glad to be alive. I felt strange.

"Franz."

"I know. I haven't answered your question."

"I have another one now."

I went back to my contemplation of Shakespeare. Good old Will. I knew what Sarah was going to tell me. Not even to ask me, to tell me. Which she did.

"Franz, this is nothing new, you've always been a terrible spoiler with children. I remember that time in Marrakech, when that German woman called the police because a sadistic madman had kidnapped her awful brats in a helicopter. The sadistic madman was you, and you stuffed those poor kids so full of licorice that after the police, the firemen, the air force, and the national guard, they had to call in an internist as well. Spoi-ler!"

Pause.

"But this is worse."

Marc-Andrea and Heidi had now joined a whole group of other children with whom they were organizing a rally. By himself, my son would never have dared mingle with other children, but with Heidi, he broke out of his shell. I had never seen him so happy. I was almost jealous.

"Franz, you have a choice. You can wait ten or twelve years and marry her."

"Clever, clever."

"You can move, we can all move to Austria, to Sankt Johann, across from the hotel that Anna and her handsome tanned fiancé are going to buy or build, I don't know which . . ."

"Buy. The hotel's already there."

"Or, you can adopt her."

Silence. All at once, I felt dead tired. I'd had enough. Since that middle of June when I'd arrived in New York to tell Philip Vandenbergh of my intention to buy a casino, I'd never stopped running. But it was finished for a good long while, perhaps for a very long while. Ahead of me was a long period in which I should have peace. Henry Chance and Caliban had remained in Las Vegas. Their presence in Atlantic City was not necessary for the time being. They would come simply to cast an eye at the hotel and the architects' renovation plans, but would then return to Nevada, where they would work on recruiting the huge, highly trained staff we would need in the spring. For my part, all I would have to do was supervise the operations. Going there once a week—to Atlantic City, I mean,—would be more than sufficient. I smiled at Sarah and pulled her toward me.

"I bet you already know where we're going to be living by next spring."

She darted at me her usual green-eyed gaze, shook her head, and returned my smile. She took my arm, and we walked together, just like an old married couple whose children were playing in the park, on a poetic, soft autumn morning in New York, under the blazing colors of the large New England trees.

"Long Island," she said.

A quick, somewhat automatic calculation—it would take me at most forty-five minutes to reach Manhattan. Long Island would be perfect.

"Have you found something there?"

She had even visited the house while I was filling my eyes with the denizens of Vegas. It was a kind of large English cottage, much of it covered with ivy, no more than ten or fifteen rooms with a porch, large garden, lawn running down to a small lake with a wooden pier. There was even a shed for a (small) boat.

"And guess who we'll have for neighbors?"

I mentioned the first name that came to mind.

"John Lennon and his Japanese wife."

"You're a pain," she said. "You guessed it."

And our rest began. For we did move to Long Island, with our two children, who got along as well, and probably better, than if they had been brother and sister. They established diplomatic relations with the very young son of the ex-Beatle, our neighbor, but as Lennon Junior was at most three years old, these international exchanges remained at the protocol stage. Anyway, Heidi ought to go to school, according to Sarah, and when Sarah was sure she was right about something, arguing with her was tantamount to trying to convince the Nile to run back to its source. She, therefore, registered our Tyrolean in a neighborhood

135

school, disdaining my offer of a tutor, which she disliked in principle.

"And who's going to drive her to that blasted school each morning?"

"You, my pet," she returned. "Don't bother, it's all settled."

And, looking at me with a sly, sarcastic pleasure, "Who wanted a regular family life? You, if I'm not mistaken."

She was right, anyway. She had made huge sacrifices, agreeing, for the first time since I'd known her, to put her professional activities in hotel management on the back burner. (She had taken a six-month sabbatical.) In a surprisingly short time, she and Heidi, two females, had established a virtual conspiracy, usually at my expense, as is generally the case. The Tyrolean had won her over, and vice versa, and I made a wonderful whipping boy for the two of them.

The house was never empty, largely owing to Sarah, who had an awesome Anglo-Saxon efficiency when it comes to organizing social activities. On certain Sundays or school holidays, everything up to and including my office was transformed into a branch of kindergarten. At such times, I disguised myself as a Newfoundlander, and by rowing furiously, reached the geometric center of the lake, where I was almost sure no one would come to ask me to repair a toy, cut a cake, or, even worse, sing something.

It must have been at the end of October, then, that Marc Lavater, who had come for the weekend, was rowing with me.

"It's about Herman Baumer," he said. "Good Lord, where do all these kids come from? Are you breeding them, or what?"

"Heidi's friends. She invited her whole class for brunch. Plus friends of friends. Marc?"

"Yes?"

"Don't ask me if I'm going to keep Heidi with us and for how long."

He smiled. Okay. But could he still talk to me about Uncle Herman, or H.B., as we called him in code? He could, I said.

"H.B. arrived in the United States in the autumn of 1941. He was twenty-three years old, almost twenty-four. He'd cooled his heels for a while before getting through Immigration. According to him, he had left Austria after a disagreement with a certain Adolf Hitler. From '38 to '41 . . ."

"Is this important, this part?"

"Not as far as I know."

"Skip it."

"I'll summarize. Two months after his entry into the U.S., the country went to war. H.B. enlisted. No pacifist, he."

"And came back with loads of medals. Was he the one who captured Hirohito?"

"No. But on his return, he was entitled to full American citizenship. He bought a hot-dog stand with his separation pay. He could barely read and write, but he made a fortune selling wieners. He bought his first store in the Bronx, then a second one in Manhattan. In '53, his first tavern. Not a high-class joint, the kind of place where you drink beer and eat Austrian and Bavarian delicacies."

"He got rich."

"Not really. Although—his customers were mainly office workers . . ."

"Is this important?"

"It may be."

"Go."

". . . taxi drivers and the like. Not bums, but not far off in some cases. H.B. gladly trusted them when they couldn't pay. Most of them, like him, were recent immigrants, from all over Europe, couldn't speak English too well. Baumer ruled over this little crowd. He was a good fellow. They cheated him, but he didn't care. He accumulated bucks anyway, probably because he spent almost nothing on himself. His sole property apart from the taverns was his studio in Greenwich Village, where he lived until the end."

"Did he go back to Austria?"

"Not for a long time. We don't know how, but somehow he learned that his sister was alive and married to a certain Moser. It was '56. Baumer went to Austria for the first time."

"Heidi wasn't born yet."

"But Anna was. She was a year old. It was during that trip that Baumer bought the timber plantation and the farm, presenting it, or rather, the revenues from it, to his sister and brother-in-law. And when the sawmill stopped producing, H.B. discreetly took up the slack. I told you. He was a good fellow."

Marc talked and I rowed for the sole purpose of keeping warm.

"Baumer came back to America. Between '56 and '72, his business continued to prosper modestly. A slightly crazy idea came to him. He wanted to buy a hotel. Not as an investment or to get rich. Just to have a good time with his buddies. Perhaps also because he had always dreamed of having his own hotel. After treating his friends to a meal, he could also then offer them a night's rest. He was a romantic in the guise of a hot-dog vendor. Nostalgia for the old days in Vienna, that sort of thing. Among his old friends were some who had known Atlantic City in its glory days. They probably told H.B. about it, for he had his heart set on buying in Atlantic City, nowhere else."

I continued to row, my feet were freezing. I was hardly interested in Herman's tribulations. I raised my finger.

"May I interrupt you?"

"Interrupt."

"This guy who wrote to Anna Moser . . ."

"Walcher."

"Right, Walcher. When does he come into the story?"

"He's there from the beginning. When Baumer bought his first delicatessen, he borrowed the money from a neighborhood bank in the Bronx. And Walcher was behind the desk. The two men had known each other since 1945 at least. They were both from the same region of the Tyrol, but Walcher was a bit older and had emigrated to the United States in 1933."

"A good year."

"Walcher acted as Baumer's accountant. And when he took it into his head to buy a hotel, he naturally turned to Walcher, who had risen in rank, for a four-hundred-thousand-dollar loan. The hotel in Atlantic City was selling for five hundred thousand."

"Walcher told Herman that he was *tob . . . tob . . .*"

"*Tobsüchtig.* Soft in the head."

"But he lent him the money anyway. H.B. was delighted. He put on a bash in his new toy with his friends, whom he brought to Atlantic City in chartered buses. He lost money, but balanced it off, more or less, with the money he made in his taverns. He was a widower with no children, and had evidently lost contact with his family in Austria. Still, when he learned—I don't know how—that he had four orphaned nieces, he beat his breast and rushed to Austria on his second trip."

"The one Anna told us about."

"The only one she remembers. In 1956, she was too young. On his return, according to Walcher . . ."

"You met him, this Walcher?"

"Yes. He didn't make a bad impression on me. Sixtyish and well preserved, reserved, not very high caliber. The model employee type. He was fond of Baumer, there's no doubt."

I was beginning to get sick of rowing, especially in circles.

"On his return from Austria, Baumer was filled with remorse. He would have liked to do lots of things for his nieces. But the circumstances weren't very good. He lost a good bit of money on his hotel. The horde of semiderelicts he'd invited had settled in for good, and they were driving away paying customers. and then above all, Herman found love."

"Would you repeat that?"

"LOVE. It was 1974, so he was fifty-six years old. Cupid struck . . ."

"Pow!"

"That's right. The lady was thirty years younger. She was a former waitress in one of his taverns. For H.B., it was love at first sight. I'll buy you a coat, honey, and here, here's a necklace, and what do you say we go on a cruise? Which he did. Walcher even put a private detective on his trail and made the trip in person to try to reason with Baumer, who was in Nassau. Nothing doing, Herman was having too good a time to come home, and to hell with the bank and his payments. Here, look."

Marc handed me one of those pictures that are taken with flash bulbs in a nightclub: it showed a sexagenarian with a flushed, laughing face, wearing a party hat, and holding onto a rather common but well-padded blonde.

"When and where was the photo taken?"

"Acapulco, January 4, 1975. The place is a famous nightclub, La Perla. Herman Baumer died four days later. Heart attack."

Marc shook his head.

"No, Franz. I sent someone down there. The death was unquestionably due to a heart attack. As proof, we have the local physician's report, as well as the remarks of an American doctor who was vacationing in the same hotel as Baumer. In addition, Walcher requested an autopsy."

"What in hell for?"

"He requested it later, when the Caltanis, or, more precisely, Olliphan, began sniffing around to buy the hotel. Walcher isn't a complete idiot. The death, and Olliphan's offer a few months later, aroused his suspicions. But the autopsy confirmed the diagnosis."

"Did the girl, the waitress, inherit anything?"

"Nothing."

"Is she still around?"

"I saw her three days ago. She's working as a clerk in a department store."

"Why did Walcher wait so long to let the Moser sisters know about their uncle's death?"

"Plain and simple. He didn't think of it. He wasn't really the executor of Baumer's will. In fact, he was mainly the guy who got his own bank to lend Baumer four hundred thousand dollars, and when Baumer began to act like a fool, he found himself in a pretty mess. Furthermore, he personally advanced Baumer another twenty-five thousand dollars. I inspected all of his accounts. On the whole, you can say he did his best to smooth things over."

"I say something unusual happened to Uncle Herman . . ." Anna's words came back to me.

"Marc, you found nothing suspicious? Nothing at all?"

"Nothing at all."

"Did Walcher know Olliphan?"

"He met him in June, 1975, when Olliphan paid him a visit to tell him that unnamed clients of his—but Walcher immediately understood that he meant the Caltanis—were interested in the hotel. A solution that seemed heaven-sent to Walcher. He was up against it, with his bank management on his back, pressing him to do something about the unpaid loan."

"When did the sale to Olliphan, or to the Caltanis, take place?"

"July, 1975."

"For how much?"

"Wait, it's not that simple. The Caltanis actually bought everything that belonged to Baumer—hotel, taverns, studio, timber plantation and farm in Austria. They took over everything. And at first glance, it wasn't necessarily a good deal."

"The taverns were doing well, you said so."

"They were doing well up to September, 1974. But in order to pay for his Caribbean and Mexican frolics, old Baumer had to dig deep. Not only did he stop his payments to the bank, he also emptied all his cash drawers and mortgaged the lot. The Caltanis got the hotel and taverns by taking over all the debts, paying off the banks and various creditors, and paying the interest and late penalties."

"Marc, HOW MUCH did they pay, altogether?"

"About $800 thousand."

And I had bought that lousy hotel for 25 million!

"Good Lord, Marc, do you realize, if Walcher had waited eight or ten months to sell, the hotel would have been worth ten times as much!"

"He couldn't wait, Franz. He had his own bank on his back, and as far as the taverns were concerned—they were all mortgaged—there was a crowd of people pressing around, howling like wolves. And we know now that gambling has been authorized, but Walcher didn't know that in July, '75."

"Unless the Caltanis told him."

"Why would they tell him? If they knew about it, it wasn't in their interest to shout it from the roof tops."

The cries of Sioux warriors from the shore: a tribe on the warpath had just captured a paleface, and they were tying him to a stake. I recognized the paleface—Yvon Samuel, a French journalist from *France-Soir*, who was also spending the weekend, and, though tied to the stake, was calmly puffing his cigar.

I said to Marc, "Come on, let's go back."

"You're the one who's rowing."

Touché.

"And I say that something unusual . . ." Damn it all, I wanted to get it off my chest.

"Marc, I'm going to ask the Englishman to take another turn around the track."

"And redo the whole investigation I've just completed?"

"Don't be angry."

"I have reason to be."

"Marc, goddammit! I've put 50 million bucks into that stinking hotel!"

Silence. He had bowed his head, his face stern. He raised it.

"Okay. You're probably right."

He even managed to smile and wag his finger.

"Your son really seems to be enjoying himself."

I followed his glance, and saw Marc-Andrea leading the Seventh Cavalry (before Little Big Horn). Despite Sarah's efforts, and despite my own much more sporadic efforts, he was a solitary little boy. Heidi's entrance into his life, into our life, had completely transformed him.

"Marc, I want nothing to do with the Caltanis."

"The transaction between you and them was straightforward. You don't have to invite them to dinner."

"But they're building their casino right next to mine."

"Loads of people are building a casino next to yours. And you're the one who wanted a casino."

I finally dropped those goddamned oars. As I walked down the pier, I intercepted the pony carrying the colonel and the lady colonel of the Seventh Cavalry.

"It's time for brunch, troops."

"We're not hungry."

They both had flushed cheeks from playing.

"There's a whole bathtub full of chocolate pudding."

They decided they were hungry.

That same evening, I managed to reach the Englishman in his ancestral castle (a real ancestral castle!). It was the second time in three months that I'd requested his services, which were outrageously overpriced, but unparalleled in their efficiency, to my knowledge. And which were equaled only by his placidness.

"Ernest Walcher, I've made a note," he said.

"I want to know everything about him. His travels in the last two years, whether he's honest, whether he's become honest or has always been that way, if he's likely to remain honest. His relations with James Montague Olliphan and the Caltani family."

"Everything?"

"Everything. Particularly if he's got money hidden away somewhere."

"You know that's practically impossible, with bank secrecy."

"Do your best. That's not all. I want to know how, when, and why Herman Baumer began making a fool of himself one fine day, for instance, by refusing to make payments to the bank that had lent him money to buy the hotel in Atlantic City. I want to know his exact financial picture in the year before his death and after his death. Apart from Walcher's statements."

"Anything else?"

"Yes. That girl whom Baumer was with in Acapulco four days before his death."

"Her life history. And whether she's got money saved up somewhere. And see whether someone didn't push her into Baumer's arms."

One of the great things about the Englishman was that he caught on fast.

"Right. And I want the ultimate on Olliphan and the Caltanis."

Silence.

"That's a lot of things, Mr. Cimballi. Some of them dangerous. And very time-consuming, at any rate."

Not to mention the insane bill he would send me! He laughed quietly, the deceptively simple laugh of an Englishman from Oxford (or Cambridge).

"And as for KGB's activities in the Western Hemisphere, you're not interested?"

I hung up. I preferred to be the one to make stupid jokes.

At the end of that October, it was four and a half months since I'd started my Crystal Palace operation. Everything had gone perfectly up to then. I had achieved all my goals—finding a site, partners, and a casino manager worthy of the name. At each stage, each day, each hour, I had taken the maximum precautions, even unnecessary ones, to ward off the only danger I truly feared—that big-time criminals would somehow get mixed up in my project.

And I had succeeded, without any doubt. By building a veritable fortress, with a Henry Chance and a Caliban posted on the lookout, backed up by Lavater, Rosen, Lupino, and Vandenbergh. And me, barricaded in the dungeon. Me with my family, for once, at last.

. . . Not having the tiniest trace of the beginning of an inkling that I myself had actually brought into that dungeon the bomb that would blow it to prices.

In truth, the Bomb herself didn't know she was a bomb.

Heidi didn't know a thing.

4. The Big Sting

15

Atlantic City, three days before Christmas. The cold was Siberian. A kind of melted snow was falling, and the wind coming from the ocean didn't help matters. I was frozen in place. So was Henry Chance, although he was wearing enough furs to contemplate hibernating in Lapland. The long, endless white line of the beach was behind us. We were facing the row of façades—hotels, art galleries, cafes, restaurants, theaters. On our left and our right, stretching almost to infinity, was the Boardwalk.

The motorized double cane-chair was still a hundred feet away from us. But it was approaching at full speed—that is, hardly faster than a man on foot. It wasn't an outlandish vehicle, or, at least, here it was common. There were hundreds of them, characteristic of Atlantic City. Except in this one were Caliban and his wife. We had been waiting for them, Chance and I, for nearly ten minutes.

"What do you think of it?"

My question, of course, was addressed to the casino manager. It wasn't his first visit to the hotel. He and Caliban had come regularly, especially in the first days of October, about a week after our meeting in Las Vegas. At the time, the construction work had barely begun. Chance had spent two full days studying the renovation plans drawn up by the architects. On the whole, he had approved them, suggesting only changes of detail. After all, the general principle of a casino-hotel was simple, bluntly simple—gambling had to be omnipresent. It was necessary that each room, each corridor, each restaurant, each bar and even the tennis courts, squash rooms, and swimming pools serve as so many subtle and tempting traps for the potential gambler. With one basic difference—this was the point Chance had harped on repeatedly—between a casino in Vegas and one here, on the shores of the Atlantic. In Vegas, the crushing heat in summer, the ever-present wind in winter, and the surrounding desert trapped customers in the enclosure designed for them, from which they could only escape as infrequently as possible. They were doomed to gamble. Prisoners of the "cordon sanitaire" (Chance used the French expression, even in English).

There was no "cordon sanitaire" in Atlantic City. That was the whole problem. He had said it before. Now he repeated it to me, with his almost obsessive mania for precision.

"And then there's the fact that the casinos are contiguous. It's certain that the gamblers will go from one casino to another, constantly, unlike what happens in Nevada."

In sum, it was a question of imagining the Crystal Palace on a basis peculiar to Atlantic City, aiming at two sorts of customers—those supplied by the hotel portion, and those who would be visiting temporarily, and would be likely to change establishments three or four times in a few hours.

In Baumer's day, the hotel had offered some four hundred rooms. When the renovation was completed, its capacity would increase to 780, plus twenty-four extremely luxurious suites.

"That will be enough, Mr. Cimballi." (He still hadn't resolved to call me by my first name.) "Assuming that all the rooms are occupied, that represents, let's say, fifteen hundred customers. Statistically, that means seven hundred people around the gambling tables."

The Lupino team had already carried out a study of that type. According to its conclusions, the "population of the gambling halls" would consist, at the busiest hours of the weekend, of 21 percent from the hotel portion, the rest being transients. Lupino's figures and those of Chance agreed. The result was clear. If seven hundred persons represented one-fifth of the room's population, this meant that we could count on three thousand to three thousand five hundred gamblers. This contingent would be replenished, mathematically, every five hours. Thus, let's say three thousand two hundred fifty multiplied by five—16,250 gamblers per day.

Who, if they had the good sense to leave us their money in the same proportions as in Vegas—and why shouldn't they!—that is, two hundred dollars per person, would thus give up three million two hundred fifty thousand dollars.

As the percentage, the famous, sancrosanct percentage, was 20 percent on this drop, this amounted to saying that this would create $650 thousand worth of profits per day.

. . . Less 20 percent entertainment costs: say 520 thousand. Again, per day.

(For years, I had loved these types of minute calculations. I enjoyed them all the more because, in general, facts subsequently showed them to be completely wrong—either I had been too optimistic, or not optimistic enough. The few times when I'd figured correctly, I'd been almost disappointed and a bit annoyed. But it was lots of fun. It was my substitute for crossword puzzles.)

Thus, $520 thousand per day. Now, the Crystal Palace, like all its counterparts in Atlantic City, would be open eighteen hours a day, 365 days a year.

Caliban and Patty's double cane-chair was no more than thirty feet away. My teeth were chattering, but the figures continued to revolve in my head (I knew them by heart, having done this calculation three or four hundred times already): one hundred eighty-nine million eight hundred thousand dollars, from which overhead costs would have to be deducted. . . .

. . . About $40 million per year.

. . . Out of which it would also be necessary, even before recording the first profit, to repay the four hundred million, plus interest, borrowed from the Philadelphia bank. So be it.

Caliban and Patty were twenty feet away. And those two oddballs, plastered against each other like newlyweds, were lustily roaring out "Tea for Two" under the melted snow.

I had finished my calculations. Marc Lavater was right. Jimmy Rosen was right. Philip Vandenbergh was right. Joe Lupino was right. And I was more right than all of them put together in throwing myself into this venture. In the worst case, even taking into account a delay in opening the hotel, and considering that some days would be very slow and that the rooms would be almost empty, even with all the imaginable reservations, the truth shone forth in all its splendor:

ONE: we would need at most forty-four or forty-five months—

the loan was over fifty months—to repay the Philadelphia bank in entirety. And as the opening was scheduled for the following April, that would bring us to November or December '81.

TWO: after November or December '81, I would collect each year, as owner of half the Crystal Palace, the equivalent of $20 to 25 million, after taxes.

Without doing a blessed thing. I wouldn't even need to set foot on the Boardwalk in Atlantic City and freeze my toes off.

At the end of my phantasmagorial, breathless coffee operation the previous year, I had pulled down a total of $90 million.

But how could that compare with what was waiting for me?

Here was a fortune—the real thing.

Here, too, were Caliban and Patty. They had finally stopped singing. They climbed out of their double chair on wheels. We entered the Crystal Palace.

It would not be an ordinary casino. It would, of course, include some features in its layout that would be unique, but its major, monumental originality would reside in the implementation of an idea I'd had, which, at the end of that December, was virtually complete.

Like other casinos, of course, this hotel would be, and was, centered on a gambling hall. More than centered—the very least of the facilities was planned around, above, and as a function of that room. It was a question of making its crossing obligatory, and its presence almost obsessive. Right at the entrance, right at the path leading into the lobby, the banks of elevators to the various floors were on the very edges of the tables. The main room extended over more than 30,000 square feet. It led into side rooms forming the first "private" areas, where gamblers could gather if they wished to be by themselves. It threw out antennae in all directions, to all the floors, even into the bedrooms, represented everywhere by slot machines whose highest jackpot was a million dollars. Represented, also, by ever-present video screens which customers could never take their eyes off, whether they were in one of the nine restaurants, eight bars or cafeterias, at the poolsides or in the sports areas, and even in the "spa," a real thermal facility filled with jacuzzis, or Roman baths, which were taken in groups in tubs of bubbling water. Owing to these screens, a customer could pick up the image at will of any

150

table of his choice and not only follow the game in progress, but take part in it himself, through a complex network of computer-controlled electronic communications.

One could likewise—even in the intimacy of one's private bathroom!—bet on this or that roulette number, on various lotteries, including that same keno I'd seen in Macao.

The main room would contain more than one hundred tables, including, for instance, sixty for blackjack, twenty for roulette, and twenty dice layouts. There would be more than four thousand slot machines. Seven hundred scantily clad, pretty girls would have no other mission but to concern themselves with the patrons of those machines, being ready at any moment to hand out perfumed towels for cleaning one's hands (repeated handling of those clicking and blinking devices blackened the palms), and, in particular, being ever on the alert to supply the required change. They would carry a shoulder bag loaded with rolls of change.

Besides the nine restaurants, eight bars, swimming pools, the spa, the squash courts, the gymnasium, the massage rooms, and the closed-circuit TV broadcasting only good news, there would also be three auditoriums, a shopping mall, a bank, a telex room, etc.

Henry Chance had been particularly influential in the matter of security. He hadn't been heavy-handed in his demands. Still he had insisted on an even stricter force than what existed in the great Vegas establishments because he firmly believed the security problems would be infinitely greater here in Atlantic City. His theory, again, of the "cordon sanitaire." As well as the fact that the police in Atlantic City, like those of New Jersey in general, were unfortunately not as well educated as those in Nevada, to whom stealing chips from a casino in one way or another was indescribably more serious than murdering fifty people with a chain saw. Henry Chance didn't believe that such sound views prevailed on the Atlantic coast. In his opinion, the local police had not understood and might not understand the full gravity of the problem. This worried him. As did his probably warranted conviction that the New York mobs were even better organized, more numerous, more vicious, and politically better protected than those in Nevada. The ideal thing, in his view—and he wasn't even kidding!—would be to erect a genuine Berlin Wall in the middle of Atlantic City, between the casinos and the rest of the city, indeed, the rest of the United States.

Although he didn't get the wall, the architects followed his other requests to the letter. A customer entering the Crystal Palace, going to the reception desk, then taking an elevator to the second floor, would assume when he arrived that he was just above the gambling room. Wrong. In fact, between the official second floor and the casino hall there would be another level, exactly equal in area to the hall, laid out in the same way, without windows, fully air-conditioned, its hidden doors reserved for "authorized personnel," with plain-clothes guards to protect the entrances. Inside what might be called the Passageway was the most remarkable array of surveillance equipment I would ever see. Enough to make the people at NASA jealous. A gambling hall is always decorated with mirrors, walls and ceiling. That's not by accident. The cameras and observers have to be placed where they won't be conspicuous. Each table would be covered by two or even three video cameras, constantly in operation, recording everything on a video recorder. Thus, at the slightest suspicion of any irregularity—and Henry Chance's suspicions were easily aroused—one could not only watch the dubious game live, but also, on a different screen, play it back in slow motion as often as appeared necessary.

Cameras everywhere, even outside the hall, in all of the hotel's public areas. Only the rooms were spared. And even then, Chance wouldn't have needed much encouragement to extend the surveillance into the very toilets! Cameras again, sweeping the outside entrances to the buildings, keeping track of the huge underground parking lot, all the access routes, including the roofs. Together with microphones that could be activated at any time from the control center, so that a monitor (who would himself be watched by a head monitor, who would be watched by a special squad controlled by Chance's assistants and by Caliban, the whole company under the infernally suspicious eyes of Chance) could, at any time, take a look at any part of the complex by turning on any of the screens at his disposal, and, if necessary, recording the scene, picture, and sound. It was madness.

In order to gamble in a casino, you need chips. The Crystal Palace would have its own tokens, with its own emblem, manufactured by experts. I would not buy my chips in Nevada, like everyone else, but in Beaune, France, from Bourgogne et Grasset. They would be shipped in small quantities by hand-picked teams of convoys. These chips had values ranging from one to a thousand dollars, the highest stake being two thousand dollars. These chips would be obtained either from the main cashier window (which was, of course, an awesome fortress, because it always had on hand $2 or $3 million in cash, plus $12 million in chips) or directly at the tables. In that case, the table manager making the exchange would immediately slip the money received into a special slot connected by a pneumatic tube to the main cashier window, without any human intervention.

A battery of computers would monitor the movements of chips at all times. Each table's operation would be counted as they went along, hour by hour. Furthermore, the chips would be counted, four times a day and not necessarily at a set time. Any irregularity would be spotted immediately. Of course, nothing could prevent a customer from buying up a hundred thousand dollars' worth of chips, putting them in a bag, carrying the bag out with him, and burying it in his garden. It was unlikely but possible. It was necessary that such a disappearance be noted immediately. And it was especially necessary, as one can imagine, that the appearance of strange chips, not hitherto counted, should be promptly detected. The bringing in of false chips was theoretically possible, even though each Crystal Palace chip (as was true in all casinos) had secret electronic devices enabling a croupier to identify it by touch alone.

This general monitoring would be accompanied, table by table, by the surveillance of trained monitors. That was one of Caliban's assignments. As first assistant manager, more specially in charge of the halls, he excelled in this type of activity. By strolling for a few seconds around a given table, he could take in at one glance the number of players, the number of chips in use, the amount of the drop (the total of the sums staked by the players). And he could immediately deduce whether, at that particular table, the casino was winning or losing and by how much.

But Caliban was a dwarf. Because of his height, he couldn't see the tabletop. Formerly, in Vegas, he had used metallic stilts, and it was quite a sight to see him get around that way. But he had something much better up his sleeve. He had ordered from Macao, in quadruplicate, in case of breakdown, absolutely fantastic equipment. Briefly, they could have been the chairs of tennis referees, but superelevated. Except at Wimbledon or Roland-Garros, no seated referee has yet been seen going around the court on wheels, making telephone calls, and communicating by radio with his family and friends. Caliban could. He could even, by simple operation of levers and buttons on the arm of his chair, turn on a given screen at the control center, transmitting the picture of a given table, and thus attracting the attention of the security force without having to utter a single word. He would be in constant contact with Henry Chance.

The rubberized wheels of his chair rolled without any noise, reversed themselves, went backward as well as forward. The electric motor was perfectly silent. And it was one hell of a surprise to hear nothing at all and then suddenly sense something or someone behind you, turn around, and discover with a shock a seven-foot-tall dwarf looking at you with his huge, dark, almond-shaped eyes.

"I really got you, didn't I!"

"For sure. And are you going to run around the room like that?"

"Just so, my colleague. And it will be good for publicity," he added, not incorrectly. He even had had an idea for improving his machine. He would add an extra seat, lower than his, where Patty could perch.

"And guess what Patty will do, Franz, while I'm cruising the tables? She'll knit. Patty loves to knit!"

Henry Chance was scowling a little. He didn't care for this kind of eccentricity in his casino. There coexisted strangely within him the most devious, most suspicious mind I would ever know along with a kind of puritanism. He was something of a soldier-monk. It was he who had personally seen to the selection of the casino's thousands of employees. He had known most of them for years, indeed, decades. But he saw them all as potential cheaters. To his way of thinking, if he had never caught them red-handed, it wasn't because they were honest, it was simply that the precautions he or other casino managers had taken had prevented them from stealing. He had already checked Caliban's wheelchairs to make sure they didn't contain any system that might, for example, distort the roulette operations. I was amazed.

154

"Henry, Caliban represents my Chinese partners. You think he's capable of cheating his employers?"

"I'm responsible to the Chinese and to you. You never know."

"And me, Henry, do you trust me, at least?"

His cold, severe gaze, "Of course not."

And I was the one who'd hired him!

But you had to understand him. It was on his shoulders alone that this huge organization would rest. Nor did I forget that the license issued by the casino control board was in his name, and only his. The law was implacable. If some poor jerk some evening managed to slip some loaded dice onto a craps table—in fact, the dice, like the chips, were electronically balanced, any croupier or table manager, not to mention the monitors, would spot the cheating immediately, at first glance, but there were always idiots—one idiot, then, would be enough, if the violation were noted by an anonymous representative of the commission, for the license to be suspended at once and the casino shut down.

"Franz, it's already happened in Vegas. The guy who brought in the loaded dice wasn't an idiot. Of course, he got six months in jail. But when he got out, he received a hundred thousand dollars. And that's not a lot, because the money was paid to him by another casino, which got rid of a competitor for several weeks that way. I don't want that to happen in my place."

On that December 21, the construction work, the shell of the entire lower part of the Crystal Palace, was practically finished. They were beginning to climb the floors of the hotel portion, redoing the façades as necessary to preserve their "style." The internal renovation had begun in some places. For the time being, the main hall was still only a vast empty lot of an acre or two, its cement floor heavily dug up for various cables and pipes. With a bit of imagination, you could see the places where the tables would be placed, owing to the mouths of the conduits that would carry the players' money, the drop, to the main treasury. This was also taking shape. For greater safety, it was being built by a special team, working out of sight behind movable partitions watched by guards.

This extraordinary wealth of precautions that Chance wanted positively delighted me. But there was something even better when it came to whetting my enthusiasm and strengthening my impression that we were building another Fort Knox.

"Shall we go down?"

I'd had various ideas about the hotel. Some of them were completely foolish, so much so that Chance and others had fought them tooth and nail. But Henry himself had accepted some of them. For instance, the idea of placing under two plate-glass windows, right in the center of the main hall and in the entrance lobby, two stacks of one million dollars, in one-dollar bills and gold coins. Over each showcase there would be a sign: YOU CAN WIN A MILLION HERE.

On the other hand, Chance had categorically rejected my proposal to have real baby elephants in the room, ridden by pretty young ladies without much on.

"How about in the garden?"

Not there either. We'd have all the animal lovers on this continent on our backs. And I wasn't about to open a zoo.

Up to then, Chance had greeted all my ideas with a reserve that, in spite of his unshakeable politeness, strongly resembled contempt. On the other hand, when I presented him with what I considered the most brilliant of my ideas, he stared at me and nodded his head.

"Interesting."

He even added, quietly, "Very interesting. I like it."

In other words, he was overflowing with enthusiasm. He wasn't, strictly speaking, an extrovert. In the grip of terminal hilarity, he'd be content to raise an eyebrow.

Good. We'd been pacing up and down the site for two hours. It was time to see what they had done with my brilliant idea. We went down.

A shoebox. Two hundred and fifty feet long by 150 feet wide. All of its walls made of reinforced concrete at least five feet thick. This shoebox was buried forty feet below the hotel's foundations and its fourteen floors. Practically on the vertical of the gambling hall. It was literally suspended in the ground. It was reached mainly by a reinforced corridor—that was the usual term—which was on a slope and divided by three reinforced doors in succession. Each of these stationary threshold doors was round and its special steel was two feet thick. According to the specialist I'd consulted, my friend Hirsch—and I believed him—this baby could easily withstand an explosion with a force of ten megatons, or one million times that of Hiroshima.

156

In short, it was a nuclear-bomb shelter.

Designed according to current standards, by the book. We had even planned, once it was finished, to have it appraised by Pentagon experts, who would be summoned to the inspection with great ceremony, and would issue a certificate that would be framed and displayed, so that each casino customer could see it.

But not all customers would have access to it. They would be allowed in only by invitation. Furthermore, between the first reinforced door (coming from the outside) and the second one was what was actually a decontamination room, but was officially termed a VIP IDENTIFICATION ROOM. There, young ladies would greet the hand-picked guests. They would check their health and physical condition by every desired method. And they would wear antiradiation suits of a somewhat special design, i.e., transparent.

Between the second and third door—the regulation airlock— would be a restaurant, bar and bedrooms. After passing through the third door, one would be in the actual shelter, in fact, the private gambling room, the hotel's holy of holies. Here there was no limit, whether in gambling or anything else. The rule was simple.

I also planned to reserve a small corner of the place for my private use. In the rear right corner I would have six rooms, an office, living room, and bedrooms. From there I could contact the control center and the outside at any time, reach Paris by phone or the New York Stock Exchange by Telex. And I would have an impregnable view of the private room as well as a picture of any part of the casino.

All of the equipment necessary for the survival of two hundred fifty persons for six months had been provided—ventilation systems equipped with antiexplosion valves resistant to shock waves and compression; devices for filtering out any radioactive dust; stocks of survival rations; electrical generators; emergency exits and evacuation routes—two of them leading to the parking lot (which, among other advantages, would enable shy VIPs to enter the private room directly without going through the hotel lobby above). All of this equipment was operated by the hotel's main installations in normal times, but at any moment, in case of alert, all connections with the outside could be severed. The shelter would then become fully self-sustaining.

As that December drew to a close, the shelter was finished, at least in its overall structure. Except for a few elements. For instance, the reinforced doors were missing, as were the equally reinforced panels of the evacuation routes. These were concrete passageways, four feet in diameter, rising to the surface at a 2-percent slope, "outside the destruction zone," in the official terminology. This meant, of course, that these passageways had to be fairly long. One of them led to the beach, beyond the Boardwalk, while three others led to the very back of the garden, about one hundred yards from the hotel, between the concrete walls of a ditch.

I entered the future private room with Caliban and Patty. As for Chance, he remained on the threshold of the third reinforced room, which as yet was only a plain round hole about two-and-a-half yards in diameter in the huge concrete wall. The vast underground room was terribly impressive in its size and in the tomblike atmosphere that prevailed. The air-conditioning, of course, was not yet working, and despite the cold outside—it was December, after all—to remain in that space, so remarkably confined, would become uncomfortable rather quickly. In back, on the right, they had not yet set up the partitions to what would be my private suite. Nothing marked the site, except perhaps a larger pile of electric cables than elsewhere.

"Your office will be here?"

The question came from Caliban, his voice echoing rather fantastically. I nodded. He made as if to sit in an imaginary chair, to look out, through an imaginary one-way mirror, on a gambling room that was still only a blueprint. He manipulated fictitious buttons on fictitious control screens.

"Like a spider at the center of its web, Franz."

"Thanks just the same."

As I've said, he had wonderful eyes, like black velvet, rimmed with long lashes and gleaming with his Asian blood. At times, he could display a wild imagination, which was both funny and vaguely disturbing, so obvious was it that he never really let go of himself, even in his silliest moments. Nothing in common with Li and Liu's natural buoyancy. But at other times, a kind of veil came over his eyes and the feeling of danger suddenly became very real. That wasn't the case at this moment. His eyes smiled at me with warm friendliness.

"The world's only antinuclear casino. The only one where you can go on throwing dice without being disturbed by those clowns throwing thermonuclear missiles in each other's faces. New York, Paris, Moscow will be flattened, there won't be the tiniest sign of life on the surface of the earth—and the casino's croupier will go on announcing that the bets are laid and time is up."

Silence. The very beautiful and almost mute Patty went to him, bent over, and kissed him on the lips. She took him by the neck with a gesture that in anyone else would be grotesque. Caliban replied with a squeeze of her hand. But it was me he continued to smile at.

"It's really a good idea, my colleague," he resumed, again with a Mediterranean accent. "A whopping good idea. With a smart publicity campaign, they'll fight to get in here. Back in Macao, they'll be happy."

He imitated an SS-20 or any other intercontinental ballistic missile whistling and exploding.

Laughing, he yelled in the tomblike silence, with echoes bouncing back, "THE BETS ARE LAID. TIME IS UP!"

16

We left the following day for Colorado. We being Sarah, Marc-Andrea, Heidi, and I, plus the Amazon who served as nanny. She was a good-natured giant, pumped up with hormones and crammed throughout her youth with anabolic substances in her native East Germany. She was probably capable of carrying all four of us on her back, and likewise capable of bursting into tears at the slightest cross word.

In Aspen, we met up with Gunther Kraus, alias Goni, Anna Moser's fiancé. I thanked him as sarcastically as possible for the present he'd sent me. The handsome Goni was abashed.

"I had nothing whatever to do with it, Franz. All I said was that you were really neat, especially with kids. Anna has weird ideas sometimes, you know."

And it was true that he wanted to buy that hotel in Sankt Johann so he could marry his Anna. Gunther was the kind of ski instructor women dream about: handsome, tanned, good-humored, and helpful. Obviously, there was every indication that in their future household, Anna would wear the pants. As for the theory of a plot against me, with Heidi as the detonator and with Gunther's cooperation, it didn't hold water. I had known him for four years, and we had skied a great deal together, skiing being the only sport I can practice without immediately setting off general hilarity. I was even pretty good at it. True, I'd spent part of my youth on the slopes of Garmisch, Kitzbühel, and the rest.

As planned, the other three Moser sisters arrived in Aspen on the morning of the twenty-fourth. We spent the holidays together, very pleasantly, forsooth. But apart from the fact that Colorado isn't the best place to carry out operations on the international financial markets and keep tabs on the construction of a casino on the Atlantic coast, another reason brought us back to Long Island. Heidi's school vacation was over, and she had to go back to class, Sarah proclaimed.

We had just returned home when, as usual, the telephone began ringing with a frenzy.

First, the Englishman. He was calling mainly to wish me a happy New Year and to tell me that he had nothing to tell me.

"Nothing, at any rate, that's really new in relation to the investigation Lavater carried out. But it took us some time to get set up. That's done. If there are any results, they won't be long in coming. One of my teams is in Mexico, the other in Nassau. Give me a little more time."

Next, Hassan Fezzali. Happy new year. He was fine, thanks. His heart was beating almost normally again. He was in Rome, after, he said discreetly, "a satisfactory stay in Cairo and Riyadh, where the prince and I settled a few outstanding problems." He didn't elaborate further, but I understood—accounts had been wiped clean, and someone, somewhere in Saudi Arabia or Egypt, had suffered Allah's justice for having deprived His

Highness Prince Aziz of his best adviser for eighteen long months. Hassan asked me if I had received the transfer reimbursing me for all the expenses I'd had in connection with the ice cream affair.

"I received it and framed it."

"On His Highness' behalf, and on my own behalf, thanks again, young Franz."

"Let's not talk about it for a few years."

Yes, he would come to the United States sooner or later. If only to admire my new toy, the casino. For naturally, he was up on all the details of my operation. Informed, but not excited, perhaps even a bit annoyed.

"You didn't tell my anything about it when we saw each other in Jersey."

"I told you about it. We discussed it."

"But you didn't offer me a share in it."

No, because I had finally turned to the Chinese.

"Would you have accepted?"

He laughed. It sounded as if he was himself again, friendly but diabolically secretive. "Allah knows," he said. I was about to hang up, to answer the other two lines which were ringing nonstop.

"Franz? Be careful."

"Of what?"

"Nothing special."

"Martin Yahl, my old enemy, is on the warpath again?"

"Not as far as I know."

A few seconds of silence. I wouldn't get anything more out of him. Hassan wasn't a man to go beyond what he had decided to say. I hung up for real, a bit perplexed.

The next call came from the Austrian consulate general in New York. And either because of the warning I'd just received from Hassan, or because for several weeks I'd had the vague but persistent impression that there was indeed "something unclear" in this whole story of Baumer-Heidi-casino-hotel-Anna Moser, I was immediately on my guard. The voice on the phone had Germanic inflections, but it was extremely courteous.

"Mr. Cimballi, is there a young Austrian national named Heidi Moser living with you at the moment?"

I hesitated instinctively, but reason won out.

"Yes, she lives here."

Could a representative of the consulate general stop by tomorrow for an interview? With me, in Heidi's presence?

At the very moment I was on the phone, I could see Heidi and Marc-Andrea playing. The gigantic electric-car loop—a gift from that idiot Lupino—had been laid out over the entire floor of the living room. You'd think you were at Castellet or Watkins Glen. Heidi was directly in the field of vision outlined for me by the door frame. Her face red, shouting in excitement, she was operating several control switches at once, pretty as a picture. She had been living with us now for three months. There wasn't a single second in which she hadn't been a source of laughter, joy, and happiness. I felt a kind of panic.

I answered, "Not tomorrow, please. Nor the day after tomorrow. I have to go away on business. Two days won't matter, will they?"

The voice remained calm and courteous.

"Certainly, Mr. Cimballi. I guess two days won't make a difference after all. Let's say Thursday, then. Is ten o'clock all right?"

"In the evening. She goes to school. Six o'clock."

The unknown person calling me on the third line had finally given up. I called Rosen.

"Jimmy, I want to know what those consulate people want from me."

He called me back forty minutes later while I was involved in another phone call, this time with Henry Chance, who had a dispute with a contractor and wanted me to intervene. I cut short his recriminations, mild though they were, and picked up Rosen.

"Franz, the consulate was served with a request from the Austrian welfare department."

Which meant what?

Which meant that, somewhere in Austria, a social worker or the equivalent felt than an eight-year-old Austrian should go to school in Austria. And that was all? It seemed like such a minor matter that I felt relieved. But Rosen took it upon himself to make things clear.

"Don't take this lightly, Franz."

"Heidi's going to school, Sarah saw to that. All we'll have to do is explain what's going on to that goddamned social worker. If necessary, by offering her a round trip from Vienna to New York."

Rage took hold of me suddenly. I wasn't going to let myself be trumped by a social worker, for God's sake! And it was up to him, Rosen, to do what was necessary. Let him handle it.

"Jimmy, one thing's for sure. As long as Anna agrees, and Heidi wants to, she'll stay with us. Period."

I didn't even give him a chance to reply. And I was still trembling with anger when, for the thirtieth or fortieth time in a row, the telephone rang.

"Mr. Cimballi? James Olliphan. When can I see you?"

It was strange. Not a week, certainly, had gone by since our meeting of the previous September 18 without my thinking of that man. With the hunch that, sooner or later, I would run into him.

"I have a personal matter I'd like to discuss with you," he said. "It so happens that I'll be on Long Island today, not far from you. It won't take long. May I stop by?"

He arrived around four o'clock. Sarah, the Amazon, and the children had gone out, since Heidi didn't have to be back in school until the following day. I was alone with the Cuban couple who took care of the household.

"What a lovely house," Montague said after arriving. "I've often thought of buying something around here."

I waited. We were in my office. On the walls I'd hung a few drawings of the Crystal Palace, the way it would be when it opened the following April. Olliphan's eyes rested on them. He shook his head.

"You've handled this business like a real pro. I'm sure your efforts will be rewarded with success. And that you won't have any problems with your neighbors."

His green eyes dropped down to me again, with that sly expression they often held, as though in our face-to-face, in our relations since the beginning, in this whole casino business, there was something very funny that he alone knew about. Toward this man I felt exceptional mistrust, and, more peculiarly, sympathy. Pity, also, to some extent. I remembered the horrible Buddha who was his wife, with her dull, glassy, toadlike stare.

163

"I'm speaking of the Caltanis, of course."

"I understood."

"They'll leave you in peace, Mr, Cimballi. They're entirely willing to establish good neighborly relations. They would have no objection to your Palace being a triumph and becoming the most popular casino in Atlantic City. Since their own place is practically next door, they figure they would collect enough of the people you pulled in to be prosperous themselves."

That made sense. But certainly it wasn't to tell me this kind of news that Olliphan had come to see me. I was still waiting.

"Of course," Olliphan continued, "I'm not here as an ambassador of the Caltanis. In fact . . . "

The sound of a car at the back of the house. Sarah was returning with the children.

"In fact, I'm here on my own behalf. Contrary to what you might think, the Caltanis are not the only clients whose interests I represent."

Wild screams. Marc-Andrea and Heidi burst into the living room, throwing themselves into my office, into my arms. I kissed them, threw them out, and closed the door behind them.

"Your children are absolutely charming."

"Thank you."

I was beginning to get impatient. And he sensed it, for he shook his head, with his strange half-smile.

"I told you I had some personal business to offer you. It consists of one word. Bophuthatswana."

It sounded as if he had just sneezed. If he was trying to impress me, he'd succeeded.

He repeated, "Bophuthatswana. It's a bantustan."

And he began explaining. A bantustan was an autonomous territory within South Africa. There were a dozen of them. Only blacks lived there. Their present autonomy was supposed to lead to independence. A rather theoretical sort of independence; these territories were so thoroughly enclaves within white South Africa—and not by accident—that their independence made as much sense as that of Clermont-Ferrand in France.

"Last October, Mr. Cimballi, the first of the bantustans to become independent was Transkei. Bophuthatswana will follow suit this year."

He reeled off this history lesson with imperturbable seriousness. At least in his face, for his eyes continued to express irony, as if to say, "How long are you going to put up with me?" Where the devil was he leading me?

"I was coming to the subject of this deal I'm proposing you go in on with me. With me and one of my South African friends, Henrik Korber. Perhaps you've heard of him?"

I couldn't even figure out if he was kidding me or not. I shook my head.

"He's completely unknown to me. At least as much as your Bophu-what's-its-name. And that's saying a lot."

After all, might as well get a laugh out of it.

"Mr. Cimballi, there are few countries in the world that are as boring as South Africa, according to my friend Korber. During the Portuguese colonial period, if you were a white South African, you went to Mozambique for entertainment. Then came decolonization, and they had to fall back on what they call BLS down there: Botswana, Lesotho, Swaziland."

A smile. He was enjoying himself.

"But these are countries that border South Africa. Unlike the bantustans, which are inside the Republic, close to the large urban centers where the white buying power is concentrated. And Rik Korber had an idea, Mr. Cimballi. Why not use the bantustans' special legal provisions to set up, let's say, another Las Vegas?"

He had finally arrived at his goal, after all. I burst out laughing.

"You came to suggest that I build a casino among the Bantus?"

He was more imperturbable than ever—that was it, exactly. Except that we weren't talking about one casino, but several, plus hotels, restaurants, in fact, a regular leisure and recreation village, which would naturally have the abundant patronage of the white South Africans, who were dying of boredom in their confoundedly Calvinist country, where ogling a seductive black woman too closely could lead you straight to prison. Whereas, in the bantustans . . .

"Rik Korber got a flat refusal from the new Transkei government. However, he's convinced that his project will be accepted by Lucas Mangrove."

"Who's he?"

"The future president of Bophuthatswana, which will become independent next December. And Bophuthatswana is barely an hour or two by car from Pretoria and Johannesburg."

Silence. I gazed at Olliphan. Perhaps he was completely deranged, and that was annoying, inasmuch as he was the one who had sold me the Crystal Palace. Or else he was trying to manipulate me, to take me somewhere, but I was damned if I could see where. Or, then again, he really believed in this Bantu business. I was perplexed, to say the least.

"And your friend Korber needs me?"

"I spoke to him about you, and he'd be very happy to meet you. You're not just anyone, Mr. Cimballi, in spite of your youth—you're twenty-seven, I believe. You're the one who had the idea of that second Disney World, in Florida, which you called Safari. You're the one who thought up Tennis-in-the-Sky, that is, using the roofs of garages and apartment buildings in downtown areas to install tennis courts. Two enterprises that are now thriving. And now, here you are in a casino venture which shows every sign of being a tremendous success. To get it off the ground, you came up with $450 million in record time. You're not just anyone to Rik. You could be the partner he's looking for—you're beginning to have some experience in the gambling field, you have accomplishments in the area of leisure parks. Financially, while you have relatively large means at your disposal, you still don't have the overwhelming power of an oil company or a Howard Hughes. And finally—"and Olliphan's smile widened maliciously—"finally, despite your Italian-sounding name, you don't have any kind of tie with, let's say, any of the Families. Apart from the fact that you bought an old hotel from one of them, of course. But I'm not in a position to reproach you for that."

This guy had an unbelievable gall! He rose.

"I hope I haven't wasted your time, Mr. Cimballi. Of course, I don't expect an answer from you right away. I'm sure you'll want to get information. Take your time. You know where to get hold of me."

He left. And I can still see him sliding, with utmost distinction, behind the wheel of his midnight-blue Ferrari 308, putting on his driving gloves. Keeping his green eyes on me to the last second, slyly, as if to say, "You don't understand anything, eh, Cimballi?"

And everything went off as if events had positively waited for my return from Colorado to register a sudden acceleration. After the first call from the Englishman, then Fezzali, then Olliphan and his subsequent visit, the Englishman popped up again, less than thirty hours after his first call.

"I think," he said, with his usual calm and his Oxford accent, "I think we're now ready to make a report on that investigation you asked me to make."

He was the kind of man who'd warn you about an imminent nuclear apocalypse by saying simply, "I'm afraid we're going to have a few difficulties in the next forty-five minutes."

So I couldn't restrain myself from asking, "You've got something new?"

"Very new," he said.

17

I suggested he meet us at the Pierre, but he refused, very politely.

"Then where?"

"If you please, Mr. Cimballi, be kind enough to do exactly what I'm going to ask you to do."

I obeyed, wondering what the hell kind of game he was playing. These former intelligence agents, which is probably what my Englishman was, were all a bit mad. He was no exception.

But I followed his orders. I drove all the way across Long Island, crossed the East River at the Throgs Neck Bridge, then across the Bronx and the Harlem River, drove down the Henry Hudson Parkway to 79th Street and reached Central Park by going all the way down Broadway . . .

. . . as far as Lincoln Center, where I had to park my car.

"Anywhere, Mr. Cimballi, and walk."

"Walk?"

"That's right, walk, Mr. Cimballi, in any direction."

Well, I was now walking, from Damrosch Park to the plaza across from the Metropolitan Opera House, in an icy rain, cursing England and secret agents afflicted with occupational disease. The Englishman finally appeared, in a Bogart-type trenchcoat and a little hat trimmed with a grouse feather, seeming very pleased with himself.

"Sorry to force you into this wild-goose chase, but we wanted to make sure you wouldn't be followed."

"FOLLOWED?"

"But you're not. Not today, anyway."

"Meaning that I have been followed, recently?"

"Very likely. At least once. Or if not really followed, watched."

As if to get out of the rain, we went into the library wedged between the Met and a theater.

"Who was following me and when?"

"On your return from Aspen, Monday last. Two men were waiting for you at the airport when you arrived with Miss Kyle, your son, the young Austrian girl who's living with you, and that giant nanny." He raised a hand to ward off my question. "I had come myself to see you land on the strength of a mere hypothesis I'd formed. And I didn't let you know earlier because I didn't know who those men were. It might have been people you'd hired for protection."

"That's not the case."

"I know that now."

From one of his raincoat pockets he drew a photograph of two men getting into a car.

"We identified one of them, and that's enough: Frank Lippi. Official occupation: assistant bookkeeper. But he works for the Caltani brothers, of course. He's already spent three or four years in prison."

For several seconds I was gripped by an indescribable fear.

"Sorry," said the Englishman.

But he still had quite a few things to tell me and show me, and he'd appreciate a nice cup of tea. We went to the Algonquin Hotel, which was one of his haunts. A car came to pick us up, driven by a man whom the Englishman didn't bother to introduce to me. Furthermore, it was one of the few times I had been in the presence of one of the members of his team, ordinarily so discreet you might think them imaginary.

In his room, he spread out photos on a table, an action he would repeat several times in the two hours that followed.

"Do you know any of these men?"

I examined the photographs one by one. They showed at least thirty different people whose sole point in common was that they were all over forty, with two exceptions, and that none of them looked like he might be president of the New York Stock Exchange. But no face reminded me of anything.

"Their age isn't all they have in common. They were all, to varying degrees, long-standing friends of Herman Baumer. You asked me to check up on him, particularly on the period preceding his death. The best thing was to compile a list of those who were close to him."

"Besides Walcher."

"Besides him. No, he doesn't know about our investigation, if that's what you were going to ask me. We did all we could so that he wouldn't know. Though one can never be sure of these things."

I was still studying the photos.

"Why these thirty or so guys in particular, when Baumer, between his pubs and his hotel, must have known hundreds, even thousands of people?"

"Because those people have an interesting trait. These men—and women, there are women among them—met with Baumer in the two weeks prior to September 21, 1974, either in the New York pubs or in the Atlantic City hotel. Nearly half of them. . . ."

"Why that date, September 21, 1974?"

"Because that's the day Baumer met Maggie Keller, his former waitress, the day he fell so in love with her that in a very short time he turned his own life upside down, went off to the tropics with her, and stayed there until his death in January '75. We had to start somewhere in our investigation, and we chose that date. On the hypothesis that Maggie Keller's turning up on that day wasn't merely an accident."

The Englishman spread out further and sorted the photos of Herman's old buddies:

"Let's come back to these ladies and gentlemen. Nearly half of them were lodging, free of charge or nearly so, in Baumer's hotel in Atlantic City. Five had been living there permanently from the beginning of September to the twenty-first of that month. At that time, as the summer wasn't completely over,

Baumer was spending a lot more time on the beach than in his pubs, which were doing very well without him, anyway. Today, of these five men, two are dead and two others have left the New York area. We had a hell of a hard time finding them. They disappeared almost without leaving a trace. But in the end, we tracked them down. One is in Florida, where he found a job as caretaker of a property belonging to one Bert Sussman."

"Never heard of him."

The Englishman smiled.

"He has interests, chiefly in an import-export business mainly concerned with olive oil, shared half-and-half with the Caltanis. As for Baumer's second former lodger, fortune smiled even more broadly on him: he's spending carefree days in San Juan as a night watchman at a luxury marina."

"Which belongs to the Caltanis."

"No. Not to our knowledge. But Caltani Senior, now dead, used to have large interests in Havana. When Castro came to power, he took those interests to Puerto Rico, where many of his old friends had also settled. No, the owner of the marina is the godfather of Joe Caltani, the elder."

"And the two that died?"

"Overdose for one of them, accidental death while drunk for the other. Mr. Cimballi, I'm not going into the details. I'm simply explaining to you how we came to be interested in what happened at the Atlantic City hotel during those days leading up to September 21, 1974. We were able to identify certain witnesses who were on the scene at the time, and we noted that two had left New York, both in connection with the Caltanis, that two others are now dead, under circumstances that may indicate that they were murdered, and that the fifth is a hard-core alcoholic who's forgotten everything, including his name. All rather interesting discoveries, but not essential. The essential thing is that if someone took the trouble to get rid of these witnesses by various means, it's because they probably saw or heard something that they shouldn't have heard and seen. Am I making myself clear?"

"Yes."

"So then we asked ourselves what it might be about. In desperation, we took pictures of Olliphan and went around Atlantic City, showing them to everybody. The man wasn't recognized, but his car was. In September, '74, he owned a white Ferrari.

That doesn't go unnoticed. Following the thread, by juxtaposing photos of Olliphan and Walcher, we eventually found someone who remembered having seen them together. Probably around September 5 or 6, 1974."

"Walcher says he met Olliphan for the first time in June '75, after Baumer's death, when Olliphan came on behalf of the Caltanis to make an offer for the hotel."

"He probably lied. And lied on two counts. First, because he knew Olliphan much earlier than that. Next, because the Caltanis' offer to buy dates not from June '75, but more likely from September '74."

"Do you have evidence of that?"

"Almost none," the Englishman said, laughing. "But if I had to make a bet—no, I have no evidence, Mr. Cimballi. I was simply told of a conversation between Baumer and Walcher, around September 6. Walcher supposedly said, 'Karl, one million is a fabulous offer,' and he appeared to be furious. Baumer replied, laughing as usual, and not taking money matters seriously, *"Ach so, you can't take it mit you."*

The Englishman gathered up the photos like a deck of cards, put them back in their envelope, and took out another envelope.

"No evidence, Mr. Cimballi. Guesses, hearsay, rumors. It's enough that Olliphan and Walcher deny ever having met before June '75, and we can't ram their lie down their throat. However . . ."

He spread out other photos, and I vaguely recognized the young woman.

"However, we've followed our initial hypothesis to its conclusion. Two dates seemed important to us. On September 5, Olliphan came to make an offer of one million dollars to Baumer for his hotel. And Baumer refused, despite Walcher's entreaties. Sixteen days later, on the 21st, Baumer was visited by one of his former waitresses and immediately began making a fool of himself. From there it was but a step to our taking an interest in Maggie Keller."

She was twenty-six years old in 1974. Born in New York. For two years, from 1968 to 1970, she worked in Baumer's bar on West Forty-fourth Street, on the fringes of Times Square.

"There's no exact evidence that there were any relations between her and Baumer, other than those of an employer and employee. But Baumer was a worthy chap, always ready to lend a hand."

So that when Maggie married in 1970 and became Maggie Keller, and left for California with her husband, Baumer apparently advanced her a little money to enable the young couple to get settled. Four years passed.

"Four years passed, and early in the evening of September 21, Maggie reappeared at the pub and asked to see Baumer. She seemed tired, drained, some even say terrorized. The Good Samaritan rushed from Atlantic City and brought the young woman into his office. We don't know what Maggie told him, but from that moment on, Baumer behaved strangely. First, he disappeared for two whole days, so that his associates became worried. On the afternoon of the twenty-third, however, he resurfaced, bustling and mysterious, but, according to all accounts, in a fairly good mood. He made a first withdrawal of some ten thousand dollars from the account of the West Forty-fourth Street bar. He left again, saying he was taking off for a few days. And that was it—no one ever saw him again. They had news of him, of course, but only through postcards."

The Englishman had even managed to track down some of those cards. He showed them to me. They were addressed "To all my good buddies," or "To the Tavern crew," or to one of his managers personally, or to one or another long-time friend. The messages were laconic, of the type, "All is well, I'm on vacation" or even "Wish you were here!" No indication of what he was doing or who he was with. Between September 30 and December 15, 1974, the cards arrived from nearly everywhere—New Orleans, the Bahamas, the Virgin Islands, Jamaica, Mexico. After December 15, silence. A silence that would last until news of his death on January 8, 1975, in Acapulco.

"We tried to retrace his itinerary. For the first blank, between the 21st and the afternoon of September 23, it was simple. He brought Maggie home to his little studio in Greenwich Village, where he had lived since his wife's death in '51. To all appearances, the Good Samaritan had fallen in love with his protégée and made her his bedmate. It wasn't exactly his style, but these things happen."

On the twenty-third, after having gone to take out money, he left for California, accompanied by Maggie.

172

"Why did we look in California? Quite simply because Maggie came from there. We assumed she had enemies out there and that she had come asking her old boss for help. An assumption that proved to be correct. Maggie kept a motel some forty miles north of San Diego, a place called Ramona. We have evidence that Baumer went through there, because he signed a check for twenty-seven thousand dollars to settle all the debts of Maggie and her husband. Who had abandoned his wife two years earlier, leaving her with a child."

Then, instead of coming back to New York, Baumer disappeared, a six-day hole in his itinerary.

I asked, "What does Maggie Keller say?"

"We haven't questioned her. We neither wanted nor were able to. I'll tell you why later. Nor did we question the two luxury retirees, Baumer ex-lodgers, now living it up in Florida and Puerto Rico. Baumer, then, disappeared for ten days. And only the cards mailed from New Orleans told his New York friends he was still alive. But in New Orleans, despite all our searches, we could pick up no trace of his having been there, with or without Maggie. In fact, he resurfaced on October 10. At the Emerald Beach Hotel in Nassau. He was with Maggie. He stayed there long enough to rent a boat, the *Blue Cypress*, with a four-man crew. Incidentally, to finance the rental he emptied the accounts of all the bars, the mortgages, and scraped together all the money he could find. Which explains that shortly afterward, his affairs were in a disastrous condition. The couple sailed off on the *Blue Cypress*. Then came two months of roaming the Caribbean, with short stops, long enough to mail those famous postcards."

"Walcher claims to have gone to Nassau to find Baumer and attempt to reason with him. He says he used the services of a private detective."

"That's true, in both cases. Walcher saw Baumer on the morning of October 11, just before Baumer left on his cruise. But his efforts were useless. Baumer went off to sail in the sunset with his sweetie. Until December 14, when the *Blue Cypress* sailed into the Mexican port of Veracruz. There, Baumer and his sweetie disembarked. They were in Mexico City on the fifteenth, the Camino Real Hotel in Chapultepec. Baumer rented a car and announced that he was going to tour Mexico. Another black hole in his biography. One of my teams searched all the hotels, motels, and other posadas in half of Mexico. Not a trace, just like in Louisiana. Baumer and the girl might have been staying in private homes, of course. We don't know. We have to wait until the night of January 3 or 4, 1975, when the couple arrived at the El Mirador Hotel in Acapulco, to see him reemerge. And that's where Baumer died, four days later, of a heart attack that seems absolutely beyond a doubt."

I stared at the Englishman. So far, all in all, he had merely rounded out the story Marc Lavater had told me. He nodded.

"You're absolutely right. But this is, so to speak, Herman Baumer's official biography in the three months preceding his death. I have another version, a slightly different one. Much less pleasant, Mr. Cimballi. Especially for you."

Because his investigators had retraced the late Baumer's footsteps. Everywhere. From California to Nassau, then in each port where the *Blue Cypress* had docked, then in Veracruz, and finally Acapulco. And because in none of those places had they found anyone who had seen Baumer in any other condition than completely drunk or asleep in his cups.

Because the *Blue Cypress* had been bought two weeks before it was rented to Baumer by one Harrison Neame, of Springfield, Illinois, who had paid for his purchase out of a numbered account in a Nassau bank. Because this Harrison Neame was totally unknown in Springfield, Illinois.

Because the four members of the *Blue Cypress* crew had mysteriously disappeared in Veracruz the very evening Baumer landed. And because the *Blue Cypress* had been sold again—at a loss—a few days later by a Mexican agency that had never even seen the owner.

Because the bank to which Maggie had given Baumer's twenty-seven thousand dollars had long been identified by the Feds as belonging to a California Mafia family linked to the Caltanis.

Because Maggie Keller had a three-year-old son who had been placed in foster care three days before Maggie arrived in New York to call on Baumer for help. Because the son was picked up by Maggie herself on September 24, and because that same day, when she reclaimed her child, Maggie was accompanied not only by Baumer, but by two other men "who looked like cops—or like hoodlums." Because Maggie no longer had her son with her when she arrived in Nassau with Baumer. Because since September 24, no one had seen Maggie Keller's son again.

And now, if I wanted to know his personal opinion, the Englishman's opinion, of what had really happened to Baumer.

"Mr. Cimballi, many assumptions but no tangible proof. But I believe things went like this: Maggie Keller was used—they blackmailed her by threatening her son's life—to draw Herman Baumer to California and give the impression of a sudden elopement. I believe that the young woman who appeared in Nassau under the name of Maggie, who accompanied Baumer during the whole cruise, and who was still with him in Acapulco the day he died, never was Maggie Keller. I believe that the real Maggie Keller, whose son was given back to her, is hiding somewhere, terror-stricken, perhaps outside the United States. We're looking for her."

"Marc Lavater saw her and spoke to her."

"He saw a young blond woman, a bit heavy, wearing glasses as in the photos we have of her. This woman told Lavater she was Maggie Keller. But she disappeared and quit her job the day after Lavater's visit. Since then, she's nowhere to be found. I think that the Baumer who ran around in those months was a man who had been drugged or soaked in alcohol, a man, at any rate, who was in no condition to react. He was taken away for the sole purpose of preventing him from conducting his business and, in particular, preventing him from paying off his debts to the Walcher bank. I think they did this in order to be able to buy, for the mere sum of its debts, the hotel he didn't want to sell. I don't think they were trying to kill him. His death was probably of natural causes. His heart gave out. Even if they helped it a little to give out."

"And Walcher's role?"

"Impossible to determine for the moment. In the story he told Lavater of his meeting in Nassau with Baumer, he said he had found in front of him a man who was obviously drunk and unwilling to listen. It's possible that he's not lying. And Baumer's drunkenness in Nassau wasn't for the purpose of surprising him. Baumer always had a bent elbow."

The Englishman put the photos back in the envelopes.

"A final explanation, Mr. Cimballi. We carried out our investigation without questioning Maggie—you know why now—and without questioning the rich retirees either, or even Walcher, much less Olliphan. I had a good reason for that. I firmly believe that if the Caltanis learn that you have, how shall I say, re-opened the investigation on Baumer, your life or your family's will be in danger."

"It may be already."

"I don't think so. The investigation Lavater carried out proba-bly worried the Caltanis. But nothing happened, and they must be beginning to calm down. At least, I hope so. Unless some-thing I don't know about gets them upset. For the time being, they're satisfied to keep an eye on you. The proof is those two men who were watching your arrival the day before yesterday. But if you don't do anything, they won't do anything. Your si-lence is your best protection. And now you understand why I took so many precautions in meeting you."

I immediately called Marc Lavater. The silence with which he greeted my information was sufficient for me to measure the se-riousness of the situation.

He said finally, "And I missed all of that. . . ."

He meant his own investigation, of which the Englishman had revealed the limitations and inadequacies.

"Marc, everybody has his own job."

"What are you planning to do?"

Nothing. Absolutely nothing. If there was another solution besides playing dead, it escaped me.

"Walcher may know the truth," Marc remarked, still stunned by the Englishman's revelations.

"Going to see Walcher is out of the question!"

Usually, Lavater's mind was sharper. He must really have been stunned.

He asked, "But why?"

"MARC! Either Walcher is in on it, and going to see him would be tantamount to alerting the Caltanis, or else he's hon-est, and his first concern would be to let the police know that somebody killed his old friend Baumer!"

"You're right. Don't say any more about it."

I exploded, "Oh, sure, I'm going to say more about it! No way! Because without mentioning the fact that any official inquiry into Baumer's death would result in raising questions about the sale of the Crystal Palace and thereby freezing the 50 million I laid out, I would also, in addition, have the Chinese on my back!"

Playing dead (figuratively) was the answer.

Of course, I could be a nice, good, honest Cimballi and go to the police myself. And say, "Officer, some wicked bandits sold me a hotel that they had stolen." What would happen? The American legal system would begin by freezing everything, my money and that of the Chinese, to gain time to sort out this whole brouhaha. It's a kind of mania that magistrates have in every country. They begin by sitting (figuratively, Your Honor) on everything that's likely to move. In the first place money. It would have taken years.

And then—do you have proof, Mr. Cimballi? Then bring us this famous English detective, we'd like to have a few words with him. And besides, where do you get the idea that the honorable Caltani brothers have anything to do with this matter? (I didn't doubt for one second that Olliphan, for a transaction of this nature, must have used a number of front companies. Tracing them back to the source would take centuries, even assuming such a thing were possible.)

Especially since, in the meantime, Caltanic killers could easily have made short work of me.

So, playing dead seemed to me to be the only solution. Hoping, as the Englishman had said, that "something" wouldn't happen to "upset" the Caltanis.

Playing dead—but only on the surface. Obviously, it was out of the question for me to remain in such a state indefinitely. I could see only two possibilities for action. First, asking the Englishman to pursue his investigation, centering mainly on Walcher and Olliphan, but to pursue it in the utmost secrecy. Second, to follow the trail that the enigmatic Olliphan himself had indicated to me: South Africa.

18

I asked Rosen to sit in on my interview with the representatives of the Austrian general consulate. The interview went off pretty well. The Austrians, who were extremely nice, conscientiously inspected the house, questioned Heidi in my absence (which irritated me), then in front of me. They interrogated me, questioned Sarah, talked with Jimmy. Finally, they went off. They would make a report, and their role would end there. And afterwards? They smiled, as affable as ever. The decision was not up to them. No sooner had they gone then I jumped on Rosen.

"Jimmy, Heidi . . ."

"I know, Franz. As long as she wants to stay. But things aren't all that simple . . ."

The words lawyers always use to tell you that you can't do something you feel like doing, even if it's honest, moral, and all the rest. And there was already one thing I couldn't do. Take Heidi out of the United States, where she had to stay until her case was settled.

Thus, as there was no question of separating Heidi and Marc-Andrea, and as Sarah did not want to leave the children in the sole care of the Amazon, it was alone, once again, that I boarded the plane to Paris, around February 10, I think. I would only stop there briefly. My real destination was good old St. Tropez. And Henrik Korber was waiting for me.

At no time, I think, was I really tempted, however slightly, to become involved in a casino venture among the Bantus. At best, the idea made me chuckle. Bantus! And in the land of apartheid, besides! In the end, it was more amusing than anything else. I'm willing to believe that I have sometimes engaged in eccentric projects—Operation Ice Cream wasn't a bad example—but there are limits.

After doing some research, Marc Lavater shrugged his shoulders.

"You're wrong. It isn't the least farfetched. Korber exists, Boph-How-do-you-call-it also exists. That is, it will by the end of the year. And in all likelihood, there will be casinos. I can even tell you that Korber's not alone in the business. The Holiday Inn chain and others are also in the running."

"Come on, don't make me laugh. Even you can't pronounce the name of that burg!"

"The venture is viable, Franz. You can do it or not do it, though in my opinion you have enough on your hands with your Atlantic City casino. But whether or not you think it's funny, there will definitely be a Bantu Las Vegas. Sooner or later."

Olliphan's Ferrari had barely crossed the gate of my Long Island house when I had called Marc, who was not very happy to be pulled out of bed at eleven-thirty at night. (I had once again forgotten to take the time difference into account.) I had told him about the strange visit by the Caltanis' *consigliere*. His perplexity was equal to mine.

He said finally, "If nothing else, we can always try to see whether this Korber story makes sense and to what degree."

"Excellent idea. Get to work on it."

"Even if it means going to South Africa?"

"Absolutely. Kiss the Bantus for me."

I now asked Marc, "By the way, did you go there after all?"

"To South Africa? Nuts to that. You're the one who likes traveling, not me."

No, he had confined himself to getting in touch with our mutual friend, the Turk, who, from his Hampstead, London, residence, which he practically never left, knew the whole world, and had given Marc the names of people to call or cable for information in Pretoria, Johannesburg, and the Cape.

"Okay, tell me about Korber."

"South African by birth and citizenship. No legal record. Made his first fortune in textiles, went bankrupt, started over, this time in overland and later air transportation. He has his own company and owns a few hotels, including a small chain in the western United States and Mexico. There are rumors afloat to the effect that this does not explain his current wealth, which exceeds 100 million rands."

"A rand is worth how much?"

"Five francs or so. More than the dollar. Sorry, but he's richer than you."

"What are you trying to do? Put me in a bad mood?"

"According to those same rumors, the man is also involved in gold. Targeting India."

"I'm familiar with that."*

*See *Money*.

Marc had come to pick me up at Roissy on my arrival from New York. We had changed airports together and taken a plane to Nice. In Nice, a rented car, Marc at the wheel. We were driving through Ste. Maxime.

Marc said, "But no drugs, no white slavery, no weapons, no pickpocketing. In short, an eminently respectable financier."

"Sarcastic, huh? And his relations with Olliphan?"

"Olliphan told you the truth. Korber employed him as a legal adviser when he bought his hotels in the Far West. The two men have known each other for at least seven or eight years. Olliphan made two trips to South Africa, each time to meet Korber. On that subject there's another rumor, even more widespread than the first. Olliphan is said to be more than an adviser, to share some of Korber's interests."

"Which interests?"

I was on the point of imagining some collusion between Korber and the Caltanis with Olliphan as intermediary. But Marc shook his head.

"I don't think so. It would seem rather that Olliphan is working on his own behalf."

"WITHOUT THE CALTANIS' KNOWLEDGE?"

"Exactly. I knew that would interest you."

A picture rose up from my memory—the terrifying silhouette of "Signora Olliphan." And suddenly my pulse began racing. Because without a doubt, if I were James Montague Olliphan, married to a thoroughly horrible Caltani and incredibly trapped in that marriage, I would have only one idea in mind—get the hell out of there, as far as possible from my wife and dear brothers-in-law. And South Africa was pretty far!

"Marc, for God's sake, do you realize what that means, if it's true?"

"I realize. In the first place, it may explain the attitude of Olliphan toward you. He sells you the Crystal Palace as a representative of the Caltanis, but immediately afterward, invites you to dinner and warns you against the purchase you've just made. And four or five months later he comes and offers you a very personal matter. If he's double-crossing the Caltanis, or at least trying to disentangle himself from them, that makes sense."

My heart continued to pound. We, perhaps, had just put our fingers on something crucial.

"And there's more. Marc! Much more!"

I was almost screaming with excitement.

"If Olliphan is really, as it seems, maneuvering very carefully to get rid of his two horrible brothers-in-law and his no-less horrible wife, the very fact of knowing that and being able to furnish proof . . ."

"Which we don't have."

"Granted. But when we have it all we have to do is threaten him. 'Ollie I'll tell your wife everything if you don't tell me everything about the Crystal Palace.' "

"And about Baumer."

"And about Baumer, Heidi, Anna, and Abraham Lincoln's assassination. Marc, we have to get to the bottom of this!"

He had the final word.

"And who's going to go to South Africa to find out if the wily Olliphan is investing there?"

I smiled.

"You said it yourself. I love traveling."

Henrik Korber had laid down the condition that our first meeting be private, saying that he was one of those businessmen who doesn't like publicity until after the contracts are signed, which was in no way unusual. He was on his way back to South Africa from Amsterdam or Frankfurt, and I was coming from New York. He suggested we meet midway, in Cannes. It was I who had mentioned St. Tropez. Where I was born, after all— and where I often told myself I would do better to stay, rather than act like a fool and build casinos or buy mountains of coffee.

On my advice, he had booked a room at the Mas de Chastelas, an elegant little hotel on the road, about five miles from St. Tropez, that had been specially opened for us since it was out of season (the owners, Dominique and Gerard, were friends). Korber was a man of forty-five or fifty, with the looks of an international playboy, two heads taller than me. I am so, so happy to meet you, he said, and I answered me-too-I've-been-looking-forward-eagerly-to-this-moment. He made the traditional remark to me, "You really look very young," and I gave him the equally classic reply, not to worry, it wasn't catching. Whereupon we exchanged the broad, warm smile of eternal friendship conceived on the spot, like two big bad wolves running into each other in a corner of the woods, each one wondering how the devil he would be able to devour the other.

181

I didn't like his looks at all. He was a shark, that was plain, and I wouldn't even trust him with my toothbrush. But I acted my role and told him that, having arranged a study of the deal he was offering me through Olliphan, I was quite ready to envision perhaps a partnership.

I had one goal, one only, in this farce—to confirm my theory about Olliphan, obtain proof that he was actually playing his private game while not giving two hoots for the interests of the Family whose *consigliere* he was, and was preparing, above all, to win his independence.

Easier said than done. First, because for the time being Olliphan wasn't the least bit compromised by his visit to me. He could always claim that as Korber was one of his clients—which the Caltanis must have known—he had merely put his client in touch with me, period. Second, because if Olliphan had really invested in South Africa, he was certainly clever enough to have done it without leaving any trace. That is to say, although I had never seen the Caltanis except in a photo (handsome Sicilian faces, by the way), I would be greatly surprised if they sniffed any misbehavior on the part of their counselor, who was also their brother-in-law. If they did, sudden death would be in the offing.

Finally, because this worthy Korber, beneath his warm and friendly playboy guise, was admirable at keeping his mouth shut. Granted, he talked, with the glibness of a salesman. He reminded me of a San Francisco real-estate promoter, a certain Lamm, whom I had once given a bit of a rough time, to punish him for having taken part in an improper solicitation of a legacy (mine). Korber talked, but didn't say what he meant. Apparently, he had made the same kind of check on me that I had made on him. There was nothing surprising in that. In fact, the contrary would have amazed me. He smiled.

"May I speak frankly?"

I returned his smile.

"Don't bother—speak as you usually do."

He gave me a slap on the back so that my lungs rattled—what jolly company I was!

"I really like you a lot, Franz. Call me Rik, of course. But one thing worries me. I know you're deeply involved in that Atlantic City venture, and . . ."

"If I go in with you, I'd be able to keep my commitments."

He smiled subtly.

"Even if you have to call in your Arab friends—yes, I'm well informed. I always find out about the people I plan to work with."

That was an opening that invited another. I plunged in.

"Precisely. Before taking this discussion any further, there are two points I would like to bring up. The first concerns my Chinese partners in Macao who are in on the Atlantic City casino with me. Whatever the outcome of our negotiations, yours and mine, I don't want them to know anything about this project. I'm relying on your discretion."

It will be noted that the statement I had just made was none other than a bluff. In fact, I couldn't care less whether the beautiful Miranda in Macao learned of my "projects" with Korber or not. For two reasons. I hadn't the slightest intention of carrying those projects through, especially since I'd been able to size up Korber. And, also, my first action would be to inform Macao myself of the offer the South African had made me and of my refusal. One can never be too scrupulous with one's partners, especially when they're Chinese.

No, in reality, I merely wanted to give Korber the impression that he would now have leverage over me, would have, as it were, a possible means of blackmail or pressure.

Which perhaps would encourage him to be a little more voluble.

"Rik, what is Olliphan's exact role in this whole matter?"

"I'm paying him to represent my interests in the United States. And I had asked him to look for a possible partner for me. He did his job."

"That's all?"

He feigned surprise perfectly, but feigned it, I could swear.

"Why these questions? Did he say something that disturbed you?"

"Because Olliphan has close contacts with people I would prefer to see only in photographs."

"In that case, I can reassure you immediately. I have no affinity with the people you refer to. In South Africa, you know, we have our own gangsters. We prefer not to import them."

He talked, but did not answer my question. Not completely,

at any rate. And he wouldn't answer it, clearly, at this stage of our negotiations. In other words, I would have to give further proof of my interest in casinos in Bantu land.

Very well, here we go. In any event, I had never been to South Africa.

We were in Capetown two days later, after a short stopover in Cairo, where I was becoming a frequent visitor, to be sure. Korber lived in a rather exceptional property planted with three-hundred-year-old oaks imported from Europe and rosebushes. The garden was filled with exotic but tame birds. The place was called Llanduno. It was to the south of Table Mountain, at the foot of what was called the Twelve Apostles. The four windows of my room, of my apartment, actually, revealed a fantastic panorama. I barely had time to admire it. Korber buried me in documentation, piled on back-to-back meetings with bankers, architects, journalists—even an anthropologist, whom I had to listen to without blinking as he explained to me that there were three races of men: the true whites, like him and me, the intermediate race, which ran the entire gamut from Arabs to southern Europeans (he put the French and the Bavarians in that category, but, curiously, not the Swiss), and, finally, the true coloreds, the Kleurlinge. He was taken aback when I told him that my name was Cimballi and that my mother had been Jewish. His sole consolation—my father was Italian, but from the north of Italy. That comforted him.

Korber called out the troops to convince me. And he nearly succeeded in persuading me that this deal he was offering was a financier's dream.

"Franz, I've seen to everything. The day after tomorrow, or the following day, we'll go together to Johannesburg and from there by car to Bophuthatswana. Barely two hours of driving. And that's not all, you understand, we're talking about building an empire of hotels and casinos. All those nigger territories are gold mines. Figuratively speaking. We're not going to build one little Las Vegas, but several. The Transkei rejected my offers, but sooner or later, it will accept them. And there's not only Bophuthatswana and the Transkei. You've also got Vendaland, the Ciskei, Lebowa, Swaziland, and others. Not yet independent, but they will be one of these fine days. Of course, by independent you get my meaning. The Kleurlinge don't have a choice. We've granted them a kind of independence, but let's be serious. It was the best way to get those guys off our back and not be forced to give them the right to vote someday. But how could they survive? Surely you don't think we've given them the best lands? They've got no choice. I tell you, it's either leave their reservations, so to speak, and come work for us as foreign workers, or accept my proposals."

Korber had at least one quality I couldn't deny—candor. A candor that bordered on the chilliest cynicism. I would seldom see better.

"Franz, you know the Dutch Reformed Church? Not exactly jolly, believe me. It won't release its hold on this country so soon. So much the better, Franz. Because thanks to that church and its bloody puritanism, you and I are going to rake in a mountain of dough. Hotels, casinos, and beautiful black girls, those gorgeous whores for whom 95 percent of Afrikaners have the hots. For almost three hundred years we haven't had the right to cop a feel from a pretty nigger gal in this country. Have you seen what our women look like? Touching a black ass here is called a *schandelijcke crime van hoerendom*, a shameful crime of whoring, and it's punishable by law. But everyone's dying to do it. And these bantustans will make the thing possible, while at the same time enabling us to set up baccarat, craps, and blackjack tables, which are as forbidden to us as black women. Franz, I'll make you a bet. In two or three years, we'll do around $400 million worth of business, you and I. And by 1985, we'll triple it.* All of Africa will come running, you'll see, both white and black."

I hadn't liked Korber from the first moment of our meeting, and my stay in South Africa in his company didn't make me cotton to him any more. The worst was that I had to pretend to be all in a dither over these grandiose plans he was hatching. It took me two days to shake him off and to make contact finally with that man whose name and address had been given to me by the Turk via Lavater.

He was a mixed-race black Malaysian, a banker by trade, who had studied in England, and whose family, he told me with some pride, already owned a townhouse on the Hout Straat

*Business volume of the southern African casinos in 1981: $350 million.

(now in the midst of the white district) in the eighteenth century, before racial segregation had really taken hold. He invited me to lunch on broiled lobster at the Homestead, a mixed restaurant in the Capetown National Park. In London, the Turk had been emphatic. If there was a man capable of obtaining information for me on any investments Olliphan might have in South Africa, it was he. His name is unimportant—I'll call him Balthazar. But when Lavater tried to ask him on the phone to start investigating, this same Balthazar had simply hung up on him.

He smiled at me over the lobsters.

"I don't discuss these matters over the telephone."

"The main thing is that you do discuss them. I'm here."

We spoke briefly of our mutual friend, the Turk, who was—there is no better word to describe him—an international loan-shark, quite capable of advancing you one million sterling almost within the hour. Provided you were really certain of paying him back down to the last penny. Otherwise, you courted risks that were not necessarily of a legal nature.

"The Turk holds you in great esteem," Balthazar told me.

"I hold him in the same. Can you find me that information about Olliphan?"

He would try. He made no promises. But in any case, not before two or three weeks at the earliest. It wouldn't be easy, and it was only because I had the benefit of hearty recommendations from the Turk that he would compromise himself this way. We agreed that he would send a coded report—if there was a report—not to me but to Jimmy Rosen, at his address.

"It would be best if you could let us know the amount of those investments, if any."

"I'll do my best."

He had a banker's traditional reserve. I wasn't quite sure what to make of him and his reliability. But there was one thing of which I was sure. If Olliphan had, in fact, transferred money to this part of the world, he had probably done so by digging into the funds of his family by marriage. A theory that made my spine tingle. In that case, should the brothers-in-law with eyes like burning coals get wind of it, another St. Valentine's Day Massacre would be in the offing. And poor little Cimballi would do well to be somewhere else when the shooting started.

186

In reality, after my meeting with Balthazar, I no longer had much to do in South Africa. Yet I didn't want to run the risk of an immediate break with Korber, the nature of whose relations with Olliphan I had not yet been able to determine. Thus, I drank the cup to the dregs. The Afrikaner dragged me to Johannesburg, and from there, due west to Boph-whatcha-macallit, to which I was supremely indifferent. My one consolation—the landscape was incredibly beautiful, and in the enormous, luxuriously appointed helicopter that he had made into his headquarters, Korber took pleasure in flying me over the Transvaal and even a part of Orange Province as far as the edge of the Kalahari Desert. Nevertheless, we eventually tore ourselves apart from one another, and with heartrending farewells and the solemn promise that I would let him hear from me very soon (indeed!), I boarded a plane in Johannesburg to Rome. A mere ruse, for instead of returning to the United States, I flew instead to Bombay on February 21. On the 22nd, I was in Macao. There I found the beautiful Miranda, to whom I related in detail my South African odyssey, without, however, telling her the real reason for it. Why tell her about Olliphan and the strange suspicions I entertained toward him, when in reality I had no proof? No point in worrying my Chinese lady over what might be only a false alarm. Better to wait until I knew more. When Balthazar had sent me his report, for instance.

Miranda took note of the fact that I was definitely not going to accept Korber's offers. She approved and gave me a big kiss as a sign of her satisfaction. She'd had excellent news from Caliban about the casino.

"I'm pleased with you, Comrade Cimballi."

Fortunately. For I believed in the yellow peril, all right.

Macao-Hong Kong-San Francisco-New York. I arrived on Long Island on Friday the twenty-fifth. Just in time to keep the promise I'd made to Marc-Andrea and Heidi on my departure two weeks earlier—to take them to see the Crystal Palace.

This happened on Sunday the twenty-seventh. You don't forget dates like that.

19

On the right Marc-Andrea, on the left the Tyrolean. In the middle, Cimballi, his teeth chattering like castanets (a forty-six-degree difference in temperature between Capetown and Atlantic City). Sarah hadn't wanted to come. She said she saw enough hotels all year round, and, besides, she owed it to herself to take a short trip to Montego Bay. Although officially on leave, it was too much for her. She had to go and take a look-see once in a while. Marc Lavater had also left us, the children and me, but it was more recent in his case, only a few minutes earlier. In fact, he was in Atlantic City like us, a few miles away, at Henry Chance's house. His presence nearby turned out to be of supreme importance.

I gazed at the huge metallic scaffolding. True, you needed a good deal of imagination to detect the future luxury in this jumble. It was ten-thirty in the morning, perhaps a little later. I had driven from Long Island with Marc, and the children. The day before, I had recounted in detail to Lavater my entire trip and my visit with Balthazar. Our mutual conclusion—the results were meager, and we could hardly see how they could improve my position, caught as I was between the certainty and intuition that I had bought a hotel that had been stolen through a kidnapping, if not a murder, and the obligation I was under not to do or say anything. At least I found some consolation in the fact that the Caltanis, for their part, had not made any more moves than I had. To all indications, they were satisfied with the situation. And I was compelled to be likewise, my only hope being a discovery by the Englishman (who was pursuing his inquiry in utmost secrecy) or some revelations by Balthazar from Capetown. In truth, I don't remember any special nervousness or foreboding on that morning of Sunday, March 27, 1977. The *joie de vivre* of Heidi and Marc-Andrea, her egging him on, had probably rubbed off on me. We had sung with all our might while crossing the Verrazano Bridge between Brooklyn and Staten Island. The car ride to Atlantic City had enabled me to see how close my investment was to New York. The hotel construction site was deserted. If you could still call it a construction site. Viewed from the outside, the casino seemed finished, except for the decorative gardens at the rear entrances, still fallow for the time being and used for storage of machinery. Inside, however, nearly all the finishing work remained to be done, both the casino itself and the floors destined for the hotel. The official opening had been scheduled for April 9, before Easter Sunday. At one point, we had even considered moving up the opening by one week, but the advertising agency in charge of promotion had shown us that this would change its campaign schedule too much.

One of the six armed guards wearing a uniform with the Crystal Palace emblem stopped us as we entered the perimeter enclosed by a temporary fence. He identified me, opened the improvised gate, crudely constructed of planks and wire, in front of my car and closed it behind us. He and his buddies had hot coffee, he said, if I wanted some.

The following second he was hopping on one foot, his left shin smarting from Heidi's traditional kick.

I explained, "It's her specialty, what do you expect?"

"They ought to hire her for the Cosmos. To replace Pélé."

"Isn't there any hot chocolate?" Heidi asked.

But no doubt the question was meant to justify her kick, for, without waiting for a reply, dragging my son behind her, she bolted straight toward the buildings. And soon that immense structure, with no other living souls and echoing like mad, unleashed both of them. They were off in a giant game of hide-and-seek, in which, of course, I was the hunter and they were the game. Seven hundred eighty rooms, two dozen suites, plus the service quarters, the living rooms, the restaurants and auditoriums, the bars and sports facilities, in addition to the casino portion itself—no lack of hiding places. The two children yelled so loudly in their excitement that another one of the guards came running. He thought there'd been an accident. I reassured him and he went away. The surveillance provided by the guards was mainly external. In theory they didn't have to be in the building, where they only made rounds.

I finally caught up with my two monsters in one of the suites. This one was practically finished, only the furniture was missing. The carpet and draperies were in place. That wasn't true of most of the rooms. The electricity was working, but the walls and floors were bare, and having tried to wash my hands I noted that the water mains hadn't been connected. Nearly all the corridors were cluttered with carpet rolls, electrical equipment, crates and boxes containing draperies and wall fabrics.

"Let's go up on the roof," Heidi suggested.

That tempted me about as much as exercises on a trapeze. With the sea wind, it must have been cold enough up there to freeze a polar bear.

"Wanna go up on the roof," Marc-Andrea announced. He was caught up in the fever and eagerly subscribed to all of the Tyrolean's proposals, especially when they were stupid (which didn't prevent him from giving her a punch from time to time).

All the elevators were working. Off we went. We came out on the roof at the place where a helicopter landing-strip had been set up. With a tyke in each hand, to prevent them from climbing over the short balustrade, I strode up and down the roof. While the cold was indeed Siberian, the view was fantastic. The weather, cloudy when we left Long Island, had now cleared up completely.

"Where's Salzburg?"

"Straight ahead of you. Just keep swimming. When you hear bagpipes, that's Brittany, and you walk from there."

Atlantic City, as its name implies, was on the edge of the ocean, at the tip of a peninsula flung to the left and right of a long string of islands and islets, marking out innumerable tiny bays. That day, owing to the wind, the air was so clear that the view stretched almost to infinity. To the south I could clearly see the Delaware Bay, to the north was the line of beaches that ended with Sandy Hook, just below New York City. And that reddish-gray blotch in the sky to the west signaled the Philadelphia metropolitan area. For a few moments I gave myself up to euphoria. Caltani or no, I was on the roof of MY casino, and I could easily imagine tens of millions of men and women, drooling with greed, rushing from all points on the horizon, from Washington, Baltimore, Philadelphia, New York, and who knows where else, for the sole purpose of feeding their dollars into MY slot machines or dropping them on MY tables. In fact it wasn't a question of money, or at least, that wasn't the main thing. What intoxicated me the most was an extraordinary feeling of omnipotence, of ultimate success—me, Cimballi of St. Tropez, straddling my new colossus.

Heidi, already so much a woman, brought me back to reality.

"Come on, let's go someplace else."

"Place else," Marc-Andrea instantly repeated.

We still had to visit the gambling rooms, and, above all, the holy of holies, my cherished baby—the antinuclear casino. Anyway, I was beginning to turn into a stalagmite from the cold. Again the elevator, heading for the ground floor.

It must have been after eleven, eleven-fifteen.

"A hundred million dollars," Heidi announced.

"See you and raise you ten," Marc-Andrea returned.

"A moment earlier, as we entered the underground room, I had been slightly surprised to find an old craps table there. Just as I'd been startled by the presence of a few old slot-machines at the head of the reinforced corridor leading to the shelter. And then I remembered that some time earlier, to celebrate the end of the major construction, Caliban and Henry Chance—the former wringing agreement from the latter—had organized a little party for all the construction workers. I hadn't been present, and for good reason—I was in South Africa.

"I get the dice," Heidi commanded me. "You rolled a three, not a four. No cheating."

And naturally, since a pair of dice still lingered on the felt tabletop, my two devils seized them immediately and wanted to play. What's more, I had to teach them the rules, which, considering my scanty knowledge of the subject, was a nice bit of bravura. Miraculously, they understood, especially Heidi from the height of her many years. As though craps were a game played from the cradle in the Tyrolean mountains. Except that she mixed up craps, poker, and war—plus a few rules she invented as she went along (but she was very good at poker, which she practiced diligently with Marc-Andrea and the Amazon, who had already lost to this fearsome duo some $15 million, represented by peanuts).

"SEVEN!" Heidi yelled triumphantly, for the ninth time in a row. "The banker pays. You're the banker, Mr. Cimballi. You owe me $400 million and you owe Andrea three hundred. This way to the cashier!"

We had no tokens, and as a marker we were using my wristwatch, which had an annoying tendency to move by itself as soon as I turned my head. In other words, I was literally swindled by my two opponents, who were in cahoots like two thieves at a fair. Furthermore, the few times that they condescended to let me throw the dice, I racked up twos, threes, and twelves with alarming consistency.

We had reached the shelter through the reinforced tunnel

which began in the subbasement, right under the ground floor. The reinforced doors had been placed in the tunnel but not yet installed. They lay on the cement floor, and we had to walk over them to get by. The air conditioning wasn't on yet, but there was adequate ventilation. Anyway, I didn't plan to stay long, in spite of Marc-Andrea and Heidi, who were glued to the table. I was hungry. I'd had only a little tea for breakfast, unlike the children, who, after a gargantuan breakfast, hastily gobbled two or three hamburgers, washed down with milkshakes, as soon as they arrived in Atlantic City. They could hold out.

"ELEVEN!" my son and the young Tyrolean exclaimed, with one and the same voice.

Their luck was really incredible. Why was I in business, after all? I could take those two to Vegas, and we'd break the bank.

"Pay, Mr. Cimballi. You owe us . . . "

About $19 billion, I knew. And I was practically starving to death, besides. I glanced at my watch on the table—twelve-ten.

It was the odor that alerted me.

An acrid smell, stinging the nostrils and soon the throat. Heidi and my son, throwing the dice so hard that they often landed twenty-five feet away, didn't seem to notice anything. Yet their eyes were watering a little. They wiped them with the backs of their hands and, with fiery cheeks, refused to be distracted.

"ELEVEN!"

I left the table. Since my last visit together with Henry Chance, Caliban, and Patty, the work had gone farther here than anywhere else. The painting was done. The light oak paneling was in place, along with the wainscoting. At the back of the room to the right, they had set up the walls around what was to be my private suite. Everything was finished, except the doors, which were missing.

I walked. There was no real alarm within me, rather a tense curiosity. I was thinking mainly of my empty stomach. And without a doubt, by sniffing, I realized that the odor was coming from the tunnel on the left, the same one through which we had entered, the one leading to the subbasement across from the elevator bank.

Behind me, "ELEVEN! Are you playing or not? Chickening out, huh?"

I climbed up on the first reinforced door lying on the ground. I advanced several feet, the odor became slightly stronger, and there was no longer just an odor. The air I breathed was filled with bluish, slightly iridescent vapors, which made me think of oil spread thinly on the sea. I was beginning to weep warm tears, my eyes were beginning to sting painfully. Okay, that was enough.

"Anda and Heidi! Come here!"

No answer, except for a triumphant "ELEVEN!," which they screamed loud enough to make themselves hoarse. I went back, quickening my steps.

"Come on, we're going!"

Marc-Andrea quickly snatched up the dice and moved away from me, merrily dancing in place, challenging me in a childish singsong.

"You can't catch me! You can't catch me!"

But Heidi stiffened, constantly blinking her eyelids. She glanced toward the tunnel and looked at me.

"Is something wrong?"

"Yes, we have to get out of here. Stay calm."

"I'm calm," she said. She yelled, "ANDA! STOP IT!"

Immediately, my son obeyed—certainly the first time that had ever happened to him. I took a child in each hand and led them toward the tunnel. The situation there had changed during these last few seconds. What earlier had been blue-violet, almost diaphanous wreaths were now long billows, rolling toward us in slow waves. We crossed the first threshold and arrived at the second one. Just beyond, the tunnel widened a little and bent slightly to the left.

"Children, quickly!"

I forced them to run. Marc-Andrea was suddenly racked by a strong fit of coughing. I yelled, "Put your co."—But they had left their coats on the craps table. "Take off your tops, quick!" And I made them cover their faces. We started again. Past the bend, I was looking at a tunnel completely filled with smoke, to the extent that I could make out anything with my burning, tear-filled eyes. A few more feet, and even before reaching the threshold of the third door, I realized the folly I was committing. The air was now barely breathable. Heidi and I began to cough, but the worst was what was happening to Marc-Andrea. He had fallen to the ground and was shaking with spasms. I nearly

193

panicked. I snatched him up, at the very second that a muffled explosion sounded ten or fifteen feet above, and a sudden reddening lit up the wall of smoke. It was no longer merely a leak, as I had thought at first, but, in fact, a fire, which was attacking all those huge cans of varnish and other liquid materials that I had seen piled up in the subbasement.

"Heidi! Get back, fast!"

I went off at a run, carrying Marc-Andrea. Only to discover, after four or five yards, that the little girl hadn't followed me. She was on her knees, coughing and crying.

"Heidi?"

I had to retrace my steps, grab her, and pull her along. We went through the middle door again. Heidi, whom I was almost carrying, pulled loose. "It's okay, Mr. Cimballi." The atmosphere was once again almost normal, except for those fumes given off by the slow-combustion chemicals. We were again at the gambling table.

"Heidi, stay with Andrea and don't move. Okay?"

She nodded, and even smiled at me, with astonishing calmness. "Okay, Mr. Cimballi." Her self-control rubbed off on me. *Okay, think, Cimballi.* We're in a giant cement shoebox which is entered by way of tunnels. Which can also be used to exit, of course. And if one of them is blocked—I went to the tunnel on the right and entered it. I didn't get very far. It was obstructed by a pile of sacks and crates of equipment, plus old slot machines. What, I wondered, were they doing there? But one thing was clear—opening a passage to the parking lot where that tunnel led would take hours.

Don't panic. There were emergency exits. One of them was in my suite. I ran back across the room.

"Come on."

The fumes had made progress, they were seeping into the room and had already crossed the first threshold. But their effects were far less noticeable as soon as we entered the suite. I knew its layout by heart, having designed it myself under the smirking eyes of an architect. What was to be my private office was all the way to the rear, at the end of a corridor that led past the other rooms, leaning against what would be a giant safe. The entrance to emergency exit Number One was there, sealed by a reinforced panel. It opened with no trouble onto a narrow passage four and a half feet in diameter, straight-sided and sloping, rather impressive inasmuch as the optical effect made it shrink to a tiny aperture a hundred yards away. I flicked the switch, and the light went on inside. I then measured the full absurdity of my situation. I was with the children inside an atomic-bomb shelter, designed to stand up to almost any disaster, and we were in danger of dying from suffocation only because I couldn't close the doors! It would have been ridiculous if it wasn't so potentially tragic. But the passageway I was looking at reassured me completely.

I rounded up the children, whose reddened eyes were the only sign of the ordeal they'd been through. "Shall we go in there?" Far from being frightening, the prospect enchanted them. I lifted them up and forward through the circular opening. They moved without the slightest difficulty since the shaft was their size. I, on the other hand, had to walk bent over, and it was only after one hundred feet that I realized I had forgotten to close the reinforced panel behind us. True, it could be closed completely only from the inside of the room, but I could at least have pulled it toward me. Too bad, I kept going.

A hundred yards farther, another round panel, also reinforced, which opened with even less difficulty since it was actually only propped in place. No sooner had I laid my palm on it than it tumbled with a rather impressive thud. This thing had to weigh a three hundred pounds! On the other side, the passageway ended and became a tiny decontamination room. A very narrow staircase, at most two feet wide, rose straight up. I knew where it led—between the cement pilings of the drain ditch at the northwest corner of the Crystal Palace's perimeter. Normally, there should have been a third reinforced closing at the foot of the staircase, but the panel hadn't been installed yet, either. It was leaning to one side against the wall. To the right of where the staircase began was a monitoring screen that allowed you to see outside. I was angry with myself for not having used the same screens that surely must have existed in the tunnel invaded by gas and smoke. That way, I could have seen if the path was clear beyond the wall of smoke. Perhaps we'd been only a few yards from the exit. But it was too late. And anyway, why worry? The open air was now a few steps away. With the children at my heels, I finished climbing the staircase. I was now in front of the last reinforced panel. It was closed, as the position of the levers showed. But it worked. I was sure of that since I had tested it with Caliban, for fun, a few months earlier. I lowered the two levers and turned them, one by one. The panel opened.

Not really. It pivoted three or four inches. But it was so thick that it couldn't be pried open enough to see outside or even to let in fresh air. *Something was blocking it.* A sudden rush of adrenalin jolted me. What was this bullshit? I pushed harder, with all my strength. I bent double. "Children, help me!" We pushed together. Without budging it an inch more. The huge round panel didn't move. There was no point in trying.

Had I been alone, I would have already been afraid. With my son and Heidi at my sides, it was blind panic. I began to pound on the steel, but that was ridiculous. I turned around. Behind us, the narrow plunge of the staircase, then the tiny decontamination room, then, on the ground, the second panel that had fallen shortly before and left the opening of the passageway gaping. I tumbled down the steps. I cast an eye at the passageway. Without a doubt, one hundred yards away at the end of that gigantic tube, the first toxic fumes were beginning to seep into the shaft. And coming toward us. It was a matter of a minute, at most. And there we were, all three of us, cornered like rats underground, trapped in a fearful array of concrete and steel! Feverishly, I tried to lift the panel I'd caused to fall, to put it back on its round threshold so that it would seal us in. In vain. It would have taken three men. A new surge of panic. Then my wits returned. The camera and the monitoring screen! I turned on the screen. Immediately there appeared a picture of the ditch, outside, in the open air . . .

. . . and the face, in large close-up, of a security guard, who was looking straight into the lens. The man smiled. He obviously knew of our presence behind the panel. He raised his hand, the forefinger pointing, and showed me something behind him, almost at his feet. I lowered the monitoring camera. Then I saw the wooden beam that had been placed crosswise, so as to block the opening of the panel. The man had crouched so that he appeared full-length in the picture. He kept on smiling ironically. Then, very slowly, I saw him place his hands on the beam, and without the slightest haste, give it a few small taps to dislodge it. The beam slid sideways and fell. Another hand signal—you can go now. The man went off, with a final smile. I rushed up the stairs, threw myself at the panel, and this time it opened, forming a wonderfully bright circle on the wide, sunny blue sky.

I lifted Marc-Andrea and Heidi through the opening. They jumped to the ground. I slid out myself, not without one last glance toward the passageway, where the first blue wreaths appeared. I swung and found myself face to face with Marc Lavater. I hadn't even had time to get over my shock. He rose before me, his face contorted with anger and worry.

"In God's name, Franz, what is going on?"

My rage was such that I could have struck him for the stupidity of his question.

I shouted, "Where's the guard? The one who put the beam in front of the panel and then removed it?"

Marc stared at me, uncomprehendingly. And then, suddenly, he did something absolutely astounding. He jumped up and ran along the ditch and in a veritable frenzy, began pulling out, one by one, the other beams blocking emergency exits Two and Three. He flung away the heavy pieces of wood. I thought he had gone crazy. I caught up with him.

"Marc, you're suppressing the evidence that someone tried to kill us, me and the children!"

He nodded, suddenly restored to calmness, panting a little.

"Precisely," he said. "Precisely."

He looked over my shoulder. His arm and forefinger stretched out. He was showing me something. A hundred yards away from us, the entire Crystal Palace was in flames, a gigantic fire.

20

"Franz, for the love of heaven, trust me! Don't say anything. You didn't see anything. You don't know what happened. There was no guard, no beam, the door of the emergency exit wasn't blocked."

Marc was whispering, a flood of words. Police and firemen

were coming toward us, accompanied and led by the guard who had offered us coffee and whom Heidi had kicked. I also noticed two cameramen from a CBS television-news team. Marc held my arm and squeezed it tightly.

"Okay, Franz? You understand?"

He whispered again.

"I beg you—no beam, no guard. The exit wasn't blocked. The fire is accidental, Franz. ACCIDENTAL!"

Police and firemen were upon us, soon joined by a TV reporter, microphone in hand. I was identified as the owner of the casino. I was surrounded, bombarded with questions, and very soon, they were filming me—filming us, me and the children. I had to show my hands, covered with bruises, my dirty and torn clothes. No, I didn't know what had happened. I knew nothing of the cause of the fire.

As often as I could, I sought Lavater's glance, and each time that glance sent me a perfectly clear message. One word was revolving tirelessly in my head: ACCIDENTAL. I knew, of course, I was absolutely convinced that the fire had been set, prepared, and very meticulously, too. Each of my actions had been foreseen. The guard I had seen on the screen was waiting for me behind the panel, in the drain ditch, certain that I would come out there as I fled with the children from the smoke and toxic fumes. Obviously, the accident theory was a sheer lie. But I stared at Marc and in those minutes replayed all the years when Lavater was constantly at my side, a model of loyalty and reliability. In one stroke, I invested all the confidence capital he had acquired.

"No, I have no reason to think that the cause of the fire was other than accidental."

Marc closed his eyes, looking infinitely relieved.

And I continued to answer the questions they asked me, under the eye of a roving lens, amid the clicking of cameras. Yes, I was in the bomb shelter when the smoke appeared, No, the children and I had never been in any danger, at any time. Since the shelter contained a number of emergency exits. Yes, of course, I was a little afraid, especially when, in my nervousness, I had turned the handles of the last reinforced panel the wrong way, but the mistake was quickly rectified. (It should be noted that Marc-Andrea and Heidi could not see the guard with the beams on the screen, and Marc had not noticed him either. I was therefore the only witness to his presence.)

In answering all those questions, I embroidered, automatically bringing attention back to myself. I took advantage of the free publicity that the occasion offered. I vaunted the merits of the Crystal Palace, the brilliant idea I'd had in conceiving of an antinuclear casino, the only one in the world. Yes, I was convinced that the hotel would soon be rebuilt and be even more beautiful, and that the millions of people who were impatiently awaiting its upcoming opening would not be disappointed. At most they would have to wait a month or two. Yes, "this charming little boy who isn't at all afraid" was my son, and this "charming young girl" was a friend of my son's.

Some twenty minutes later, in the car where Marc and I had taken refuge, in front of the cafeteria where Heidi and Marc-Andrea were stuffing themselves:

"Franz, I saw in your eyes that you understood, while they were interviewing you."

"I think I understood—the insurance."

"The insurance. The hotel is insured against fire. But let it be discovered that the fire was of a criminal origin, and the insurers, under the terms of the contract, won't pay. Even if you had been reduced to ashes, and the children along with you, that wouldn't change anything. It would have proved your innocence, or your clumsiness as an arsonist, that's all. The insurance company wouldn't pay."

"Marc, by removing those beams, by destroying the evidence they represented, and by persuading me not to mention the guard I saw over the television circuit, you're involving me in an insurance fraud!"

"You have no choice. I didn't have one, either. Those beams, the way they were placed, were damning. And anyway, there's something else."

At eleven forty—he was sure of the time, and Henry Chance, whose house he'd been at, would confirm it—Lavater received a phone call.

"The man who called me introduced himself as the head guard of the Crystal Palace. He supposedly had a message to give me from you. I was to come and meet you as soon as possible, here in this cafeteria. I left immediately. I had hardly entered the place when another phone call came from the same man. He said, and this is practically word for word, 'A fire has broken out at the Crystal Palace. Mr. Cimballi and the two children are at present trapped in the northwest corner of the garden, in one of the emergency exits of the bomb shelter, exit Number One. We think we can free them. Please come quickly.' He hung up before I could say a word. I rushed there and saw first Marc-Andrea and Heidi, then you, just as you were coming out."

"But you saw the guard? The one who removed the first beam and who probably put them all there?"

"I didn't see anything."

"Marc, that's impossible! Fifteen or twenty seconds elapsed between the moment he went away and the moment I saw you in front of me!"

"You can go far in twenty seconds. And he could have slipped behind a pillar of the ditch."

I was silently enraged.

Marc said, "They weren't trying to kill you, Franz. Everything was planned, down to the smallest details. They waited until you and the children were in the underground room. I don't know how they went about starting the fire."

"They may discover in the next few minutes that the fire was criminal. And my lie won't have served any purpose."

"We'll see. No, I think they were only trying to make you understand something."

"To keep my nose out of the late Baumer's life, for instance."

"Exactly. Think, they even took care to make me rush to the site."

"To prevent my telling the police."

"To prevent you from doing something stupid. Franz, everything went through my head very fast as soon as you mentioned that guard and those beams. I acted by reflex. I don't regret anything. If I had to do it over again, I would. This fire is going to cost millions. Without reimbursement from insurance, how are you going to pay? You'll have the Philadelphia bankers on your neck. We can convince them to stretch out the payments by a month or two, but that's all they'll agree to. You'll also have the Chinese to deal with. They're going to demand an accounting, insurer or no, reimbursement or no. You told me so yourself. At best, you'll only be financially dead. You have only one chance. Get the hotel going again, by any means. Even through an insurance fraud, and I know what I'm saying. In my life I've never committed the smallest crime."

"Me neither, shit!"

"Well, this will be our first crime. And if your conscience bothers you as much as mine does, there's no reason why you can't go to your insurers some day, tell them the truth, and pay them back. But for that you need the Crystal Palace, you need it intact, renovated, able to provide you with the means of being honest. It's your only chance, Franz, your only one. Otherwise you're cooked!"

I had no intention of making Marc Lavater bear the sole responsibility for what happened. Even though there's no doubt that Marc more or less forced me into that first false statement to the police that I hadn't noticed anything unusual. I had just gone through a terrible experience. I was nearly dumbstruck. I obeyed his order to keep quiet without at first understanding his motives. I obeyed him for the sake of the confidence I had in him.

But I could have revoked that initial lie. I could have explained that I'd been shocked, traumatized, who knows what else, and that now memories were coming back to me.

I didn't do it. Not in the hours that followed, nor in the days afterward. I continued to lie. And it was remarkably and ludicrously easy. Everything helped to convince me to back up my lie. The amount of damage, first of all. It was initially estimated at $100 million, then quickly figured at $150 million. Where would I get it? And the fact that the two children had been with me played its part. Who could imagine for one second that I had been anything other than an innocent victim of that fire?

After all, the only thing I had to do was tell the story as it had happened, simply leaving out the episode of the grinning guard I'd seen on the control screen and forgetting the whole business with the wooden beams. Heidi and my son had seen nothing. Their testimony confirmed my own, before television cameras and thus before tens of millions of viewers on the evening news. How could my statements be placed in doubt? In fact, I was sympathized with, pitied. The newspapers opened their columns to me. Our game of dice, our panic, our flight into that dramatic tunnel, the toxic fumes advancing in a compact mass as we retreated, all of this made great "human interest." The big innocent eyes of the two children, the humor and cheerfulness of Heidi, whose tongue had never been more agile, did the rest.

The advertising agency in charge of promoting the Crystal Palace phoned me to say that the effects of the adventure on the public were better than any campaign.

Sarah returned from Montego Bay on Monday the twenty-eighth, two days sooner than planned, anguished and mad with rage.

"Not on account of you, Cimballi. On account of the children. You could have been roasted alive, it wouldn't have made any difference to me."

"That's a nice way of putting it, Sarah."

"But your having dragged Anda and little Heidi into that insane episode and your filthy casino—that's beyond me!"

There followed a tongue-lashing, a tirade, in short, a bawling-out, in proportion to the fright she'd had. Eventually I got carried away myself—yet without telling her the truth. Perhaps because of that, above all because Marc and I feared that our enemies wouldn't rest there, the decision was made that Sarah, the Amazon, and the children would make the trip to visit to Li and Liu in San Francisco that had actually been planned for some time. (Marc-Andrea couldn't tolerate the New York winter, being accustomed to Jamaica, and the doctor had suggested a change of climate.) On March 1, Sarah took the little crowd away, it being understood that I would join them as soon as possible.

Events ran together with lightning speed after that.

First, on Wednesday, March 2, there was another visit from the representatives of the Austrian consulate general. They had seen the television and newspaper coverage, had recognized their national, and were alarmed. Moreover, they had shown up after I had had hours of consultation with the architects and the contractor who were supposed to get the Palace back in shape and was then in the middle of discussions with Caliban. A tense, cold Caliban. For him, the situation was clear. The fire that had ravaged the casino would delay the opening by two months, at least.

"It's a serious gap to overcome, Franz. Miranda isn't at all pleased."

"And I'm delighted, maybe?"

"Under the terms of our partnership contract, you're responsible for management of the casino. You and your assistants— Henry Chance and all of his staff, including the guards who were unable to prevent the fire."

"I can't be held responsible for an accident."

The dark eyes with their glittering pinpoints did not let me go.

"If it really was an accident, Franz. Which I hope it was for your sake and the sake of our friendship. For otherwise, if Miranda were to lose money on account of you . . . "

We were on the point of exchanging unfriendly glances when the Austrians from the consulate were announced, with God knows what papers. This was too much. I firmly and simply threw them out.

"Where is Heidi Moser, Mr. Cimballi?"

"That's my business!"

The next day, Thursday, March 3, a full day of nervous harassing discussions with the people from the insurance company, Getchell & Harkins New Jersey Insurance. I could do nothing else but take them head on, like a man who has nothing to reproach himself for.

"When will you pay?"

"As soon as our investigators have turned in their report."

And those same investigators, whom I had already met two days earlier, put me on the grill again, made me repeat my entire story. Plus there were new questions. Had I received threats of any kind? Did I have enemies who might have started the fire merely in order to injure me? Did I know competitors who might be inconvenienced by my casino? And so on. They knew everything about my former businesses and the means by which I had bought the hotel. (Except, of course, the two-stage payment—they didn't know about the second phase, the $15 million transferred to Curaçao). It took five to six hours of intense questioning before they finally decided to release the information I wanted. From their initial inspections, it appeared that the fire could—"Note the conditional, Mr. Cimballi, it's only a hypothesis"—could only be accidental. Which was tantamount to saying that they would then agree to reimburse $150 million, not to me, but to the Philadelphia Bank that had advanced $400 million. They even consented to tell me what, according to them, might be the origin of the disaster: one of the old slot machines stored in the subbasement, not very far from the entrance to the reinforced tunnel, could have been plugged in where it wasn't supposed to be, probably by a worker. Hence overload, hence short circuit. A spark might have fallen on the cut carpet, the fire might have spread to the elevator cages and the large vertical ventilation shafts, attacking the large cans of varnish and other synthetic pastes.

"In that case, Mr. Cimballi, it's entirely possible, even probable, that the fire started several hours before your arrival. It was smoldering."

"When will you pay?"

A vague answer. But I wasn't unaware that American insurers, unlike certain of their brethren in other countries, were fortunately inclined to settle their debts rapidly. They paid with marvelous promptitude, as soon as they were convinced that they could not do otherwise. They made me sign my statement and made Marc sign one, also, since he had been on the premises. (He explained that he was coming to get me for lunch and thus arrived at the site by accident. A lie that went unnoticed since help—police, guards, firemen, and onlookers—were just arriving when he entered the hotel compound. No one had paid attention to him in the midst of the crowd and general hubbub.)

They went away, leaving me alone with Lavater, Rosen, Vandenbergh, and Lupino, at once exhausted and optimistic.

"It's almost in the bag," Marc told me, looking me in the eyes.

At which point, the worst happened. The final turn of the screw. A telephone call on the evening of that same Thursday, March 3.

"Mr. Cimballi? James Olliphan. I think the time has come. We'll be waiting for you tomorrow, Friday, at ten o'clock, on the corner of Fifth Avenue and Fifty-fourth Street. No, not in front of the St. Regis, but on the other side, if you don't mind, at the entrance to the Gotham. Be there at ten o'clock sharp."

He wasn't asking for a meeting. He was summoning me. For that matter, his "I think the time has come" was enough to make everything clear to me. As did the peculiar tone of his voice. He wasn't alone when he dialed my number. And I could guess the identity of those who were with him.

21

A long black car, one man seated next to the chauffeur, another in back opened the door for me and had me seat myself between him and Olliphan. The car started up.

I said, "I can imagine the headlines tomorrow, in the *New York Times*, *Var-Matin Republique*, *Nice-Matin*, and *Le Meilleur*: ST. TROPEZ'S GREATEST FINANCIER KIDNAPPED ON 5TH AVENUE."

"And with his consent, besides," Olliphan remarked, smiling.

His green eyes shifted away from me to rest with emphasis on the man to my right, then on the one sitting next to the chauffeur, who hadn't even turned his head when I climbed in and maintained a dense silence. Olliphan's warning was clear. "Watch what you say in front of these two." And perhaps also, "Cimballi, don't think of bringing up other subjects than the purpose of our meeting today. Don't even think, for instance, of mentioning Korber's name or of telling me about your trip to South Africa." (Which he surely must have known about, Olliphan, that is, by way of Korber.) But perhaps I had too much imagination. Especially since it was me Olliphan was looking at once more and continuing to smile at.

"For you do consent, don't you, Mr. Cimballi?"

"To the trip? It was my dream. I'd have come begging."

I was dead tired. In all, I hadn't slept an hour the previous night. Rosen and Lavater were still with me when Olliphan had called. Vandenbergh and Lupino had just left. We'd only been able to reach Vandenbergh, and I made him come back. And all together, through hours and hours, we had considered the unappealing features of the situation. It being understood that Olliphan's call, and the summons he had transmitted to me, were in the order of things. In fact, we were almost expecting it. And I knew already what Olliphan (and through him, the Caltanis) would say to me. That is, I was expecting an ultimatum which it would be quite impossible for me to refuse.

For the simple reason that, having lied to the insurance people, having even signed a false statement, I had perforce given Olliphan the rope with which to hang me. Such had been the conclusion of Rosen and Vandenbergh, Marc's also, all three of them equally appalled by the situation. I told them that I hadn't been hung yet. And even this morning, tired as I was, I continued to believe in my chances of extricating myself.

We would see.

We saw. The car had headed north, up Manhattan, across the Bronx onto the New England Thruway toward New Rochelle. We passed the exits for New Rochelle, Larchmont, and Mamaroneck, where I remembered having gone sailing with the Rosens. To my left, Olliphan filled up the silence with a monologue in his pleasant, cultured voice. He talked about himself, leaving nothing out—his childhood memories, his youthful ambition to become a concert violinist, his discovery that he didn't have enough talent and would have had to content himself with playing in an orchestra. And then, as time went on—perhaps to prevent me from talking—he came around to discussing Cimballi, what he had read in the newspapers about that interesting character, from my triumphant I AM HAPPY, when I defeated Martin Yahl financially for the first time, to those famous commercial spots on American television screens, in the not-so-distant time when I was up to my neck in the coffee deal.

"I must say you're anything but a conventional financier, Mr. Cimballi. Sometimes I wonder, do you really take finance seriously?"

"As much as you do."

He broke into laughter.

"That says it all."

My tension was rising. It increased when the car finally left the highway near the small town of Harrison. We were now on a small road, charming enough, bordered by luxurious private properties. We turned into one of those properties. The house—of stone, not wood, which was unusual—was at the very end of a long driveway, behind a thick curtain of trees and bushes. Two other cars had arrived before ours. Two men were cooling their heels, marking time. They followed us with eyes that expressed nothing.

"This way, please."

Three of us got out—the three of us who had occupied the back seat. But only Olliphan and I entered the house, whose door was opened for us by what was obviously a chief bodyguard, with eyes like a rat, a blue beard, and charcoal eyebrows. I gave him a big smile.

"Hired killer or tap dancer?"

The rat's eyes went over me without appearing to see me, while Olliphan gave me a charming smile of friendly reproach.

"Come now, Mr. Cimballi."

We entered the house and were in a vast living room decorated by a monumental basalt fireplace. Most of the furniture was covered with cloths. Two men were waiting for us. I had never met them, but I had seen photos of them and recognized them instantly—Joseph, known as Joe, and Larry Caltani, wearing their fleshy Sicilian faces over worsted wool suits that were worth their weight in bank notes. The Caltanis greeted me with a simple motion of their heads. You could tell how much warmth I inspired in them. They had me sit in an armchair in front of a small, roll-up home-movie screen. It was almost the same as what had happened to me in Macao. But physically, I preferred Miranda.

The curtains were drawn over the bay windows looking out on the grounds. The projector was turned on. It was the Caltanis, and they alone, who conducted the discussion that followed. Olliphan took no part in it, confining himself to watching the scene as a silent observer, his green Irish eyes lit up, as usual, in the gloom. Ditto for the beady-eyed carbonaro, the fifth man in the room.

"Look, Cimballi."

As the pictures began to roll, I understood that the filmmaker must have been stationed at a window in one of the buildings adjoining the Crystal Palace (but not in the Caltanis' casino). He had operated at a distance, using a telephoto lens to get a view from above, from top to bottom. A wide shot of the ditch, where three of the emergency exits of the bomb shelter ended. Then, a close-up of each of those exits, giving a clear view of the beams driven into the ground which blocked the opening of the panels.

"End of the first series, Cimballi. Here's the second."

Marc Lavater was the star. You saw him running into the Crystal Palace compound, running toward the hotel, away from the crowd that was beginning to form, consisting of the Crystal Palace's armed guards, bystanders, and police. He headed straight for the ditch. He removed one beam, dragged it away, lifted it with a violent thrust of his whole body, and threw it into the distance. He ran back, repeated the operation with a second beam.

207

"Third series, Cimballi. The best one."

The pictures, the following pictures, were in close-up on the emergency exit Number One, the one I had used. You saw the panel blocked by a beam, and, immediately afterward, the same panel (but the beam had disappeared), the same panel opening, Lavater was in the shot, his back turned but clearly identifiable. You saw my hands, helping Marc-Andrea, then Heidi to jump down. You recognized me when I pulled myself out through the emergency exit, when I began to address Marc. A specialist could probably reconstruct the first words of our conversation by reading our lips.

But the film ended abruptly at the instant when I was about to tell Marc about the guard.

The latter at no time appeared in the picture. Thus, owing to the way the film had been edited, it clearly looked as if Marc had acted alone, had removed the three beams and thus saved our lives, the children's and mine.

The carbonaro drew the curtains again and light returned.

"What do you think of it, Cimballi?"

Joe Caltani's voice was very soft, a bit husky, and in no way unpleasant. I tried to catch Olliphan's gaze but the lawyer was strictly expressionless.

I answered, "An excellent film. I especially appreciated the quality of the editing. A great director is first and foremost a great editor. Hitchcock said so."

But I couldn't go on making jokes forever. I shrugged.

"The way you present them, these pictures prove almost beyond a doubt that someone tried to kill me and the children who were with me. And without Lavater's very timely intervention, his going right to the emergency exit without worrying about the fire, all three of us would have been asphyxiated."

"They also prove something else."

"When you see Lavater's behavior, not worrying about the fire, you might think that Lavater was expecting the fire, that he and I are accomplices, that we're aiming for arsonists' credentials. That's not all."

It wasn't the easiest thing I'd ever done in my life, but I managed a smile.

"They also proved that I lied, and Lavater ditto, to the police and reporters."

"And to the insurance company."

I nodded. A short silence.

"Last question, Cimballi" (Joe Caltani pronounced my name "Chim-bah-li," Italian-style, an idea that had never occurred to me). "What would happen if this information got into the hands of your insurance company's investigators?"

"I'd like a cup of coffee," I said. "No milk, please. It's fattening."

A head signal. The carbonaro went off toward what I assumed was the kitchen.

"Cimballi, if this document gets into the hands of your insurance company, your chances of being reimbursed for the 150 million in damages are zero. Right?"

"Right."

"You might even go to jail, Cimballi. You and Lavater."

However prepared I may have been for this interview, it was nonetheless one of the worst moments of my life. It was a hard pill to swallow. I smiled.

"That's a very plausible hypothesis."

The carbonaro, as warm and friendly as ever, returned with the coffee. I tasted it. Absolutely nauseating. It wasn't my day, that was for sure. I put down the stoneware mug.

"And how much is all of this going to cost me?"

Fifty-one percent of the Crystal Palace shares.

No more, no less.

Oddly, I felt almost relieved. I was expecting even more outrageous demands, and the worst thing was that these gentlemen had the means of getting what they asked. I'll explain.

On Sunday, February 27, 1977, when I arrived at the Crystal Palace with Marc-Andrea and Heidi, I felt I had no reason to fear a violent reaction from the Caltanis. Lavater's inquiry on Baumer had irritated them, of course, but as the results Marc obtained were fairly meager—the fact that I hadn't acted proved that—they had calmed down in the end. That had been the Englishman's opinion, and I concurred. The only danger I was courting, then, had to do with the Englishman's new investigation. But I was sure of his absolute discretion.

Yet the Caltanis had reacted, in their brutal fashion. They hadn't tried to kill me, that was clear. If that guard (who wasn't part of the team of six hired by Chance) had come to free me after placing the beams there himself, it could only be by order of the Italian-Americans. Conclusion: they had wanted to frighten me, delay the opening of a rival casino, and, above all, urge us to mind our own business and forget about Baumer.

That had been Marc's and my analysis on Sunday evening. We had wracked our brains to try to understand what might have motivated this dramatic warning. Without success. We hadn't seen what was staring us in the face, and what I would understand only much later. Furthermore, we had made the mistake of not closely examining the reasons for the two phone calls Lavater had received. Why, in such a meticulously calculated plan, had they taken the trouble to make Marc rush to the scene? And not just anywhere. Precisely in front of exit Number One. It took us twenty-four hours to find the answer. And even then, accident had played a part. The CBS reporters had arrived on the scene barely a few minutes after the fire broke out (it was mere coincidence that they were in Atlantic City). The cameramen had taken acres of film, no doubt overjoyed by the windfall. It's not every day you can get a burning casino on film. But on Monday, I suddenly had cold chills down my spine. What if, by evil luck, Lavater had also been filmed in the process of removing the beams? I viewed the film in New York and was reassured. Marc was nowhere to be seen in it. But suddenly, I had a hunch. "Marc, the Caltanis must have photographed you removing the beams. That's even the reason they made you come, brought you down there!" From that point on, imagining what was going to happen was simple. Sooner or later, Olliphan or the Caltanis would call me to set up an appointment at which they would dictate to me the terms of total surrender.

But it was one thing to understand the workings of the trap I had fallen into and another thing to find a way of protecting myself, especially permanently. For the time being, drinking that dreadful coffee, I hadn't found it.

I said, "I'd have a hard time selling you 51 percent of the shares. I only have fifty."

"You'll have to convince your Chinese partners."

Joe Caltani's tone was calm as ever. He didn't threaten, he was talking business, he was making me "an offer I couldn't refuse." Olliphan had changed places. Only a few moments before, he had been sitting on my right. I only had to turn my head a little to see him. Now he was seated in a chair behind me, so as to make me understand—I'm completely outside this matter, my role was limited to bringing you here.

"Let's assume," I said to Joe Caltani. "Let's assume I give in to your blackmail."

"You have no choice."

"If those photos go to the insurance company, I'll certainly be in a lot of trouble. But I won't be the only one. My insurers will give the film to the police, who'll reopen the investigation, assuming it's been closed or will be closed someday. The criminal arson theory will be definitely confirmed. It's you, Caltani, who started the fire. I'll shout it from the roof tops. Sooner or later, they'll find the evidence."

The two brothers stared at me, blank faced. My threat left them cold. To tell the truth, they looked as if they didn't give a damn. I was sure that the real arsonists must not have been amateurs. After all, the insurance company investigators seemed to have been fooled already.

I continued, "Furthermore . . ."

And I stopped short, as though struck by lightning. I had been about to brandish the threat of revealing all about the Baumer affair. But it was absolutely out of the question that I make the slightest reference to the inquiry the Englishman had carried out once before, which I had asked him to reopen, centering this time on Walcher and Olliphan. I'd be risking my hide. If I had the slightest chance of getting myself out of this trap, it depended on two factors—the Englishman's searches and any action I could undertake against Olliphan by way of the South-African connection. In both cases, I had to keep silent.

Keep silent. The two Caltanis stared at me, surprised by my sudden immobility. Behind me, I heard Olliphan get up and walk around the room. He entered my field of vision, went to one of the bay windows and became engrossed in looking at the grounds. I wondered if he had understood what was going through my mind. I had the strange, inexplicable hunch that he had.

"Yes, Cimballi?"

The question came from Joe Caltani. I was still unable to utter a word, and it was probably the first time in my life that had happened to me. I realized how I must look, my mouth open, frozen in my chair, my hands trembling. To try to get a grip on myself, I also rose and walked around the room, like someone who's choking with rage and having murderous impulses. I went back and forth in front of the rat-eyed carbonaro in total silence. And, as always at the most unexpected moments, it was like a blinding intuition in a chess game that makes you see eight or nine moves ahead, so sharp and fleeting, however, that it sometimes takes hours or days to trace it back to its source. I could have yelled, for I had barely sensed it when it nearly escaped me, and I had to struggle harshly to keep it on the surface of my thoughts.

I controlled myself, more or less. I turned to face those men who were looking at me.

I said, in a low voice, "Okay. I'll try to convince my Chinese partners to sell me back their shares."

"Trying isn't enough."

"I'll need a little time. Obviously, I'll have to go to Macao."

"Two weeks."

"A month."

"It's March 4. You have until the twentieth."

Something fantastic was happening inside me. At the same time that I negotiated bitterly, that embryo of an idea that had suddenly emerged continued to run through my head, both fantastically seductive and extremely childish by turns.

"A month. March 31, at least. Not before. I need time to convince the Chinese . . ." (I was improvising) ". . . and also because I have to—*we* have to wait for the insurance company's report. If it refuses to reimburse the damages, there'll be nothing more to buy, the Crystal Palace won't be able to operate without additional financing of 150 million, which I don't have and neither do you."

That last statement was only a guess on my part. At that time, I had only rather incomplete information on the Caltanis' real financial resources. I knew that in order to finance their casino, they had made use, as I had, of a bank loan for some $300 million. That didn't prove they were broke.

Joe Caltani consulted his brother with a look.

What he saw must have convinced him, for he said, "Okay. Wednesday, March 30, at noon."

"On condition that by then, the insurers have agreed to the reimbursement."

"Okay."

Silence again. Olliphan, still looking at the grounds, coughed slightly. That may have been some signal, for Joe Caltani continued, "We're businessmen, Cimballi. Respectable businessmen. We're going to pay you for what you're selling us. We'll assume our share of the debt to the Philadelphia bank, and we'll pay you 51 million for the 51 percent we're buying from you."

It was too good to be true.

And of course, it wasn't true. For he added, "At least, $51 million will be the amount entered on the deed of sale. For we won't consider the transaction complete until you've retransferred thirty of those millions to us at a Panama bank whose address we'll give you. After all, we have to make a profit, Mr. Cimballi."

I was rising in status, here they were calling me "Mister." But that promotion didn't hide the truth. All in all, I would receive $21 million for 51 percent of the Casino's shares. And that was assuming I could first succeed in buying back from Miranda what I wasn't at all sure she wanted to part with. And if I didn't wind up with a big knife a foot long between my shoulder blades, I would have the pleasure of losing $30 million (and more, for I'd have to pay off Macao). Things were getting better every minute. I raised my hand.

"I accept, on three conditions."

"No conditions."

I made a gesture to get up and leave the house.

"Fine. In that case, send the film to whomever you like. I'm ready to be blackmailed, but only up to a point. That point is reached."

Silence. I wasn't bluffing. I was really ready to break off the negotiation—if you could call it that. Larry Caltani, the smarter of the two brothers, it seemed to me, asked, in an even softer and huskier voice than his older brother's, "What would those conditions be?"

"One—the transfer will take place in two stages. First, on March 30, or forty-eight hours at the latest after the insurance company has given a favorable report, I will transfer to you forty-nine . . . "

"We said fifty-one."

"You'll get it eventually. I'll transfer you the additional 2 percent."

"When?"

"Three months to the day after the Crystal Palace goes into operation."

"One month."

"Two."

"Okay."

"So much for my first condition. I said there were three. Here's the second one. I want that film, and any copy of it that may have been made, deposited this very day in the safety vault of a bank of your choice, so long as it's a real bank. That vault will be sealed in my presence and can only be opened in the simultaneous presence of myself and either one of you or one of your representatives. Naturally, from this second as I'm speaking to you, we won't part from one another until that film is safe."

Olliphan's voice, his back still turned to us. "That type of vault, no matter what arrangements you make, can always be opened by a court order issued by a judge."

"I know."

"And there may be other copies hidden."

"I'll take that risk. I don't believe you went to the trouble of having other copies made. Did you?"

"The answer would be no, in any event," Larry Caltani softly remarked. He was immediately followed by Olliphan, who spoke as he faced the wintry landscape of the grounds.

"And our clients will merely have to file a complaint against you, especially if they're the hotel's shareholders, in order for that vault to be opened by the police and for the documents it contains to be handed over to the court."

By God, Olliphan's helping me! I knew it!

I said, "So your clients are risking nothing by agreeing to my request."

"Correct."

A pause.

Larry Caltani: "But why put them in a vault? Mr. Cimballi, the mere fact that we become your partners guarantees you against those documents reappearing on account of us."

"I don't want that film to get lost, whatever happens. And I also want that film, as well as the copies that may be found between now and then, destroyed in my presence the day I assign you the additional 2 percent. As for my third condition . . ."

My hands were sweaty.

"I want the transfer deed for the first 49 percent, as well as the pledge of sale I'll sign for you on that March 30, for the last 2

214

percent, I want all those documents to be antedated February 25, 1977. The twenty-fifth because on the twenty-fourth and previous days I was outside the United States."

"The twenty-fifth was two days before the fire."

"Exactly. In that way, I'll be assured that those films, or this film if there's only one, will never reappear on account of you."

Silence. I didn't dare look toward Olliphan, who kept his back turned to us. I wondered to what extent he guessed what I was up to. I would have been extremely surprised if he had. I didn't entirely know myself.

I added, "What are you afraid of? You tell me you don't mean to use that film if I give in to your terms, and on the other hand you seem absolutely convinced that the insurance company will never uncover the criminal origin of the fire."

Silence again.

Olliphan's voice: "I'd like to speak with my clients, Mr. Cimballi. Out of your hearing."

My pulse must have been close to a hundred fifty, but I did my best to appear in control.

"I'd like that film removed from the projector."

The carbonaro obeyed at a sign from Joe Caltani. He placed it in a box which he laid on a coffee table.

I said to Olliphan, "Okay, talk with your clients. On condition that you remain where I can see you and have no contact with anyone else. For instance, you could go outside, and I'll stay warm and watch you, with this paragon standing over me."

I indicated the carbonaro. Olliphan and the two Caltanis went out to the yard at the back of the house, off about sixty feet, and began to talk. I heard nothing, of course. At no time, respecting my request, did they seem about to leave the path where I had a good view of them and made no attempt to contact the other men, bodyguards and chauffeurs, who were in front of the house. Behind me, without even needing to turn around, I sensed the carbonaro's iron gaze. It wasn't a pleasant sensation. I believed him entirely capable of putting a bullet in my neck if I took it into my head to touch the film.

As the minutes went by, my pulse reached a record speed. Joe Caltani gesticulated and talked, though I couldn't make out any of the words he uttered. He almost always had his back to me, and I couldn't even read his lips, something I would be incapable of doing anyway. Larry, his brother, spoke less frequently. Olliphan talked more, his face blank, in profile from where I stood.

I was afraid.

One of the major pawns I was playing was Olliphan, or, more precisely, his attitude at that moment. The conditions I had placed on my acceptance of the Caltanis' ultimatum did not conceal any trap. For the time being. Mainly because I wasn't yet able to concoct a trap. I hadn't even imagined it, didn't know what it might be, knew still less if it might exist one day. But I knew that nothing would be possible for me if my enemies did not accede to my arguments. And I needed Olliphan not to contradict me. Twenty or thirty minutes passed. Finally, the three men came back toward me. I had promised myself to not look the green-eyed lawyer in the face, but it was too much for me. As soon as he crossed the glass door, I stared at him, and what I thought I could read on his face almost made me lose my nerve, or what was left of it.

"Okay, Mr. Cimballi. We agree."

With one small change, or better, with an additional precaution on their part. The film would be placed in a cardboard box. That box would be deposited in a bank vault, which could only be opened in the simultaneous presence of two persons. I would be one, but the other would be neither one of the Caltanis nor Olliphan. The Caltanis had chosen a certain Kowalski, Peter Kowalski. I fully understood the purpose of the maneuver. The Caltanis would not appear in any way. If one day, for any reason, the film came to light and into the hands of the police, the Caltanis could claim they had never heard of it. And thus, they would have a chance to get back at me legally.

"And where is this Kowalski?"

"We're going to call him in your presence. And you'll go with him to deposit the box in the vault."

I gave my consent. Once again, I checked the film to make sure it was the right one. I placed it in the box and secured the box with adhesive tape.

Olliphan: "You may keep the box with you, Mr. Cimballi. Until you deposit it with the bank.

"I'm honored that you trust me."

But, obviously, they didn't mean to take their eyes off me. I wondered if one or more copies existed or not. In their place, I'd have made them.

216

As for my other conditions, they accepted them. What part Olliphan had played in that acceptance, I didn't know. But my conviction was firm. He had pushed the Caltanis to grant what I was asking. Exactly as I had hoped he would. My major pawn had performed to my complete satisfaction.

I thought about those conditions they had agreed to. On March 30, in twenty-six days, assuming that in the meantime the insurance company had given the green light to repayment of the $150 million, I would assign 49 percent of my own shares in the Crystal Palace to a front company. In the meantime, I would have to show proof of having bought the shares from the Chinese in Macao. And on that March 30, I would also sign an irrevocable pledge of sale for another two percent, which sale was to take place two months to the day after the opening of the Casino. The transfer deed and irrevocable sale pledge would be antedated, they would in fact be fully valid as of February 25. And the day my sale pledge was executed, the box would be withdrawn from the vault and destroyed along with the film it contained in the physical presence of the Caltanis and myself.

It was clear. Even though no trap was visible, the Caltanis would probably have refused to bargain if Olliphan had not, for a reason I didn't yet know, played my game.

While I was at it, I might have concocted some adventurous plan to recover the film before it was deposited in the bank. I could have sent in a mercenary squad, the Salvation Army, or something else equally ridiculous. But they hadn't given me an opportunity, and anyway, it was possible other copies were floating around. In that case, my life wouldn't have mattered much to the Caltanis!

Actually, there was another reason I didn't try anything, the true one. I didn't give a fig about that film. Provided, of course, that my insurers didn't get hold of it!

The car that had taken me to Harrison brought me back to Manhattan. Olliphan didn't make the return trip with me. I was treated to the company of just three men, a chauffeur and two others who flanked me on the back seat, one of them the carbonaro.

On the sidewalk in front of the entrance to the bank, two other men were waiting for us. One of them introduced himself as Pete Kowalski. He and I entered the bank, followed by the carbonaro who kept a hand in the right pocket of his overcoat.

But maybe he was only holding a pipe. The formalities were quickly dispatched. Ten minutes later, we were outside again.

"Good-bye, Mr. Cimballi."

In a few seconds, I was alone again. The first bar I passed was good enough. I went in to have a drink, not usually a habit of mine, but the circumstances were not exactly ordinary. But the whiskey didn't calm the fluttering of my stomach. If the truth be known, I was in a kind of weird exalted state in which quite a few feelings were mingled—fear, of course, but also a cold elation and an uncommon ferocity. I had just been subjected, and had had to give in, to the most deliberate, the most coldly cynical blackmail. It had been laid out and executed with something like courtesy. "We're respectable businessmen, Mr. Cimballi," Joe Caltani had said.

Okay.

I had been stung to the highest degree, there was no other word for it. But during those few seconds when I had remained mute, silenced, frozen under the slightly surprised stares of the "respectable businessmen," a lightning bolt had flashed through me, through my little gray cells. It wasn't yet a shield. Not THE shield. At best, an embryonic idea. Which I would now have to develop and, if possible, bring to term, assuming it were viable.

Then we would see who had stung whom.

5. He Who Stings Last Stings Best

22

In all good adventure movies, there always comes a scene, during the seconds, minutes or, better yet, the nights leading up to the final big battle, whether the evil Indians are preparing to attack, or the hero has to lay siege to some inaccessible and particularly impregnable fortress, when you see the hero sweetly and calmly giving the heroine a hug. Under the moonlight or against a sunset.

Sarah chuckled.

"And that's me, the heroine?"

"You, Marc-Andrea, and Heidi. It's a triple role."

I had left New York in a whirlwind on the first plane to California on the evening of March 3, several hours after my summit meeting with the Caltanis. It was, among other reasons, the best way to avoid endless discussions with Lavater, Rosen, Lupino, and Vandenbergh. I had confined myself to a brief telephone call to let them know I had nothing to tell them. They hardly appreciated my terseness. It even worried them.

"Let me have a few days," I had said.

Sarah gazed at me.

"Are things all that bad, Franz?"

"They could be worse. I could have metastasized cancer, Heidi could have fractured the shin of the president of the United States, Marc-Andrea could have an earache, and you could decide to enter a convent."

"The convent can wait," she said. "Come and make love to me, my pet. It's good for what ails you."

I obeyed, and she was right that it would relax me. So much

so that I repeated it at regular intervals over the following three days, doing nothing else except taking walks through San Francisco with my Irishwoman and the children. Li and Liu, with whom we were staying, were away. They were in France, Monaco, actually, trying out their latest invention, an underwater forklift, an outlandish contraption with which you could take samplings of the ocean depths in order to recover the precious metals which litter the ocean floor, as everyone knows.

"Franz, do you know how much gold there is in the sea, in colloidal suspension alone?" they were to ask me. "About nine million tons!"

"Nutty Chinks, are you going to sift all the oceans? You expect to get rich that way?"

"We're already rich, pal, we're as rich as can be. We just want to have some fun."

They returned to San Francisco on March 7. Just in time, for I was beginning to get bored waiting for them. For me, the advantage of coming to California, besides enabling me to rejoin my little family, was that it allowed me a little breathing space. I wanted to be alone to work out my embryonic idea at leisure. In other circumstances, I would have fled to St. Tropez. The house where I was born, La Capilla, was the only place in the world where I really felt at home. The prohibition against my crossing a border with Heidi had prevented me from going there, and I was less willing than ever to part from her. Thus, I had to be satisfied with San Francisco, but, all things considered, I had made the best use of this respite, far from my counselors who would probably have knocked themselves out to show me I was irredeemably crazy. I had developed the embryonic idea. I had made something of it that, seen from a distance and in a thick fog, almost resembled a shield against the blackmail to which I'd been subjected. Li and Liu were among the first persons to whom I revealed my plan. And for good reason—I needed them desperately. I explained my plans.

Silence.

They weren't laughing in the least.

A moment before, with that delirious humor that was theirs alone, they had been giving me a demonstration of their goddamn whale-lift machine, which resembled both a cricket and a Model T with the engine removed and replaced by pedals. They explained that by the mere fact of rivers and streams flowing into the sea, there was a yearly accumulation of 3.5 billion tons of various minerals, which had been going on since the world began, a rather long time. And they further showed me that with at most 600 million machines identical to theirs, it would take no more than seven or eight billion years to become the kings of all existing minerals, not to mention those that weren't known yet.

They were no longer laughing. Their clowning stopped at once. Within a second, they turned back into the cold and methodical businessmen they knew how to be when circumstances demanded it. (The two of them were worth almost 300 million.)

"It won't work, Franz. It's the most vicious scheme . . ." Shaking their heads, "Too vicious, in fact. It won't work."

"It's my only chance, don't you agree?"

"Drop it. Sell your 50 percent of the Crystal Palace to the Caltanis, take the 20 million they're offering you, and get the hell out."

"I'd rather croak. And anyway, those sons of bitches want fifty-one, not fifty. They're not stupid. They want me to get the Chinese out of the game before they get into it themselves. No, I don't have a choice. And you'll have to help me convince Miranda. You know her, she'll listen to you, and maybe she won't have me chopped to pieces right away."

"Or else we'll all be swimming in the China Sea along with the sharks. Franz, even assuming that Miranda can be convinced, if there's the slightest hitch in your crazy plan, you'll wind up a minority shareholder in the Crystal Palace and the Caltanis will be the majority. On top of that, they'll have 100 percent of the casino next door. It's easy to guess what they'll do—combine the two establishments in one, of which you'll have only a little less than one-quarter of the shares. From then on, they'll bleed you dry. Between repayments to the banks and all the new investments they'll be sure to make, you won't touch a single penny of profits for thirty years. Liquidated, Cimballi."

Did they think they were telling me something new? I had never held any illusions about the fate the Respectable Businessmen had in store for me.

I said, "One more reason to try something else. Those guys stung me, I want to sting them back like nobody's business. And I think I've found a way to do it."

To understand the reasons that would impel Li and Liu to take part in the highly acrobatic *combinazione* I was proposing to them, it was necessary to realize that I had known the two Chinese from San Francisco from the beginning, mine and theirs. At one time, I had done them a favor that had almost cost me dearly. They had built the better part of their present wealth on the $60 million my natural honesty had handed them on a platter. When I found myself in a desperate situation two years before, they hadn't been able to help me, their hands tied by the investments they had just made. That was no longer true now. They had ample means with which to come to my aid. But never mind the sincere friendship between us. In the jungle of finance, friendship isn't listed on the exchange. Although, sometimes—they cared for me a great deal and felt themselves somewhat indebted to me. But, knowing them as I did, I tended to believe that in the final analysis, it was the very outlandishness, not to say the madness, of my plan that seduced them.

For they nodded their heavenly heads and said, "The first thing to do is to talk with that dwarf, Miranda's cousin. What's his name again?"

Caliban. Who met us in San Francisco on March 8, with his blond wife inevitably at his side. He was nervous, suspicious, and worried at the same time. Over the last few days, he had seen the team of investigators from the insurance company at work, combing through the more or less ashy ruins of the hotel, with fantastic attention to detail. And when I told him the truth, that the fire was indeed arson, that I had the proof, and that, unfortunately, I was not the only one who had it, and finally, that I was—we were—in one hell of a mess, his face, already rather grim, became downright ferocious.

"I knew something was up. These last few days you weren't acting normal. I let Miranda know. And it is about time you set me straight, I was beginning to lose patience."

Incredible, the sense of danger this little man could arouse! Good God, I was really in a fine mess, stuck between a Caliban and his Chinese bosses on the right, and the Caltanic killers on the left! It was still six months to my twenty-eighth birthday—if I lived that long—but no question about it, when it came to getting myself into innumerable scrapes, I kept setting records!

"You should have let me know right away," the Corsican-

Chinese dwarf continued. "I represent the half-owners. I count as much as you!"

It took me two full hours of vehement discussions to appease his rage. There had been two times when we almost came to a final break, meaning his immediate departure for Macao to incite a mass uprising against Cimballi. Fortunately, each time, Li and Liu's intervention succeeded in bringing the dwarf and me back to the negotiating table, on the strength of arguments in Chinese of which I understood not one iota.

And I again saw Caliban sitting in an armchair, his tiny legs folded under him, as always. He called Macao and spoke interminably. Behind him, through the bay window, the red silhouette of the Golden Gate Bridge was shrouded in an ever-shifting mist. Caliban, having finally spent all his rage, asked me to repeat for him once more the smallest details and necessary stages of my future plan of attack. He never interrupted me, remained strictly impassive, never took his eyes off me. I had finished. He was silent for a few dozen seconds more and when he finally decided to open his mouth, spoke Chinese. Li and Liu answered him in the same tongue, their discussion going on at length.

Finally, I remarked sourly, "I can do without dubbing if I have to, but I'd appreciate subtitles, at least."

The next day, March 9, twenty-one days from my first deadline—when I would have to assign 49 percent of my own shares to the Caltanis—I flew to Hong Kong. Not alone. Two-and-a-half Chinese were with me. Li and Liu were on the trip, but I could hardly count Caliban as a whole Chinese. After all, his father was Corsican.

A new round with Miranda, in Macao. In every sense of the term. First, because I had to present to her, my third audience in a row, the detailed phases of my strategy, outlined first for Li and Liu, then Caliban. I was beginning to know my speech by heart, and I embellished it with additional explanations, even anecdotes. It was like the Arabian Nights. And Miranda, dressed all in black (as though already in mourning for me), listened with extreme impassiveness.

A new round because next, after my new presentation, I was treated to the same interminable chatter in Chinese. Except now there were four of them, exchanging ideas in Cantonese. Except now it lasted an hour and a half, not the few minutes it had in San Francisco. Except now while I was still worried about Caliban's possible reactions, I was actually in deep anguish waiting for Miranda's comments.

I was scared. It was one of those moments when you sense intuitively that everything will be decided in an instant.

Apparently, they had all but forgotten my existence. All of a sudden four pairs of almond-shaped eyes turned and stared at me. And then I saw an expression that I knew well appear in Li and Liu's eyes. It wasn't long in coming—helpless laughter overtook them. And that wasn't the biggest surprise—there was Caliban, overcome by hilarity as well.

They laughed till they cried. But Li (or Liu, who knows) told me all the same, between two convulsions, "Cimballi, he got some clazy head on his shoulder. In other words, my dear Franz, you're probably more Chinese than any of us. We've just taken a vote—we decided to write to Peking to ask them to naturalize you."

Finally, she stood up.

"Would you please follow me, Mr. Cimballi?"

I desperately looked for some indication of what was waiting for me, but Li and Liu's faces were totally sealed. As for Caliban, he was smiling blankly, dark red lips on very white, sharp teeth. His smiling meant absolutely nothing. I had seen him in Atlantic City go into a rage at a trainee croupier who was trying to show off his virtuosity in handling dice. Caliban had begun by smiling, then he lashed the man's face, in an incredibly swift movement, with a razor-sharp blow of his fingernail. It took three men to calm him down, and a heavy price had to be paid to get the croupier kicked out.

"This way, please."

The door closed on the three men who had come with me from San Francisco. I wasn't alone with Miranda, however. Two or three of the girl bodyguards had appeared and surrounded me. An isolation maneuver, after which we found ourselves in the bedroom.

"Sit down, make yourself at home."

I sat on the edge of the bed; Miranda lay down. Other bodyguards appeared, bringing the total to five. It was a mobilization. Working in teams, they began undressing Miranda and me. They finished in record time.

"That's the advantage of being a woman, Cimballi. What better time to discuss business with a man than when he's making love to you?"

I didn't have the slightest idea what Li and Liu might have said in Chinese about my plans and my chances of carrying it off. There were supposed to explain—I gave a start on the bed. Not content with having stripped me naked, the bodyguard ladies were making advances!

"The main thing," said Miranda, "is to put your partner in a weak position. In a business discussion, that's crucial."

CONCENTRATE, CIMBALLI! Let's see, where was I? I was telling myself that Li and Liu must have explained what they knew of my past, maybe even offered their own guarantees . . ."

This time, if I didn't jump, it wasn't because I didn't feel like it. But I had every reason in the world to remain motionless, absolutely so. For suddenly, some of the five lasses were holding minute silk slipknots and others had razor knives—all instruments used by Chinese barbers in a high wind. And, punctuating each motion with kisses and gentle pats, they began to shave that part of my anatomy where it would certainly had never occurred to me to use a blade.

"Let's see," said Miranda. "The best thing is to go over everything from the beginning. You're going to explain to me again, not why I should sell you my shares, but how you expect to compensate me for giving up a deal that, in spite of this fire . . ."

Chinese barbers love to use silk slipknots to pull out their customers' hair. All you have to do is encircle the hair as close as possible to the skin, tighten the knot, and give a short tug. It almost works if you're nearly beardless. I wasn't. In that place even less than everywhere else. And the razors that the others were using to perform a kind of harvest, like reaping wheat, dissuaded me from jumping.

"It would be better if you don't squirm too much, Cimballi," said a naked Miranda, kissing me. "And let's talk business. So you're buying my shares . . ."

"That's it, exactly."

"On what date?"

"February 23. Because the deed of sale to the Caltanis will be antedated to the 25."

She kissed me and caressed me affectionately.

"Don't wriggle so much, an accident can happen so fast, with those razors. And how much are you paying for my shares?"

"Sixty million."

"So I'm already making ten million?"

"Right. In addition, I'll pay your share of the profits, if there are any, in the first two months that the casino's in operation . . ."

While speaking, I followed—when Miranda wasn't kissing me—the razors' movements.

". . . after deducting the payments to the Philadelphia bank figured over fifty months."

"You think there'll be profits in those first two months, Cimballi?"

"Frankly, no."

"So for only ten million, I'm supposed to give up a deal I helped set up and that promises to be very fruitful?"

"There's the second part of my plan. Which will bring you infinitely larger profits."

"If it ever comes to pass. If you're still alive to put it to work."

"I'll do my best. To remain alive, especially."

"I'm going to accept, Cimballi. To refuse would force me to contend with the Caltanis myself. I may do it one day, especially if they win out over you. Kiss me, please, you don't seem very enthusiastic. I'm going to accept for that first reason, and also because your friends from San Francisco seem to think you're entirely capable of bringing off such a ridiculous operation."

A razor mysteriously appeared in Miranda's hand. She placed it against my throat. The girls moved away. *Are they going to stand there and watch?*

"Kiss me, Cimballi. No, I don't intend to let go of this razor. I have too much of a desire to use it. Without your friends from San Francisco, you'd already be dead. Kiss your ex-partner. Better than that, better than that, please. There. You see, you can when you want to."

It was simple. Well, almost.

Forced to submit to the Caltanis' blackmail, I had to give up 51 percent of the casino's shares for $21 million.

To do that, I had to buy back Miranda's shares. And buy *all* of them back. For two reasons—because the Caltanis had demanded that I be the only one in the deal with them by March 30, to the exclusion of any other partner who might prove too curious, and because (obviously, the Caltanis' didn't know about

228

this second reason) I desperately needed to face the Caltanis alone after August 4, the date on which I would execute my sale pledge for the last 2 percent in order to carry the plan I had dreamed up to its conclusion.

To convince Miranda to sell me her 51 percent, I had offered to buy for $60 million what she had paid fifty for. Her profit— ten million. That wouldn't have been enough to persuade her. But my plan, if it succeeded, would be worth infinitely more to her. She believed in it and didn't believe in it. But she didn't have much of a choice. By refusing to sell, she would have prevented me from granting the Caltanis what they demanded and, therefore, would have had to face the insurance company along with me. She would lose everything, or just about, with no recourse other than a lawsuit against me, which would take years to pay off, and might never pay off, because, in the meantime, the Caltanis—or she, giving in to rage—would have bumped me off.

There remained (Miranda having agreed to the sale) a major problem. Financing this first phase. In June, 1976, when I undertook my casino venture, I had a little more than $80 million dollars. Let's say $82 million. I got back ten million more from Liechtenstein through Fezzali's release. Up to ninety million. Of which I spent fifty for the purchase and "personal funds" for the Crystal Palace. There remained some 40 million (I had had expenses, with the Englishman, for instance). But I had just promised to pay Miranda sixty million. I made it with the help of a loan from Li and Liu. I would pay them back on March 30, as soon as the Caltanis had paid me the twenty million in exchange for the 49 percent I was assigning them at that time.

As can be seen, it was VERY simple.

And in addition to that marvelous simplicity, this first phase of my plan was characterized by the shape it left me in, financially speaking (leaving aside the very thin pink line Miranda's razor had printed on my throat): I was almost completely bankrupt. To make ends meet and keep at least enough to live and travel on— and pay the Englishman, always!—I had had to liquidate all my positions on the financial market, halt all my ongoing operations, sell off, for instance, my Canadian and Australian bonds. I wasn't yet ready for the soup kitchen, but when I thought that only nine months ago I had been peacefully tanning myself in the Jamaican sun, without a care in the world, with enough to live on for at least three hundred fifty years—well, it was enough to leave me speechless.

We returned on the same plane to the United States on March 14, Li, Liu, Caliban, and I. Caliban's presence was in response to a demand of Miranda's.

"Cimballi, I don't know if your, let's say, unusual plan is going to succeed. I have my doubts. But it occurred to me that you and the Caltanis might be accomplices, joining forces to get rid of those poor stupid Chinese from Macao. That, along with my feeling bad about breaking up that touching friendship between you and Caliban, I feel Caliban should remain with you at all times. You'll keep him informed of your smallest actions. If he notes any tendency on your part to make a fool of me, he'll make mincemeat out of you. And besides, he's an expert in the casino business, your Henry Chance agrees. Have fun, Cimballi."

Here I was, flanked by a bodyguard/spy of little more than three feet tall. And before launching into the battle that awaited me, I had another problem, the problem of Sarah and the kids. The farther they were from the theater of operations, the better.

Li and Liu: "Are you afraid the Caltanis will go after them?"

How could I not try to foresee everything, with enemies of that stripe? A Martin Yahl, at least, didn't maintain a full battalion of killers! Nor would he have gambled with my life and those of the children by setting a casino or any other building on fire. No, in view of what I was setting up for the Caltanis, the possibility of physical danger, unfortunately, could not be ruled out.

I would have preferred to have Sarah and the children leave the continental United States. For Jamaica, if all else failed, or even better, France, St. Tropez. But I couldn't take Heidi across any borders. So they would stay in San Francisco, under the discreet watch of Li and Liu.

That was what I strove to convince Sarah of on our return from Macao. Not so easy. In cases like these, her Irish temperament soon showed its explosiveness.

"You mean I may have to stay here until the end of the year?"

"Nothing's stopping you from going to Jamaica to take care of your fucking hotels."

"And leave Marc-Andrea and Heidi behind?"

She was foaming. By St. Patrick, why wasn't I like all other businessmen? With a fixed residence, an office, a secretary to ogle, office hours, a membership at the local country club? Why was I always launching into idiotic ventures that forced me to run senseless risks? (Why, anyway? I wondered myself.) And how had I managed to be a multimillionaire one day and practically bankrupt the next?

"And besides, you've just told me that your son's life and that little Austrian's, not to mention my own, are now in danger? Franz, there are days when I could strangle you!"

Her, too! I certainly inspired tender sentiments in women. And the worst, what enraged Sarah the most, was that she was forced to give in, to stay with the children for the sake of the semimaternal affection she felt for my son and little Heidi. How could she leave them, knowing they were in danger? She even had to give up her professional career, perhaps forever. She had asked for and obtained a six months' sabbatical. She would have to extend it for another six months, without being sure, however, that everything would be over by the following September. I was ashamed of what I was doing to her and the position I was putting her in.

The following morning, March 15, she nevertheless succeeded in getting enough of a hold on herself to accompany me to the airport.

"Who are these people you're dealing with, this time? It's not Martin Yahl again, is it?"

I almost missed him!

"No, it's not him."

"But it's worse?"

"Yes."

Her gaze flowing beneath half-closed eyelids, her face tilted slightly backward.

"Are you going to win, Franz?"

"Absolutely."

"My foot. You're scared shitless, aren't you?"

It was all I could do not to break down suddenly, at that moment, in the lobby of San Francisco's airport. I suddenly felt the crushing weight of the incredible nervous tension built up over the last weeks. And the prospect of the weeks to come, with the frenetic activity awaiting me, offered no relief. I pulled Sarah toward me, kept her there for a long moment, as though to ask her forgiveness and perhaps also to find a bit of courage.

"Sarah, after this, I'm quitting. Whatever happens."

She nodded, her eyes wet. I climbed on the plane for New York, heading for battle.

23

March 30, 1977. Noon.

On one side of the table, Vandenbergh, Rosen, Marc Lavater, and me. On the other side—not the Caltani brothers, who were conspicuous by their absence and obviously did not wish to appear officially—on the other side, Olliphan and two men, one of whom was an Italian-American business-lawyer. The second man next to Olliphan was named—let's call him Weisman. With regard to him, Jimmy Rosen had passed me a note a few moments before, when the meeting had not yet officially begun, since Olliphan was late: *Weisman. A front for the Caltanis in several enterprises. Formerly of Vegas. Casino manager for fifteen years. License taken away. Hates Olliphan. Dangerous.* As always in such cases, I crumpled the message and burned it in an ashtray—under the eyes of Weisman, who wore glasses with dark lenses that did not soften the intensity of his gaze.

"When you're ready, Mr. Cimballi," Olliphan said, smiling as usual.

Philip Vandenbergh took from his briefcase documents which certified that, owing to the transfer from my former partners in Macao, I was now the sole owner of the Crystal Palace. He spread the documents out on the table and pushed them toward the enemy camp. A total silence while, one by one, in order, Olliphan, the Italian-American lawyer, and finally Weisman took note of my transaction with Miranda. Olliphan spoke first.

"I'm glad to see that your former Chinese partners accepted your buy-back offer."

"That fire worried them. It was too much for them. They don't like casinos that burn down."

"But you did tell us your insurer had concluded the fire was accidental?"

Jimmy Rosen became energized and presented photocopies of the report turned in by the insurance company investigators, as well as the letter sent to me on March 24, six days earlier, by Jack Getchell, chief executive officer of the Getchell & Harkins New Jersey Insurance Company. In the report, the investigators concluded there had been an accident (a short circuit caused by faulty wiring) that was not the fault of the casino security force. In the letter, Getchell told me that he would, as provided in the contract, proceed to reimburse all damages caused by the fire and the subsequent intervention of the firefighters. He indicated, however, that while the estimate of the damage was not yet complete, the total reimbursement would be close to $150 million. In the meantime, he was enclosing a transfer notice for $75 million to the Philadelphia bank, with which we could begin the renovation work.

Olliphan, "My client, Mr. Weisman, was concerned only yesterday about the outcome of this insurance business. This will reassure him, I dare say."

I glanced at Weisman. He looked as if he couldn't have cared less about our conversation. Which, of course, was a sheer farce. Olliphan and thus the Caltanis were the first, after me, to be informed of the green light given by the insurer. Since that green light was the prerequisite for today's meeting. But it was a question of observing formalities. And even if none of us sitting at that table were fooled, we made believe this was an ordinary transaction.

The rest went rather quickly. I placed my signature on the deed dated February 25, 1977, by which I sold to Weisman 49 percent of the hotel's shares. Weisman signed likewise. I received a certified check for $49 million. The formalities were completed. Everything was in order. Weisman and I shook hands.

Whereupon, as agreed, Vandenbergh and Rosen left us. I remained alone with Lavater, facing the trio.

At first, as soon as the insurers' official decision was made public and the date and arrangements for the meeting were set,

Olliphan had objected to Lavater's presence for the second part of the transaction. I had categorically refused to cooperate except in the presence of my French attorney.

"I have no secrets from him. He knows everything about my affairs. And if something happened to me . . ."

"What the devil do you expect to happen?"

"I might have an accident as 'accidental' as the hotel fire. Lavater will be there."

He was there. Silent but present. And the fact that he was there seemed to annoy Olliphan's lawyer-colleague. So much so that he took Olliphan aside in a corner of the room, and they both began whispering. Olliphan, very calm and smiling, succeeded in pacifying his companion. (He certainly had above-average persuasive powers.) They both came back to the table from which Weisman hadn't budged.

"Let's get this over with, Mr. Cimballi. You've received $49 million in exchange for 49 percent of the Crystal Palace. There are two operations remaining for us. Your irrevocable promise of sale for the additional 2 percent on August 4, on the one hand, and on the other hand, you're supposed to transfer $30 million for us to Panama, the bank . . ."

I did my best to stimulate incomprehension.

"Thirty?"

A smile from Olliphan, "Because under the terms of the agreement you made with . . . you know . . ."

"The Caltanis, not to mention any names."

I winked at Marc.

"A couple of real creeps, incidentally. You should have seen their faces."

"Yes, so I've heard," said Marc, imperturbably.

Olliphan didn't raise an eyebrow. His smile was bigger than ever. I could have sworn he was enjoying himself, as well. But not his lawyer pal, who was scowling. As for Weisman, he was as distant as ever.

"No names," said the pal.

Olliphan resumed, as though nothing had happened.

"According to those agreements, you undertook, after signing an official contract, to restore to your buyer the difference between the official price and the real price. The official price is fifty-one, the real price twenty-one. The difference—thirty. Mr. Cimballi, you are really getting—not just officially—$19 million

today and $2 million more on August 4 when you fulfil your irre-
vocable promise of sale by transferring the last 2 percent, which
will make my client, Mr. Weisman, the majority shareholder of
the casino known as the Crystal Palace."

All of this was poured out at a mad pace. Come on, it was a
cinch—he was enjoying himself too.

I said, very suavely, "I'm not entirely in agreement. I want
$20 million right away, plus $1 million on August 4."

I had a good reason for this demand. Li and Liu were friends,
but I couldn't allow myself to keep them waiting when it came to
paying them back the twenty million they had lent me so I could
pay Miranda. It was already a substantial gesture of friendship
on their part not to charge me interest. (I had offered to pay
them a million on August 4, but they had refused.)

"No way," Olliphan's pal stated forcefully. "Nineteen now and
two on August 4."

I nodded at Marc. He opened his briefcase and took out ham
and cheese sandwiches and the Thermos of coffee.

I explained, "We're not leaving here without that $20 million.
And we have plenty of time. Which do you prefer, Olliphan,
ham or cheese?"

This time, it was Olliphan who took his pal off in the corner.
Whispering. Return to the table.

"We agree on twenty," Olliphan said.

But I had the feeling even he was beginning to get impatient.
I had probably gone a tiny bit too far. The remainder of the
meeting went off without incident. I signed the promise of sale
by August 4 for the other 2 percent, subject to the condition that
the Crystal Palace opened for business on June 4, as planned. I
settled the arrangements with Olliphan for a transfer of $29 mil-
lion to a numbered account at a bank in the Bahamas, from
which the money would no doubt be rerouted to Panama or
other fiscal paradises. And it was finished.

Marc and I were the first to leave. The meeting took place in a
suite rented for the day at the Drake Hotel, corner of Fifty-sixth
Street and Park Avenue. The Pierre was not far away. After two
hundred steps, I asked Marc, "Did you understand why I
wanted you to be there?"

"Olliphan?"

"Yes. What do you think?"

235

"Strange. How should I put it? He has a kind of nonchalance, an almost devil-may-care attitude, which is rather surprising in a Mafia lawyer. And he helped you out, twice. By convincing the other lawyer that I could stay, and especially in the matter of the $20 million instead of nineteen. Without him, your bluff wouldn't have succeeded. With or without sandwiches and coffee."

And Olliphan had come to my aid before at the meeting in Harrison, by persuading the Caltanis that my three demands could safely be accepted.

Marc continued, thinking out loud, as it were, "It's the devil-may-care attitude of someone who knows he's doing to die of cancer or some other incurable disease. Or else he's playing a strange, incomprehensible game. And I can't see where it's leading him."

"It may have something to do with Korber and South Africa."

I grabbed Marc's arm to stop him in his stride.

"Marc, that half-caste banker in Capetown, Balthazar. Normally, he should have contacted Rosen in case he found out something about Olliphan . . ."

To return to the Pierre on foot, we had briefly followed Madison Avenue, then turned left. Tiffany's was on our left, across the street. I froze.

"I asked Balthazar to tell me whether Olliphan wasn't, by any chance, getting ready to emigrate to among the springboks, lock, stock, and barrel, without his dear wife whose maiden name is Caltani, but with, perhaps, a little cash borrowed from his brothers-in-law. But Balthazar hasn't replied, and that's annoying."

"And you'd like me to go and nudge him."

"Yes. But first you'll see the Turk in London. You know the Turk. He's my friend, but he's also the worst piece of garbage in the world. If there's something rotten about Balthazar which is likely to make him open his mouth if we so much as dangle it under his nose, the Turk ought to know about it. So go see the Turk in London, and make it short. Ask him how we can force Balthazar to talk. Then split for Capetown."

I crossed the street we were on, which happened to be East Fifty-seventh.

"And tell the Turk I'll pay him next year. I'll pay him 10 percent of all the sums I know and can prove were transferred by

Olliphan from the United States to South Africa."

"If Olliphan transferred a billion, you won't look so good."

"Olliphan couldn't have stolen a billion from the Caltanis. If he stole anything. Come on."

I went into Tiffany's, with Marc on my heel, and bought two pairs of earrings, one gold, one with diamonds.

I left my card and a check for one hundred thousand dollars. Or about one-fifth of what I had left. We went out through the door on Fifth Avenue.

"Have you decided to wear earrings?" Marc asked.

"The gold one's for Ute Jenssen in London. She'll convince her old man, the Turk, to do me this favor I'm asking. Even if she had to hit that traveling gypsy over the head. The other one's for Sarah. Marc?"

"Yes?"

"Watch out when you go to Capetown. We don't know what Olliphan's game is. I'm not going to South Africa myself because I'm afraid the Caltanis are having me watched. They could do the same to you."

"Okay."

We approached the Pierre. I felt good, light, airy. I felt like dancing.

"Marc?"

"Mmmm."

"I'm going to win."

24

April, the entire month of May, and a good part of June. Nearly three months in all, and for me, a period of reflection and waiting. Which I interspersed with short visits to the Crystal Palace and stays in San Francisco, where Li and Liu went beyond my own precautions, setting up a massive guard around my little family. You saw Oriental faces everywhere, as though the sixty thousand Chinese in San Francisco had been mobilized.

Li, Liu and Caliban were the only ones besides Lavater who knew about and were following the preparations for what I called my sting operation. Caliban often accompanied me when I went to San Francisco. In the first place because Miranda had ordered him not to lose sight of me, second because he had taken a liking to Li and Liu and was planning to start some venture with them, which they subsequently did.

This period, extending approximately from April to June 20, was, above all, one of preparation for me. A slow, methodical, and especially furtive preparation. The machinery to be worked out was manifold and incredibly complex. And it required, of course, the utmost secrecy.

There were two kinds of travels, then. First those that everyone could know about, including Olliphan and the Caltanis. And the others. For those, I did not use public transportation, on which it would be too easy to track me down. I called on my old friend Flint, the billionaire pilot from Palm Beach—a billionaire in large part through me. I had helped him make piles of money by creating Safari on the formerly swampy land he owned in Florida. He put his airplane and himself at my disposal.

Visits to the casino, trips to San Francisco, and preparation. And something else with which to fill that period—meetings.

After the signings on March 30, ten or twelve days elapsed in which nothing else happened. Construction work resumed with a vengeance. We would be ready by the evening of June 3 for an official opening the next day. Thus, all was going well. Except for Henry Chance. I informed him of the change of partners on the evening of March 30. He reacted immediately.

"Weisman? I knew an Abe Weisman in Vegas. Dark glasses, about fifty-five, thin lips, practically never talks."

"That's him."

"In that case, Mr. Cimballi, you no longer have a casino manager. I'm leaving."

"That's out of the question."

"Weisman is only a front man."

"I know. Just as I know who's behind him. But I need you to stay, Henry. I need it desperately."

"Sorry."

I must have argued until I was blue in the face, hinting that I

238

expected an imrovement in the situation very shortly. I didn't say what that improvement would consist of, and, in fact, I said nothing at all about my plans. I begged him. Because it was true I had an absolutely vital need for the casino to be a success, and from that standpoint, Chance was essential to me. He finally gave ground a little.

"Three months, Mr. Cimballi. Three months from the opening. After that, I'm leaving Atlantic City and going back to Vegas or Monte Carlo."

I couldn't have asked him for more. Three months from the opening would take us to September. And by September, one of two things would have happened—either I would have slain the Caltani dragon, or I would be completely reduced to ashes.

An annoying incident in the same period. Which took the form of a particularly official missive from one or another Austrian ministry, ordering Mr. Franz Cimballi to produce young Heidi Moser with all deliberate speed. "Drop dead!" I snorted, and tossed the letter into the wastebasket. I had other things to worry about, and my position with regard to Heidi had not changed, except in a sense directly opposite to that of the Vienna authorities. I no longer wanted to be separated from her. Anna Moser, her guardian, was in full agreement.

But I had not reckoned with the admirable persistence of the authorities. Ten days after I received the letter, an American plainclothes man appeared at the Pierre. He wore an old raincoat and workboots and kept a cold half-cigar in his mouth at all times.

"It's about that little Austrian girl. You have to hand her over, so to speak."

"She's not here."

"And where is she?"

Absent, so to speak, I answered. But if he wanted to search the closets . . . He looked around the apartment, even under the beds, in the closets, and in the bathrooms.

"Not here, huh?"

"I just told you that."

He sucked his cigar stub and a bit of nicotine mixed with saliva dribbled from his lips. Nauseating.

"As far as I'm concerned," he said, "you can do what you want with this Australian . . ."

"Austrian."

"Whatever. But the law is the law. You hand over the kid, and you'll have no problems. You don't hand her over, and you will have problems. I'm in charge of the investigation, so to speak. Don't you want to tell me where she is?"

I would have refused even if he looked like Robert Redford. But the looks of this fourth-rate cop didn't help matters. This whole story seemed simply grotesque to me. It was time to put an end to it. I made my decision that very day, based on my love for the child.

"Jimmy, I want to adopt Heidi, officially. Get the ball rolling, find out what has to be done. AND DON'T TELL ME IT'S NOT SO SIMPLE!"

"You shouldn't have kicked the people from the consulate out. Their report on you isn't very nice. You have no fixed residence, you're not married, and you run a casino."

"And what about my drug trafficking? I'm a mafioso, right?"

"For a judge in some Tyrolean village, hearing the story from the people you kicked out . . ."

"Jimmy, I want to adopt Heidi. I've been thinking about it for a long time. Let's do it. Anna Moser will surely agree, so will Heidi and Marc-Andrea. To work."

I hung up. I had already spent too much time on preliminaries and extracurricular activities. The Englishman was waiting for me. The date: April 16.

In order for our meetings to be private, he had simply taken a room at the Pierre himself, and we pretended not to know each other. There was a wealth of precautions which I found slightly ridiculous, but he insisted on.

"It's about Walcher. Walcher is an old friend of Herman Bau . . ."

"I know who Walcher is. I mainly want to know whether or not he was an accomplice to Baumer's kidnapping. Yes or no?"

He hesitated. I felt that he, too, was going to tell me it's not so simple.

"It's not so simple," he replied. "For two months now we've been following him step by step. He went to Nassau twice. Both times, he met with a banker, the same one, whose name is . . ."

"I don't give a damn."

"One of those two meetings took place in a hotel room. Where someone had the happy idea of installing a bugging system. The full recording . . ."

"What does it say, mainly?"

"Walcher has $2 million in a numbered account."

"He could have inherited it or won it at canasta."

"Or dug into his bank vaults. But he didn't do any of that. If you would take the trouble to read the transcript of his conversation with the banker, you would see that Walcher says at one point, 'That money's been lying around for two and a half years now,' and he announces his intention to put his capital to work at last. Two and a half years, Mr. Cimballi. Figure it out. That takes us back to October '74."

That sounded familiar. The Englishman smiled.

"It was in October '74 that Baumer reappeared in Nassau, after having disappeared. It was on October 14, '74, that Walcher himself went to Nassau, in order, as he put it, to try to talk some sense back into his friend Baumer. My opinion is that he used that trip to open a numbered account. Walcher is a banker. No banker would leave $2 million in an account without trying to make it grow. Unless he had excellent reasons."

"What's the date of that conversation you uncovered between Walcher and his Nassau banker?"

"April 2."

In other words, the Saturday immediately following my signing the deed transferring the 49 percent. The coincidences were becoming enormous.

"Another thing," said the Englishman. "By the greatest of accidents, Walcher's personal telephone is connected to a listening device. On the evening of March 30, Walcher received an interesting call. Interesting and brief. Here's a transcription of it. 'Ernie? It's Abie. Just to let you know it's all settled. See you soon.' We tried to find out who that untalkative Abie might be. We had to go back more than a month in our files. On February 12, Walcher had dinner with one Abie Weisman. Does the name mean anything to you, Mr. Cimballi?"

I nodded. And how! The Englishman and his team's work on Baumer had already given us some strong hints. For me, things were now clear. Walcher had been the Caltanis' accomplice in Herman's kidnapping. That wasn't the only conclusion to be drawn. In paying $25 million to the Caltanis, I had, without

241

meaning to, deprived the lawful heirs of Uncle Herman—the Moser sisters. Including Heidi. Who, like her sisters, would now be in a position to sue all of us!

Whichever way I turned, I was sitting on a powder keg. What an imbroglio!

Marc Lavater's absence had lasted more than three weeks in all. Of course, he had phoned me, to keep in touch—first from London, then from Paris. Then silence, as we had agreed, for reasons of caution.

He returned to New York on April 20. A mere look between us was enough. He had obtained results. He waited to speak until we were alone in the car bringing us back from Kennedy Airport (where we had met—I was on my way back from Europe). What he had to tell me consisted of few words, but those were the words I was waiting for.

"Olliphan has been transferring money to South Africa for years already. Fourteen million dollars in all. The transfers were made by a very circuitous route. Everything was done to preserve the utmost secrecy. Franz, you've gotten me used to some pretty fine juggling when it comes to transferring funds, and back when I was valiantly protecting the interests of the French treasury, I saw a good share. But never like this. As far as sorting out how much of that $14 million actually belongs to Olliphan and what he embezzled behind the Caltanis' backs—it would take years. And the Caltanis' cooperation."

"The main thing is that I have a way of putting pressure on Olliphan."

"You have. I brought back a few very sketchy documents. Balthazar spilled everything he knows. He hates us now, you, the Turk, and me."

"What's Korber's role?"

"He's the one who manages Olliphan's interests. The two men have been partners in quite a few enterprises under Korber's name. Franz, if you tell the Caltanis a tenth of what I've found out, Olliphan is a dead man. You've got him."

I was trembling so hard with excitement that I had to stop the car and turn off onto the shoulder. In the state I was in, I might cause a smash-up. And I had enough problems as it was. But it was a blatant fact that one of the vital mechanisms of my scheme had just slipped into place.

Marc asked, "And where are you at, on your side, with your efforts?"

What he called my efforts—and I termed my preparations—were well under way. I gave him a run-down. We looked at each other, in a car shaken by other vehicles stirring up huge air currents as they passed us. The memory of my first meeting with Lavater was very clear in my mind. It was during the summer, July, 1970, I think, and over the telephone, without ever having seen him, I had set up a meeting at Trocadero Square in Paris. I was fresh from Kenya at that time, all puffed up, like the kid I was, with my first success. Since then, Marc Lavater had been through all my campaigns. He smiled at me.

"Let's not start that old army buddy stuff. Everything is ready, if I understand correctly. To be frank, I hardly believed it could happen. But it's happening. When are you getting in touch with Olliphan to hit him with the news?"

"I'll wait till the last minute. I don't want to give him the time to turn around."

On June 4, the Crystal Palace opened for business. In its first days, it was a smashing success. True, everything had converged to make it so, starting with the fire itself and the numerous appearances I'd made on television screens, recounting the dramatic moments I'd gone through with Marc-Andrea and Heidi.

By June 15, Henry Chance himself conceded that this casino was likely to break records. The organization he had set up was operating beautifully. In New York City alone, he had opened three branches, which were, in fact, a kind of bank and travel agency combined. All anybody had to do was make a thousand dollar deposit (immediately registered by a computer terminal), and the potential customer would be credited an equal sum in Crystal Palace chips, available in Atlantic City. Food and drinks would then be offered free of charge. With a ten thousand dollar deposit or more, the gambler received free travel and lodging as a supplement. Similar branches were opened in all the major U.S. cities and in Montreal (with a contemplated expansion of the arrangement to all the great capitals of the world).

There remained Chance's famous card file, in which he had been recording, for maybe twenty-five years, the names of all the big gamblers on two hemispheres. "Mr. Cimballi, I'll guarantee that your success will be complete the day I see those big players in my casino." For these special customers, he had worked out a special plan. They could either occupy one of the Palace's suites or stay in New York, in any one of the Manhattan deluxe hotels. In that case, a special helicopter shuttle fleet, luxuriously outfitted, maintained the link between Fifth Avenue and the Boardwalk in Atlantic City. Better yet, a Boeing 747 chartered by the casino and bearing the Crystal Palace emblem was placed at the disposal of West Coast gamblers every Friday evening, departing from Los Angeles—which was really the last word!

Of course, I had every confidence in Henry Chance's professional competence, but—unlike Caliban, who supported him—I wondered if he weren't making the mistake of applying to Atlantic City techniques that had been proven only in Vegas. I was wrong. It was proved to me in the first days of July. Flint's plane, which was bringing me back from a new "discreet journey of furtive preparation" had landed at Newark Airport in the greatest possible secrecy. Since my absence had lasted a bit more than a week this time (but I had just tightened the last screw on my sting), my first concern was to call Chance to find out where we were at. He answered my question with another question.

"How much did you estimate the casino's future annual profits would be?"

"About $40 million."

"Then figure on 50 percent more. They're here."

THEY, meaning the big gamblers, the high rollers. For the first time since it had been placed in service, the chartered 747 had, for two consecutive weeks, carried a full load of customers over the great plains of America. Even the Japanese were there, and the Hong Kong Chinese, who were capable of leaving you a million dollars in three days. Not counting a few princes from the Middle East!

I decided to let myself have eight days of vacation in San Francisco. There I heard from Jimmy Rosen, who had managed to halt the proceeding begun against me by the Austrian government and obtained a court order from a judge, granting me temporary custody of Heidi. Thus, I stayed longer in California than planned. I returned to New York on July 22, thirteen days from my meeting with the Caltanis, set for August 4, to keep my promise to sell the last 2 percent. The Englishman was waiting for me at the Pierre. He had kept Olliphan under surveillance for months and confirmed that I was ready to nab the *consigliere* at any time. But I choose to wait a while longer.

I told the Englishman, "It would be ideal if I could meet Olliphan in a public place, where our meeting would go completely unnoticed. I don't want to put his life in danger."

An Oxonian smile.

"Nothing easier, Mr. Cimballi. By another lucky accident, we know about our man's schedule as he passes it on to his secretary. What day in particular would you like?"

"Monday the first, Tuesday the second, Wednesday the third."

That is, three, two, or one day before I would be face to face with the Caltanis. And, by the force of things, three, two, or one day before the ignition of what could really be characterized in several ways—my very personal finish to an operation that had begun on June 14, 1976, when I told Philip Vandenbergh that I wanted to buy a casino; my attack; or, yet again, the final phase of a sting that I had been preparing now for twenty-five weeks.

June 14, 1976–August 4, 1977. Those might be the dates to inscribe as my epitaph, on my slot-machine shaped tombstone, if the slightest hitch occurred in my defense plan. I had counted. It came to 412 days.

The Englishman, after consulting his notes, said, "Tuesday the second seems convenient to me. As you know, Olliphan is a music lover, but he's also a collector of contemporary American painting. On Monday, August 1, there's an exhibit opening at the Museum of Modern Art which he planned to attend on the following day, according to his calendar. He'll be there around five o'clock."

"Me, too."

"How much time will you need to spend alone with him?"

"Fifteen minutes, at most."

But it didn't even last that long. It was almost five-thirty on the afternoon of Tuesday, August 2, when, preceded and guided by one of the Englishman's assistants, Olliphan joined me on the fifth floor of MOMA. When he saw me, he raised his eyebrows slightly, looking almost amused. That would be his only sign of surprise.

"But I'm not so surprised, Mr. Cimballi. I was expecting something of the sort."

During the next four or five minutes, he listened to me with his strange half-smile without once interrupting me, while I was explaining everything I knew about him, and what I expected from him in return for my silence. He kept quiet even after I had finished.

Finally, shaking his head, "I don't know what you've planned for the Caltanis, but you've undoubtedly taken huge risks."

"That's my business."

He hesitated briefly, then asked, "And do you also mean to settle accounts with Ernie Walcher?"

"While I'm at it. And you have fifty seconds left to make up your mind."

He began laughing, looking inward, so to speak, as though laughing at himself and the comical stupidity of humanity in general.

"But I've made up my mind, Mr. Cimballi. What do you think? I put you on notice last September 18, when you came to my house. And I'm the one who told you about Korber. I gave you the rope to hang me with and waited to see if you would be clever enough to pick it up. Do I have to say any more to you? I don't know to what degree you've come to hate the Caltanis, but it would be impossible for you to come up even to my ankle. Very well, of course I accept all of your conditions. For Walcher, it'll be very simple. I can give you the proof you need. There again, I don't know how you're planning to cook his goose, but whatever you do, he's earned it. It was his idea to pull Baumer out of circulation."

Suddenly, he became garrulous, and I sensed he was entirely ready to spill the rest of the story to me. But it wasn't the time or the place. I cut him short. With less than forty hours before my showdown with the Caltanis, the worst thing that could happen would be for this confab I was having with Olliphan to become known. He admitted that, as well.

He asked, "And what have you planned concerning, let's say, my confession?"

He would record it that very evening on cassettes. Then, at four o'clock the next morning, someone sent by the Englishman would come to pick up those cassettes, turn them over to a battery of typists who would transcribe the recordings. Rosen and Vandenbergh would be in his office at nine-thirty, bringing copies of the cassettes and the typed manuscripts.

"All three of you will listen to the cassettes, read the transcripts, and make any additions or corrections my lawyers feel are necessary. You will sign the transcripts. The official reason for your meeting with Rosen and Vandenbergh will be to put the final touches on the documents that the Caltanis and I will sign the next day."

And as soon as Rosen and Vandenbergh, after checking everything, and with the signed confessions in their hands, announced to me that all was in order, he, Olliphan, would be free to leave the United States, to go anywhere—to South Africa, for instance, to join his friend Korber. Hoping, for his sake, that the Caltanis wouldn't be able to find him. Olliphan again nodded his head, smiling. It was true he had something Irish in his eyes—a sort of poetic madness, so to speak, filled with a humor that bordered on savagery.

"And I won't be present at that meeting on Thursday? It's out of the question. In the first place, because Joe and Larry, noticing my absence, would be very inclined to distrust me. I've been fooling them for fifteen years and more, trust my experience. And then, I've another reason for being there. I want to know what you cooked up for them. I'm eaten up by curiosity. As a mere mental game, I tried to imagine how I might have helped you get out of that merciless trap I helped to put you in. I tried to put myself in the place of a Lavater, a Lupino, a Vandenbergh, or a Rosen. What would I have advised you to do? I couldn't find a satisfactory answer. And yet it seems you've found a way. And I should miss a spectacle like that? To see those two creeps, my dear brothers-in-law, Joe and Larry, get their asses kicked for once? No way, Mr. Cimballi. In fact, I'm praying for your success."

The next day, Wednesday the third, shortly before noon, Vandenbergh and Rosen met me at the Pierre. Everything had gone off as planned. With them they had Olliphan's "confession," recorded, typed, and signed. They had even put the original in a safe place, carrying only a copy with them. Nothing was omitted. There was the whole story of the Crystal Palace, laid out in its entirety for the first time—from the initial buying offer—for one million dollars—made by Olliphan to Baumer and vigorously declined by the latter, to Walcher's intervention, followed by Baumer's kidnapping (carried out by the Caltani strongman whom I call the carbonaro), Baumer's death (accidental, but scheduled for later, in any case), the purchase of the hotel by the Caltanis operating under cover of a front company, the resale of that same hotel to a certain Cimballi.

Then the first anxieties of the Caltani clan and of Walcher, as well, when they discovered young Heidi Moser's presence around me. For it was indeed Heidi's appearance on the scene that set off everything.

Rosen: "Franz, it was your first inquiry, the one made by Lavater, that put Walcher on the alert. He panicked, especially when he saw that you were keeping Heidi with you, and when he knew you had gone to Austria to meet the other Moser sisters. Walcher wasn't sure what Anna knew—Baumer had seen her shortly before he was kidnapped. Walcher and the Caltanis decided that you were getting ready to take up the fight for Heidi and her sisters by revealing the entire scheme to the police. It was necessary to shut you up and executing you wouldn't have done any good, too many people around you seemed to be in the know. No, it was necessary to insure your complicity in the fraud."

"Hence the fire."

"Which was prepared by a special team from Chicago. Two men, of whom we know at least their whereabouts, if not their names, through Olliphan. It won't be too hard to identify them. But the fire was calculated not to threaten you physically. They wanted to put you in a situation such that you could no longer tell the truth without being seriously compromised. Which wouldn't have prevented you from being eliminated if you'd been pigheaded."

As I've said, those who knew the arrangements for my Big Sting of the following day, August 4, were extremely few in number. Rosen and Vandenbergh, as well as Lupino, had been kept out of the secret. They would surely have opposed such a crazy maneuver. And in any case, I didn't need them in my preparations.

It was, thus, quite logical that as lawyers they should insist on Olliphan's confessions being turned over to the police, even though they recognized that the big lies Marc and I had handed the insurance investigators did, in fact, pose a few problems. But Vandenbergh had a solution.

"Your insurers have nothing to gain by coming down on you. I'll take it upon myself to convince them to make a deal. You and they will claim that you acted in concert in order to trap the Caltanis. With Olliphan's confession . . ."

And he went on developing his arguments. I barely listened to him, out of politeness, mainly. In truth, I was unbelievably nervous as the hours went by and the moment slowly approached for meeting the Respectable Businessmen. I had been preparing for this showdown for twenty-five weeks, no one could talk me out of it any more. It was too late. Furthermore, I was convinced my solution was better than any that could be offered to me. And finally, as strange as this may seem, I wasn't after Olliphan's hide, whatever his role had been. He had helped me, for reasons that were entirely personal. In spite of everything, I had sympathy for him and a kind of pity still. It was enough that I had his confession—which I would only use if things turned out for the worst tomorrow—and had neutralized him, depriving the Caltanis of their wiliest adviser and the one most dangerous to me.

For the third or fourth time, I replied to my two New York counsels that I was sticking to my original decision—there was no question of making use of Olliphan's confession. Philip Vandenbergh was the first to leave, hiding his anger under his usual icy courtesy. Jimmy Rosen left as well, keeping his eyes on mine until the last minute. While he didn't have the slightest idea of my real intentions, he knew that within twenty-four hours I was going to pull the biggest coup of my life, and surely the craziest. He didn't resent my having kept him in the dark. He shook my hand and smiled.

"Good luck, Franz. Or rather, *merde*, as you say in French."

After they left, it began to seem a bit like the night before battle. Only Lavater and Caliban had remained with me. Speaking French, more like foreigners in New York than ever before, we went to a movie, but to this day, neither Marc nor I can remember the title of the film. That tells you that we must have been pretty tense, the two of us.

The meeting with the Caltanis had been set for eleven forty-five in a suite at the Plaza Hotel.

25

An hour earlier, I had gone to the bank on Nassau Street and had withdrawn from the vault the box containing the film. I wasn't alone, of course. Accompanying me, besides Lavater, were Kowalski and two bodyguard types. We had signed the documents allowing the vault to be opened, and everything had gone off without incident.

The box was now on a low table between the Caltanis and me. Joe Caltani shrugged his shoulders and remarked in his husky voice:

"You weren't risking anything, Cimballi. We wouldn't have used that film."

"No way," his brother Larry chimed in. "Once we had come in as partners . . ."

In short, it would have been suicide for them, they told me in unison. It was touching as hell, but I shrugged my shoulders, with the painful-furious-resigned face of one who had to swallow a pill and found it decidedly very bitter.

"I don't like it when someone puts a loaded revolver to my head, even if they tell me they're not going to use it."

There were six of us—Marc and me, the Caltanis, Weisman, and Olliphan. Kowalski had disappeared, a mere pawn whom they'd kicked off the chessboard. As for the carbonaro, I had seen him on arriving. He was keeping watch in the next room, together with two of his "soldiers," since he seemed indeed to be the Caltanis' minister of war.

"Let's get this over with," I said.

The Plaza suite overlooked Central Park. Just under the windows, I could see two or three horse-carriages waiting for customers. The weather in New York was extremely hot and humid, indicating a storm.

"Franz?"

Lavater was calling me. He had opened the box and withdrawn the film and was examining it. His face darkened as he discovered the extent of its revelations.

He finally remarked, bitterly, "In other words, I would have been the first to go to jail."

"But not since we've all agreed to destroy the film," Olliphan remarked, smiling and most affable.

Somewhere a metal wastebasket had been found. Marc and I cut the film to pieces with scissors and threw the pieces into the basket. A small container of lighter fluid was poured on the debris. It caught fire immediately, and while it was burning, there was silence. Soon there was nothing left but ashes, which Marc was careful to pulverize.

"But nothing proves that no copies were made . . ."

Joe Caltani broke into laughter.

"Oh, come on, now . . ."

Weisman grabbed the wastebasket, showed its bottom, and went to empty the ashes into the toilet. During the next few minutes, we went on to what was, after all, the main purpose of the meeting—that I execute my promise of sale for the additional 2 percent. A final demand on my part—I asked for a full discharge of directorship between February 25 (the official date of the transfer of the 49 percent, actually transferred on March 30) and the present. This request was granted. I initialed the transfer deed, which henceforth made Weisman, and thus the Caltanis, the majority shareholders of the Crystal Palace. It must have been about ten minutes past twelve. I got up, looking like someone who had taken a laxative. Joe Caltani interrupted my motion—look here, now that we've settled all our business, why not try to bring a little human warmth into our relations?

"Cimballi, we're partners now. Aren't we? We have to celebrate this. Franz, you have Italian blood, like us, that creates bonds. So call us Joe and Larry. And Ollie. We're going to work together in confidence for years, yes, yes."

For that matter, "Ollie"—Olliphan, of course—had had a great idea. Why not all go together to visit the casino, take a tour of it as owners? Ollie had prepared festivities for us down there. One of the hotel's helicopters was waiting for us at the Wall Street heliport. Weisman and Lavater would put one copy each of the documents we had just signed in a safe place and then join us. In the end, I agreed, a bit sulkily, but everything indicated I would wind up making the best of the situation. No, I didn't speak Sicilian, but Italian, yes, a little. *Andiamo.*

And everything went off exactly as planned. It was one-thirty when we landed at the Crystal Palace, greeted by Henry Chance, who in his capacity as casino manager was receiving his shareholders. (He was icier than ever, but from time to time, his gaze sought and met mine, which was indecipherable.)

Vintage French champagne for me, Italian specialties in the name of our common heritage for them. We feasted. Weisman reappeared around three o'clock, joined us half an hour later. It was around four o'clock when the telephone rang.

We were sitting in the living room of my private suite way at the back of the bomb shelter (the private room did not open until six o'clock every evening, unless the big gamblers insisted on using it). Henry Chance was giving us his report on the casino and the wonderful prospects that everything seemed to indicate. It was he who picked up the phone. The phone had rung several times before that, and there was no reason to think that this call was more important than the previous ones. But it was. It was crucial, in fact. Chance's face, an almost imperceptible change in his voice, made this clear.

Chance said to his caller, "And they know that Messrs. Cimballi, Caltani, and Weisman are here?"

A pause, then, "Very well. In that case, send them down."

He hung up, and explained, to a deathlike silence, "Three men who say they were sent by the Getchell & Harkins insurance company. They say they know for a fact that all the owners of the Crystal Palace are gathered here. They demand to be seen. They say there are exceptionally grave reasons for their visit."

Here I ought to clarify three points.

1. While I was expecting—and with reason—such an action by the Getchell & Harkins company, I was totally unaware of how and when it would take place and what form it would take.

2. Those three men who had so rudely interrupted our merry celebration were in no way my collaborators. They were genuine private detectives who had no reason to give me any presents and would not do so, anyway. To them, I was as responsible, at least to the same degree, as the Caltanis, for the monstrous fraud they had uncovered.

3. Henry Chance didn't know anything about what was going on. Still, to use the phrase he had used in Vegas, he wasn't "a man who is easily fooled." And I had asked him to wait three months after the opening before carrying out his resignation threat. Thus, while he was totally ignorant of the ensuing drama, I would swear he guessed at that second that I was the instigator of it. It was enough to see his eyes.

252

All three of them had the cold assurance and calm indifference of hangmen proceeding with an execution. Only one of the three would speak. He introduced himself. His name was Yarrow, he had forty years' experience in investigations of damages. He was small, stocky, with very thin lips and a tiny mouth. He wore steel-rimmed glasses. He resembled a math teacher I'd once had, whom I'd hated.

"Never to this day," he said, "have I had to work on such a difficult case. Nor, at the same time, a clearer one."

In the first minutes after his entrance, he had asked Chance to leave the room. Then, he had mentioned all our names—Franz Cimballi, Joseph and Larry Caltani, Marc Lavater, Abraham Weisman.

"We've never met, you and I, but I know each and every one of you."

He continued, "I was placed in charge of the investigation into the fire at the Crystal Palace more than three months ago. Hence, I took over from the company's regular investigators, who had concluded the damage was accidental. They were wrong. The fire was of criminal origin. And I can prove it."

His assistants went into action. They set up a projector and a portable screen. (It was the third time in the history of the hotel that I'd been shown a film.) Right away, I recognized the images—they were from the film made by the CBS reporting crew. Exactly the same as what had been shown on every American TV screen.

"Yes, millions of people saw them, gentlemen. I studied them over and over again —before discovering something abnormal."

I thought I was going to have to play a role. But I didn't have to. I felt an actual cold chill run down my spine, and from the sudden tenseness of the Caltanis sitting next to me, I knew that they too had just taken a big blow on the head. For the person that Yarrow had just singled out among the crowd of police, firefighters, and spectators contemplating the burning hotel, the person on whom the frame froze, was the guard I had seen through the control screen at the emergency exit, the one who had placed the beams and then removed at least one of them, while smiling at me ironically.

Yarrow: "On that Sunday, February 27, the day of the fire, the Crystal Palace was obviously under surveillance, being under construction. Six guards in all. We know their names and their faces. We've taken their testimony. We've reconstructed their movements at the time of the fire. You see all of them on the CBS film at one time or another. But look closely at that man in the middle of the crowd—who's wearing the uniform of a security guard—and who's moving away with the greatest indifference, far from concerning himself with the fire."

The film, which had stopped on one image, began again. But it stopped on one image after another, in a terribly impressive slow motion.

"He was moving off and going away. Notice, gentlemen, that he seems rather in a hurry to disappear. And that's the first bit of evidence. There were officially six guards watching over the hotel. But this one? Where does he come from? Where does this seventh guard come from? And what was his role?"

The film went backward and stopped again on the man's face. The picture was suddenly enlarged.

"And who was he? It took us weeks to identify him. Now we know his name—Frank Dindelli. Frank Bruno Dindelli, to be precise. Convicted twice, once for assault, another time for racketeering and assault. Which didn't, however, prevent him from finding a job. Last February, he was still working as a chauffeur and delivery man for a company that imports chiefly olive oil. A company belonging to whom?"

To Joseph and Larry Caltani.

"Naturally, we wanted to meet this Mr. Dindelli, to ask him what he was doing in Atlantic City, wearing a guard's uniform to which he had no right. And we found him. But not in the United States. He had, in fact, left American soil for Sicily, where he now lives, very peacefully, near Taormina, off the revenue of a hotel and restaurant he paid for in cash. The date, moreover, of his return to the country of his ancestors is no less interesting. Dindelli left New York for Rome on Sunday, February 27, in the evening."

I looked at the Caltanis at that moment. They were frozen, but you would have had to be blind not to notice their growing nervousness. A wild joy came over me—so much for the Respectable Businessmen!

Yarrow again: "Of course, we were able to establish a close tie between Frank Bruno Dindelli and you, Mr. Joseph Caltani. We have the evidence on the books of your generosity toward Dindelli. And incidentally, since you used one of your regular front men, Mr. Weisman here, we also established, if there were still any need for it, the ties that exist between you Mr. Caltani and Mr. Weisman. But that's not all. There's something else still more incriminating. In Dallas at the time of President Kennedy's assassination, several amateur filmmakers recorded the scene. The same is true for what happened at the Crystal Palace on Sunday, February 27, between eleven a.m. and one p.m. We found no fewer than seven persons who had their cameras running. It was a Sunday, and many tourists had come from New York. Among the pictures taken at random, one film in particular caught our attention."

The scene that the "amateur filmmaker" had recorded was short. It lasted barely seven or eight minutes. The John Ford, so to speak, of that Sunday had slowly swept the perimeter of the hotel, filming perhaps without realizing it. Still, he had captured for all time the simultaneous presence of five persons in the ditch outside the shelter's emergency exit Number One.

"Do you recognize yourself, Mr. Cimballi? Do you recognize the two children beside you? And that man carrying a beam, ten or twelve feet away from you, is beyond a doubt your French lawyer-adviser, Mr. Lavater here. While the guard you can see walking away on the left is, you will agree, clearly identifiable, though you can see him only from the back. He is, indeed, Frank Bruno Dindelli."

The projector stopped. One of the assistants switched on the lights. Yarrow faced us, a ray of triumph in the depths of his nearsighted eyes.

"And I have a third piece of evidence, gentlemen. There are very few experts capable of organizing a fire like that at the Crystal Palace down to the last second, so that regular investigators from an insurance company would be fooled and conclude it was an accident."

So few that Yarrow claimed the ones involved had been identified. There were two of them, brought in specially from Chicago. Yarrow had their names and photographs. He knew when Joe Caltani and Abie Weisman had contacted them, how much Joe Caltani had paid, and by what method. He piled up so much evidence that for the Caltanis and Weisman to deny their responsibility for the arson and fraud would be simply ludicrous.

As, for that matter, it would be for Lavater and I. No doubt and no possibility of defense—we were all guilty. Accomplices.

Yarrow had even constructed a very probable theory to explain our collusion. Joe and Larry Caltani, Abie Weisman, James Montague Olliphan, Marc Lavater, and Franz Cimballi, like the jolly bandits we all were, had deliberately set the hotel on fire in order to convince the Macao Chinese to withdraw from the deal.

For him, it was an open-and-shut case.

He wasn't wrong.

And I can still see Olliphan's face, staring at me in the restored silence. A look that, as far as I could read it, asked me two questions—"In God's name, Cimballi, how the devil did you do it, and above all, *what's your plan?*"

26

Here, a few necessary explanations.

The idea of a film supposedly shot by an amateur filmmaker— that idea came from me. I was rather proud of it, in fact. When I explained it to Li and Liu, it didn't fail to set off their usual convulsive laughter. As former special-effects men in Hong Kong, working on blood-drenched Kung-Fu films, they were in their element. It was simple to reconstruct the exact setting—it still existed. We copied it scrupulously as it had been on February 27. For the actors, no problem. Marc, Marc-Andrea, Heidi, and I had played ourselves (and had quite a jolly time of it). As for the fake Dindelli, the seventh guard (who, I admit, I hadn't noticed on the CBS film), a Los Angeles actor had played the role, facing away from the camera.

That was how we forged one piece of evidence.

As far as identifying the "experts from Chicago," we had relied on Olliphan's confessions. The hardest part had been to give their names to Yarrow without Yarrow finding out the source of the information. As a last resort, we fell back on the traditional "informer"—another actor—whom Yarrow paid.

On the other hand, I had absolutely nothing to do with the third proof adduced by Yarrow. All the credit for spotting Dindelli on the CBS film went to him. And even if I helped him a little, he still carried out his own investigation. Thanks to which he was, that August 4, in a position to send us all to jail— the Caltanis, Weisman, Marc, Olliphan, and me.

Why had I helped him?

The answer came from Yarrow himself.

"Before speaking," Yarrow said, "I asked Henry Chance to leave. Deliberately. He's not implicated. His reputation is above all suspicion, and our investigation showed that that reputation was deserved. But perhaps some of you . . ." (I noted with pride that it was me he was looking at, in tribute to my stunning intelligence) ". . . have already understood what I'm getting at. The situation is clear. If the evidence against you goes to the police, I will have the great satisfaction of seeing all of you behind bars. In fact, if my employers had given me free rein, I would have come with police. And arrest warrants. But I received different orders and I'm obeying them."

With regret, obviously.

He went on. Let's skip the details, as he said himself. He was offering us a bargain on behalf of Getchell & Harkins, which had hired his services. And we could take it or leave it. We (the Caltanis and I) had fraudulently received $150 million. We would have to return it. That was the least we could do. But we would also have to pay interest. Ten percent. Or an additional $15 million.

"Furthermore . . ."

Yarrow's thin lips formed the sadistic half-smile of a math teacher posing a third-degree equation to an inveterate dunce.

". . . furthermore, of course, you will pay a penalty of $75 million. Or a total of $240 million. You'll divide this debt among yourselves, as you like."

Yarrow's assistants had put away their equipment. They left. Yarrow gathered up his own briefcase.

"Two hundred forty million, gentlemen. It's Thursday, August 4. I'll expect you at our Newark office next Monday, August 8, at nine forty-five. You'll have until ten o'clock to hand in certified checks for that amount, all together or by one of you. If you're late, even by one minute, for any reason whatsoever, I won't wait. I'll leave my office and file a complaint immediately."

He slammed the metallic latch of the attaché case and departed.

You had to admit, it was a fine exit. Worthy of Shakespeare.

My part required that I scream in rage. I screamed. I told the Caltanis what I thought of them. What, they hadn't even been able to organize an act of arson without leaving signs of their horrible infamy? And who had used Dindelli? Who had sought out those two so-called experts from Chicago? Me? And who had left that film lying around, of which Yarrow had shown us a portion? Because, after all, they didn't expect me to swallow that story of an amateur filmmaker? Yarrow's film was the same one that they, the Caltanis, had shown me in Harrison! Yes, the same one! I had no trouble simulating fury. I really hated those thugs who had tried to sting me and who, for now, might have succeeded, by dragging me into an adventure that was still likely to end in prison. And in spite of Marc, who tried to calm me down (but it was a game worked out between us), I lost my composure.

"Listen to me, Caltanis, and you, too, Olliphan! What do you think I did, after you showed me the evidence against me? Do you think I waited calmly for my execution? I looked for ways to defend myself. And I found them. Perhaps not sufficient to make you leave me alone, but enough to sink you along with me when the time came. I also compiled evidence. And I'm warning you—you're going to pay Yarrow that $240 million, you'll pay every last cent of it, or I'll blow it all sky-high. I'll be the first to go to the cops. And the cops will be talking to you not only about the arson, but about your blackmailing me, and the Baumer affair, the whole Baumer affair, not to mention the business of tax evasion in your saloons! Kidnapping and fraud—you'll have the Feds on your back!"

Whereupon, still following the script Olliphan, Lavater, and I had worked out, they asked me to calm down, to try to talk about the situation without getting excited. The situation was serious and everyone wanted to find a solution.

Let's talk money, for instance. Yarrow's asking us for $240 million. Olliphan suggested that settlement of the sum be prorated according to our respective shares: 51 percent for the Caltanis, 49 for me. Or $122 million 400 thousand and $117 million 600 thousand respectively. I began screaming again in rage—who had started the fire, who was responsible for this bullshit? The Caltanis. So let them pay.

Four hours later, through the good offices of Olliphan and Lavater, the good apostles, we reached an agreement that ostensibly made me grit my teeth: I would pay a hundred million and the Caltanis a hundred forty.

I even managed to talk about my utter bankruptcy while making my eyes fill with real tears.

Why were the Caltanis going to pay?

That, of course, was the crux of the matter, and the part of my plan about which first Marc, then Li and Liu, and finally Miranda had expressed the greatest reservations. Only to wind up agreeing, however, that I was probably right.

The Caltanis would pay because they had no choice. The phrase is proverbial. To understand it, you had to know their situation. I knew it. Since last February, with his awesome tenacity, Jimmy Rosen had been working furiously to gather the maximum amount of information on my opponents. The Caltanis had, if not an empire, at least a good number of earthly possessions. In that beginning of August, 1977, they held 51 percent of my hotel, plus one hundred percent of the adjoining casino, plus a chain of saloons and restaurants in New York, plus interests in three or four import-export businesses (olive oil, mainly), plus a share (fifty-fifty with a Chicago Mafia family) in a casino in Vegas and another one in the Bahamas.

For them, not to pay Yarrow by ten o'clock on August 8 would be suicide, and, in any case, madness.

In the first place, the insurance company was behaving reasonably by asking us to pay a penalty of $75 million. The truth was that in the event of a lawsuit, we would probably be sentenced to pay more than that. The penalty might have been set by the judge at the equivalent of the stolen sum, or $150 million. We would have had to line up $315 million instead of two hundred forty.

Second, at least one of the Caltanis, if not both, would have gone to jail—along with me, of course, but I could hardly see how this would have consoled them, friendly chum and good buddy though I was.

The third consequence, at least as important—they would have been prohibited from taking any part, in any form whatever, in running a casino. Thus, they would have had to withdraw, not only from Atlantic City, but also from Vegas and Nassau. Without any possibility of ever going back.

My threat of calling in the FBI was a bluff. I had no proof in regard to either Baumer's kidnapping or tax evasion in the saloons. But I KNEW that, in both cases, they had something to worry about. The Caltanis didn't know how much I knew, and they weren't at all eager for the FBI to examine them too closely.

And, finally, by paying—even under the dramatic circumstances in which they would do so—they salvaged the essential thing—Olliphan would strive furiously to convince them of it, and he was their best adviser—that is, the chance of starting over. As the saying goes, they cut off an arm but saved their neck.

They had no choice.

How would they pay?

Yarrow's ultimatum took place on Thursday, August 4, in the late afternoon. Let's say six o'clock in the evening. Payment of the $240 million categorically had to be made on the following Monday by ten o'clock. An eighty-eight-hour reprieve. Forty-eight of which would be taken up by the weekend, which didn't make things easier when it came to finding cash, as one may imagine.

The Caltanis didn't have $140 million in the bank. Who the hell does, anyway? According to Rosen and Vandenbergh's closest estimates, they could mobilize in such a short time at most $10 or $12 million, which was already a lot.

One hundred thirty million were still needed.

What bank would lend it to them? For it would first be necessary to explain to a banker WHY they needed such a sum so fast. And in three days, including the weekend? Impossible.

Borrow from their partners in Nassau and Vegas? Even assuming that those partners had such large amounts of cash immediately available, the remedy would perhaps be worse than the illness. There's certainly no love lost among financiers, but among the Families, it's an outright balance of terror. To show your weakness is to condemn yourself to perish.

No, the Caltanis had only one possibility, a single one . . .

The Swiss group.

I knew all about the Swiss group. And with reason. I was its founding father. Call me Papa.

The Swiss group had appeared on the market last April. It was one of the very first processes I'd set in motion in setting up my Caltani sting operation. The Swiss group was in Zurich. It represented very large financial interests, and had officially authorized two men, one of them being Paul Hazzard,* American, the other named Adriano Letta, Italian, to carry out its business. Hazzard and Letta said they had funds which they wished to invest in the North American market. Through Olliphan, they obtained a meeting with Joe Caltani and made him a buying offer for the casino in Atlantic City, the one that adjoined the Crystal Palace. Caltani refused. That was expected. It didn't discourage the ambassadors of Swiss finance. They returned to the attack regularly, on two or three occasions. Adriano Letta spoke painful English, but he knew Italian and the Sicilian dialect as well. He did his best to form personal ties with the Caltanis, and succeeded. He was even invited to family dinners. He shared the spaghetti of eternal friendship and returned to Rome (this took place around July 20), regretting once again that the Caltanis had turned down his clients' offer and making it clear that one never knew, if one day . . .

Thus, the trap was laid.

And the Caltanis could do nothing other than spring into it. Pressed for time, and above all, urged on relentlessly by Olliphan, they called Letta in Rome. At that moment, it was ten o'clock in the evening in New York, on Thursday the fourth, and thus four o'clock in the morning on Friday the fifth in Rome. They announced to Adriano that they had decided to accept his offer, but, they said, the matter was extraordinarily urgent. Was he empowered to negotiate immediately? Could he fly to the United States at once? As always, Adriano followed my orders to the letter. He objected, of course, argued the near-impossibility of winding up a deal in such a ridiculously short time and finally gave in to the almost panicky entreaties of the Italian-Americans. At 6:50 in the morning (in Rome), he boarded a plane that landed him in Paris just in time to hop on an Air-France Concorde. He was in New York at 6:35 in the morning (Eastern time). Discussions began immediately . . .

Discussions in the course of which the Caltanis went so far as to offer Adriano a million-dollar bribe to get him to persuade his clients to close the deal, and to close it that very day! A bribe

*The Texas oilman who had given me Henry Chance's name.

which Adriano accepted (he gave me all of it, and I let him have his regular 10 percent commission, but that's merely an anecdote) and which did make him willing to undertake the task of convincing his "Swiss clients." He made lengthy phone calls to Zurich, argued until he was blue in the face, in the very presence of the Caltanis, who were biting their fingernails.

(Let us note in passing that the "Swiss" to whom he telephoned was none other than Cannat, Lavater's aide, who had acquired a superb German accent for the occasion.)

Adriano finally hung up and smiled at the Caltanis. "That's it. They agree." It was a quarter of ten in the morning in New York, and thus 3:45 in Europe. Letta defined for the Caltanis the terms on which the deal would be made. The Swiss group would take the Caltanis' shares in the Crystal Palace for $40 million, and their shares in the adjoining casino for another $80 million. One hundred twenty million dollars in all. In addition, the Swiss would take over the mortgages on the two casinos.

That $120 million would be paid by certified check on Monday, August 8, at nine-thirty a.m. "I can't do any more," Adriano explained, "we'll sign all the documents at that time." It was only after another, very heated discussion that the Caltanis got Adriano to move up the closing of the deal, and hence the remittance of the check, by one hour. You can understand the Caltanis' agitation if you remember that they had to be in front of Yarrow, in Newark, on the other side of the Hudson, BY ten o'clock and not one second later. (In fact, that Monday, Adriano would PURPOSELY delay as long as possible, until Joe Caltani had been brought to the brink of insanity, being required as he would to cross the Hudson at meteoric speed in the panicky fear of standing up Yarrow.)

You take your revenge any way you can.

What had the Caltanis sold to pull down that hundred twenty million?

First, their own casino. They had invested $85 million in it and had contracted a loan for $320 million. The Swiss group paid eighty and took over the mortgage. The Caltanis' loss: $5 million (plus the million-dollar bribe). But they lost more than that in reality, for they had sold at less than cost a business they had created, which in four months of operation (the Caltanis' casino had opened for business two months before the Crystal Palace) had proved to be an excellent money-maker, and which was actually worth 20 percent more than the initial investments. Their loss of income could thus be estimated at 20 percent of $450 million, or nearly $90 million.

The Caltanis had also been forced to give up 51 percent of my hotel. They made forty, they had given me twenty-one. They earned nineteen.

This last point annoyed me tremendously. But even though I repeated my calculations a million times, there was nothing I could do. That nineteen million was my bait, concealing the enormous hook.

And I, Franz Cimballi of St. Tropez?

One thing was clear. So as not to evoke the slightest suspicion on the part of the Caltanis, I absolutely had to pay my share. And pay it for real, without shuffling papers. Both because the Caltanis were fully capable of checking my operation and also because I had Yarrow on my back, who wasn't a chum.

Thus, I had to line up a hundred million dollars. And in eighty-eight hours. (With, however, a huge advantage over my codefendants—I'd been expecting it for twenty or twenty-five weeks.)

Sixty-five million dollars came from the Turk. He had, very officially, bought my shares in the Crystal Palace. With a mere telephone call and in the name of our old friendship (ha-ha-ha). Sixty-five million dollars was the real price, anyway, in August 1977, of 49 percent of the casino's shares, after two months of more than satisfactory operation.

Thirty-five million came, again very officially, from my sale to Li and Liu of my rights in two businesses I'd created with them—Safari and Tennis-in-the-Sky. In reality, it was ages since I'd had the smallest interest in either of those two businesses. But who knew it, apart from my two Chinese friends and me? As always in such cases, we had made heavy use of front companies in the financial structure of the two businesses. To pick up my trace in such a forest of impersonal and exotic corporations would take years, at best.

I wagered, without taking too much of a risk, that the Caltanis would have other things on their minds besides trying to figure out how I had been able to keep my share of the bargain.

On Monday, August 8, 1977, 9:45, I appeared in front of Yarrow with my two certified checks, one from the Turk, the other from Li and Liu. The Caltanis were there, waving the certified check signed by Letta's clients, plus $20 million of their own money. And I had to agree that we looked like real idiots. You might have taken us for little boys, caught red-handed stealing apples and forced to make honorable amends. Yarrow gave a sniff of contempt and probably regret, as well. No doubt he would have preferred, for his part, that the whole matter should be taken to the courts.

"But," he said again, "I'm only carrying out the orders that were given to me. You're getting off lightly."

Looking more disgusted than ever, he gave us, in return for our checks, the documents by which the Getchell & Harkins New Jersey Insurance Company guaranteed us the withdrawal of any action. All in all, it was a kind of final discharge which acknowledged us, the Caltanis and me, as models of financial probity and virtue.

The meeting with Yarrow lasted barely twenty minutes. Larry Caltani arranged to leave with me. Even if I had the tiniest ounce of sympathy for him—and I didn't—my role in the drama required that I give him a dirty look. I didn't cheat myself. Especially since, beyond this play-acting, I felt disgust for what had happened. The excitement that had carried me all these last months suddenly collapsed. Even if it was the result of a plan I'd been working on for a long time, the fact remained that I had found myself, across from Yarrow, the Honest and Implacable Policeman, in the very unpleasant and humiliating position of a crook forced to make amends. I hadn't liked it at all.

"Tough back there, huh?"

That was perhaps the worst. Here now was a Caltani, showing sympathy for me! With a very Latin gesture, he took my arm. I pulled myself away with an unfeigned fury.

"The less I see of you in the next two hundred years, the happier I'll be!"

"You'll never hear from us again, Cimballi."

"So much the better for you. Don't forget, I still have that evidence on Baumer and the tax evasion."

The two brothers' dark eyes pinpointed me.

"Bring it out, Cimballi, and you're a dead man."

"I won't bring it out. As long as you stay out of my sight, and, I'll add, I'm in good health."

Their bodyguards drew near. Larry Caltani held out his hand.

"As a peace offering," he said.

"Go fuck yourselves."

They climbed into their long black limousine and drove off toward the George Washington Bridge.

As for me, I took my time. It took me a good two hours to get back to Manhattan. I didn't get to the Pierre until around one o'clock. I called Sarah in San Francisco. I told her that everything was fine, that it was over, that we would soon be together, she and I and the children. I hung up, and turned to face the man who had been waiting for me.

He licked his ice cream.

"These American ice creams are overcooked. They're not even as good as those lousy Yemenite strombolis, in the final account."

"Speaking of accounts, shall we go over them?"

He showed me the $240 million in certified checks that Yarrow had brought him an hour earlier and smiled:

"Yes. I think the time has come."

27

Not for one minute had I thought that Hassan Fezzali—and behind him, Prince Aziz—would not come to my aid, because I, after all, had pulled Hassan out of a tight spot. But good finance doesn't depend on good feelings. The friendship between us, which the ice cream episode had strengthened, enabled me at best to get a hearing.

In mid-March, no sooner had I obtained Miranda's agreement in Macao than I secretly met Fezzali in Rome. He listened to me, indeed. But waited without comment.

I said, "Of course, what I'm proposing is a deal. It's not without risks, but what business doesn't have them, especially in view of such large profits? Because when all's said and done . . ."

"If all goes well."

"When-all's-said-and-done-if-all-goes-well, you'll have invested one single little billion dollars, out of all those billions of petrodollars you manage. And that billion will bring you about 30 percent in less than a year. I have spoken. *Amen.*"

"You are obsessed by the desire to increase your riches . . . but very shortly you will know . . . you will see hell, and you will be asked for an accounting of the pleasures of this world . . . Sura 102, verses 1 to 8."

"We will await the outcome. You too shall wait, and you shall learn who among us follows the right path, and who is led astray. Sura 20, verse 135, if I'm not mistaken."

He bent his head.

"Someone's been studying his Koran, looks like."

"One mustn't neglect anything in a matter like this."

Physically, Hassan had fully recovered from his captivity. He looked as he was destined to look for eternity—the face of a melancholy old camel on a huge carcass of interlocking bones. Plus an enormous tongue for licking ice cream. He scratched the bridge of his big Bedouin nose.

"And I should buy that insurance company, according to you? The Herschell . . ."

"Getchell. The Getchell & Harkins New Jersey Insurance Company. It's not a very big company. The payment they had to make of $150 million put them in a little difficulty. Their balance sheet suffered. Furthermore, the current chairman, Jack Getchell, is an elderly man without immediate heirs. He'll sell."

"Assuming he does, then what?"

"Then, the man you'll place at the head of the company to represent your interests will immediately, in secret, reopen the investigation into the Crystal Palace fire. He'll entrust this new investigation to a certain Donald Yarrow. I've asked around. Yarrow is the best private cop in this field."

"And Yarrow will find out that the fire was of criminal origin."

"Yes."

"And he'll have you put in jail."

"No."

"Too bad. And why won't you go to jail, young Franz Cimballi?"

"Because Yarrow will obey the orders—extremely precise ones—given to him by the new chairman of Getchell & Harkins, that is, your representative. He'll obey because he knows that any insurance company would a hundred times rather have a poor settlement than a good trial. And anyway, Yarrow won't have a choice. He'll obey, or he won't get paid."

"So then, this insurance company that I'll have bought will receive $240 million from the Caltanis and you?"

"Correct."

"One hundred twenty million each?"

"I think I can convince the Caltanis to pay a hundred forty. After all, they're the ones who set fire to my casino."

"And you'll pay a hundred million?"

"On the button."

"But you don't have it."

"The Turk will buy out my shares in the Crystal Palace for sixty-five million. That's the real price."

"The Turk doesn't have that much money."

"He'll get it. When you've given it to him. In reality, it'll be you, not he, who'll buy my 49 percent of the hotel."

"I see. But you still need $35 million. Where are you going to get it?"

"Li and Liu will lend it to me at 15 percent."

The Son of the Desert chuckled.

"That confidence which those Heavenly Fools have in you always surprises me. They're almost as crazy as I am, listening to you rave. And what else do I have to buy?"

"The rest of the hotel from the Caltanis, and all of the other casino, also from the Caltanis. By way of a supposed Swiss group that we'll establish for the occasion, with Adriano Letta as commercial manager."

"The Prophet forbids gambling."

"The Prophet surely said something about the Caltanis somewhere. And about the fate that should be meted out to them. Likewise, he probably recommends rewarding the nice Cimballis."

"That wouldn't surprise me," my favorite Bedouin replied. "He said so many things."

But he spoke somewhat absently. And I could almost see the figures parading through his brain, the brain of an old carpet dealer recycled into high finance. Never had I seen him use so much as a pocket calculator. Everything in his head. Which he now leaned to one side.

"And then sell everything afterwards, eh?"

He was thinking out loud. I knew then that he would accept.

No, it wasn't really simple. But neither was it frightfully complicated. In order to understand what interest Hassan Fezzali had in coming in on my sting operation, one has only to line up the figures.

First, what he laid out, in other words, his investments.

He bought an American insurance company. In this field, investments are rarely adventurous. In the case of Getchell & Harkins, however, it might appear hazardous, inasmuch as the company was in difficulty following the payment of $150 million. But after my intervention, translating into Fezzali's buy-out and Yarrow's arrival on the scene, the company would recover its $150 million, plus $15 million in interest, plus $75 million in penalties. Operating at a deficit in March, Getchell & Harkins would be amply profitable in August. Fezzali would have made a resoundingly good deal.

He bought the Crystal Palace. To that end, he paid $65 million, using the Turk as a cover. Plus forty to the Caltanis. Plus assuming the current bank loan, or (including interest) $440 million. In fact, by August the Crystal Palace had been operating for two months, and two payments had already been made to the Philadelphia bank. The total paid by Fezzali for the Crystal Palace: sixty-five plus forty plus four hundred forty: $545 million.

He bought the neighboring casino, the one properly belonging to the Caltanis, for $80 million, plus assumption of the bank loan (this second casino had been open for four months, and four installments had been honored on the initial loan of three hundred twenty plus interest, or $368 million), which by August was $338. The total paid by Fezzali for the second casino: eighty plus $338: $418 million.

Or, in total for the two casinos: $963 million.

Now, the profits.

And a remark at the outset, illustrated by an example, that of the Crystal Palace. How much had it cost? Exactly $100 million in personal funds (my $50 million, plus the fifty invested by Miranda), to which must be added the $400 million borrowed from the Philadelphia bank—$460 with interest. Total cost: $560 million.

Hassan paid $545. Already, he was carving out a first profit of fifteen million.

But to figure it that way would be stupid. For the real value of the hotel in August, 1977, was no longer $560 million. The hotel was worth more. Because it had begun operating two months earlier, because it was run by the formidable Henry Chance, and because it had proved to be more than profitable. It was a solid-gold enterprise. Its real purchase price by that time had thus gone up by about 20 percent (and that's a modest estimate). It was thus at least $670 or $680. Say $675.

The story was exactly the same for the other casino, which had been open four months, and which, while not as powerful as the Palace, was also a good business. If it were to be sold in August, and sold under normal circumstances, not with a knife to the throat, as the Caltanis had done, it would have been worth, beyond any doubt, between $530 and $550 million. Say $540.

This is to say that by adding the real selling prices (a perfectly possible sale, potential buyers were not lacking): $675 plus $540 equals $1,215 million for the two establishments.

For which Hassan, once again, had paid $963.

The potential profit in August, assuming Hassan resold immediately, not in haste but within thirty or sixty days: $1,215 minus $963 million: $252 million dollars.

Not bad, eh?

AND IT GETS BETTER!

For one would have to be downright simple (which I didn't think I was, at least not all the time, and which Hassan surely was not) to sell the two casinos *separately*.

Obviously, they had to be grouped together, made into one, through one or more passageways, bridging the gap, the no-man's-land of barely one hundred yards that lay between them.

I then came up with something gigantic.

Which was worth (much) more.

Which was worth, in fact, one billion dollars more. Precisely one billion $640 million dollars. Such, indeed, was the price

Hassan Fezzali received in April, 1978, when he sold it all to an oil company that wished to gain a foothold in Atlantic City, after Vegas, where it already owned two casinos.

And where was that nice Cimballi in all of this?

I was satisfied with a modest 10 percent on the proceeds of the final sale in April, 1978. The same 10 percent that Miranda received, pursuant to the agreements she and I had signed in Macao. I, thus, received $164 million, which Hassan paid me down to the last penny, the first payments being made in advance, by monthly installments, beginning August 9, 1977. (I was short of money.)

He could afford it. Going over the figures once again, it will be seen that by subtracting from that $1640 million made in April 1978 the $963 he had invested in buying the casinos, the thirty he needed to spend to unite the two buildings, the $164 for Miranda's commission and mine (1,640 − 963 + 30 + 164 + 164), he was nevertheless left in the profit column with the modest sum of $319 in profit, for a real investment of $963.

I had led him to expect a 30 percent return. The result was even better.

Especially when you think that he had made an additional profit on the insurance company, even deducting the $15 million in interest and the $75 million penalty.

Three hundred ninety-four million, therefore, by combining the profits on the casino operation and that of the insurance company.

That's why Hassan Fezzali listened to me and followed my suggestions.

And that is why Allah is great!

28

Walcher. I had to wind things up on him. He had ignominiously betrayed his old friend Herman. He had more or less been responsible for his death. He had left the Moser sisters penniless. And, finally, he was the source of my own woes. Without him, there might not have been a casino, and I wouldn't have been forced to engage in those breathtaking acrobatics.

I settled his account in one hour. I went to see him with the Englishman, who had made up his file. We laid the evidence before him, and I told him in addition (pure bluff, but he believed me) that I was going to tell the Caltanis that everything I knew about the Baumer affair, I had gotten from Walcher.

The Englishman had warned me. "Walcher's a mediocrity. He doesn't have a nervous system equal to his dishonesty. He'll break down right away." Walcher broke down. That very evening, August 8, two of the Englishman's men put him on a plane to Buenos Aires, asking him not to return for ten or twelve years, and giving him for all his traveling expenses only the forty-odd thousand dollars he had in his personal account. Before that, he had signed a transfer order for the $2 million (which the Caltanis had paid him for his collusion in the Baumer kidnapping) he had hidden in Nassau. I recovered that money. The reason why will be explained.

Henry Chance. I had wanted to tell him myself about the changes that had occurred, and to do so, I went to Atlantic City for the last time, as soon as the Walcher business was finished. Henry Chance heard me out, not blinking, distant. But from the slight gleam in the depths of his pale eyes, I guessed that I was preaching to the converted.

"You knew about it already, didn't you, Henry?"

"I knew you were cooking up something against the Caltanis. That something has happened. The game is over, and you have won. The games goes on. With other players."

"You'll never see them again. I mean the Caltanis."

"Nor will you."

"Nor will I."

We were side by side in the long, low hall that was straight above the gambling rooms. Numerous screens were sending us pictures from every nook and cranny of the Crystal Palace. It was seven o'clock in the evening. The crowd around the tables was thick and high-spirited.

"Henry, I have good reasons to think that those who bought the hotel are the same as those who acquired the Caltanis' old casino."

"And they're going to unite the two buildings."

Was there anything he didn't know, this man who was so courteous, so quiet and at the same time, all but inaccessible, so far away?

I added, "In any case, you'll be responsible for the overall supervision."

He didn't even seem to have heard me. He was watching, turning on one screen after another as the girl moved about in the room below us, one of the girls whose job it was to supply the slot-machine addicts with change. Suddenly, he snapped his fingers, summoned one of his assistants, gave an order. The girl was to be kicked out immediately. No, no explanations, a casino manager doesn't have to give any. He rules and decrees. He looked at me with his clear eyes.

"Franz, can I give you some advice?"

It was the first time he had used my first name.

"Why not?"

"Don't mess with casinos any longer. You got away this time . . ."

". . . but by a fraction of an inch. I agree." I shook his hand.

"You'll always be welcome at the Crystal Palace."

"You know very well I'll never set foot here again."

He nodded and seemed to have forgotten me already, his eyes on the screens, a soldier-monk posted on the battlements, his whole life compressed into this watch. It was the last image I retained of him, for I never saw him again.

Olliphan.

I returned that night from Atlantic City. It must have been a little after midnight when I turned over my car to the Pierre doorman. Upon my entrance, the front desk handed me a message that was waiting for me. I opened the letter. It was from Olliphan. It read, word for word: "I have one last revelation to make to you and a crucial one. Whatever time you come in, please come see me."

I hesitated. I all but threw the message into a wastebasket.

But curiosity won out—a curiosity not unmixed with caution. I pulled the Englishman and Marc out of their beds. They joined me and we left together.

On East Sixty-fifth Street, the crowd was beginning to break up. There were two policemen there, keeping the last gawkers away from the big spot on the pavement, straight down from the sixty-fifth floor of the building. "An accident?" "Two dead. They fell all the way from the top and landed in pretty bad shape." Not only because of the fall, the policeman obligingly explained. In his opinion, it was chiefly the acid that had done the most damage. No, they hadn't yet been identified—he meant the corpses.

Marc plumped for an immediate retreat, but nothing on earth could have stopped me from going up. I found the armed guard who had shown me Olliphan's private elevator eleven months earlier. He said, the policemen who are still up there wouldn't let us in, unless we had good reasons to be there. We went up.

There was, in fact, an entire police brigade on the sixty-fifth floor. By way of a pass, I showed them Olliphan's message. They questioned me, but what could I say? I knew nothing. They ended by explaining to me that at this stage of the investigation, there was only one conclusion.

"No witnesses. All the servants were fired this very day, according to the Puerto Rican butler whom we were able to reach, and who should be here before long. No witnesses, but the evidence tells the story. He threw acid at his wife, doused himself with it, either by accident or deliberately. Then they both went out on the goddamned incredible sloping balcony without a railing. A sixty-five-story fall to finish the job of the acid, what do you think is left? You have a statement to make?"

No. We went back down. It was a warm, damp night in New York. It was only when we drew in sight of the Pierre that the Englishman said to me, "This business with the acid sets me thinking. There's something I can do to find out the truth. In Rio, in the islands opposite the city, there's a doctor who changes faces. If you like, I or one of my men could fly to Brazil tonight. Just to find out if a man formerly called Olliphan didn't make an appointment with the doctor. Or else, I could also make a quick trip to see Korber in South Africa."

I glanced at Marc. He shook his head. That was my opinion, too.

I said to the Englishman, "No. The story of the Crystal Palace is finished. And I really don't want to know what happened to Olliphan. Thanks just the same."

"Don't mention it," replied the Englishman.

Caliban and Patty, and Li and Liu, and Miranda. They're still alive, though under different names. Caliban divides his time between Atlantic City and California. He still spends time there.

And Heidi.

After numerous round trips between Austria and the United States, Jimmy Rosen eventually achieved a kind of first initial beginning final arrangement. I had to go to Vienna and Salzburg four times to negotiate with an incredibly stubborn social agency, and I even had to finance a trip to San Francisco for an Austrian official determined to see with his own eyes that Sarah and I did not intend to deliver our Tyrolean into prostitution. That official earned a double kick in the shins for his pains. But the adoption procedure was set in motion, and it came to fruition in June of the following year, 1978.

At least in the meantime we could all cross borders in unison. That was why, in September, 1977, I proceeded to a roundup of my family in my house, La Capilla, in St. Tropez.

"Can I take all my clothes off?" Heidi asked.

"What next?"

"Everybody here is naked."

"Not everybody. I'm not naked. Sarah's not either."

"As far as you're concerned," she grinned, "it's a good thing. You'd better keep your clothes on, the way you look. But Sarah's not even wearing a top."

"Neither are you. That's because you have nothing to show."

"Very funny."

She ruminated. At the poolside, Li and Liu and their respective spouses (I hoped at least their wives could tell them apart) were snoozing peacefully in the September sun of the French Riviera. Caliban and Patty likewise. Sarah was in the house. She had taken it into her head to make one of those unnameable Irish puddings for my birthday. The mere sight of it curdled my blood. That, together with bacon and eggs, represented the whole of her culinary repertoire.

Marc-Andrea was sitting next to me, copying me or doing his

best to copy me, which means that he kept adding up what he thought were figures.

"Mr. Cimballi?"

I raised my head and met the cornflower-blue eyes.

"Yes, Heidi?"

"I love you, Daddy."

Whereupon, she put on her clogs and went off on a chase, digging up the beach sand. I went back to my accounts, which I had nearly finished. And I was fairly sure of the result obtained. Here it was nearly the 250th time I'd started over. It was very simple. If I deducted from the $164 million I had received or would receive from Hassan, the sums I owed to Li and Liu plus interest, plus the $25 million I would restore to the Moser sisters, plus the bonuses for the Turk and Balthazar, plus Marc's fees, plus the Englishman's lavish salary, plus renting Flint and his airplane, plus all my expenses, what I had spent for the Crystal Palace in all categories, since June 14 of the previous year . . .

A scream came from the beach, followed immediately by Heidi's clear, triumphant laugh. "It's my specialty!" she yelled.

. . . If I subtracted all of that and looked at what remained, I realized that I was in possession of $91 million 823 thousand 641. That is to say, exactly what I had on the morning of June 14, 1976, when I had boarded the New York plane in Montego Bay, Jamaica, in order to tell Philip Vandenbergh that I wanted to buy a casino.

What I had that morning, increased, however, by my profits from the casino sale. Which profits came to precisely $157.29.

Before taxes.

A second furious scream from the beach. And Heidi again burst out laughing, again proclaiming her *joie de vivre*. I put away my pen and took Marc-Andrea's away from him.

"My dear colleague," I said to him, "supposing we abandon finance and beat it before the Irish pudding arrives?"

He nodded vigorously, as appalled as I was by the imminence of the pudding. We adjourned the meeting. I took his hand, we crossed the garden and went down to the beach. On the beach, three men—one resembling Yves Mourousi, one Gunther Sachs, and one Johnny Halliday—were dancing on one foot and rubbing their left shins.

I took Heidi by my other hand and all three of us went off at

275

the same pace to the edge of the beach and lazy waves, rather pleased with ourselves on the whole.

Then they let go of my hands, Heidi turning somersaults on the wet sand, her golden hair sparkling in the sun. My son followed her in a mad whirl of laughter and dances. I had run all over the world in search of what was in front of me, and which no silver sword or golden key could give me. Looking at their little tanned bodies, dripping with foam, I told myself that it was here, MY FORTUNE.

The True. The Only. Heidi and Marc-Andrea's laughter rang within me like a flawless verity.

> St. Tropez–New York–Las Vegas–
> Atlantic City
> July 1981–January 1982